The Do[...] Namdarin, Part One.

Michael Porter

Copyright © 2017 Michael Porter

All rights reserved.

ISBN:154807344X
ISBN-13:978-1548073442

DEDICATION

For Bandit Queen, who planted the seed.
For my wife Jackie, who watered it and watched it grow.
For John Kenny and my local writers group, who nurtured the bloom.

"Not matter how evil may assail you.
Remember, there is still love in this world."

CHAPTER ONE

The dead lord stood on the hill looking down on the ashes of his life. His family dead.   His house destroyed.   His honour ended.

His name was Namdarin, he angered the mages of Zandaar by refusing their demands to surrender his son. They sent the black fire to raise his home. His house burns and he sits on the hill looking down from the raised platform of old, old stones. His horse carries the carcass of the wood buck that today's hunt brought. Without the hunt he would have been in the house when the fire came, but he still thinks of himself as the dead lord of Namdaron.

He sits on the stones and weeps for his dead. He still sees no reasons to give the only son of his fifteen year marriage to the black wizards to use or train as they see fit. The son, the wife, the servants, the house, the yard, the dogs, all are dead.

Namdarin takes the horse and says. "Why do you still live when all else is dead?" The horse snorts at the smell of death in the wind, a westerly with a hint of rain for the evening to come. Namdarin drops the girth and releases the horse's load saying. "Run free from the death I could not prevent."

The big grey, nearly white, stallion runs down the hill and rolls in the green grass, happy to be free of it's cargo. He drinks at the stream and eats the grass while his master watches and returns to the stones.

As the sun descends the lord sits in a despondent trance, not alive, yet not truly dead.

He sits through the dark desolation of the night, alone, truly alone. As the sky lightens with promise of coming dawn his mind begins to function after an unusual fashion, he thinks, 'If my life is over the vengeance of the house of Namdaron is not necessarily finished.' Rising with the sun comes anger. Rising with the sun comes hatred. Rising with the sun comes fear. Arising with the sun comes Honour. He stands on the old altar, takes from his belt the hunting knife his father gave him so many years ago, cuts free the coat and shirt from his upper body, revealing a muscular, trained, torso used to hard work and much swordplay. He stares into the rising sun and swears, "All who hear me now witness that I, by my name and the dead that surround me, do swear that I shall forever find and destroy the black mages of Zandaar. I shall hunt them to the ends of eternity. Bear witness and hear my oath." While speaking he carved the shape of a heart upon his chest. "Let this be all the heart I shall have until this is ended." Thus did he swear though it was not exactly as he intended he did not realise the enormous nature of his error. The dead gods of the old altar bore witness. The dead spirits of the house bore witness. The spirit of the dead wood buck bore witness. The live grass and horse bore witness. The wind and the sky and the rain bore witness. The sun and the moon bore witness. He fell to the stone and his blood fell on the altar. Consciousness ended.

As the sun past the zenith he awoke. The oath was in place. The future set. His course plotted. He called to his horse "Arndrol come!" He came. The lord Namdarin mounted and rode bareback down the hill, passing the whitened bones of the wood buck. He enters the ruins of the castle Namdaron. All is ashes and death. White bones and melted, blackened stone are all there is to see. He goes to the cellar steps thinking that something may survive there. The stone trapdoor looks undamaged. Hope springs. He fastens his belt to the ring of the door give the end to Arndrol and says "Pull my large and only friend, pull for me." As the horse pulls the heavy door rises on its black iron hinges and a dark passage becomes visible.

"Is anybody down there?" He calls thinking. 'Anybody at all.' The door crashes to the courtyard and the horse skitters away, frightened by the noise.

"Is anybody down there?" There is still no reply, so he must enter to be sure that there is nothing that can be of use on the quest he knows is to come. Namdarin takes a deep calming breath and descends the darkening steps, when he is halfway down he hears a loud thudding sound and a snorting behind him, he looks back and sees the horse peering into the hole, "Don't worry my friend I will be back." As he reaches the bottom he hears a more regular thudding and stops to listen. He laughs "Frightened by my own heart!" In the darkness he feels around for a torch or candle. He pulls a torch from its holder and a tinderbox from its niche below. Hearty sparks brighten the gloom and soon the pitch pine torch burns to cast its flickery illumination about. There seems little damage down here below ground, though the smell of smoke and death is still quite strong. Searching he finds no bodies, no-one made it to the safety of the cellar, the other stairway from the inside of the house is blocked by smoking rubble. In the store room he finds some concentrated travelling food, a mixture of oatmeal, dried fruit and fats, which would keep indefinitely and keep him alive for a long time. Amongst other things he discovers maps and a small chest containing some gold and jewels.

"A war chest, a small war chest, but all I need for a one man army. This talking to myself is a sure sign of madness, but who is to say what is mad and what is sane. I feel saner now than ever before. I think I will need some help to defeat the wizardry of the Zandaar, I'll go to the eastern mountains and look for Granger the magician, he may help." Taking his supplies he returned to the surface and the desolation that was his home. Arndrol was waiting nervously shifting his weight from one foot to another. "Come friend, let's go and get your saddle then we can take our war to the Zandaar." They rode out of the castle and up the hill to the stones. Namdarin sat on the horse looking down at the saddle resting on the ground near the old altar, for the first time he realised that the wood buck he had killed only yesterday had been completely stripped of flesh, its bones still in place and tied to the saddle.

"Something very strange is going on here. This must be magic." He dismounted, untied the bones and buried them near the altar. While digging the hole, he felt the scabs on his chest crack with the effort. Examining the self inflicted wound on his chest he found that it had healed completely, the scabs fell away to reveal a bright pink scar. "Whatever took the flesh from the wood buck seems to have helped heal me." He said, very puzzled, as he placed the bones in the hole and covered them up.

"I hope this will appease the gods of this place, and absolve any offence I may have caused to these old and un-named gods." Once Arndrol was saddled and bridled he was much more settled. The saddle was needed for the comfort of the rider and its luggage carrying capacity, the bridle was un-necessary as Arndrol was a well trained war horse it just made him less nervous. They descended towards the ruins as the sun approached the mountain tops in the west.

"Well boy it's too late to start today, we'll rest for another night and start out at sun up." Arndrol flicked an ear as if in agreement. He camped in the lee of the ruins of the west wall. His fire was broken furniture, his food was half a salted pig, his drink was Wandras, a distilled liquor, all from the cellar. He toasted the family of Namdaron, the servants and retainers whose names he could remember and the castle itself. He drank the Wandras until he fell asleep.

Namdarin awoke to a miserable day with a miserable headache. He staggered to the stream and washed his head by simply immersing it in the icy water, this didn't help much. "Arndrol!!" he shouted. The big grey came cantering round the ruined wall and trotted up to its master snorting to say "Good morning." or so it seemed to Namdarin. After loading the horse and closing the cellar door they set off in a roughly easterly direction along the road through the estate of Namdaron or more accurately the remains of Namdaron. Although the farm lands were unharmed the houses were burned to smouldering rubble. As they cleared the boundary of the estates the rain started as if to deepen the gloomy attitude of both man and horse. Namdarin picked the pace up from a slow walk to a steady trot. Very easy for the horse but tiring for the man, after an hour or two of trotting the man's headache and misery were reduced to a background nagging. As they came over a ridge Namdarin noticed another group of travellers on the road ahead and that he was catching them very quickly. Without dismounting he strung his bow, checked that his sword and dagger were cleared and ready for action, and slowed the horse to a quick walk. Nearing the travellers he observed that they were not farmers carrying produce, nor merchants or dealers, the only goods they had were swords and knives. Their somewhat dishevelled appearance marked them as possible brigands definitely not soldiers or warriors of a recognisable organisation, so Namdarin nocked an arrow to the string and prepared to fight.

When the travellers heard the horse behind them they stopped, turned and spread out across the road. The middle one of the five shouted "Good morning fellow traveller, who are you and where do you go?" None drew sword or knife, though their hands rested lightly on hilts. They did not seem to anxious to initiate a fight so Namdarin relaxed a little.

"I am Namdarin ex-lord of Namdaron and who be you?" Called Namdarin whilst checking the area and seeing no more men concealed about. The road here was narrow but surrounded by open fields so if necessary he could ride around these un-mounted men.

"I am Jangor, we are mercenaries looking for work. How can you be ex-lord? For we passed around Namdaron but three days ago and all was fine there, they certainly had no need of our services."

"The Zandaar sent black fire to destroy my house and to my shame I was out hunting alone. Now I will always be alone."

Jangor paused as if in deep thought, looked at the man next to him who nodded, then spoke "Why not join us? Its not an easy life, it has risks and occasionally good rewards."

"No thank you. I have a purpose. I go to destroy the Zandaar."

"That will be a mighty task. You could hire us and we could help you in this."

"I have barely enough funds for myself let alone six men."

"Then there is nothing to be said except good luck in your task and pass freely friend." The men all stepped to the side of the road to allow Namdarin to pass.

"Thank you for your good wishes. If you feel like becoming farmers the farms of Namdaron are profitable and can be made habitable quite quickly. Since I will probably not return you are welcome to make use of them."

"Thanks for your kind offer. Farming is not really for us .Too many oarly mornings and not enough drinking time."

"The offer stands. I hope this will help make your journey slightly better." said Namdarin tossing a flask of Wandras to Jangor.

Jangor caught it, opened it, tasted it, and said "This is good. Many thanks my lord." Namdarin kicked Arndrol into a canter and passed the men quickly.

Once he was well clear of the mercenaries he slowed to a trot again. By nightfall he was approaching the forest of Drangor, a dark and forbidding place. So he camped for the night on its outskirts. The night sounds of owls and prowling predators made Arndrol nervous so he stayed close to the fire and his master. When the sun rose they broke camp and headed east again. Into the forest they went, once inside the initial barrier of the undergrowth the ground level foliage became quite sparse, probably because of the lack of real light. The high canopy blocks out most of the light except were an old tree had fallen, here an oasis of sunlight brings a fierce competition to grow. Arndrol soon became used to the noises of the forest the constant hiss of wind in the canopy, the songs of the birds, and the noises of frogs and toads. The day started to pass as a mind numbing tedious progression of trees, each the same as the last, in unchanging monotony. Then they entered an area where the noise gradually faded to nothing. No sounds at all. This caused some measure of alertness but not for long.

    Suddenly Arndrol stood still shocking Namdarin to attention. "What's wrong?" He said, not really expecting a reply, just as a man on a rope swung past the horses head waving a large sword very threateningly. Namdarin yanked his sword from its scabbard, cleared his dagger and turned the horse towards the first man to come out from behind the trees. Namdarin veered left and hit the man with a wide forehand sweep that split the man's head almost completely in two. As the body fell the horse kicked it hard towards the next in line who stumbled, fell, too close to Arndrol's hooves. The horse stamped on the man and screamed joyfully, this is a horse trained to fight. A wild horse armed with teeth and hooves, he kicked and bit to defend his master, who slashed right and left, stabbing any portion of flesh in range. Together they knew this would be to the death, so they fought on. Six attackers lay in the leaf mould, limbs removed by a flashing blade, heads smashed by a crushing hoof, when Namdarin's sword jammed in the leather armour of a brigand's gourget and he was heaved from the horse. As he fell the horse spun and trampled the villain in question. Without guidance the horse was unsure what to do he still fought the brigands, they could not catch him nor mount him, to get too near was to tempt death so they allowed him to escape. The man fought on. He was covered in blood, most not his, although several small cuts were bleeding quite profusely. With his back to a tree his thoughts were of the Zandaar and their lucky escape as his quest would die here. 'No. Such cannot be. I must fight.' He thought. With the renewed energy of anger and hatred he took the battle to the brigands stepping over three corpses he advanced step by step, hewing like an axeman, chopping like a madman, howling like a demon. Until his sword jammed in a belt and this time would not come free. The brigands took him by the arms and spread-eagled him upon the forest floor, the leader placed his sword in the middle of Namdarin's chest and slowly pushed it down through his coat and shirt, through flesh and ribs and heart and spine. Namdarin felt an icy hand on his chest and heard a roaring in his ears .The darkness closed in with dreadful finality.

Jangor was walking quietly through the forest of Drangor thinking, worrying, his men would begin to get hungry soon, as the money was almost gone. He hated this dreary place, Kern was scouting ahead, Mander was trailing behind, yet despite these precautions everybody's hand was on the sword hilts. All talk was whispered, everything was uneasy. Kern whistled the warning, it was repeated to Mander who ran forward with sword in hand, to find his friends creeping towards Kern with swords drawn. Kern was hiding in some thin brambles, they huddled together .

"Ahead are some bodies on the ground." Said Kern, pausing uncertainly.

"And?" Said Jangor.

"I don't know. They look strange and feel wrong!" Jangor had long since come to respect Kern's feelings.

"Kern, Andel, Stergin you go round that way. Mander and I will go this way and when we meet on the other side we'll decide."

They crept around the scene of a fight, checking carefully to be sure that none of the protagonists were still about to cause more mayhem. Finding nothing alive at all they decided to investigate more closely. They approached the scene slowly careful not to disturb any of the tracks. Kern spent some time examining the tracks.

"Well Kern. What happened here?" Asked Jangor.

"Men on foot attack man on horse, over there, man on horse killed six, then he was dragged from the horse, the horse escaped that way with men on foot chasing it. The man from horse made a stand with his back to that tree, he killed another three, he was very good or very lucky. He lost his sword in that one and the rest killed him. Then the men on foot left after the horse."

"When did this happen Kern?"

"That's the strange part. The bloodstains say today, probably mid-morning. The bodies say five maybe ten years. Every living, or dead, animal within ten paces of the horseman is now bones. The men that attacked him, the lizards and mice in the leaves, all bones. The horseman was the man we met on the road two days ago, his body is not bones. This is powerful magic and I don't like it."

"I'm not bothered about the magic, I see swords and armour, metal and money that will keep us from starving for a few more days. Strip those bones and lets see what we've got."

They set about systematically stripping the bodies of valuables, swords and knives, the occasional jewel or stone of worth, but they stayed away from the body of Namdarin. Before the grizzly task was finished the quiet of the forest was shattered by an awful scream. They spun, drawing steel, looking for a foe. Namdarin staggered to his feet, casting about for a weapon, snatching his sword from its last victim, he howled as if in pain. The mercenaries retreated out of reach of Namdarins whistling blade.

"Stand and fight." Shouted Namdarin. "Fight and die like men, you bastards."

"My lord, we have no quarrel with you." Said Jangor. "We will not fight you unless we must."

"I remember," muttered Namdarin, falling to his knees, "I am dead. They plunged a sword through my heart. Oh, the pain."

"He was definitely dead." Said Kern to Jangor, who walked over to Namdarin's crouching shape, removed the sword from Namdarin's shaking hand, took Namdarin's head in his hands and said tenderly.

"Namdarin you are now afoot and without your supplies, if your quest is to continue you must join with us for a little way at least. We can discuss this strange magic later, once we are away from this place." Jangor released him and stepped back hoping that Namdarin would recover quickly.

Namdarin knelt in the leaves looking at the hole in his clothes and said. "What kind of magic is this? Why me? This is almost too much for the mind to handle. Oh, the pain. Maybe I am not without my horse." He stood and whistled loudly, shouted "Arndrol come!!" There was no sound of reply. "It seems you are right. Though I am sure that my horse will return if he lives for I reared him and trained him from birth, I am more his mother than any horse ever was. Which way are you fellows heading?" Jangor was amazed by the speed of Namdarin's acceptance of his situation, and astounded by the bloodstain on his clothes.

"We head east, hoping for employment in Mandroth, where I hear there is some strife over a river boundary." Answered Jangor.

"Then it appears we travel together for a while. When do we leave?"

"Immediately, Kern point is yours, Mander behind. Let's move but keep it quiet."

They resumed their previous formation except that the middle contained an extra man. After an hour's slow marching things began to relax a fraction.

"Namdarin, are you any good with that bow you carry?" Asked Jangor, quietly.

"I use it mainly for hunting game." He replied, remembering the good feeling of bringing down a wood buck, to take home to his wife. "If I am going to be hunting men I will have to change my arrows."

"Why change them? They look good to me."

"The ribs of game are vertical so the head is set vertically, men's ribs are horizontal so the arrowheads need turning so the points slip between the ribs."

"It will be good to have a bowman to help provide food for us, you see, we are swordsmen only. Perhaps you could teach one or two of us the bow as we travel."

"Gladly. Isn't it a bit unusual for mercenaries like yourselves not be proficient with all weapons?"

"We were only recently .. ..released by our lord."

"Outlawed?"

"Yes. After a fashion. Our lord Morndragon was having a dispute with some hill people over a few cows, the hill people stole them. Morndragon wanted them back, or the hill people punished, he wasn't bothered which. The hill people were hidden in a forest and Morndragon decided to send in the troops, us. I being a captain pointed out to him that if we charge up that bare slope waving our swords above our heads shouting our battle cries as he ordered none would reach the trees. These hill people are excellent bowmen. We are not. Morndragon had me arrested, charged with treason and sentenced to hang before we returned to the castle. Four of my friends decided that it would be politic for us to leave his service as soon as the sun went down. We did. Here we are. Looking for another lord to serve, who has more brains than the last one. You would fit the bill, except for this quest of yours, we could return to the house of Namdaron, secure it, and start to rebuild, the choice is yours."

"My course is set, my oath was sworn, I must continue."

"How do you intend to fight these black magicians?"

"I am going to the eastern mountains to find the wizard Granger and see if he will help me. It is known that he has no love for Zandaar."

"On foot we will be in this forest for another two or three days and our supplies are low, if Kern sees any tracks will you hunt for us?"

"Of course, and I will show Kern how to make a bow."

"Thanks Namdarin, this could be a useful partnership."

Here the conversation stopped for a while. Namdarin walking with his new friends checked his arrows, he had twenty-four. He started to unbind the metal tips of ten of them to use for man killing, thinking 'I never would have thought that I would set arrows to kill a man.' He used threads teased from the frayed edge of his shirt to rebind the tips, by the time he had finished it was beginning to get dark, when Kern whistled the warning again.

They froze and listened, Kern was coming towards them, he had obviously discovered something that posed a hazard.

"What's the problem?" Asked Jangor.

"Man tracks, lots of them, all of a sudden. We must be near their camp."

"Namdarin, how many attacked you?"

"I am not sure. I killed nine or ten and that can't have been more than a quarter of their force."

"A raiding party of forty or fifty, so this must be a large camp, we can't kill them all but we could steal some provisions, maybe some horses. Right Kern and I will go and investigate the rest of you stay here, Stergin don't sharpen your sword, because the sound travels hundreds of paces even in these woods."

Jangor and Kern left the other four behind, and within five minutes Stergin was fiddling with his whet stone and fingering his sword hilt. Namdarin looked at Stergin and laughed softly, saying "Jangor certainly knows you very well."

"I am not very good at doing nothing, I was always awful on parades. Only Jangor kept me in Morndragon's troops, because I am quite good with a sword." Mander snorted. "Morndragon wanted him out because Morndragon always lost fencing tournaments to Stergin. It really upset him, sometimes for days."

Andel was already asleep so Mander said "That man is at least half cat, he will sleep anywhere, anytime, even standing on his feet." The rest of them settled down to try and catch some sleep leaving Namdarin to stand guard. He was feeling unusually awake, very alert, considering how tiring today had been. Just before the sun went down completely Jangor and Kern returned.

"It's quite a large village really, about fifty or sixty houses formed in two rings about a circle of standing stones. I saw no visible garrison, nor any real soldiers, but I did see heads mounted on posts around the perimeter, these people are obviously unfriendly, after dark we will sneak in and see what we can find. So let's get a couple of hours sleep first. Who wants first watch?"

"I'll take it." Says Namdarin, "I'm not sleepy."

"If you get tired wake Andel he's probably had an hour by now." He laughed. The five mercenaries settled down to sleep leaving Namdarin to his thoughts. 'I seem to have fallen upon some good friends to have here,' he thought, 'they could be very useful, I will need a new horse at least or this quest will take forever. I still don't understand how I come to be alive, it is extremely disconcerting remembering death, the pain makes the memory hard to recall, what of the bones all around my mended body? Is there a connection to the bones of the wood buck by the old altar? These are all questions for the magician Granger. More immediate is the problem of food and a horse, a new dagger would be a help. This village sounds very strange to me, why keep heads on posts? To warn unwanted visitors away, visitors like us. Is it a bluff or does the village have the protection of something that collects human heads? I will have to see these standing stones in this village to be sure, not that I know much of such magic. I wonder if these new friends can be convinced to follow my purpose to its final conclusion? It is now very dark and the moons will not rise for at least two hours, now we must move.'

Namdarin woke Jangor saying "Its dark and there are no moons."

"A good thought. Wake up you lazy useless dolts, there is work to do."

The group collected themselves, drank from their flasks.

"I don't suppose there is any of that Wandras left, is there?" Asked Namdarin, hopefully.

"Just enough." Said Jangor, passing the flask round, the warming fluid ran down their throats, warming their bellies and their minds. They moved off quietly towards the village heading for the south side because of a hill that would give an excellent vantage point to observe from, before going in. They arrive at the hill and lay on the top looking down into the village. The villagers are up and about still, they are having a late night procession around the village. They are marching slowly and chanting, three times around the centre, then into the standing stones where the chanting became louder.

"If they are all occupied this should be easy." Said Jangor. "Let's go."

The six crept down the hill towards the houses as they approach the heads on the posts they could see that the heads were in various states of decay. Most without eyes, many without hair, all with a strange look of life.

"Yuck. How horrible!" Whispered Andel.

Kern went first through the ring of posts. Immediately the two heads on either side of him started to scream. A piercing howl, like the damned of hell.

"Out!" Called Jangor. They ran away from the screams until they came to a small ditch like depression in the fields, here they crawled eastwards around the village away from the noise. Four villagers armed with axes came running to the screaming heads.

"Thank the gods." Muttered Jangor. "Those are only alarms and not more communicative, then we could have been in real trouble. We'll wait for things to quieten down again." After nearly an hour in the cold damp ditch Jangor decided that the coast was clear and a new plan of invasion was needed.

"If we can set off as many of those evil heads as possible they won't know were we actually are, so if some one runs round in and out of those poles the noise should cause much confusion."

"Better still if two people run one each way, then duck inside, the centre of the noise will be difficult for the villagers to locate, so they won't know where to start looking." Said Namdarin.

"Good idea. Mander you go that way, Andel you the other, we meet at that house, the one with the odd shaped shed at the back. Everybody clear."

A general agreement of nods and whispers. They crept towards the village again, nearing the ring of heads Jangor said. "Go!" Mander went left, Andel right, the rest ran straight inside to the house picked by Jangor. Kern went to the shed with the strangely high roof and broke in the door, with a simple push of the shoulder. Inside it was dark and dank, damp and smelly, like wet rags or fishing boats. The four settled down to await their friends. Mander arrived first by a couple of minutes. After only a few minutes waiting the chanting resumed. Jangor lead the way into the house which seemed to consist of one room with beds, well straw mattresses on the floor, at one end and table at the other. The appearance was very rough, with no real care taken of looks or function, the whole aspect was one of carelessness.

"Let's try another one." Said Jangor. They opened five houses and sheds and found nothing of any real interest, only a barrel of salt beef, some of which Stergin took.

"That large building could be a stable, that's next." Said Jangor, getting depressed by this dreadful village. Opening the large doors they found that he was right. Namdarin stopped dead in the entrance, for there in the middle of the large central area was a big grey horse, tied down. A rope to each leg, one to his tail, and two for his head. With a hiss of steel Namdarin drew his sword and slashed the ropes holding his friend, flung his arms around the horses neck and hugged him, saying "They caught you, my friend, but they had brains on their side. You are free now, to run with me again." Arndrol tossed his head, lifting Namdarin clear of the ground, and causing a quiet chuckle amongst the others.

"Someone you know?" Asked Jangor.

"Yes .A very old friend."

There were only eight other horses in the stable so they decided to take them all. With six horses saddled, and three for pack the opened the doors and lead the horses outside. The chanting appeared to be over, going as quietly as horses can they went to the outer ring of stones. The crowd were concentrating on a man in the centre, standing on a raised dais, waving a knife over his head, praying in a loud voice. A tall man in a long black robe, with a cowl over his head, hiding his face in darkness. Namdarin saw red rage rising before his eyes, his hand took a man killing arrow, nocked, pulled, released, three times in four seconds. Three feathers sprouted from the black robe and it fell into stunned silence.

"Ride!!!" Shouted Jangor. The six mounted and headed south out of the village. Arndrol rapidly overhauling the smaller horses reached the perimeter first and charged the axe wielding guards, knocked them to the ground with his broad chest, reared, and stamped them to pulp, until his front legs were red to the knees. Finally he reared and screamed in defiance, turned and raced after the others who were almost to the top of the hill. The five paused at the top to wait for Namdarin to catch up, seeing no immediate pursuit they set off at a much more reasonable pace.

"Your friend seems a little unhappy with those people." Said Jangor.

"Yes. The stable was obviously not up to the standard he is used to."

"Why did you kill the priest? We could have escaped un-noticed."

"Zandaar." Was Namdarin's answer. A single word, carrying all the hate and anger, it even caused Arndrol to skip a stride and snort loudly. Now the horse hates them as well.

"If we ride through tomorrow we should be clear of any followers. Then we should reach the inn at the Red river ford. I just hope you haven't committed us to your cause by killing that priest, Namdarin." Said Jangor.

"I'm very sorry if I have." Replied Namdarin with feeling and doubt.

They stopped briefly at dawn, by a stream, to eat. Letting the horses rest and graze, while they ate salt beef and wild mushrooms that grew nearby. As the sun came up and warmed them, the fullness of their bellies caused them to lie in the long green grass and relax.

"Namdarin, what do you know of the bones of the men you killed?" Asked Jangor.

"Well. I'm not sure, but something similar happened to a dead wood buck, which was near by when I made my promise to end the

Zandaar. I had killed it that day, and was taking it home, and dropped it near the stones, when I saw the wreckage of the castle. I swore to kill the Zandaar, and then there was blackness. I woke about noon the next day, and went down to the castle ruins, the wood buck was only a skeleton by then. That's as much as I remember."

"These stones, what did they look like?"

"Some big boulders with a flat slab resting on top, why?"

"Did you spill any blood on the stone?"

"Well, yes, I did get somewhat extravagant in my grief." He replied showing the heart shaped scar on his chest.

"Hell!! I think you may have accidentally called on the old gods. Absolutely anything could happen. Granger should be able to determine the exact nature of this oath you swore, maybe the gods protect you, and maybe they cursed you. We have no way of knowing. I suggest that after Red river you go find Granger as quick as you can." Jangor looked a little worried. He wasn't bothered about people being after him but irritated gods he could do without.

Jangor looked around and saw the other four fast asleep and said "Let's rest for an hour or two." Then went to sleep himself, soon followed by Namdarin.

Namdarin was woken by Andel shaking him saying "Wake up, the horses have escaped, wake up."

Namdarin stood and whistled. Arndrol came trotting up and nuzzled his master. "Good morning, my friend." Said Namdarin. "Go and fetch the other horses for us please." Arndrol flicked an ear and trotted off, to return in a few minutes with the other horses in tow.

"Now we can continue our journey." Said Namdarin to the other men.

"He's a handy fellow to have around." Said Mander, pointing to the grey horse. They mounted and set off through the forest towards the Red river. The forest started to thin out as the trees separated and the grassy patches in between got bigger. In the middle of the afternoon they came over a ridge on to a grassy plane that descended to a broad river.

"The Red river." Said Jangor. He was right it was a definite red colour. "The colour is caused by the iron rich mountains the it flows from, it has only one problem, and it tastes horrible. Even horses won't drink it."

"What does the man at the inn make his beer from then?" asked Namdarin.

"Most of the feeder streams are quite good. He uses the one just upstream from the ford, which is sweet and pure. He grows his own barley above the flood plain of the river, and his hops come upstream on barges. His beer is the best is the world, without a doubt."

"I have heard of the inn at the Red river, I just haven't been this far from home before. I had no cause to, until now." Said Namdarin, wondering if he would ever return to his house. "Any way, how can we afford to buy beer or rooms at the inn? My gold was take by those villagers and you are short of funds, you said so." Asked Namdarin.

"We have some armour and swords that we scavenged from the men you killed. The blacksmith by the river will buy them, we won't get a good price, but he'll give us enough for some beer and food and maybe a room with a real bed for the night. If the metal isn't enough we have a couple of spare horses. If the innkeeper doesn't feel like riding them he can always put them in a stew. How many spares are there?"

"Three, no four, I'm sure we only had nine horses when we left the village. Where did that skinny piebald filly come from? Do you know Arndrol?" Asked Namdarin. The grey just flicked its ear and nickered softly.

"Does he know?" Asked Jangor.

"Probably," answered Namdarin, "he does tend to collect horses were ever he goes, specially fillies, it can be very embarrassing sometimes."

"So we have four spare horses, we could eat for a month on them."

"Or Stergin could drink for a night." Said Mander, causing some laughter.

"Or buy Mander a wife." Replied Stergin.

"Enough." Said Jangor, before things start to get ugly.

This kills the conversation completely for a while. As they get nearer the river they can see the smithy, downstream of the inn, which is a large square house around a courtyard, about fifty paces on a side. Smoke billows from the big chimneys on the inn and the small one of the smithy.

"We'll go to the smith first," said Jangor, "and see what he wIll offer for this metal."

The smith is, as all smiths, a large and red-faced man called Smith, surprisingly enough. After perusing their wares the smith says, "I'll give you three gold pieces for the metal or twenty for the grey."

"The horse is not for sale." Said Namdarin.

"Seven for the metal." Said Jangor.

"Robbers. Four is as high as I will go."

"You steal the food from our mouths, six."

"My poor starving babies. Five."

"Deal." Smith and Jangor shook hands and the deal was struck.

On the way to the inn, now with enough money for a bed some food and some beer, Jangor looked puzzled. He had a thoughtful frown on his face.

"What's wrong?" Asked Namdarin.

"We should have got three gold for that metal, no more. Steel must be in short supply around here at the moment. But why? The mines are upstream and there is generally plenty to trade. The miners swap metal for beer at the inn. This is very strange. Everybody stay awake for any news once we are inside." They went to the front door of the inn, a double door three men wide, only one side of the door was open, which is unusual on a hot day. In the door way stood a man, like two of the smiths twins together.

"Wadda ya want?" he demanded.

"Room and board for six." Said Jangor, looking the hulking brute in the eye. The doorman was a little slow, while the six watched he checked the door, he checked their weapons, he checked the position of his friends inside, he was in the process of deciding whether to attack. Luckily for him, the decision was taken for him before he completed his deliberations. A voice shouted from inside. "Let the gentlemen in, Herm. I'm sorry for the doorman, gentlemen, but we've been having some trouble recently with bandits. What can I do for you? Rooms? Food? Beer? All are ready and waiting. My name is Killion. Come this way, won't you?" Said someone who could only be the landlord, ushering them into the main common room. Killion talked in an endless stream, never seeming to take a breath. Jangor interrupted him mid flow.

"Room and board for six, stabling for ten horses, and we will see the rooms now."

"Of course, gentlemen, right this way, the first floor I think, oh yes, those will do nicely for such fine gentlemen."

They went up the stair from the corner of the common room, along a dimly lit passageway to the end and entered the last door on the left. A sturdy door with a large bolt on the outside. Inside the door were two rooms separated by a grubby brown curtain. Each room contained three beds with little space for anything else.

"Nearly." Said Jangor, looking at Kern then the bolt.

Kern pushed his dagger behind the bolt and levered it away from its slide.

"Now these are just right. One night. We leave in the morning."

Jangor and the landlord haggled. Agreeing on five silver pieces. After the landlord left Jangor said "We could be in more danger in here than in the forest. We stand watches as usual. I don't trust this place any more."

"I'll go and see to the horses." Said Stergin.

"And I'll have a look around the rest of the place." said Kern.

"Right. Half an hour in the common room, understood!" Answered Jangor.

"Right." Said Kern. Stergin just nodded. The other four left in the rooms searched thoroughly, turning all the beds over, tapping all the walls, and checking the floorboards. They found nothing to indicate any danger at all. But this did not ease the feeling of nervous edginess they all felt. When the search was finished they went down to the common room. Two other people were sitting in the common room at a table by the fireplace, they were deep in thought and paying no attention to the newcomers. Jangor went to the bar and banged his hand down shouting "Service!" A young and pretty barmaid appeared, her face reddened probably by nearness to a cooking fire, she said, "Yes sir, what do you wish?"

"Six tankards and a jug please, my lovely."

She blushed, and got a jug full of foaming beer from beneath the bar, then she left again. The four friends stood near the bar drinking their beer slowly. Jangor was beginning to worry about Kern and

Stergin when Stergin came in from the courtyard.

"The horses will be fine, the stables are good and the hands seem to know what horses need. Arndrol is a little unhappy if not stroppy, though he hasn't bitten any body, I think he might. To get there you go out the door I just came in, turn left, third door along the wall. The big door out of the courtyard is barred and guarded, the quickest exit, even mounted, is probably through here." Reported Stergin. Then he poured himself some beer and drank. While Stergin was speaking Kern came down the stairs.

"This place is a fortress and it's on alert, something is definitely going to happen, and happen soon." He said, looking somewhat disturbed.

"We'll have those two tables over there by the wall, push them together to clear some floor space, then we can see both doors and the stairs." Said Jangor, to his friends then "Waitress! Another jug and some food, if you please."

The young girl came quickly with a new jug of beer and said, "We have some beef ready if that will do gentlemen?"

"Of course, that will be fine." Said Mander, turning on the smile that always pleases the ladies, "When does business pick up around here?" he asked.

"The miners generally start to arrive soon after sunset." She replied, departing quickly. Before long she returned with six platters of sliced beef, in thick gravy, then a bowl full of steaming potatoes, and a basket of warm bread buns. "Will that be all, sirs?"

"For now." said Mander, with the smile, and a wink. She almost ran off, blushing bright red. While the food was being delivered the doorman, Herm, came in from the courtyard, glanced round the room, and took his station by the outer door.

"I wonder were he's been, all this time?" Said Jangor.

"He's been picking up his spare daggers, there are at least three more in his belt." answered Stergin. "And he's probably had some specific instructions."

"I like this less and less, I think we ought to leave, after we've eaten of course." said Jangor.

"I agree." Said Kern.

"I'll saddle the horses then we'll be ready." said Mander, taking a large stack of beef and three buns with him.

"Waitress!" shouted Jangor. When she arrived he told her that they had changed their minds and decided to continue their journey, so she went to find the landlord. Killion, the landlord, appeared in moments saying, "What is wrong, gentlemen? Why the sudden change of heart? How have we offended you? Please stay in my house for the roads are not safe after dark anything..."

"We are leaving in a little while." Jangor was forced to interrupt, "It is nothing to do with your service or house and I think the roads will be alright for a group as large as ours. We will certainly pay for the room, though we won't use it and the food and beer. How much do we owe you?"

"Forget the room, call the bill one gold piece, but at least stay and have another jug on the house."

"Here's your gold piece. We leave now." Said Jangor, getting from his seat and moving towards the courtyard door. The others followed him. As Jangor went into the courtyard he shouted, "Open the gate!" Mander came out of the stable leading the horses. Namdarin called "Arndrol come." and his horse came as usual. While they mounted Jangor demanded that the gate be opened again. As no one was moving to open the gate he wheeled about and headed for the common room door. He ducked under the lintel and rode inside, the others following. Herm was unhappy. His instructions did not cover horsemen in the bar. He bellowed "Stop." and drew a knife from his belt. Herm was a bit slow, as Jangor had time to draw his sword and slap Herm on the head with the flat, thus rendering Herm unconscious. No one then delayed them further, they departed at a gallop, straight across the ford and up towards the eastern hills.

"What was all the rush for?" asked Namdarin.

"When a landlord offers to neglect an agreed charge and offers free beer, always run away, he intends to surprise you, probably with a stabbing pain in the back." Replied Jangor.

"Also," added Mander, "someone had offered him a lot of gold to keep us there. Alive or dead, they weren't fussy."

"How do you know?" Asked Namdarin.

"The stable boys were talking as I entered the stable, I wasn't sure it was about us, so I had to convince one of them to tell me. Word came through just before we arrived for six men, one on a wild grey horse."

"How did word get there ahead of us?"

"I don't know, but the Zandaar have their ways."

"I'm sorry, my friends, it seems you may be involved in my battle, unless we separate right now, then the horse that everyone is looking for would not be with you. I certainly will not give up Arndrol."

"Right," answered Jangor, "we head south while you go east to find Granger. I wish you luck in your task."

"Good bye my friends," said Namdarin as they turned south, "I wish you all the best luck in the world." Then he kicked Arndrol into a full gallop such that the smaller horses of his friends could never match, and was gone.

CHAPTER TWO

Eastwards he rode as fast as the great horse could comfortably go. Sometimes he thought of Jangor and the others and hoped that they were free of the Zandaar. For a few days he avoided the farms and the towns he came across, he hunted as he went, for the game was plentiful, deer, rabbits, birds and even the occasional fish shot with a tethered arrow. The mountains drew nearer, the terrain more rugged and colder. He finally decided it should be safe to enter a town, many miles from any incident involving the Zandaar, so with a large deer hanging across the rump of the horse, he chose a small village by a river. Riding into a strange village always attracts some attention, so Namdarin was not surprised by the stares. He rode to the inn, little more than a large house but obvious for all to see. He asked the landlord to trade the deer for cash or goods. The landlord gave him five gold pieces for the deer, and sold him bed and board for one gold. The food was good, the beer fair, the bed wonderful, Namdarin slept until mid-morning. He asked the landlord if any one would know were to find Granger. The landlord suggested he try the monastery in the hills to the north-east. Namdarin offered his thanks and left with a new heading, and new hope.

Into the mountains went Namdarin, climbing higher, into the cold. He was wearing his blankets most of the time just to stay warm. Both man and horse were losing weight, becoming thinner as body fat disappeared. Snow began to make travelling difficult and foraging hard for the horse. As they climbed to a high pass Namdarin came to a decision and said to Arndrol, "If the summit of this pass shows no signs of the monastery we go down were it is warmer." The horse flicked any ear but made no other comment. The last section of the rise was so steep that Namdarin dismounted and let Arndrol find his own way up. On the crest he stopped to catch his breath, and looked about at the beautiful snow covered peaks, the white clouds in the crystal blue sky, the trees in the valley ahead, and a column of smoke rising from a large stone structure, with a tower. Could it be a monastery? Descending into the valley at a quick trot, Namdarin was thinking of his home, which looked a lot like this monastery ahead. A square stone building around a large courtyard, surrounded by a moat, not yet frozen, no doubt containing good water and fish. The walls were not high, only twice Namdarin's own height. In the middle of the yard was a small round structure, most likely a well. About the moat were fields, most bare soil, already harvested, but in the corner of one field some monks were pulling potatoes. Monks in black hooded robes. Monks of Zandaar. Hot rage filled his brain, red mist covered his eyes, he reined the horse sharply, and stood still until the heat of anger subsided.

"I want to kill them," he whispered, "but they are many, if I kill the ones in the field the others will be alert and secure inside their walls. I need a plan, but first I need information. I must remain calm and lodge with these evil priests for a few days." Breathing deep and slowly, to calm his racing heart, he approached the monks.

"What do you want? Strange horseman." asked one of the black robed figures. From close distance there was still nothing to distinguish one from another. 'How do they tell each other apart?' Thought Namdarin, saying, "I wish lodging for a few days, if you can spare the room and some food, I have some money but not much."

"You have travelled far. What do you seek?"

"I seek the hermit Granger. Do you know of him or his house?"

"What can you want with a wicked old witch like him?"

"I want some magic with which to win the heart of a lady. Have you a map that shows his house?"

"We have maps and such in the monastery. Granger can not help you because his magic is evil, and comes not from the great Zandaar."

"May I see the maps, as I have no wish to trouble Zandaar over so trivial a matter?" Said Namdarin thinking, 'I must get inside that wall to find some weakness, but I mustn't press too hard.'

"How can a trivial matter bring you so far from home?"

"It is not trivial to me, but gods work a much bigger stage."

"You are a travelling actor with a lust for a rich man's daughter."

"How do you guess so closely the truth?" Lied Namdarin, to give the monk some pride in his own intelligence for apparently outwitting the traveller.

"You may follow me into the courtyard, but the abbot must decide the rest."

"Thank you." Answered Namdarin with a very quiet sigh of relief.

Silently the monk lead the way, without once revealing a hint of his face, seeming pleased with his deduction of Namdarin's purpose. As the two approached the gate it swung slowly open. It was a foot thick, hard old wooden planks, bound with wrought iron ties, a real siege door. Namdarin tied the horse to a rail beside a doorway that smelled like a stable.

"Wait here. I will fetch the abbot." Instructed the monk, going into a door. Namdarin wandered over to the circular structure in the middle of the paved yard, and found that it was indeed a well. Next to the well was a large wooden barrel, taller than Namdarin and at least five feet across. A storage tank that would only need filling once a day. Two monks came out of the door, possibly his guide and the abbot. Observing the two closely Namdarin discovered that one was obviously older, by his walk, and his shoes had golden buckles. Glancing about the yard he found that the stable hand had black lace up boots, the guards by the door had black boots with white laces, the guide, who appeared to have been in charge of the potato pickers, had black shoes with silver buckles. So their ranks were determined by the footwear, presumably their power as well.

"You want food and lodging, we don't generally welcome strangers. However you may sleep in the stable, food will be brought to you. Do not try to enter any other building. You must leave tomorrow. Is that all clear?"

"Yes, your reverence. I thank you for your hospitality." Replied Namdarin, watching the old abbot return to the door and his guide to the fields. Entering the stable he found it to be just like any other, stalls for the horses and the brown cows, native to the area, a large sturdy pen at the back with some black pigs, beside the pig pen was an open door, which seemed to lead to a dormitory, the ends of two beds were visible from were Namdarin was standing, hay storage above in a large loft, that would make a good bed, but everywhere the black cowled monks watching. Namdarin put Arndrol in an empty stall, un-saddled him and gave him a good rub down, which seemed to please the horse greatly. Filling the manger in the stall with hay he looked round for a water trough to fill a bucket, there wasn't one.

"Where do I get water for the horse?" he asked a nearby stable hand.

"From the big barrel by the well." Was the answer.

"Does all your water come from the well?"

"The barrel is filled every morning and blessed by the abbot, thereby all the water we use is holy water."

"Thank you for your help." said Namdarin thoughtfully. A plan of action was beginning to come together in his mind. Poison was the answer. Poison the water and kill them all. No, that would not work, some would die but the others would realise the water was poisoned. It's a good idea but it won't work like that. He filled his bucket and gave it to a grateful horse. Namdarin got three big armfuls of hay down from the loft so that he could sleep near Arndrol. Settling down in a nest of hay he watched the monks about their business through the open stable door. As the sun went down the monks started to return from the fields, they came in through the big door, bowed to the guards, went to the well, took a drink of the water in the barrel, made a strange hand gesture, then went into the main building. The sunset bathed the whole scene in bright red and gold light, the tower showing red at the top fading to purple towards the bottom. The bell rang loudly and the monks went inside, even the guards by the gate, though, they locked it first. When the bell stopped ringing a muffled chanting came from inside the main building. This was the weakness Namdarin needed, no one to watch the walls, no one to watch the doors, no one about at all. Now is the time to climb a wall and kill them all, but how. A drug to make them all sleep, that is what is required. He thought, put them to sleep then sneak in and cut off all their heads. But what drug to use, something tasteless, odourless, colourless, and available. Valerion, mother used it to help grandma sleep when she was sick. In the valley he had seen the tall pink flowers, on a hillside above a stream, they will do nicely.

About an hour after sunset the monks came out of the main part of the monastery and performed some sort of purification ceremony at the well, which involved washing in the cold water and then drinking it. 'Just wonderful,' Namdarin thought, 'they all use the water, and it can put them all to sleep.'   Soon a low ranking monk in black-laced boots came to Namdarin with a tray of food, the monk offered the tray but said nothing, the food was plain but good. After eating Namdarin settled down thinking about the way his mother used to process the valerion, he tried to remember the songs she sang to increase the potency. He was lying in the hay humming the songs to himself when four monks came into the stable and started to put out the lamps, close the shutters and make sure that all the animals were secure, then the four retired to the back room and closed the door. In the darkness, listening the steady breathing of the animals Namdarin was very soon asleep.

With the rising of the sun the monks rang their bell again and went to their prayers. By the time a monk brought breakfast Namdarin had the horse saddled and loaded, feeling an urgent need to set about killing these monks. As he was finishing his meal the abbot arrived, saying, "I see you are ready to leave, that is good. I urge you to cease the search for Granger, he is a charlatan, and will not help you. But if you must look, I hear that he lives in a high snow filled valley to the north of here, a valley so inaccessible that no sane person would go there, especially with winter so close. Granger has only the white grouse and the white foxes for company."

"Thank you," said Namdarin, "for the hospitality you have given and your directions to the home of Granger, though I think I will take your advice and not seek him. I have seen enough snow to last a lifetime."

"A wise choice, go in peace with Zandaar."

These words were nearly the abbots last. Namdarin's hand flew to the sword hilt as he smothered a cry of rage with a cough and forced the hand to release the sword. When the coughing fit subsided the abbot said "It is good to stay out of the snow when your have a cough such as that." Namdarin mounted Arndrol quickly and left in a hurry, not knowing how long he could keep control of the hate growing in his belly. Galloping up the hill away from the monastery he drew his sword and chopped the tops off shrubs and bushes and saplings, finally giving vent to the anger that had built up all night. At the crest he stopped and shouted, "I will kill you all." Then dismounting he lead the horse down the steep and difficult slope into the valley where he knew the plants he needed were growing. The extraction of the useful part of these plants would be time consuming and not easy. He sang the songs again to be sure he had them right before he started the extraction process. The green parts of the plants were pounded into a mush then boiled gently in water, after an hour or two the mixture was cooled and sieved, leaving a clear, sometimes green tinted liquid. As he went down the valley he looked for a place to use, thinking about a cave or a trapper's shack, he couldn't remember seeing any such on the way up, but there was sure to be something of use. In a group of trees, too small to be called a copse, he found a small shack, no a hut really. Going in he found one room with a good roof, a stone fireplace, even some pots and plates. Unloading Arndrol he said. "Go on, have a good run before we start hauling the wood and plants here, go my friend." Arndrol snorted and galloped off through the trees, kicking and jumping, glad to be free of his saddle. Leaving the horse to its joyful play Namdarin set about sorting his possessions and collecting wood for a fire. Here below the snow line there was plenty of grass for the horse, not the lush summer grass of his home, but good enough to fit his needs. With a roaring fire blazing in the hearth Namdarin settled on the rough cot in the corner, wrapped in his blankets he drifted off to sleep.

A loud bang on the door woke Namdarin with a start. He jumped to his feet drew his sword and shouted. "Who is out there?" The only answer was the stamping of hooves. Namdarin pulled his dagger from the top of his boot and moved towards the door, he lifted the latch with the dagger point, stepped to the side and flung the door wide, he stared up into large brown eyes set on a wide grey forehead, he laughed, "I bet I look a bit stupid." He said to Arndrol, "Threatening my only friend with a sword and dagger. What's wrong? You want to come inside, don't you? You're not used to sleeping on your own any more, are you? Well come in, but don't step on anything and don't make any mess, is that clear?"

The horse nodded and pushed his way in, being very careful he turned about to face the door again. Namdarin looked around the hut and said. "It certainly looks like a stable now. Let's get some sleep shall we?" The gentle snuffling of the horses breathing soon lulled Namdarin back to sleep.

It took Namdarin three days to make enough of the sleeping drug for all the monks in the monastery, he ended up with a flask containing two pints of green viscous fluid, of hopefully extreme potency. On the fourth day after his arrival at the hut he left it, in much the same condition as he found it but with a string of dried fish fastened to the chimney stack by way of payment for the real owner of the hut. It was afternoon before he reached the ridge, the deeper snow making travelling more difficult than last time, he stayed on the ridge, well out of sight, until the bell started to toll, racing ahead of the darkness he descended to the monastery, when he was still about half a mile away the bell stopped. Namdarin pulled the horse to a quick halt, so that the pounding of hooves would not alert the guards at the gate. Standing very still the only sounds that Namdarin could hear were the thumping of his heart, and the panting of Arndrol from the run down the hill. Approaching the walls at a walk he peered through the descending gloom knowing that the guards had gone but still not really trusting just one observation. He rode quietly over the bridge to the gate then inside the moat along the wall to the lowest point of the southern side of the courtyard. He leaned forward and whispered, "Stand still my friend." into the horse's ear, then climbed onto the saddle and then up on the wall. Lying along the top of the wall he listened very carefully for any sound other than the chanting from the main section of the buildings. There was no noise in the yard at all. "Go and hide." he said to the horse, who waded across the moat and into a field were he found some tasty winter cabbages, which he set about with a will. Namdarin chuckled at the crunching of greens and thought 'Well the monks will have no need of them, I hope.' After climbing slowly down the wall he crept across the yard to the well house, and then inside. Peering over the edge of the barrel he found that it was just under half full, "Good that means they won't fill it up tonight, they will only have to fill it in the morning, that will make the poison stronger." He whispered to himself thinking 'This talking to myself is going to have to stop.' He sprinkled the potion on the surface of the water then stirred it in with a ladle used to fill buckets, then he emptied all the buckets that still had some water in them, so that every one of the monks would have to use the water in the barrel. Sneaking back across the yard and over the wall he made good his escape. He found the horse by simply following the noise of crunching cabbages. Namdarin had planned to return to the ridge for the night but Arndrol in swimming across the moat had soaked all the firewood. So they headed for a stand of trees to the south in the hope of finding a place to stay warm until the morning, as it was they were lucky to find a small dell and enough dry wood for a small smokeless fire. Namdarin had little sleep, thinking of the battle to come, he spent most of the night honing dagger and sword, checking arrows and bow and touching up his arrowheads with a small whetstone ground for the purpose.

Before the dawn Namdarin was concealed in the undergrowth at the edge of the trees, awaiting the dawn bell to call the monks to prayers. The sky lightened and the bell was silent. The sun edged over the hills and the bell didn't ring. The sun cleared the hills and started to burn the mist from the moat and still no sound nor motion from the monastery. A fierce joy filled Namdarin's heart as he called his horse and galloped up to the gate. Climbing over the gate he found the guards fast asleep at their posts. He stabbed them through the heart with a cruel smile. Opening the gate he wedged it with a guards spear then broke the shaft so that the gate could not be easily closed. "Go and eat some more of those cabbages," he said to the horse, "but be ready, I may need to leave in a hurry." Namdarin checked the well house, it was empty. Into the stable, to where the stable boys slept in their small dormitory at the back. Three swift slashes with the sword and three of the four were dead, the fourth was struggling to wake up when Namdarin cut his throat with a single sweep, then watching the blood spraying up the wall, Namdarin giggled. "This is going to be easy." On the way out of the stable he butchered the squealing pigs in their pen.

He ran across the yard to the door, it was unlocked, inside a corridor went left and right, which way? He decided to go right towards the tower, where the chapel and other major rooms should logically be. At the end of the corridor was a large studded door, again unlocked, beyond it was a large room, with an altar at the far end, the chapel. Two monks seem to have fallen asleep facing the altar, they were dispatched rapidly by a red soaked blade. In the corner of the chapel was a small door. "The tower." muttered Namdarin. Sure enough, it opened on to a narrow winding stairway up to a small room containing a large bell and two more sleeping, snoring monks, they soon snored no more. On his way back down to the chapel Namdarin wondered if any of the monks in the tower were on watch the night before when he sneaked in over the wall, if they were, they were asleep then as well. Once back in the chapel he checked the other two doors, one led down a corridor to what smelled like a kitchen, the other to a row of many small doors, probably the monks cells. "The kitchen first I think", mumbled Namdarin, to no body in particular. He was wrong about the kitchen, down the corridor and through the door he came to the refectory, rows of long tables with hard wooden benches alongside. No one about, the smell of food gets stronger so the door opposite must lead to the kitchen, this time he was right. Here there were six monks, one was trying to wake up the others, with no apparent success. The monk saw Namdarin and grabbed a large knife from one of the tables then charged, straight onto Namdarin's sword, the black robed monk gurgled, spitting blood all over Namdarin, coughed, and died. The other five monks were beheaded at the table were they slept, their blood pooling on the table and pouring off the edges in thick red streams. The storerooms and larders off the kitchen revealed lots of food, and wine, but no more monks, so Namdarin returned to the chapel and the corridor to the cells. Opening the first door along the corridor there was a sleeping monk, then he was dead. The second door the same, and the third, fourth, fifth, all the same small rooms containing a bed, a table, and a monk. In the sixth room the monk was awake, or very nearly, and kneeling praying in front of a symbol on the wall. The symbol was five yellow lightening bolts and five red flames radiating from the centre on a blue background, the whole seemed to twist and turn, rotating first one way then the other, the centre pulled the eye in and grew into a whirling vortex. Namdarin snatched his eyes away and chopped the monks neck, his arm felt weak and it took three strokes before the head thudded to the floor, then Namdarin noticed the monks shoes, shiny black with bright golden buckles, a high ranking Zandaar indeed. Looking up the symbol on the wall was only a painting, static and quiet. "Ah, resistance at last, this was a magical snare to entrap my mind. You will have to try harder Zandaar." Said Namdarin as he went on to the next room, being more careful. On down the corridor he went, and found only sleeping monks in all the others, until at the last door he paused, hearing a mumbling noise from the room. As he opened the door he saw a large snake, its head the size of a large dogs, its body blue, red and yellow diamond shapes, it hissed loudly and advanced. The coils of the serpent seemed to fill the room behind it, and it poured through the door like a wave. Namdarin ran backwards up the corridor, the snake raised its head almost to the ceiling and full fifteen feet up, then began to creep towards the man. Namdarin backed off until he was thirty feet from the snake, sheathed both sword and dagger, took his bow from his back and an arrow from his quiver, pulled and shot straight for the snake's eye. "Thirty feet, an almost stationary target, how can I have missed?" he said. Taking another arrow he fired again, very carefully this time, watching the arrow all the way. The string twanged, the bow thrummed the arrow hissed through the air, into the snake's head, then thud. "Thud? Try again." Said Namdarin confused by the delay in the sound. Another arrow the same result, into the head, wait, then thud. "Figment, illusion." Shouted Namdarin, "At the end of this corridor is a door with three arrows in it. This evil snake does not exist." Putting his bow on his back he drew sword and dagger again, and charged straight at the snake, as the flesh of his hand, not the sword but living flesh, passed through the snakes head it dissolved like the nightmare it was. At the end of the corridor was a door with two arrows in it. "Only two, where's the other? It's not lying on the floor so it didn't strike the wall." He opened the door and there before him on the floor was another of the high ranking Zandaars with an feather in his eye. The feather of the third arrow. "Did touching the snake or this arrow make it disappear? This is an important question if they are going to use these tactics again. I must remember to ask Granger if I ever find him." The cooling monk paid no attention. "Right that is every where to the right of the main entrance cleared out. Let's see what surprises are the other way."

Off the corridor to the left of the main door there were only two rooms, the first, with a large double door, was a library, many books no monks, the other room had a single door, the first one to be locked. Placing his ear against the hard wood of the door Namdarin could just hear something, but he couldn't tell what it was, talking, singing, chanting, parrots in a cage, it could be any of these. The hair on the back of his neck started to tingle and prickle like when somebody was watching him. 'It's the abbot in there and he's up to no good.' Thought Namdarin. 'They burned my house so I'll burn theirs.' He went to the library and started moving the books to the abbot's door. In the middle of the library was a lectern on which rested a very large book, its thick yellowing pages bore a script the Namdarin had never seen before, the illumination of the pages and the beautifully carved leather cover showed that this was important to the Zandaar, "I will take this one with me it may be helpful for Granger if I survive this day." said Namdarin. All the time he was piling the books against the abbots door the feeling that he was being watched got worse, he kept turning round and suddenly looking over his shoulder to try and catch some one behind him. He knew from the lay out of the rooms that there was no other exit for the abbot as his room was in the corner of the building, unless there was an underground section, Namdarin could not remember seeing any trapdoors in the floors he had crossed, but that did not mean they weren't there. "The storerooms and the wine cellars are all above ground so there is no need to dig a real cellar, I hope." said Namdarin, getting more and more nervous. He set fire to the books outside the abbot's door, and waited until they were fully alight and the door started to smoulder, then turned to leave. The day suddenly became very dark, like a thundercloud had just covered the sun in an instant. Namdarin's skin started to itch like hot lime had been poured all over him, the light continued to fade, now down to twilight, he ran, to the library to get the book then out of the door into full darkness, "Is this what the black fire feels like?" he moaned. Staggering to the well house he covered himself in cold water from the barrel, being careful not to drink any, but this did not help the burning sensation that was consuming his whole identity. In complete blackness him stumbled into the stable, his sense of smell and hearing were unaffected, he could smell burning hair and cooking flesh, he could hear crackling flames. He fell screaming to the floor, he fell into a deep black well full of pain, darkness and burning knives, the agony increased until his brain could stand no more, it turned off the pain, then it too turned off.

A strange thought tumbled through Namdarin's unconscious brain, 'Cabbages.' The darkness returned but the struggle to reality was started. 'Cabbages.' An unusual thought, not a thought, a smell. Gradually awakening he asked "Cabbages?" Again a warm breeze heavily scented with cabbages blew across his face. He opened his eyes to see large yellow and green teeth only inches from his nose, two great pink pits blew cabbage fumes into his face, above them two enormous brown eyes stared down. It's a horse, which at least begins to make sense of some sort. It's Arndrol. Namdarin reaches his arms around the horse's neck and hugs him tightly, Arndrol backs away and lifts his friend to his feet, Namdarin staggers, then looks down at his unruly knees to tell them to start co-operating. He is completely naked, not just without clothes but also without hair, the patch of ground were he had lain was blackened and charred, all around were the bones of horses and pigs, the stable was a ruin of black destruction. Shivering in the cold air Namdarin clings to the horse and guides him to the well house, they both drink cold water from the well. Namdarin picks up his sword from the floor, were he had dropped it, wiped the black soot from the hilt, he noticed the Zandaars book on the floor, and then began to feel a little more confident.

"Wait here, my friend." He says to the horse, "I must get some clothes from inside. I won't be long." Still unsteady on his feet he goes into the main entrance. "First some food." he mumbles, wobbling towards the kitchens. Once there he takes bread and cheese and some meat and fruit. Sitting at a clean, un-bloodied table he thinks. "I have died again, but returned to life. Died by the Zandaars black fire, oh the burning, the memory of it causes pain to course through the muscles. Awakening I see the bones of once living animals, like the wood buck, the villagers and now the animals of the stable. The pigs were already dead, I remember killing them, but the horses were alive and now they are bones. This is indeed a mystery, some magic that involves me and the old gods. I need food and clothes, these monks around me have need of none, and so theirs will have to do. The abbot and whoever else was in his rooms, I must make sure they are dead or word of what happened here will escape too soon. The strength returns to my limbs quickly, I must be getting used to dying. What an awful thought. Time to move." He gets up from the table and goes to cells to see what clothing the monks can lend him. In the cupboard in the first cell he finds soft underclothes and stockings, some good woollen jackets, and the long black robes, that the monks normally wear. Putting on the clothes and the monks long black boots, he gathers a few extra garments because he knows that he must go up into the snowbound mountains to find Granger the magician. Wishing for a suitable scabbard for his sword he pushes it under his belt and goes towards the abbot's rooms. As he approaches he sees results of his handiwork, the door is a pile of ash on the floor, grey ash in the black ash of burned books. Peering through the now open doorway he sees a room blackened by fire, completely destroyed. Bookshelves around the walls must have fed the fire he started, the carpet, the furniture was all gone to charcoal, the smell of overcooked meat hung in the air.

"It looks and smells like the bottom of a barbecue pit." He says to himself. The window frames still contained broken fragments of glass, heat blurred on the edges, all still closed. "No body went out of the windows, it seems that there were only the three of them in here," said Namdarin counting the skulls he could see about the floor. Returning to the kitchen he gathers some dried meat and biscuits, some fruit and bread, some wine and spirits, and from the back of one of the dark store rooms a longbow and quiver of arrows. Carrying all his booty he goes to the courtyard to meet Arndrol, who is getting very restless by now. Once the horse is loaded he mounts and goes out of the gate. Standing on the bridge over the moat he thinks. "East or west." He can't go directly north to find Granger he has to use the passes into the mountains, "The eastern side I know nothing about, the west I know to be hard to climb, I think the west is the best, the prevailing wind dumps its snow on the western slopes and the abbot mentioned snow grouse and white fox. West it is." The decision made he set off up the slope to the pass by which he had come upon the den of Zandaar. At the crest he turned and shouted. "I said I would kill you all, and I did." Forgetting for a while that they had killed him as well.

CHAPTER THREE

Knowing that his way was generally northwards he set off down the valley along the northern wall looking for the first usable pass into the next valley. After trying two passes that ended in sheer rock faces, the third was more productive, it climbed steeply until it reached a high plateau, with a small tarn, some trees, and some deer, one of which he shot with his new bow. The accuracy and power of the bow were not up to the standard of the bow that had burned in the monastery, but it would have to do until he could make or buy a better one. With the best cuts of the deer fastened to the horse he set off down into the next valley. Only a few minutes down the hill he heard a loud roaring like an angry lion, only somehow bigger. Deciding to investigate the source of the noise he galloped into a small off shoot valley which climbed to small col. Against one sheer rock wall stood a tall red headed woman, shouting and fighting for her life. Standing facing the woman was a white bear, a full eight feet tall, howling with pain as the woman slashed its forepaw with a long dagger. Namdarin approached the bear carefully, quietly dismounting and pulling his sword from his belt. When he was nearer he could see the remains of a sword in the bears right front leg, which was hanging uselessly. The fur clad woman was hard pressed keeping the bears slashing claws away from her, the wicked point of her knife weaving a glittering cage of steel between her body and the bear. Namdarin stood un-noticed behind the bear, took a good grip with both hands on the hilt of his sword, kissed the blade, said a quick prayer and struck. A slicing two handed stroke that cut the hamstrings in both of the bears legs, it screamed and fell forwards, in the instant that the sword struck the woman rolled to her left under the bears useless right foreleg, before it hit the ground she was on its back, calmly she pushed her knife into its neck between the skull and the first vertebra, then gave the knife a savage twist. The huge white bear twitched and died. The woman withdrew her knife, wiped it on the white head, and sat, panting, watching Namdarin very carefully. Namdarin looked into her blazing green eyes, the deep colour of priceless emeralds. As neither spoke the tension in the air rose, she gripped the knife tightly and watched his sword, he stared, lost in her eyes.

"Thank you", she said, "for your un-needed help. If you want the pelt of my bear then we must fight now." She rose to her full height and stood ready. Namdarin looked straight into her eyes, as she was very nearly as tall as him.

"I have no intention to claim any of the bear, nor to make war on a woman who thinks she could beat that monster with only a poignard. Why do you take on such a large bear on your own?"

"I had hoped it would be sleeping and I am alone and have no choice."

"Even a sleeping bear is difficult to kill, why go after a bear at all?"

"The pelt will keep me warm through the winter, the meat is good and there is plenty of fat stored to last the bear through the cold. These are the prizes, so the risk is small."

"I am called Namdarin, I am glad that I was of some small help in your struggle with this useful bear, please tell me how I can be of more help, you are going to need some because not all the blood on your clothes is from the bear. Where is his cave? We will need some shelter from the weather."

"The cave is over there behind those boulders, it is quite large to have only one bear in it." She was beginning to tremble as the rush of adrenalin started to subside. Namdarin whistled loudly. Arndrol galloped up and stood near the bear sniffing and shifting from one foot to another, uncomfortable so close to a large predator, even a dead one. Namdarin tied a rope the hind leg of the bear, then passed the other end three times round the saddle horn. "Pull hard, my friend. Its not far to go, come on, pull." The horse's haunches rippled with the effort but slowly and jerkily the bear began to slide towards the rocks that concealed its den. The woman looked on in amazement as the horse dragged the bear, which must have been the heaviest of the two, across the rocky ground with only the man's words driving it on. Arndrol's nose was almost touching the rock-face above the bear's den when he stopped. "Well done, my friend." said Namdarin, as he unfastened the rope and then all the other baggage, and finally the saddle. "Go and rest and eat and play, you have earned it." He said patting Arndrol's flank and sending him on his way. Down to the pass trotted the horse, to find good grass to eat and the cold clear water of the tarn to drink.

Namdarin sorted through his luggage then set to starting a fire in the small mouth of the cave, which was about three feet high and four wide. The woman seemed very unsure of Namdarin despite his help with the bear approaching slowly she spoke. "Why the sword and not an arrow?"

"An arrow might not have got through its back to the heart, which would have been the quickest kill, I chose the sword because it gave a very good chance of completely immobilising the bear with one stroke, as was the case. Had I known how you intended to kill it, I would merely have tapped it on the shoulder to make it turn round so that you could finish it with that little knife. It will soon be dark, if you start work on the bear, skinning it, butchering it whatever you want to do with it, I'll go and get some firewood, so we wont get cold." This said Namdarin walked off, not only to get some wood but also to give the woman time to settle down and get her thoughts in order, to realise that he meant her no harm. She didn't seem to want to trust him. When he returned with his arms full of dead wood she had slit the bear open from throat to anus and removed most of its internal organs, she carried its intestines and stomach some way off because they would give off a very unpleasant smell before the morning. While he built the fire up she lifted the enormous liver out of the almost empty bear, carefully she laid it on the ground and cut it into two almost equal pieces.

"Come and take your pick, hunters must always share the choicest bits." she said, looking him straight in the eye. He was again astounded by the deep emerald glow of her beautiful eyes. He chose the smaller of the two pieces saying, "I'll have that one, thank you very much. The bear is all yours. I would never have the courage to hunt such on my own." She picked up the other, larger, piece of liver and began to eat it raw, taking huge bites and swallowing them almost immediately. When she was half way through her share, she glanced up to see Namdarin's puzzled look.

"It is really good, still warm and bloody like this." She said. Namdarin cut a small section off his share and ate it, he was surprised how good it did taste, he had never before had liver this fresh. He looked at the woman and saw that she was covered in the bears blood on both arms up to the elbows on the face and chin and down her front, she was bright red, and happy. When she had finished her liver Namdarin still had a lot left, though it was going quickly. Namdarin looked at her and said. "Have you any belongings hidden somewhere?" She jumped up, startled, "Oh, I forgot about that." Then she ran off. Namdarin put down his liver deciding to save some for later, took a burning log from the fire and went to investigate the cave, inside the opening it widened out until it was about fifteen feet wide and ten feet deep, the roof was twenty feet high in the middle and the walls came down from the highest point to leave an almost cone shaped cavity, plenty of room for three or four bears, or two people but not both. He wrapped some of the bedding that the bear had brought in for his winter sleep around a branch, then set fire to it to make a torch, which he wedged in a crack in the wall, this illuminated the cave quite nicely. He split the bedding into three piles, one for him, one for her, and one for Arndrol, who would have to sleep outside. He went back outside to see if the woman had returned, the sun had gone below the mountain tops and still there was no sign of her, Arndrol came back and settled in his bedding as instructed, near the fire and the entrance to the cave. Namdarin sat by the fire, fidgeting, wondering why he was worrying about a complete stranger who had already proved her survival abilities. Staring into the flames he thought about her, she was almost as tall as him, though much lighter, she had curves in all the right places, she had wiry muscles and lightening speed, she had real agility and courage, she had a beautiful face and eyes full of wild green fire. "No." He said. I mustn't think these thoughts I have a family to avenge and an oath to keep, I don't have time for such dalliances with women. The thoughts of her would not go away, he could see her as a large wild cat, cornered and defending her kittens, savage and angry, attacking with a total disregard for her own safety. Arndrol snorted. "What's wrong my friend." he said, looking around to find the woman returned and standing only five feet from him, "How did you get so close without me knowing?" He asked her. "You were watching the fire and almost asleep, which is a quick way to die in these mountains, there are lions and leopards hereabouts you know." She replied putting down her large rucksack, she had obviously taken time to wash the blood from her face and arms, her long red hair was tied back by a leather strap, that looked strangely wide and sturdy for such a simple task.

"My name is Namdarin", He said "of the house of Namdaron. Which is many miles to the west of here. Who are you?"

"I am called Jayanne, and I have no house nor people to call my own."

"My house is destroyed and my people dead. But I will not give up my name until my task is completed."

"Well Namdarin, the task of the moment is the butchering of a large white bear, if you wish a share of it you must help me to first skin it then dismember it. Are you willing, lord?" she asked with an acidic emphasis on the last word.

"Despite your cruel mocking of my fate, I will help you. If only to look upon your beautiful face for a while longer." He replied smiling, almost cheerful.

Together they set about cutting the skin from the bear first from the head then down the body until after half an hours hard work it was off in one piece. Butchery was easier he chopped the difficult bits with his sword, and she carved the meat from the bones.

"Surely its easier to cook with the bones in." He said.

"Yes, but bear bones are very heavy to carry if you're going any distance."

"I'm going north to look for a magician called Granger, where are you going?" He asked, hoping that she was going the same way.

"I go south, heading for warmer country, to look for a new life."

"What happened to your old life?"

"My old people, who have disowned me, believe that a woman belongs to the man her parents chose as her husband. They chose wrongly for me, they picked a coward and a bully, he was bigger and stronger than me, he hurt me, I killed him."

"Only a few words but such a sad tale, how did your parents come to make such a fatal mistake?"

"He was the son of the chief elder, he showered them in gifts and promises he did not keep, they saw only a large increase in status, for me and indirectly for them. They denounced me because the chief elder told them to. The brave men of the village chased me off with spears and swords, but they will not have forgotten the gifts I left them with. No, they'll not forget."

"Well if you're going south, head westwards my old home is that way, it's burned and probably still empty, but it has great potential, it was once rich and beautiful."

"I may go that way. I can help you a little, I have seen Granger in the last few days, his home is in a wide valley just north of here, as you go north its the third valley you will come to. He said I should go east as there is a monastery in one of these valleys, where I can get further directions and perhaps some help."

"The monks cannot help you now, their monastery is dead and empty. This Granger is he likely to help me? I have a difficult oath to fulfil and I think I will need some magic just to survive."

"He seemed a reasonably helpful person, but what is this task of yours?"

"My home and people were destroyed by some evil priests, I have sworn vengeance upon them and I will kill them all. They wanted a good portion of my lands to build a monastery, I said no. They wanted my son to become one of their acolytes, he said no, so I said no. They twice sent mercenaries to take my son. Then two priests came and demanded that I give up my only son or they would bring my house down. In the struggle one priest died, the other got away. A few days later I returned from a hunt and the house was ruins, everyone dead. The buildings they destroyed but the house of Namdaron lives on in me. While I breathe they will pay, pay with life after life, until I, or they are no more. The monastery that Granger told you of was one of theirs, I have been there."

"What are these priests called?"

"They are the priests of Zandaar, they wear long black robes and black shoes."

"There was such a man staying with the chief elder in my old village. He really made me nervous, I don't know why, but he did."

"It is very dark now, I suggest we get some sleep, the cave is big enough. Arndrol you can keep watch. Wake us up if anything or anyone comes near." Said Namdarin to the big grey, who snorted in reply and settled deeper into his bedding. Namdarin and Jayanne went into the cave and wrapping themselves in heavy blankets went straight to sleep, as it had been a hard day for both.

Namdarin was woken by the singing of birds, he looked across the cave to were Jayanne was sleeping to discover that she had gone. He went outside and Arndrol was gone as well, in a momentary panic he glanced round the area about the cave, finally he saw Arndrol by some boulders eating the lush green grass that grew were a small spring came from beneath the rocks. The fire was built fairly high and some of the bear was roasting beside it, Namdarin turned the meat to help it cook evenly, then put the remains of his share of the liver beside it to cook for his breakfast. He wandered over to Arndrol to see if there was a pool big enough to wash in, finding one suitable he drank then washed, all the while wondering where Jayanne had gone. Her rucksack was still there by the fire, so she can't have gone far. Suddenly Arndrol stamped his feet in alarm causing Namdarin to look round for what ever had disturbed the horse, all he saw were three large black weasel like creatures, coming down the rocks. The three scampered over to were Jayanne had left he bears innards, and began to fight over what they considered the choicest bits. After a few minutes of their squealing and squabbling, Namdarin decided he didn't want to share his campsite with such noisy and troublesome neighbours, so he ran towards them waving his sword and shouting to scare them off. The three stood their ground and snarled at the man, who stopped short amazed that the small creatures would threaten him. Namdarin didn't want to get to close to the brave little carnivores, but he also didn't want to waste arrows on them. An arrow would go clean through their small bodies and probably break on the rocks. So Namdarin looked around for some rocks to throw at the little monsters. As soon as he bent down to gather a few stones Jayanne came running up. She had heard him shouting and came at once. She saw the weasels, she snarled much as they did, her right hand snatched the strap from her hair, her left hand dived into her pocket, three times the left hand went to the strap, three times to strap spun, three times something flew rapidly through the air, three times a weasel was hit, crack, crack, crack, quicker than it can be said.

Jayanne ran over to the weasels, two were dead, the third was trying to run away but its back was broken, Jayanne approached the last living weasel with dagger drawn, the weasel threw itself on the point of the blade in an effort to bite her hand, it died scrabbling at the guard of the knife with its long bloody claws.

"How I hate these thieving little fiends." She said.

"What on earth were they? They didn't seem to know the meaning of fear."

"They are black devils, they are savage, vicious, monsters, who fight with any animal or man for food, they're not frightened of fire, or noise, or smoke, or wolves, or bears, or thunder, or lightening, their only saving grace is the pelts. They are soft and fine, really warm, and collect no frost in winter, so they makes good hoods."

"I have never seen their like anywhere."

"They only live in the high mountains, or the far north where the weather is much cooler."

"I have not seen a sling used to such good effect either, was that the gift you left to the men that chased you from your home?"

"Yes, though I did not cause them serious injury, just enough pain to teach them not to come too close."

"Have you any other weapons concealed that may surprise me, or is that the only one?"

"My sling is the only weapon that I ever conceal. I am good with a bow, quite good with the sword, when I have one, I can beat about half the men in the village at the fencing tournaments, but the strong ones just beat my blade aside and I am done. I can fight very well at close range with a knife, were speed is more important than strength. I ride horses to hounds occasionally. Other than this I am a poor defenceless woman, struggling to survive the harsh wilderness." She smiled and her green eyes flashed in the sun.

"I hope the wilderness survives the struggle, for it is almost as beautiful as you." He replied laughing. They shared the joke for a while then she showed him how to skin the black devils. Namdarin thought about a woman alone in the winter and her chances of seeing the spring, finally he said "Jayanne. If you wish to return to your village, I am sure it could be arranged. There is a Zandaar there and I will kill him, if you go back there with me they may accept your return."

"I would like to see my parents again if only to show that I am still alive, despite everything that they could do."

"Right, before you go back to visit you will need weapons and a horse, these might be obtained from an old monastery that I know of. Do you agree?"

"Yes, but before we go there I must finish curing the bearskin, it will make an impressive cloak, don't you think?"

"Oh yes, most impressive, a shame though that we cut off the head, with the bears head resting on yours looking down on people with its empty eyes would make them tremble and shake with fear. Perhaps we could sew it back on."

"I don't think sewing the head on will look right, but if we smoke the skin over the fire and rub some of its own fat into the inside, it should be usable before tomorrow."

"I had forgotten something, where were you when I woke up?" He asked.

"I went to collect some wild carrots from just over the rise, to go with the bear meat, that smells like it's burning." She ran over to the fire and quickly turned to meat over and Namdarin's piece of liver. Wrapping the carrots tightly in dry grass she put them near the fire to bake. She tied the bearskin to a couple of straight sticks and draped it over the fire, then put some wet leaves on the fire to make some smoke. She moved with complete efficiency, no wasted effort at all, as if she had been doing this all her life. Sensing Namdarin's interested stare she said. "It makes a change having someone else to think about, in the five weeks since I left my village I have spoken only to Granger, and that only for a few minutes of one afternoon."

"What sort of new life are you looking for?" He asked thinking about places she might go.

"Being alone has been fun but there can only be so much excitement, already I crave company, travel and new things to see and do, once my parents know that I am not going to try and come back they might realise how much I hate to be tied down to one place."

"Why don't you come along with me? I intend to travel the whole world if necessary, it may be hard going at times, the excitement may be more than you could want, but it certainly will not be boring."

"We certainly seem to be going the same way for a while lets see how things turn out when it is time to leave my village."

It was nearly noon when the meat and carrots were ready to eat, so they ate and settled down for an afternoon nap. Arndrol rested standing up nearby, his digestion working overtime on the glut of grass that he had been eating all morning. Namdarin woke in the middle of the afternoon to find Jayanne rubbing half melted bear fat into the bearskin with a rib bone donated for the purpose by the bear. In the warm sunlight she had removed most of her furs and was wearing a small tight cloth jacket and short breeches, she was working hard leaning on the rib pushing the fat backwards and forwards working it into the skin, Namdarin watched the play of light on the muscles of her arms and legs as they tensed and relaxed. He saw the red freckles on her skin, and her long red hair, that swung to and fro refusing to be tied in place by the sling. Unbidden he thought of her naked working the hide, and he felt a sudden rush of blood. If the quest were over this would be the woman to rebuild the house of Namdaron, a wife to him and mother of his children. Looking about her he saw her knife, handle upright in the grass only inches from her right hip, and a pile of round stones only a foot from her left hip ready for the sling. She is battle ready at all times. Something attracted her attention, possibly the harshness of his breathing, she looked at him and recognised the fire in his eyes and the passion in his belly. She knew the meaning of this look, she remembered the whips and the ropes and the pain. She knew that she would never again suffer this at the hands of a man, staring coldly into his eyes she took her knife firmly in her right hand and waited. He felt the ice in her eyes, saw the white knuckles holding the knife, he knew that his daydream of her would not be easily fulfilled, so he rolled over to face away from her and let the tension of the situation subside. When his passion had decreased he went to relieve himself, then returned asking, "How is the hide coming along? It looks very good."

"It is nearly finished and yes it will be a good skin, which should be worth a lot of money in a large town." She answered calmly, showing that she wanted to forget the incident of only moments ago. Namdarin saw that if he wanted this woman he would have to win her very carefully, or he may wake up with that sharp knife in his back. He began to look on this as a second quest to be delayed until his war with the Zandaar was over. By the end of the day they had both forgotten about his awakening, and relaxed into a sort of routine typical of campsites everywhere. They tidied their belongings in preparation for the journey that would start the next morning. They ate cold bear meat for supper and went into the cave to sleep. By the flickering light of the torch on the wall Namdarin could she her lovely red hair spread out like a halo around her head, he also saw from the position of her right shoulder that her right hand was underneath her head and he knew it must still hold that wicked knife, this thought did not seem to effect the way his body felt about her, his manhood rose hard and throbbing and absolutely refused to go down. After a few minutes of discomfort Namdarin took himself in hand and rubbed himself to a rapid climax. This was the first time he had cause to resort to this method of gratification in many years. His thoughts were still of Jayanne as the deep blackness of sleep overcame him.

As the sun came up in the morning he awoke feeling a little guilty about his actions the night before. The thought of the family destroyed by the Zandaar, of his wife who had attended to his every need, and of his only son, the joy of his life. He closed his eyes to help him visualise the face of Althone, his wife. To his amazement and extreme discomfort her face seemed to be blurred around the edges, as if he was forgetting how she looked. The harder he tried to bring the picture of her into focus the more it faded, to be replaced by Jayanne's pretty features, and her savage independence. He left the cave to find Jayanne and to start packing up the horse so they could leave soon, outside the ground was covered with a thin layer of snow, and a few flakes were still blowing in the wind which had move to a northerly direction and was decidedly cooler. The puddle where he had washed the day before had a thin film of ice on it, which he broke without thought, drinking and washing as before.

When he stood up Arndrol came trotting towards him, tossing his large head, shaking his thick mane, and stamping his heavy hooves, the horse knew they were going somewhere today and was anxious to be off.

"Yes my friend, we will go as soon as we are ready and all your fidgeting will not speed things up, so relax and behave yourself."

The horse went back to eating the grass. Namdarin went to the edge of the col to see if Jayanne was anywhere about, she was by the stream digging, 'Probably carrots.' he thought going back to the fire and calling to Arndrol. By the time Jayanne returned with her crop of carrots the horse was saddled and nearly loaded. "Only the last of the meat to load, then he's ready." He said.

"Let's eat the rest of the cold meat for breakfast." She said, slicing it into large chunks. In a few moments breakfast was finished. Namdarin mounted, checking the loading and that there was enough flat space behind him for Jayanne to sit, he reached down with his right arm and lifted her up on to the horse. As her weight settled onto Arndrol's back the horse laid his ears back and stepped sideways quickly. "Settle down boy." Said Namdarin reaching forwards and patting Arndrol's neck.

"Are you ready?" he asked Jayanne, as she reached both hands round him.

"Yes, I suppose so," she replied nervously, "he looks a lot bigger from up here." Namdarin laughed quietly and turned the horse towards the exit of the col, setting off at a slow walk to make sure the horse would get used to the load. As they turn south into the pass Namdarin was thinking of Jayanne, the way her warm body pressed against his back, every footstep bouncing them nearer together, the way her breasts rubbed against him meant that he had problems thinking of anything else. When they were walking through the high bracken around the tarn their passing frightened a pair of grouse into the air. The loud clattering of their wings caused Arndrol to sheer away, turning very sharply and rearing, this caused the load on his rump to slip. As the luggage became entangled in his hind legs the huge horse panicked. When the horse started to bolt Namdarin knew he would be uncontrollable so he reached behind himself, grabbed Jayanne firmly with both hands and dived into the bracken. The two landed in a tangle, with him underneath. Jayanne got to her feet immediately to see Arndrol galloping away, bucking and kicking, scattering their luggage over a wide area. She looked down at Namdarin's still figure on the ground, unmoving like the dead. She touched his neck and felt a pulse, so he was still alive. Slowly she straightened out his arms and legs, which all seemed to move in the right places, no broken bones were obvious. Then she turned him over and saw the blood on his face. Wiping the blood away with her bearskin cloak, she found only a small wound, above his right eye, just were his eyebrow should have been.

Feeling around the wound carefully she noticed that the eyebrow was just beginning to grow again, as was the hair of his head. The wound was caused by a rock hidden in the litter of the bracken. She looked down on to his strong and handsome face, thinking that he might have made a good husband, even though he was filled with hate. The gentle stroking of the fur on his face brought Namdarin back to alertness, he opened his large blue eyes, his pupils contracting rapidly to pinpricks because he was looking up into a bright sky, he said "Are you hurt?" Jayanne shook her head.

"No, but you are, so lie still for a while. You were unconscious for a couple of minutes and may be concussed. Do your arms and legs hurt?"

"No more than could be expected falling from a horse. I do feel a little dizzy though. Were has that horse gone?"

"He ran off. How is your vision? Any blurs?"

"No, you look just fine." He replied with a smile.

"Does Arndrol often do that sort of thing?" she asked blushing a pretty pink.

"No. He is generally very trustworthy, obviously all that luggage and two people was just asking too much of him. He will run for a while until he calms down a bit, then he will come back looking guilty and very sorry for himself. He thinks that he is better than other animals and should control his feelings more, but he is still a horse, and horses occasionally bolt."

"Let's see what we can find of the luggage then we can be ready for him when he returns. You take things slowly, that bump on the head may make you a little unsteady." Namdarin tried to stand up, he half succeeded then sat down again with a thump.

"I think I will rest here a while, if that's all right with you?" he said.

She smiled and walked of along the trail of scattered packages, parcels and food. In a matter of moments she found his water bottle and her rucksack, she gave Namdarin a drink and took a bandage from her pack to wrap around his head. Binding the wound tightly soon stopped the bleeding, though she knew that as soon as she took the bandage off it would start again. She returned to her task of collecting, almost everything was recovered undamaged, the only important exception was Namdarin's small tent, it now had a new ventilation hole in the middle, which would have to be patched before the tent could be used. While she rummaged around in the high brown bracken he whistled for the horse. When the pile stacked around Namdarin was nearly complete, he felt good enough to stand up. He was shaky and unsure but at least he was upright, standing with his hand on the hilt of his sword made him feel much better, but whistling still made his ears ring. The two people sorted their belongings out for the second time that day, and waited for Arndrol's return. Jayanne started thinking about the things she would have to leave behind if the horse did not come back. By midmorning they had sorted everything out, and it was all ready for packing on the horse, who remained stubbornly absent. They settled down in a depression in the bracken to get out of the wind. Every few minutes Namdarin would whistle for the horse. Long before the sun would have reached its zenith, if they could have seen it, they heard the thunder of hooves that preceded the horse's return.

Namdarin stood up, so that Arndrol could see him, the horse slowed to a trot, then stopped a few feet away, he was sweating profusely, his flanks covered in white foam. Arndrol hung his head almost to the ground as if tired or ashamed. On the horses back was Namdarin's saddle, with his bow and quiver still attached, tied behind the saddle was a haunch of a deer, these items completed their original stores, so nothing was actually lost. Namdarin calmed the horse, rubbing him down with some dried brown bracken.

"We shall have to let Arndrol carry all the stores while we walk, that will be quickest." Said Namdarin to Jayanne.

"Yes, we can still make good time if we are carrying nothing." She replied helping lift the bear meat onto Arndrol's back. When the horse was loaded again Namdarin gave him a pat on the shoulder and talked quietly to him to make sure he would not panic again. Then taking the reins in his hand started walking south toward the valley with the monastery. He began to feel quite comfortable with Jayanne walking to his left and Arndrol walking calmly just behind and between them. At about midday he saw ahead on the track a small dog like creature, which was half white and half brown.

"Do you know what sort of animal that is?" He asked.

"Yes. It is a fox." Answered Jayanne

"It's a strange colour for a fox."

"No, it's an in-between fox."

"In-between?"

"Yes. The foxes on the foothills are brown and stay brown all year, the foxes in the high slopes are white and stay white all year, the in-betweens live half way up and are brown in the summer and white in the winter, so its an in-between fox. They are the best ones to hunt, because in winter the tip of their tails stays brown, or sometimes red, and the pelts make good decorations."

"That one is not a scout for a pack, is it?"

"No. They are all loners. Its the wolves that hunt in packs round here."

"Wolves are the same everywhere."

"Up in the high mountains the wolves are different, they are very big, almost half the height of Arndrol at the shoulder. Thankfully they are rare, and usually advertise their presence by howling. I haven't heard any."

"I've never heard of wolves that big before, I hope we don't hear any, ever."

The multi-coloured fox continued on ahead of them for a while before disappearing into the brush, obviously chasing some scent. By the middle of the afternoon they had made good progress and were coming down into the valley that lead to the pass for the monastery.

"I know a small hut were we can stay tonight," said Namdarin "we can't make it to the monastery today."

"Lead on. I don't like the idea of sleeping in the open, at least not on the ground."

"Where do you sleep then if not on the ground?"

"I generally climb a tree and tie myself to it."

"That's a good idea. It wouldn't help Arndrol much though." said Namdarin laughing at a picture of the horse stuck up a small tree. Jayanne laughed too. Walking through the brush toward the hut Namdarin started to collect firewood so save a job when they got there. On arrival he discovered that the hut was exactly as he had left it with the dried fish still on the chimney breast. They were quite comfortable that night, Jayanne slept in the bed, her first for a long time, while Namdarin slept on the floor, and Arndrol was very unhappy to be left outside, even though he was wrapped up in a heavy blanket. The morning brought more fresh snow, which blew around the hut on the freshening north wind.

"We should have no problems getting to the monastery, providing that the snow doesn't get too much worse." Said Namdarin while the horse was being loaded, this time the load was covered by the blanket to help keep Arndrol warm. The people wore almost all the clothes they had and still felt chilled when standing still where the wind could blow icy fingers in through the gaps in their garments. Especially Namdarin's head, the hood of his robe did not keep the wind out. Jayanne's bearskin gradually acquired a sugar like frosting of snow, Namdarin's sword became so cold that he was forced to wear his gloves just to touch it. Arndrol started to get very skittish because his tail turned into a frozen mass that kept banging against his legs and making him step forward quickly. Namdarin cut the frozen hair off the tail saying "You really won't need a long tail until summer by then it will have grown again." The horse seemed glad to lose the weight from his tail but a little unhappy to lose such a beautiful decoration. Long before midday they cleared the ridge of the pass and looked down on the monastery in the valley, the third visit for Namdarin and the first for Jayanne. "It looks quite a nice place." said Jayanne as the sun broke through the clouds and picked out the walls and the fields surrounding them. Namdarin thought he saw something moving in the courtyard, but he was still too far away to be sure. The two companions and their horse plodded slowly down the hill and up to the gate. Across the bridge over the moat Namdarin observed the hoof prints of one horse in the snow, they looked very fresh, the edges were sharp and the bottoms of the print showed very clearly the details of the horse's foot, no snow had blown into the print since the horse had made them.

"Be careful." He said. "Somebody is in there ahead of us. Move quietly, and that means you too." he said nudging the horse in the ribs with his elbow. Arndrol blew gently and rested his chin on Namdarin's shoulder. They followed the prints across the yard and into the stable to find a bay mare tied in one of the stalls, still saddled, loaded and breathing fairly hard. Leaving Arndrol in the stable Namdarin and Jayanne went outside and turned towards the door to the main building, following the footsteps of the rider of the other horse they crunched through the snow. They were still some way from the door when a black clad monk came out of the open door and down the steps then he looked up.

"What has happened here brother?" he said seeing a fellow monk in black.

"I know not, who are you brother?" Namdarin asked, noticing that the monk wore a good-looking sword at his hip and silver buckled shoes on his feet.

"I am brother Jorgarna from the abbey at Westfordham, and you brother?"

"I am Namdarin, I come from west of here, what has happened inside?"

"You are no brother of Zandaar. What do you want here? Who is that witch in the white fur?" Answered Jorgarna, pulling his sword halfway clear of its scabbard.

"I want to kill you, as I did the others here, she wants your sword and horse. I will allow you to draw your sword and fight like a man, which is more than I did for your evil brethren." Said Namdarin drawing his sword from his belt and setting his feet in the snow. Jorgarna whipped his sword clear in a fast arc and lunged towards Namdarin, who rather than taking the charge on the point of his sword, side-stepped and struck the monk on the backside with the flat, sending Jorgarna sliding across the ground in the slippery snow. Namdarin took the bow and quiver from his back, tossed them to Jayanne saying "If he runs put an arrow in his legs." While the monk struggled to his feet Jayanne walked across the yard, and nocked an arrow. Jorgarna watched her, but she was already too far away for him to reach her before her arrow reached him. Turning to face Namdarin he said. "Why did you do this dreadful thing?"

"You and your people destroyed that which was me, now I will destroy everything that is you. Let us see the standard of sword play taught in these places, if you fight well you will die fast." The monk knew that he was no match for Namdarin, so he attacked savagely, hoping to overwhelm the older man and get in a lucky stroke. Namdarin stood stock still in the snow, parrying with lightening speed. For three whole minutes and some of the fourth the monk sustained the onslaught, nicking Namdarin twice, once in the left side, and once in the right thigh. Both men were breathing hard when the monk caught Namdarin's sword in a bind and came in close pushing both blades high over their heads, as they struggled each to push the other off balance, Jorgarna reached for the knife in Namdarin's belt, only to find that Namdarin's left hand was already on it. Jorgarna jumped back from the bind and for the first time in the duel Namdarin moved, he stepped forwards and slashed, the tip of his sword took the monk in the right forearm, Jorgarna looked down at the blood pouring down his arm, covering his hand and sword hilt in a sticky mess, while he was so mesmerised Namdarin slashed the sword just above the hilt, it shattered and fell to the snow, Namdarin recovered and plunged his sword into the monks elbow joint and the monk quickly followed the remains of his sword.

"Go on, kill me." Said Jorgarna, kneeling on the snow, watching the red patch near his hand grow.

"No, you did not fight well enough for a quick death, in fact the only quick death you could have won was an arrow in the back having first killed me. I want information and you are going to give it."

"No. I will tell you nothing at all." The monk looked Namdarin straight in the eye hoping that Namdarin would believe him. The tip of Namdarin's sword touched his throat and the monk pushed towards it only to find it had gone. Jorgarna was still looking for the sword tip when Namdarin's boot hit him full in the face sending him sprawling on the cold ground. Jorgarna tried to shake his head to clear his vision but found movement restricted by the presence of Namdarin's heavy left boot on his neck. With the point of his sword Namdarin cut away the monks clothing, and nicked him a few times, these cuts bled little in the cold air. Namdarin looked down on the shivering naked monk, who had a large tattoo on his chest, the symbol of Zandaar. Namdarin pricked the mans nipple then ran the tip of the sword down his body to his genitalia. He pushed the monks penis from side to side a few times then laid the edge against its root, the cold steel caused the monk to hold perfectly still. Namdarin looked into his eyes and smiled. The monk knew fear. Namdarin removed the sword from its warm resting place, and plunged it straight into the monks knee joint, with a savage twist of the wrist the joint was destroyed, Jorgarna screamed and struggled, to no avail. The other knee got the same treatment. Another scream but less struggle. Namdarin heard a noise across the courtyard, he looked up to see that Jayanne had dropped his bow, and was kneeling in the white snow, emptying the steaming contents of her stomach. Namdarin went back to his grizzly task. The monks left elbow went the same way as his knees. This time the scream was only a gurgle and Jorgarna closed his eyes. Namdarin rubbed snow on the monks face to wake him up. Jorgarna became conscious after a fashion. The monks horrific wounds were bleeding but not enough to threaten his life, at least not immediately, Namdarin spoke, in a calm, cold voice. "Tell me what I want to know and the pain will stop." Then he tapped a ruined knee with the flat of his blade. Jorgarna howled. "Tell me about your priesthood, who runs it? Where from? How does news get about so quickly? What is the meaning of the book on the lectern?"

Jorgarna talked and talked and talked, for almost an hour he told of their god Zandaar, known to be five thousand years old, the commander of the order, he told of the city where Zandaar lives, now called Zandaarkoon. He told of the magic of the abbots, which allows the transmission of messages over great distances. How the loss of contact with this monastery had brought him to investigate. He told of mental subjugation. He told of illusion and the death in dreams. Eventually he was talking merely to hear his own voice.

"You have earned your death." Said Namdarin, stepping away and removing the monk's head with a single stroke. Namdarin wiped his sword on the monk's chest then put it back in his belt and went to see where Jayanne had gone. In the stable he found her, she was in one of the stalls, curled up in the hay. She looked up at him with fear in her eyes.

"How could you do that sort of thing to a man?"

"How could they burn a house full of women and children, just for some land?"

"How could you enjoy torturing him so much? You were smiling."

"It had to be done. I need to know whom I am fighting, how they fight, and most of all where they are. The smile was for him, I needed him to fear me, the more he was afraid the quicker he talked and the quicker the pain stopped."

"It is still not right, it's a horrible thing to do."

"I agree. Why don't you get a fire going and I will go and see what supplies are still here that can be of use?"

"I suppose so." she replied somewhat petulantly.

"Don't forget, the water in the barrel is poisoned so get it from the well." said Namdarin leaving the stable and going into the main building. Jayanne broke down one of the stalls and used the wood to make a fire in the doorway. Before Namdarin returned she had some bear broth bubbling gently over the fire.

"Look what I have found." he said holding up two weapons. The first was a bow, double recurved, and made of bone carved with may representations of animals and a full eight feet long. The second was a war axe, four feet long, with a double head, both heads curved blades in clean steel. The haft of the axe was a piece of very plain wood, it looked out of place with such an unusual blade, almost the sort of haft to be found on any wood cutters axe, though it showed no signs of wear or even use it was clean and very white.

"These will certainly make an impression on your people." He said giving his new treasures to her.

"I definitely can't pull that bow and I can hardly lift the axe."

"You wont have to pull the bow just carry it, and the axe, with a bit of practise you should be able to swing it, if not fight with it. I am sorry I couldn't find you a sword. The only sword around is his," he waved in the direction of the courtyard, "and it's broken." Namdarin took the axe and held it by the wrist strap at the end of the haft, he tapped the blade with the handle of his knife. The axe rang like a bell, for three or four seconds it hummed a beautiful clear note.

"That is very good steel," said Namdarin "only really good steel rings like that. I wonder what that monk was carrying." He went to the mare in the stall and removed the bags from her saddle. Rummaging through the contents he found some food, clothing and a book, a book written in the same script as the large one fastened to Arndrol's saddle. "If this is a smaller version of the teachings of Zandaar, then it can be of as much use as the large one, I can even afford to loose one now." He mused. "Jayanne, how many days on horse back will it take to get to your people?" He asked.

"About four or five, or more if the weather is really bad. We have to go back the way we just came, and then north through the western foot hills."

"That should give you plenty of time to get used to the axe and your nice new horse, she seems quite docile. I'll go and find some arrows for the bow and then we can leave soon because this place is going to start to smell very bad."

"Right, the food will be ready on a few minutes." She answered, stirring the pot just to be sure the broth didn't burn. She looked up and watched Namdarin walking across the yard to the main building, she was still a little afraid of him, but not really sure why. He had not done anything to hurt her, he had only helped her, yet the way he dealt with the monk showed that he was capable of extreme savagery. Thinking of the monk, she glanced at his tattered corpse in a puddle of red snow, her stomach clenched, but she fought to control it. 'I hope he never hates me like that.' She thought. 'I know about hate, how else do I describe the way I felt about my husband. I know savagery, how else do I describe sticking a knife in him while he slept. Everyone is capable of fighting for their lives or their loved ones.' These thoughts calmed her and made her much more tolerant of Namdarin's behaviour. When he returned with a quiver full of long arrows she smiled, he looked strong and handsome, he might have made a good husband for me, she thought. They sat near the fire eating the bear broth, it was rich and tasty. Namdarin stared at the body of the monk and decided to conceal the evidence of torture by burning it, he collected some large armfuls of hay from the loft and piled them on top of the corpse, when the pyre was big enough he lit it. By the time he had completed this grizzly task Jayanne had loaded the horses and was ready to depart. Namdarin held on to the head on the monks horse while Jayanne mounted, then released it, he was ready to grab the reins if it became unruly. The bay mare was calm and obviously used to many riders. Namdarin mounted and they set off over the bridge through a swirl of stinking smoke, the stench of burning meat made them both gag. Up towards the pass at a quick trot they went stopping only to collect some cabbages from the fields.

CHAPTER FOUR

Together they rode through the snowy landscape towards the bear's cave where they met. Being mounted they made very good time and were passing the tarn long before the sun went down. Their idea was to spend a night in the cave again. Quietly they walked their horses into the col which had changed since they last saw it, the ground was covered by a carpet of snow that was two feet thick, the spring seemed to be frozen solid, and the trees were festooned with snow and glistening icicles. The entrance to the cave showed no tracks but Namdarin was still wary, another bear could have decided to hibernate there. He knelt by the opening, listening and sniffing the air, he heard nothing and detected no odour. Tossing his bow and quiver to Jayanne, he said with a big smile, "I am going in. If I come out running put an arrow in whatever is chasing me. Try not to hit me, I might get a little angry."

He turned and carefully pushed his way through the partial barrier of snow that had accumulated across the entrance. The white snow outside reflected a great deal of light into the cave, it was much clearer inside than the last time he had crept in. The bedding had been disturbed but looked free from any large inhabitants. Drawing his sword he stirred the bedding and found no small creatures either, "The smell of the bear must have put any visitors off." he mumbled. Without thinking he walked out of the cave and looked straight at the tip of an arrow, he froze.

"The cave is empty," he said quietly, "you can put that arrow away."

Jayanne slowly released the pressure on the string, and replaced the arrow in its quiver.

"You should have shouted from inside. If my fingers had slipped you would be dead." She said angrily, throwing his bow on the ground, and stamping over to the horses to begin the unpacking. She wondered at her own thoughts, why am I so disturbed by the idea that this man could be dead? Am I becoming attached to him? I would certainly miss him if he suddenly disappeared. I have only known him a few days and already I have got very used to the way he looks after me, and protects me. Namdarin left her to get on with the unpacking and cleared their old fireplace of snow then built a fire. Filling a pot with snow he set it by the fire to melt. Wood was going to be in short supply, so he said

"Jayanne fetch your axe, its time for some practise." Taking the axe from its place hanging from her saddle horn she followed him to a small stand of pine trees on the slope down to the valley. Namdarin pointed to a tree about two feet in diameter and said. "That one I think. Chop it down."

"What do we need a whole tree for?"

"We don't need a tree but you need to build some muscle to swing that axe."

"Why not a smaller one?"

"Too easy. In a few days you may be fighting for your life with that axe."

She looked at him, and felt angry that he was right. She swung the axe high then struck the tree about a foot from the base, the axe cut deep into the rough bark, then she wrenched it clear.

"No. No. No." he said, "Not like that. Let me show you." Taking the axe he planted his feet so that the axe head touched the trunk of the tree at full arms reach.

"The first stroke hits the tree going upwards." he said swinging the axe round and up to hit the tree just above waist height. The head buried itself two inches into the tree, he pulled it out.

"The second stroke hits the tree going downwards with full force, striking above the first." He lifted the axe above his head, then swung it down, pulling all the way to the tree. The head whistled into the tree, six inches deep. A wedge shaped chunk of tree flew out, landing three feet from the trunk.

"I love this axe, it's really good. That's how you chop down trees. Now you try. For axe practise though you have to be able to cut both ways, so that's four strokes forehand and two backhand." He returned her axe, and watched her first few strokes. She lacked his strength but every strike hit its target. Soon there were wood chips everywhere. Her backhand was very weak but that was only to be expected. He left her to deal with the tree on her own and went to make a meal for them both, he knew she would be very hungry by the time the tree fell. The snow in the pot had melted so he added some more, until the pot was nearly full with cold water, leaving the water to warm he went to collect such firewood as was lying about. When the water was warm and the deer meat added along with the vegetables and grain he went to the trees to see how well Jayanne was progressing. As he approached he could hear the thud of the axe, it was irregular but still sounded powerful. Through the trees her saw her standing beside the target tree, her furs scattered about were she had thrown them, she was sweating despite the coldness of the air, her upstrokes were weak, her down strokes still had some power, her backhand was forgotten. The top of the tree began to wave about in a none existent gale. He knew it would fall soon. He walked towards her to warn her about falling trees, when an especially powerful downstroke buried the head of the axe six inches deep in the remaining ten inches of trunk. She tugged and wrenched at the axe but it would not come out. She put her foot against the trunk and heaved, the tree swayed alarmingly.

"Wait." shouted Namdarin running towards her. She stood back from the tree until he got there.

"The weight of the tree is resting on the axe head, so you wont be able to pull it clear. What you have to do is use the axe as a lever to push the tree over." He explained taking a firm grip on the haft with both hands and pushing upwards. "The tree should then fall away from you. I hope. If it starts to fall towards you, you must wait until you are sure which way it falls, then run to the side. Another way when you have a hole cut this deep into the tree is to bang an iron wedge in with a big hammer, that will push the tree away as well."

Gradually increasing the pressure on the haft it starts to rise, the tree starts to groan like a wounded man, then cracks shoot up the trunk, and it starts to fall. "Run." shouts Namdarin grabbing Jayanne's arm and dragging her ten fast paces away from the tree. He steps behind a smaller tree, putting it between himself and the scattering splinters of the falling tree. When the noise stopped they went to the upright stump of the tree, Jayanne started to collect her furs.

"Now we have plenty of firewood." Said Namdarin picking up the axe from beside the stump, then chopping off a few good sized branches, this finished, he checked the edge of the axe and found that it was completely unmarked, not one sign was visible to show that it had just been used to cut a tree. He ran his thumb along the edge and it was still so sharp that it cut him without him feeling it, as he sucked the blood from his thumb he noticed that the axe showed no sign of blood at all.

"This is a wonderful axe. I wonder who made it." He gave the axe to Jayanne, picked up the branches and together they walked back to the cave.

"How do your arms feel?" He asked.

"Very tired, and my back. Chopping trees is very hard work." She answered with a deep sigh.

"It will be easier tomorrow."

"I don't want to think about that just now." Her muscles went into spasm just thinking about cutting down some more trees, the cramps made her groan and squirm about trying to relieve the tension in the exhausted muscles.

"Once you get used to cutting down trees, you will find that cutting down men is in one way easier, men are not as hard as trees but they do move quicker."

Later whilst sitting around the fire they chatted about their earlier lives until long after the sun had gone down, they stayed near the fire to keep warm.

Namdarin was no longer bothered by his feelings for Jayanne, he accepted them and tried not to fight them. Namdarin told Jayanne how his father had died when he was only fifteen, leaving him as lord on the house. How he took a wife, Althone, who was beautiful and young, and together they started a family, their first and last child, a boy called Naron It might have been the fact that Althone was only sixteen when she gave birth that prevented her having any more. Naron was only fifteen when the Zandaars came. Jayanne told Namdarin how much she had enjoyed the games she played with the boys, and how she hated the girls and their silly attitudes, Jayanne much preferred to climb trees and fight rather than tending animals or cooking. She learned to use a sling when she was only nine years old, and she practiced constantly. As the conversation began to flag the two friends retired to the cave to sleep.

The morning arrived with no new snow, but a clear, sunny if cold day. Mounted the two people set off towards Jayanne's village. After about an hours travelling Namdarin said. "Get your axe out and start swinging it about, try not to hit your horse with it. Chop at imaginary heads either side, first one then the other."

"My arm is very stiff," she replied, "from cutting trees."

"I know it will hurt, but you must do it, or your arm will not be strong enough when we reach your village."

"Don't you ever get tired of being right." She said with a sigh.

"Yes, its just another load I have to carry." He said with an enormous grin and a wink to prove he didn't believe it any more than she did. Within ten minutes she was sweating again, but the stiffness in her arm soon went and the axe strokes flowed with a smooth and graceful rhythm. Arndrol started to get excited by the axe work, almost as if he thought they were going into battle.

Half an hours practice with the axe was enough for Jayanne's arm, her grip on the haft started to slip so Namdarin called a halt. By the middle of the morning they had come a long way down the mountains, the snow had started to thin out and much more greenery began to reappear.

"Things certainly seem to change very quickly" ,said Namdarin, "as we move down these mountains."

"Yes, it generally only takes a few miles of travel, at this time of year, to find grazing for horses, or food for the pot. Once the winter deepens the snow will come right down into the foothills, my village usually has snow lying in it for about two months." She replied, with a smile on her lips, from thinking about the happy times she had spent trapped in her parent's house when the snow was so deep it covered the doors.

"In my home we hardly ever see snow at all, let alone snow that lies around for months."

"The thaw is more of a problem than the snow, it makes the ground just a sea of stinking mud. Travelling is easier while the ground is frozen solid."

That evening they stopped in a small group of trees, and while Namdarin set up the tent he had Jayanne cut down a bigger tree. She found this slightly easier than the first tree, as her arm was getting stronger all the time. She returned to the camp site with three large logs cut from the tree after it fell.

"Our supplies of meat are running low." Said Namdarin, "I think we must do some hunting tomorrow, it shouldn't slow us down to much."

"There should be some deer in that forest somewhere." she answered pointing to a large expanse of conifer trees off to the west.

"I would like to try that big bow, if that's all right with you?" he asked, looking at the bow fastened to her horse and thinking about the power it must possess, the arrows were four feet long with heavy iron tips, set for vertical penetration. To himself he said. "I wonder what game that bow was intended to hunt." He did not realise that he was soon the find out. They spent the night huddled together in the small tent, Jayanne slept until the sun was up, but Namdarin's rest was disturbed by a dream of running, he was running from an un-known and un-knowable terror, something hideous was following him its fang filled jaws slobbering. He woke to the sound of a straggled scream, his own.

Jayanne did not awake and Namdarin lay sweating for some time before sleep again took him. In the morning they packed up their camp and headed into the forest, to hunt for food. Walking the horses down the middle of a small stream they scanned the banks for signs of deer that had stopped to drink. Seeing some large cloven hoof prints they left the stream bed and followed into the forest proper. Visibility was seriously restricted be the closeness of the trees, sometimes the horses could not pass between them. The deer they were following left a very clear trail in the mushy rotten needles beneath the trees. Namdarin knew that they were catching up with the deer quite quickly as the tracks became fresher and fresher, "Give me that big bow, I'll see how good it is for deer." he said to Jayanne, who handed over the bow saying. "We must be very quiet if we are getting that close." Namdarin nodded, and then walked the horse on. Moving much like the deer would the only unusual sound was Jayanne axe clinking against her stirrup. "Put the axe in your lap." whispered Namdarin. This stopped the clinking and made Jayanne just a little more ready for action. Within a few minutes Namdarin pulled Arndrol to a fierce halt.

"Something has frightened that deer, it suddenly started to run very fast, we probably can't catch it now, we'll just have to look for another to follow."

He said, glancing meaningfully at Jayanne's battle axe. As he turned towards where he thought the stream should be, they heard a faint scream. Namdarin assumed it was someone in difficulties so headed straight towards the noise, as quickly as the trees would allow. The scream came again this time accompanied by a howl and the barking of dogs. Approaching the noise, they began to hear words in the screams, and the howling became a little pained on occasion. Throwing caution to the wind Namdarin kicked Arndrol into a gallop, leaning low over the horses neck he ducked under most of the branches, he let the horse decide the best course through the trees, and held on tight to his dodging and jinking mount, the scream was beginning to sound very desperate. Suddenly he was in a clearing left by the fall of a large old tree. Namdarin gripped the horse tightly with his knees, Arndrol slid to a halt. Over the fallen tree trunk Namdarin saw three large black wolves feasting on the bloody remains of a horse, pulling one of the long arrows from its quiver he saw five more black shapes that appeared to be attempting to climb a tree, to get at the youth who was now half way up, and still going. Namdarin nocked the arrow, pulled to the limit of the bows strength, and released. The arrow fair howled through the air, screaming it hit the biggest of the wolves, the one with the white muzzle, standing on its hind legs up against the tree. The arrow struck in the chest, tore clean through the wolf, and buried itself in a tree some yards further on. Before the wolves noticed their fallen leader another arrow was in the air screaming death to a wolf, this one was pinned to the tree by an arrow through its head. The wolves turned towards Namdarin to attack the intruder who was after their food. The three wolves from the tree came forwards quickly, Namdarin hit another in the throat, the arrow ended sticking out like an extra tail. Namdarin threw down the bow and drew his sword. The pounding of hooves told of Jayanne's arrival on the scene. Jumping her horse over the fallen tree she landed amongst the wolves slashing right and left with the axe, chopping a head here, a back there, the axe seemed to be whining in anticipation of the blood it was to drink. Jayanne stormed into the three eating wolves, Namdarin watched the axe carefully, it turned bright red with each strike, and was clean steel before the next. Arndrol jumped over the tree, so that Namdarin could be near enough if Jayanne needed help, as the grey's hooves hit the ground Jayanne sliced the last wolf completely in two, through its ribcage, with almost no effort, or so it seemed.

Namdarin didn't take his eyes from the axe, as the blood of the wolf appeared to be gradually absorbed into the blade, until the shining steel was once again utterly clean.

"May I see the axe?" he asked. Jayanne passed the axe to him without comment.

"It looks sharper than before and feels a little lighter." He said with a mystified frown on his forehead.

"After the first strike it seemed to become weightless. I thought of where I wanted it to be, and it was. The effort of the battle was entirely in controlling the horse, the axe was nothing." She replied equally confused.

"There must be magic in this blade." He said, "Be very careful, it might do almost anything." Taking the axe back she nodded, then looked up the tree.

"You can come down now, Morgan." She shouted.

"You know him?" Asked Namdarin.

"Yes. He comes from my village."

Namdarin went to collect his arrows, the first was buried two inches into the tree that had stopped it, and Namdarin took his knife from his belt to dig the arrow out. Holding the shaft of the arrow gently in his left hand he started to cut into the trees hard bark around the shaft, then the arrow came free, long before the head was visible it just slid out of the wood. Going to the second arrow, he held it in his right hand and pulled slowly, the arrow slid out of the tree and the wolf's head, like the two were only a straw target. The third arrow was almost out of wolf already so it presented no problem either.

"These arrows are magic as well." He said to Jayanne, who was watching a young man of less than twenty years climbing slowly down the tree. The young man dropped the last ten feet from the lowest branch to see a woman he knew and a strange man, two horses chewing on the sparse grass around the base of the fallen tree, and the chopped up remains of a wolf pack. His own horse had been torn apart by the hungry wolves.

"Thank you, Jayanne, and you stranger for my life."

"How is every one at home?" asked Jayanne.

"Things have changed since you, er," he paused, "left. The chief elder has decided that we must build a new temple to a new god called Zandaar. Dorana, the man in black, is to be the high priest of this new god. A few who have spoken out against them have just died. My father died three days ago, he was strong and healthy, but he went to sleep and never woke up. He refused to hand over his share of the silver from the mine, he said that he had no need of expensive gods like Zandaar. I was going to find help against this god."

"What help?" she asked.

"I don't know. I just wanted to find somebody who knew how to fight them."

"Maybe, help has found you." Said Namdarin.

"You know how to fight them?" Asked Morgan, looking hopeful.

"I know how to kill them, they die just like everybody else."

"But you will not be able to get close enough, Dorana is always guarded by the chief and his family, they never leave him alone."

"Then they may die as well." The coldness of Namdarin's response caused the young man to shiver.

"So you plan to kill Dorana?"

"We shall see, we still have food to find, let's continue with the hunt. Morgan you can ride double with Jayanne, we'll take you home in a few days."

"Thank you, you may have to go a long way to find deer, those wolves will have scared them all away." said Morgan while Namdarin mounted and settled the bow and quiver. Namdarin looked down on the carnage about him, there was not enough left of Morgan's horse to make a meal and he wasn't hungry enough to eat the tough rank flesh of the wolves. When Jayanne and Morgan had settled on Jayanne's horse he said,

"Let's head back to the stream, we might pick up some more tracks." They returned to the stream and plodded down it looking for any signs. Namdarin kept his eyes on the soft banks of the stream, and his ears listening for any sound that came over the noise of the wind in the trees and the whispering of Jayanne and Morgan behind him as they caught up on the gossip of the village. Though his eyes and ears were occupied, his brain began to wander, to thoughts of Dorana. Why did the Zandaar want the silver from the mine? They were not short of funds. Were they being greedy? Or did they have a specific purpose for it? Should he ride into the village and put an arrow in the priest, or try and question him first? What ever he does information is now a bigger part of the war than mere death.

"Namdarin, what are these tracks here?" Asked Jayanne, shaking Namdarin from his reverie, he looked to here she was pointing, and said,

"They are the tracks of wild pigs, very tasty. Be cautious if we catch up with them, they can be extremely vicious." He followed the tracks with no further explanation as to why he had missed them. Once away from the soft verges of the stream the tiny hoof prints of the pigs were difficult to follow. Through the dense undergrowth, through the litter of pine needles, over tree stumps and boggy ground they went, wherever the pigs had gone. After an hour chasing the pigs they finally heard them snuffling about in large bowl shaped depression in a hillside, they looked like they were digging for mushrooms or last years pine cones. Namdarin put an arrow to the long bow and nodded at Jayanne to do the same, picking the biggest pig in view, Namdarin pulled the huge bow and looked over to see if Jayanne was ready, her bow was drawn, and she was tracking a large boar. Namdarin checked that he was still on target and whispered, "Fire." Two bows thrummed, two arrows flew straight and true, two pigs died where they stood. In the ensuing chaos Namdarin hit another large pig, and Jayanne got three smaller ones with her sling, even so at least fifteen pigs made it into the cover of the forest, disappearing into the gloom, squealing in alarm. Jayanne and Morgan jumped to the ground to make sure that none of the pigs recovered enough to attempt an escape, but they were all dead. Namdarin sat on his horse watching the other two gutting the pigs, he was thinking about this huge bone bow.

"Jayanne," he said, she looked up, "Do you mind if I keep this bow, it seems to fit me perfectly?"

"Of course you can keep it, I certainly couldn't pull it, and can I keep this one?"

"I think that is a more than fair trade." answered Namdarin with a big smile, getting down to help the others with the pigs. Once the pigs were cleaned Jayanne said,

"Let's go back to the stream and camp there for the night, at least we'll have water available, and some grass for the horses."

"Right," said Namdarin, "Morgan help me load these big pigs then you two can take the little ones." Between them they stacked the pigs on Arndrol's rump, and tied them on very tightly. Back at the stream Namdarin turned up stream, heading for a clearing they had passed through earlier that day, where he knew there would be more than enough grass for the horses. Long before sundown they were sitting around a blazing fire, watching the horses rolling in the grass, smelling the sweet scent of piglet roasting, and listening to the birds chattering in the trees.

"Morgan," said Namdarin, "Are your villagers going to be difficult about Jayanne visiting her mother?" The young man thought for a few moments before answering, "Probably not too difficult, they won't want to fight a warrior such as yourself, and while they are deciding what to do, I will tell them how you saved my life. That will put my mother on your side immediately, she will, most likely, offer you bed and board there and then, so if she does you accept, and go to our house before anyone can complain. I don't know how you are going to kill the priest."

"I will have to wait until I can see the village and how things are done, I may even wait and see if he wants to try and kill me. If your villagers are as frightened of warriors as you suggest, he will have to kill me himself."

"How can you be so sure he will want to kill you?"

"Because I am going to do everything that your father did, I am going to speak out against this monk, and his ways. I will ask awkward questions about the uses to which your silver is being put. Is it just to line the priest's pockets? Or is it something worse? I am going to stir up as much trouble for this monk as I possibly can. I will force him to act."

"He may kill you instead of the other way around."

"That is certainly a risk, though one that must be taken at sometime."

Namdarin lapsed in to a thoughtful silence, he was considering his chances against a properly trained monk as should logically be assigned to the take over of a village. The monk is likely to be trained in both combat and magic, or possibly a blend of the two, this could make a fight very hard on Namdarin. Sitting across the fire was Jayanne, staring into the flames, with a distant look in her eyes, and a tiny smile on her lips.

"Jayanne." He said quietly, she looked up. "It's time to practice that axe some more, you pick a tree that you think will be a challenge." She looked around the clearing and picked a tree that could only be described as huge, eighty feet tall, and with a trunk four feet across. Leaving her fur coats by the fire she took a firm stance beside the tree, soon enormous chips of wood were flying about the clearing, some landing almost in the fire.

"Hey. Watch where the splinters are going, please." Shouted Namdarin, to no apparent effect. In a matter of only ten minutes the tree was beginning to sway most alarmingly. Then it fell, crashing into the forest with a thunderous roar, smashing down smaller trees as it went. Jayanne came across the clearing towards the fire with her axe over her right shoulder, as if it had always been there, three smashed branches in her left hand, a big smile on her face, and not a sign of sweat anywhere.

"Namdarin, you were right about it getting easier, that tree took almost no effort at all."

"I think that axe likes a diet of blood." He answered looking more than a little perturbed, "I wonder how long it will wait to be fed again. It may not be fussy whether the blood it drinks is friendly or not. I find this thought somewhat frightening."

"What about that long bow? Since you got it you have fired five arrows, three of which have been shot in a hurry, you never even came close to missing. Even an expert bowman can miss when under pressure, pressure such as a hungry wolf charging straight at him. Did you actually aim those fast shots or did you just point and release?"

"I don't know about consciously aiming them, but I am a very good bowman. I put three arrows in a Zandaar priest from a distance of seventy yards. I fired them so quickly that at least two of the arrows were in the air at a time."

"Yes. But you weren't under pressure, he was too far away to cause any concern at all, if the priest had fallen when the first struck him, the other arrows would have missed him completely."

"So the arrows may be magic, if they are they must be guided by the thoughts of the archer, therefore I must be careful who I think about when firing the bow."

"You be very careful. I don't want an arrow in the back because you are thinking the wrong things again." She said with a meaningful stare, thinking about the lustful look she had seen in his eyes.

"We don't know that the arrows are magic, the axe certainly is, because it gets sharper as you use it, but the arrows may just be lucky."

"I want nothing to do with that bow," she said angrily, "the axe I can cope with because it is always in my hand, but an arrow can go anywhere once it is launched."

"You keep the other bow then, I am sure I can control this, so called magic bow and I assure you that you will come to no harm from me." He said getting to his feet and gesturing wildly with his hands. Both seemed to be getting very irritated about something.

"Hey." shouted Morgan. "Let's not start a battle over a bow that may or may not have some form of magic properties. You two are getting excited about nothing. Am I missing something here? Is something going between you two that I don't know about?" He grabbed Namdarin by the arm and pulled him down to sit again by the fire. Jayanne took a deep breath and sat cross-legged opposite Namdarin, the blazing fire and blazing eyes between them.

"Maybe we are just nervous about going into that village of

yours," said Namdarin, keeping his voice under very tight control, "It certainly gives much cause for fear, I am afraid of Dorana, and Jayanne must be afraid of her families' reaction to her return. We must not let these fears come between us." Jayanne nodded in agreement, though she did not trust her voice enough to say anything.

They sat around the fire until the sun went down, and then ate the well-cooked piglets. With warm food inside them they all calmed down, Namdarin put up the tent and looking closely at it he said, "This is definitely not big enough for three of us at once, so if we take turns at watching, one can stay outside to keep the fire going and watch out for wolves and such while the other two sleep. Do either of you want the first watch?" he asked, getting no real show of any preference from the others he said, "Right I'll go first, then Morgan, then Jayanne." He looked at the others waiting for some reaction, but they did not seem bothered by his decision at all, taking their lack of objections as agreement, he said, "You get some sleep and I'll look after the horses." He looked around for Arndrol and whistled the grey came pounding out of forest in only a few seconds, trotting across the clearing, tossing his big head, and shaking his mane. "You go find the other horse and bring her back here where we can both keep an eye on her." Arndrol snuffled loudly and came up to Namdarin and put his large head under Namdarin's arm as if to say he wanted some attention, for a change. Namdarin rubbed the horse's ears, scratched his nose, and stroked his neck. "There you are you big soft baby, now go and find that mare before she gets lost." Arndrol wheeled about and galloped off into the forest, to look for his new friend. While the others settled down in the tent Namdarin wandered into the forest to collect some more wood for the fire, when he returned to the fire Arndrol was already there, along with the bay mare. The horses settled into the long grass back to back, so as to keep watch for themselves, Namdarin sat by the fire, trying not to get too comfortable, he stared into the dancing flames, and thought of the times he went camping with his father. On one particular occasion, they went deep into the old oak woods and found a clearing much as this one. Sitting up most of the night they talked about bows and hunting, Namdarin was only thirteen years old but was already quite good with a bow. That very day he had shot his first wood buck, a small and slow one, but he hit it and killed it, though they did have to follow it for half a mile until it actually dropped. Remembering the smell and taste of his first wood buck, Namdarin smiled. His father taught him many things, hunting, fishing, and fighting. He taught Namdarin about soldiers, and the best ways to deal with them. Between the age of ten and fifteen Namdarin learned many things, he learned tactics, and battle planning from his father, who also ensured that he learned to read and write from a local monk. He learned fencing and wrestling from his father's master at arms. Then suddenly at the age of fifteen he was left to learn how to run an estate, the grief of his father's death still burns in his heart. The crackling of the logs on the fire, the wind whispering gently through the upper branches of the trees and the water of the stream bubbling over the rocks, these sounds all added together to produce a hypnotic effect that soon lulled Namdarin into sleep, a sleep filled with awful dreams. Blazing fire filled his mind, both the black sorcerous fire of the Zandaar and the ordinary fire of burning wood, out of the fire came the faces of the people he had killed. Many had no names that he knew, but some came with their names on their lips, a whispering catalogue of death. Behind the fire he could see a cowled figure, a tall black cowled figure, from beneath the figures robe a flaming sword appeared which flew straight towards Namdarin's heart, with a shout Namdarin woke up.

Jayanne scrambled from the tent, swinging the axe and looking for a foe to strike, Morgan came from the tent at a run with a bow in his hand and an arrow strung.

"Sorry my friends, I must have fallen asleep, and a terrible dream woke me."

"You get some sleep," said Jayanne with a kindly look, "You must be very tired, I'll take the next watch." Namdarin went into the tent without another word, and fell asleep immediately. He didn't even wake up when Jayanne changed places with Morgan, and his dreams were untroubled. Namdarin was finally wakened by the smell of roasting pork. He slowly opened his eyes, to see a bush of bright red hair directly in front of his face, he felt a warm body pressed hard against his, his left hand was rising and falling with the breathing of the woman because it was resting on her hot naked belly. His manhood rose with typical early morning passion, it pressed itself hard and throbbing against the small of her back.

Namdarin froze, desperate not to wake her up, her reaction to this totally innocent situation could be exceptionally violent. What should he do? The thoughts raced through his mind, pretend to be asleep, or try and get out of this strange predicament. Very slowly he removed his hand from her stomach and started to roll away from her, all he needed was a quarter turn then he could wriggle out of the tent. She must have sensed the warmth of his body going away and followed it pushing him hard against the wall of the tent, pressing her buttocks against his hip, she grabbed his right arm that was trapped under her head and wrapped it about her neck, then began to squirm her body against his, pushing and wriggling in a most disconcerting fashion. "What is she dreaming about?" he thought, unable to move at all, thinking about her dreams brought some of his own fantasies to the fore. With a tiny moan she woke, and froze. Namdarin shut his eyes and snored loudly, praying that she would believe that he was still asleep. She carefully untangled his right hand from her hair, and moved away from him. Namdarin kept his eyes tightly shut, rolled towards her and curled up into a tight foetal ball, sighed and relaxed as if asleep. Listening to her harsh breathing he became a little worried, after a few moments that seemed like hours, she pulled her clothes tightly about herself and left the tent. Namdarin listened to her talking to Morgan about breakfast for a few minutes then made a big show of waking up, lots of yawning and groaning and stretching.

"By the gods," he said loudly, "I slept like a baby. That food smells good."

Going out he caught Jayanne's eyes and she looked away, into the trees.

"How far to your village now?" he asked Morgan.

"On horseback, two days maybe one. It is quite easy going from here."

"I suggest we get moving as soon as possible, for some reason I feel an urgent need to face this monk, and I believe he knows of our coming and purpose."

"How do you know that?" asked Morgan, with a deeply puzzled look.

"That dream I had last night, that was his work I think. Forewarned is forearmed, I will be ready for him next time."

"What can you do against a dream?" asked Morgan.

"With a dream, anything you want. Let's eat then leave."

Morgan divided the cooked pig into three equal portions and handed them round. When the horses had been loaded, they set off in a north-westerly direction, soon leaving the pine forest behind. Crossing a plain of withered brown grass they came to a large river. The water looked deep and swirled violently over hidden rocks.

"We can't cross here." Said Namdarin, "Is there anywhere better, Morgan?"

"Yes there is a ford many miles down stream and a bridge a few miles upstream. The bridge is nearer to our route, but has a small problem, nearby is an inn that is frequented by vagabonds and cut-throats, it is a hazardous place to travel. The ford could add a day to our journey, but is as safe as anything is out here in the wilds. The river is impassable anywhere else at this time of year."

"I think we'll take the bridge, there are three of us, we have weapons and are more than willing to use them. Even a large group of bandits should think twice before attacking us." Said Namdarin hoping for agreement from the others.

"Yes." Said Jayanne. "I hope in one way that they do attack us, I wonder how my axe will like human blood." she smiled mischievously. Morgan shivered.

"Do you two have to be so blood thirsty?" he asked. Neither replied, they just turned their horses upstream and trotted off in the direction of the bridge. At midmorning they dis-mounted for a while to rest the horses and continued on foot, the going was quite easy. The long grass hid no potholes, or boulders. The smoothly undulating ground gradually tended upwards, and the banks of the river became a gorge, that slowly became very deep indeed. The river was restricted by the narrowness of the gorge, so it roared and grumbled as it smashed its way over huge rocks, and around tight bends, the noise faded to a mere whisper as they climbed higher. The sun came out from behind the grey clouds as it started to descend from its height, and the afternoon started to warm up. Before long the bridge came into sight, it was a large wooden structure, of many tall tree trunks lashed together and spanning the narrowest point of the gorge, rails had been fitted to the side of the bridge each about three feet high, probably to guide people across in the dark of the night. On a hill top across the river from the three stood a large house, with many horses tied up outside.

CHAPTER FIVE

"That is the inn I mentioned, it is called The Dark Crow." Said Morgan.

"It seems to be very busy, should we drop in for a beer?" Asked Namdarin, "the hot sun on my face has made me extremely thirsty." he continued with a strange smile on his thin lips.

"Yes, let's." Answered Jayanne, kicking her horse to make it trot across the rough wooden deck of the bridge.

"You two are crazy." Said Morgan, shaking his head.

"It could be that somebody will give you a fine horse, then you wouldn't have to ride double." Said Namdarin.

"That is not at all likely."

"Then maybe they will leave it to you in their will."

"Why do you want to pick a fight with these people?"

"If this place is know for its bandits then the local lord should have done something to terminate their activities. He has not done such, so he is most probably in their pay. This sort of corruption cannot be allowed to continue. If I can do anything to stop it I will, and I might catch a few Zandaars while I am at it. Any way I am not trying to pick a fight, what I want is for a few of them to follow us and then we can fight them. If we win, we will have horses and food and who knows what else. Also when news gets back to the bandits of our victory they will be much more careful in future."

"So what exactly are we to do?" asked Morgan.

"We will go inside, have a drink, show some gold then leave. Its very simple."

"What if they don't need our gold?"

"If they don't want gold then at least one of them will want my horse."

"How can you be sure?"

"You shall see."

Climbing the hill towards the inn was easy for the horses, even Jayannes, which was carrying two. A man standing on the porch looked them over and went inside as they started to dismount. Fastening their bows firmly to the saddles so they could not get lost, the three friends checked their weapons, Namdarin slackened his belt enough to give himself a quicker draw and Morgan loosened his sword in it's scabbard, Jayanne hung the axe from her shoulder, Namdarin tied Arndrol's reins to the saddle horn and took the reins of Jayanne's horse and put them in Arndrol's mouth saying "Go for a walk, but not too far." The big horse tossed his head in agreement and wandered down the hill away from the inn and its noisy crowds of people.

"Right, let's go in and get some food, shall we?" asked Namdarin expecting no denials. Jayanne face was filled with a wicked smile, "Yes I think we shall." She said very quietly. The inn was a large two-storey structure with thick stone walls, small windows, and a single heavy wooden door. Climbing the wooden steps to the covered porch they passed between two lines of horses tied to the porch rail, about ten horses in all. Namdarin pushed the door open then walked confidently inside, choosing a table near to one of the four front windows, he took a seat with his back to the window and facing the rest of the room. Jayanne sat to his right giving her a good view of the door, then Morgan sat facing the window. Namdarin found that his sword made sitting in the low chair very un-comfortable so he took it off and propped it up against his thigh. Morgan's shorter sword was no problem. While they were settling into their places at the table the general level of noise in the room dropped until it was almost silent. Namdarin looked at the large fat man, who was standing behind the bar and shouted. "Landlord, service if you please." The fat man's eyes flashed to a large black bearded man in the far corner, then back to Namdarin. The fat man dropped the cloth he had been cleaning the bar with and came over to Namdarin.

"My name is Brin, this is my house. How may I be of service?"

"What foods have you available?"

"There is only mutton stew ready at the moment, but I do have some beef cooking that should be ready in an hour or so."

"Mutton stew for three then and a jug of beer." said Namdarin brusquely and waved the man away.

"That will be three copper pennies, sir." Said Brin. Namdarin looked the fat man in the eyes and whispered, "We shall see about that after we have tasted it."

"Very well sir." Said Brin, leaving in somewhat of a hurry.

"Morgan do not look round, because if you do they will know that we are talking about them, is that understood?" asked Namdarin, Morgan nodded.

"The black bearded man in the corner is the one that everybody in this place looks to for instructions and that includes the fat landlord. Jayanne you are in the best place to keep a close eye on him, watch who he talks to, and if any of these leave the building warn me, but try not to be obvious. Morgan you watch out of the window and try to keep an eye on the horses, or any one moving around out there." The two nodded in agreement.

"How much further is it to your village?" asked Namdarin in a voice loud enough to carry across to the tables nearest them.

"We still have about a day to go." Was Morgan's answer.

"So we should get there sometime tomorrow morning, that will do very nicely. Things should really start to happen before nightfall." Brin arrived at this point, his arms full with three large steaming bowls of stew, a plate of bread, a jug and three beakers. He managed to put all the items on the table without a single drop of the contents being spilt.

"Well done," said Namdarin "have you ever thought to take up juggling, you could be very good." Namdarin tasted first the stew then the beer. "Very good indeed, although I am so hungry that anything would taste good. Thank you my good man, call that a silver piece shall we." He tossed a silver coin to the fat man who snatched it out of the air with surprising speed, he bit it to ensure its value then disappeared it, though he had no pockets or purse visible, the coin vanished about his person somewhere.

"Thank you, my lord." Said Brin' bowing then departing

"Namdarin," whispered Morgan, "there are three men outside looking closely at the horses, Arndrol doesn't like them and he has gone further away."

"Is he still taking Jayanne's horse with him?"

"Yes."

"I am sure he can look after both of them with no problems, it will take a lot more than three to catch him." The heavy stew was rich with carrots and mushrooms, so the three had a good meal, and the beer was passable, almost as good as the inn by the red river. The other people in the room very quickly returned to their conversations, with only the occasional glance in the direction of Namdarin's party. Though the black bearded man never took his eyes off them.

"One of blackbeard's friends has just gone out through the bar." said Jayanne in a very hushed tone.

"Someone just called the three who were annoying the horses and they are coming back to the inn." Muttered Morgan.

"I've finished," said Namdarin, "so you two hurry up. We have many miles to go before we can rest for the night." This loud statement brought a flurry of looks, and a sudden change in many of the voices around them. Many glances went to blackbeard, but he made no response. Morgan and Jayanne finished the last few mouthfuls of the stew in huge gulps. The three stood up, Namdarin put his sword back into his belt, Jayanne swung her axe up to it's usual resting place on her shoulder with a simple flick of the wrist. Morgan stuffed the last two bread rolls down his shirt. "They will do for later." He said.

"Don't you think of anything but your stomach?" asked a smiling Namdarin.

"Erm." Thought Morgan, pausing for a few seconds, before stating "No." Namdarin shook his head and laughed quietly, then shouted. "Good day landlord, thanks for a good meal."

"Come back again, my lord." Said Brin.

"Maybe we will." Said Namdarin taking a last look about the place, fixing Blackbeard with a cold stare. Morgan opened the door and went out on to the porch, Jayanne followed, and Namdarin came last. He stood in the doorway and whistled, Arndrol came galloping up the hill still holding the reins of Jayanne's horse firmly between his teeth. Namdarin patted his horse on the neck and rubbed him between the ears, just were the horse liked to be scratched the most. "Thank you my friend." He said quietly.

"Well, we certainly attracted some attention." Said Jayanne, "I wonder who Blackbeard is?" She asked, of no one in particular.

"I have heard of a huge bear of a man who is possibly the

leader of the bandits hereabouts." Said Morgan.

"I think we just met him." Said Namdarin, "Let's get some distance between us and them before they decide what to do." He jumped up onto Arndrol's back, and waited while Jayanne and Morgan mounted the other horse. Together they set off at a good quick trot away from the inn. Once they had come down the hill on which the inn stood the land was very flat and featureless for a few miles, as they approached the first of many depressions, that made the land look like a slow heavy sea that had suddenly frozen solid, Namdarin stopped and looked back, as far as he could see there was no-one following them from the inn. This did not mean that they were not there, it just meant that Namdarin could not see them.

"It seems clear behind." He said with no confidence at all.

"They are there," said Jayanne, "they want this bearskin, it was my horse they were after not yours."

"Could be. I do feel that prickling on the back of my neck that usually means someone is watching." Said Namdarin.

"Well I for one hope that they have left us alone." Said Morgan with real feeling, "I don't share your fondness for conflict."

"Morgan," asked Namdarin, "Is there any where near by that would be good for an ambush?"

"Yes, the path we must now take goes through a narrow gully, though we could with some effort go around the gully, over tops of the crags the paths are really only fit for mountain goats."

"I think we will tempt them into attacking us."

"I think you saved my life only to waste it." Said Morgan.

"You will not die, but you may get a horse and a new sword."

"I don't want a sword, this is my fathers sword, and his fathers, and so on backwards in time for many generations, this sword is a thousand years old and cannot be replaced by anything newer."

"Then it is time it was christened in blood by its latest owner."

"How do you know I haven't bloodied it already?"

"Just a guess. One that you have confirmed." Morgan looked away in disgust. Then turned back to Namdarin and said angrily, "Some of us are not as blood thirsty as you."

"Some don't have my motivation." The cold rage in Namdarin's eyes stopped Morgan, but only for a few moments.

"I have motivation as well you know, my father was killed by a Zandaar."

"You still have a mother to protect, I have no one." When Namdarin had said this he realised that he had lied, now he had two to protect. One of which he had absolutely no intention of losing, though she would not be lost in battle, she could be lost by the wrong words and actions. These thoughts brought home to him the fact that he was indeed falling in love with Jayanne, he tried to picture his life without her, he saw only darkness, blacker and deeper than the current hurt that filled his heart. The thoughts of another love for his life did not abate the wish of vengeance by one iota. His battle would go on and if Jayanne chose to fight beside him so much the better, if not then he would fight alone.

The horses were walking across the undulating grass land for at least two hours when they arrived at an almost sheer escarpment, the rugged green tinted rock faces reaching two hundred feet up into the blue sky, a crack in the rocks was clearly visible a mile or so to the north.

"That is where the gully is." said Morgan. They turned towards the gully, the ground around the exit point of the gully was littered with rocks and boulders caused by the massive run off of rainstorms. The gully followed a fault line in the rocks, where the rock was softer it had eroded and made a stream, then a river, and now the river only flowed in the harshest rains, and brought with it enormous quantities of mud and other debris to deposit on the rolling grassland below.

"Once we reach the top of the gully we are fairly high up in the mountains and will be only a few hours from the village." said Morgan.

"Is there a way around that the bandits could have used to get here ahead of us?" asked Namdarin.

"I don't know for sure, there are many ways into these mountains, but we have certainly taken the shortest and quickest, so to be here first they would have needed to flog their horses almost to death."

"Well, judging by the hoof prints in the dust and the damp patches that may have been caused by the foam from a tired horse, I would say they have been here about half an hour."

"Oh, God." said Morgan, "It looks like we will have to fight."

"Perhaps they will see reason and let us pass in peace." Said Namdarin with an extremely sarcastic tone.

"Morgan, are you any good with a bow?" asked Jayanne.

"No."

"Right, get your great old sword ready for battle." Namdarin unfastened his bow from the saddle and strung it, nocked an arrow, and declared. "I am ready."

Jayanne set and arrow to the string of her bow, checked her axe and declared, "I am ready." Morgan held his sword in a trembling hand and said, "I will never be ready for this." Proceeding at a slow walk they continued along the gully.

Upward into the mountains they went, the walls of the gully got progressively lower as they gradually approached the upper plateau.

"Morgan was right," muttered Namdarin to himself, "This is a perfect place for an ambush, a hundred men could hide in the walls and never be found." Then louder, "Jayanne watch the right side, I'll watch the left, Morgan, watch every where, we might miss something." Walking slowly up the slope of the gully bottom the two horses began to get nervous, Arndrol was very jittery, constantly side-stepping and hopping from one foot to another. When the walls of the gully were only a hundred feet high, which meant they were two thirds of the way to the top, a man appeared standing on a rock, he was outlined against the sky. The man's bow was clearly visible, he pulled it. Namdarin stood up in the stirrups and turned Arndrol's head towards the man, pulled his bow to its prodigious limit, both bowmen lined up their respective targets, both acquired their targets at the same time, the man on the hill released first, then made the mistake of watching his arrow fly, Namdarin moved the tip of his arrow upwards to allow for a two foot drop, because a hundred feet up is a long way even for this bow, Namdarin released, the string twanged and the arrow leapt from the bow, a green fletched thunderbolt screaming up into the sky, Namdarin did not wait, he kicked Arndrol in the ribs with his right heel, the horse jumped four feet to the left. The man on the hill saw his arrow hit the ground and was disappointed, then he saw a green blur as Namdarin's arrow plunged into his right eye, the point smashing through the orbital bone and then out through the top of his head, scattering splinters of skull and brains. The bowman on the hill slumped out of sight, Jayanne guided her horse over to the arrow in the dirt, grasped it by the feathers and pulled it up then placed it in her own quiver.

"That's a trade of a sort", she said.

"I don't like losing arrows," said Namdarin. "Stay alert there are more of them." Another man jumped onto a rock, this time on Jayanne's side, he didn't even get his bow pulled before Jayanne's arrow took him in the chest, ending his life in a rich red fountain of blood. Now the attackers came into view all around, Namdarin's bow sang its deadly song four times, Jayanne's only three before the brigands had descended to the gully floor. Ten of the men finally jumped to the ground and ran towards the horses, Jayanne dropped her bow onto the saddle horn then slid to the ground, whirling her axe about her head and screaming like a banshee,

"Come my axe thirsts for your blood." Namdarin and Morgan remained mounted, Arndrol charged at three of the men, knocking one to the ground to be stamped to death, the other two died their heads chopped by Namdarin's sword before they recovered their balance. Arndrol wheeled about and charged over to where six men had surrounded Jayanne, none of them could get close enough to strike her because of the whirling axe, the circle about Jayanne closed in slowly, one man stepped in too far and was struck, a rapid forehand stroke hit him just above the belt, his hard leather armour didn't slow the blade, nor did his shirt nor flesh. The blade came through the man and was clean and bright, flashing round in a long arc to discourage the other five. The man dropped his sword, grabbed his belly and fell to the ground moaning, he looked unhurt, the impact with the dusty floor caused his wound to open and his guts came flowing out, like so many strings of sausages, he lay there in the dirt trying desperately to stuff them back were they belonged. The brigand next to him looked on hypnotised, until Morgan came up behind him and chopped his head clean off, the sword of his fathers was blooded with a real flourish. While all the carnage was going on the leader of the brigands a large black bearded man stayed in the rocks about halfway up the wall of the gully, he knew his men had lost and started to climb up to where their horses had been hidden. The four remaining on the ground saw Blackbeard leaving and tried to follow him, as they scrambled towards the rocks Jayanne cut them all down from behind, striking limbs and heads from bodies, leaving the gully to look like a slaughterhouse. Jayanne threw back her head and howled like a wolf, then shouted. "Come back you coward. Come back and die like your friends. Are you frightened of a mere woman?" Namdarin put an arrow to his bow, pulled it, and scanned the lip of the gully waiting to see Blackbeard to go over the top, he saw a quick flash of somebody's head but could not shoot his arrow fast enough.

"Well I think that is over, they are dead or gone. Is any one hurt?"

"I am fine." answered Morgan, looking down from the horse at a head staring up with blank dead eyes.

"That was a fine stroke, well struck," said Namdarin, "Jayanne how are you?"

"I am uninjured, but I want more foes to strike, why do they run away?"

"They are unused to a wild woman, wielding a wicked axe, and screaming for blood. You frightened them away like rabbits from a hound. Now calm down, we really ought to get out of here, there may be more of them close by."

Namdarin dismounted, and searched the slain until he found what he was looking for, a scabbard and belt into which his sword would fit. "That's better." He said settling the scabbard on his left hip, the belt also came with three sheaths for knifes, all full. Remounting he looked down at Jayanne, who was standing amongst the dead swinging the axe gently to and fro, "Come on Jayanne, we must leave."

"Why do I feel so angry at them for running?" she asked.

"Could be that you have been spoiling for a fight for a long time and they denied you the opportunity." Said Namdarin as Morgan rode over to her and passed her the reins of the horse, then leant down to help her into the saddle. With a sulky look she grasped his hand and jumped into the saddle in front of him.

"Let's go and see if they left us any horses." She said, kicking the bay hard and making her jump forwards. Namdarin let her go for a moment or two, while he thought about the arrows he had lost. "They are up there, in those rocks." He whispered pointing towards the rocks with his right hand, "I wish I could get them back."

There was a strange tugging sensation in his arm, as if he was trying to pull something towards himself, the sensation decreased to a smooth steady force, and descending from the rock came a long, green fletched, blood dripping arrow, it approached Namdarin slowly and settled gently into his right hand, then it was followed in sequence by four others. He was completely astounded, putting the arrow back in its quiver he turned to followed Jayanne, at a discreet distance. He was worried about her attitude, she seemed unduly anxious to fight, he thought she might even have fought with him. In a line astern they trotted up the gully with no further incident until they reached the plateau. There, about half a mile away on the northern side of the gully were four horses that seemed to be roaming free, obviously ones that Blackbeard could not control. Once they were near the loose horses Morgan dropped to the ground and between the three of them they soon had all the horses rounded up, and tied together. Morgan picked a big roan stallion for himself, and was very glad not to have to ride double with the bad tempered woman any more. Fastened to the horses they found a selection of weapons and some supplies, all of which would have their uses. So riding three horses and pulling three horses they set off at a fast trot across the plateau heading for the mountains, which contain the home village of both Morgan and Jayanne. Before nightfall they had reached the mountains and climbed a little way up the pass that Morgan had pointed out as the one that leads to his home.

Camping for the night they now had two tents, and more than enough food, still Namdarin was wary of Blackbeard and his men, so watches were set and the night passed slowly but uneventfully. They rose with the sun, to a cold clear day, climbing the pass was easy, as the snow was very shallow but Morgan said that it would get very much deeper in a few weeks, once winter took its grip.

Namdarin kept an alert eye on the trail behind them but saw no signs of pursuit. When they came to the crest of the pass, the snow filled vista that stood before them was totally breath taking, they stopped for a few minutes and just looked, amazed by the beauty that was before them.

"It's a wonderful sight." Said Namdarin.

"Yes, it is very pretty, especially if it is your home." answered Morgan.

"And frightening even if it is your home." said Jayanne.

Down in the valley they could see the village complete with the deep pits of open mines, the gaping holes in the sides of the mountains showing the shafts of drift and deep mines. The spoil heaps of used ores were obvious for any to see, but the overall effect of the mining on the valley was minimal. There were still open pastures and good-sized stands of trees, more than enough to support the villagers. Though the village was in plain view it was still many miles away, it would be almost midday by the time they reached it. The approaches to the village caused much comment by Morgan, many new things were visible, a large building was being put up that had not been started before he left.

"This is a strange time of year to start a new building, we usually do that in spring, when we know that bad weather is not going to interrupt the work." He said, thinking that somebody must be in a hurry to see that finished.

"It will be that Zandaar, he wants it up fast, we must find out why." Said Namdarin. The path leading into the village was almost wide enough to be called a road, It was smooth and well drained.

"Do you get a lot of travellers through here?" asked Namdarin.

"Many people come to buy the silver, it is much sought after. Some travel for months just to buy our silver." said Morgan.

"Why? Silver is rare but not that rare."

"Our silver is different from everybody else's, it works easier, and it doesn't lose its shine as fast as others. Sometimes when you get the sunlight on it at just the right angle it glitters in many colours, it is very pretty."

"Perhaps it has some other properties that you don't know about." When they had only half a mile to go Jayanne put on her white bearskin cape and put her axe across her knees.

"That is new." Said Morgan pointing at a gate across the road, just on the out skirts of the village. "I wonder why they have put a gate there, is it to keep people out or in."

"The fence only goes a hundred yards or so each side of the road, so it is only a symbolic barrier at best. Its probably to keep a check on strangers coming in." Said Namdarin thinking that he was just such a stranger, and that Jayanne was definitely designated as undesirable. The barrier across the road was a simple single pole affair, which had to be removed by two men before any one could enter, anyone not riding a good horse. As the barrier was only four feet high a horse like Arndrol could almost step over it, any horse in good health could jump it, it was merely a symbolic barrier. The two gate keepers appeared from their small hut to the right of the road way, they were tall men dressed in black, not the black flowing robes of the Zandaar but black none the less.

"Halt. Who are you?" said the tallest of the two.

"I am Namdarin, lord of the house of Namdaron, and these are my friends."

"What do you want here?"

"I come to buy your famous silver."

"We have no silver for sale."

"But this town has always sold its silver, how else is it to survive?"

"We no longer sell our silver, you must go." At this point Morgan became very impatient.

"Edran, is that you in those dreary black clothes."

"Morgan, we had thought you dead in the mountains."

"I would have been if not for these good people, kindly remove the gate and let us in, I wish to see my mother."

"We are not allowed to let any strangers in."

"You will not stop me from going into my home and I will take my friends with me so that my mother can thank them personally. If you do not stop this foolishness somebody will get hurt."

"We have very specific instructions not to let any one in."

"Who gave you these ridiculous instructions?"

"Dorana, the high priest."

"What not the chief elder, Kironand?"

"No, he has been unwell for some time and Dorana has taken over."

"Dorana was elected as chief elder."

"Not really, he just took over."

"Enough. I refuse to be ordered about by that insane priest. Open the gate or we break it down."

"We dare not."

Morgan looked meaningfully at Jayanne, who understood his intent immediately, she lifted her axe high over her head and swung it down with all her strength, the head of the axe hit the pole of the gate and went clean through, chopping the gate into two pieces, which fell to the ground with dull thuds. Namdarin walked Arndrol through the gap thus provided, followed by Jayanne then Morgan who said to the frightened gate keepers,

"Go and tell Dorana that I have come home, and that I challenge his right to keep me away."

Edran nudged the other gate keeper in the ribs very hard with his elbow, causing the man to scamper off into the village as fast as his legs would carry him. Once they were out of earshot of Edran, Namdarin said.

"They didn't recognise you Jayanne, did you know them."

"Yes," she replied, "not well but I did know them and they knew me, I wonder if Edran still has a limp."

"One of your gifts?" he asked, to which she just nodded.

"Everything seems to have changed since you left, Morgan." Said Namdarin.

"Yes. If the people here aren't allowed to sell their silver then the village will starve this winter, we don't grow enough food for everyone, the silver buys us everything we need. Dorana must be stopped and quickly before it's too late."

"Which way to your mothers house?"

"Follow me." said Morgan taking the lead. Riding slowly down the narrow streets Namdarin realised that this was indeed a prosperous settlement, most of the houses they passed were in good repair, and well built of quality materials. Some had ornate carving on the doors and walls, some had fancy windows with balconies, and stained glass. After a few turns they arrived at Morgan's mother's house, it was only a single storey, but it was extensive, it looked plenty big enough for a large family. Morgan jumped from his horse, tied it to a post beside the front door and banged on the door, While his friends dismounted he opened the heavy wooden door and shouted. "Mother, it's me, I'm home." Then to the others. "The stable is around the back, we can put the horses there in a little while."

A small grey haired woman came to the door almost at a run, she looked like she was about fifty five years old, she peered at Morgan with her bright, clear blue eyes, she checked him up and down, then in a creaky voice said, "Where have you been? I have been worried sick. You may have been dead for all I knew. Running off like that without a word, indeed. You are an irresponsible young hooligan." The tirade showed no signs of slowing so Morgan threw his arms around her and hugged her and kissed her, saying, "I am back now and I have some friends for you to meet, they saved my life."

"Well put me down and introduce them properly." Morgan let her go and she smoothed the creases out of her long grey skirt and her blue shirt.

"This is Namdarin who comes from far away, and this is Jayanne who comes from right here."

"I am very pleased to meet you Namdarin," she said with a small bow, "and you young lady should not be here, so come inside quickly before anybody recognises you." The old woman herded the three inside and shut the door, then barred it with a large oak beam. "Morgan, you get the other doors." She said.

"I'll see to the horses first." He said. Morgan went out of the front door, which Namdarin barred behind him.

"Come in and sit down," said Morgan's mother, "My name is Bettice but most just call me Betty. I thought it was wicked to chase you from your home just because you killed that monster, he was truly evil."

"Thank you Betty." said Jayanne.

"I don't think that anyone will recognise you, Jayanne, because you have changed so much, you are thinner and somehow wilder than ever."

"When I see the way things have changed here I feel even angrier than when I left."

"Yes, a lot has changed since that Dorana came, my husband died only a few days ago. He was not the only one, a least six outspoken people have died in their sleep in the last five weeks." A small tear started to roll down the old woman's face. "There have been far too many funerals this year, most of them very recently."

"Perhaps we have come at the right time to stop Dorana." said Namdarin.

"You think you can stop him?" she asked.

"I know that he can die, and I know that I must try."

"You are a brave man even to think a thing like that, some say that Dorana can hear thoughts that are against him, though I think he has spies that listen at peoples windows."

"How many people of the village actually support him?"

"Only a few actively support him but most of the rest are too frightened to act against him."

"Do you know what he wants the silver for?"

"Not exactly, it is taken to the foundry and cast into the shape of lightening bolts and flames. What these are for who can tell." At this point Morgan came into the room saying, "The horses are in the stable, all the doors are bolted and all the windows locked, we should not be disturbed."

"Oh. My son," said the old woman, "what has been happening to you?"

Morgan told her how he went to get some help, how Namdarin and Jayanne saved him from the wolves, of the fight in the gully, and how they came through the gate into the village. He did not mention Namdarin's cause, leaving that for the man himself to decide. When the story was told, she looked deep into Namdarin's eyes, took his hand in hers and said, "I thank you a thousand times for the life of my son. If he has chosen to stand beside you in this fight with Dorana then I will stand with you, I may not be much in physical combat but you must stay here so that I can feed you and keep you safe during the dreadful darkness that is night time here."

"Why is the night so frightening?" asked Namdarin.

"Every one suffers from evil dreams, and some appear to die from them."

"That is one of the Zandaar's normal tactics, so I have been told."

"Anyway, to the practicalities of life," said Betty, "It is almost time for tea, I will go and see what I can find in the kitchen, I was not expecting so many so I am afraid that rations may be a little short."

"I am sure that Morgan has already brought in the supplies from our horses. These we will gladly share." said Namdarin. Betty left the room and they heard the clattering of cooking pots, and a quiet singing from the kitchen.

"Are you going to tell her of your cause?" asked Morgan.

"No, I don't think so, it will only complicate matters, and I would rather she look upon me as knight in shining armour." he answered with a big smile.

"Of all the conceit." said Jayanne, "You men are all the same, you don't want her to know the immensity of the battle she is getting involved with, you think it will frighten her off. She has lost her husband and thought she lost her son, now that he has returned she will fight to her last breath, in any way she can. Your dismissive attitude makes me so angry that I almost want to kill you both. You are so stupid!" Her eyes flared bright green with her anger, her right hand resting casually on the haft of the axe, and her right foot was tapping softly but quickly against the floor. Namdarin saw that his joke had been in extremely bad taste.

"It was only a joke," he said, "I meant no offence to either of you, don't forget that I have seen you take on a bear single handed. I know how hard women will fight for their loved ones, this brave old woman shames most of the men in this village because she is willing to take a stand, if only because her hothead son says so. It is the bravery of people like Betty that proves to me that the Zandaar cannot win, even if I fail, some will fight on." Jayanne calmed down a little but her foot didn't stop tapping, she looked hard into Namdarin's eyes, but she said nothing. The silence reached out for what seemed to be hours, but was only seconds, until, "Right, I will tell her." said Namdarin.

"That's better." Said Jayanne, with a sigh. Betty came back into the room saying. "The food will be ready in about an hour."

"Betty," said Namdarin, "there is something I must tell you. I started this fight against the Zandaar long before I knew your village existed, they destroyed my home and my family, I swore that I would kill them all, I did not come here specifically to help you, this is a visit of pure chance, if by killing the Zandaar that is here I help you then so much the better, but by helping me you could become embroiled in a much larger battle, you could end up fighting them all. If you do not wish to take this risk speak now and I will leave you to your peaceful life."

"Young man!" She answered in a clear and loud voice. "My life has never been peaceful, we are miners, we fight with the earth for her treasures, we live in the mountains and fight with the seasons for food, and when we have won our treasures from the bowels of the earth we fight with the merchants for a profit to keep us alive. I have been fighting for more years than you have known. One more threat makes no difference to me. The only reason that Dorana is doing so well is that we have not found a way to beat him, yet. He has promised the greedy ones more silver than they can carry, he has promised the frightened ones that others will dig for them, and he has promised the religious that Zandaar will provide for them. He promises anything to anyone, but means none of it. The young and the strong ones are dead, only the old and weak are left but I for one will not surrender. You think of me as an old and frightened woman, you are right, but I will fight on. Perhaps a chance will come to put an arrow in his head, or poison in his food, or a spider in his bed. One Zandaar or all Zandaars I care not, I will fight the world for my sons heritage."

"Old woman, you shame me, please accept my humblest apologies for doubting your courage. I will help you if I can, then when Dorana is gone you must keep this village from the rest, will you do that?"

"Of course. Now, how do we kill Dorana?"

"If I can get close enough I will shoot him with an arrow."

"That is not at all likely to happen, he almost never comes outside of his new church."

"Then I will stir up as much trouble as I can for him, and make him come and fight me." said Namdarin with a grim look of determination.

"We must see what we can do about that." Said Betty, returning to the kitchen to check on the food. A few moments of silence descended on the room, giving Namdarin a chance to look around, the room was fairly large and very tidy, it was obviously the house of prosperous people, the curtains on the windows, the ornaments scattered about the walls all spoke of wealth. Namdarin's quiet appraisal of his home caused Morgan to comment, "Yes Namdarin, my father was an excellent miner, he could smell silver through a thousand feet of rock. We were definitely one of the richest families in the village, now that is ended. I have no talent for finding silver, and once our small stockpile has been exhausted I will have to find another way of keeping my mother from starving." Namdarin nodded because he knew that Morgan was going to find it very hard to earn money in a village that is taken up by mining. Just then there came a loud banging on the front door, followed by a loud voice shouting, "Open up, old woman. Bring out these strangers that you are harbouring, they attacked the gatekeeper and must answer to Dorana for their sins." Morgan went to the door, he peeped through the small grill in the door and said, "I am Morgan and this is my home, how dare you call me a stranger, the strangers are my friends. They did not attack the keepers they only broke their silly gate. Now go away Lorik and leave us in peace."

"I have specific instructions from Dorana to bring the strangers to him."

Morgan closed the grill for a moment and said quietly to his friends, "This is when things get a little exciting." Opening the grill he looked out saying, "If Dorana wishes to see my friends he can come here to visit, that is if he is not to frightened to leave his nice new pigsty." Lorik spluttered with shock, but quickly recovered his powers of speech.

"Dorana says that you have a hoard of silver here that must be surrendered immediately, or we are to come in and take it." Morgan shut the grill again and said, "Be ready to fight." As he opened the grill to speak to Lorik again Namdarin went and stood at one side of the door and Jayanne stood at the other both had their weapons drawn.

"If you and your four friends come in to take my families silver I will cut you down like the common thieves that you are, but you Lorik I will not kill, no, you I will bury alive in a small coffin." Lorik went a deathly pale, his ashen features showing quite clearly his terror. Morgan knew that Lorik could never be a miner because he had a dreadful fear on enclosed spaces, the mere thought of being buried alive made him tremble and shake. Morgan took advantage of Loriks sudden seizure, he lifted the bar from the door, flung the door wide open, the five men outside stepped backwards at this sudden move, so Morgan drew his sword and stepped through the opening, Namdarin followed and stood to one side.

Jayanne stayed in the doorway, with her axe dangling casually from her hand.

This was too much for the detachment of Doranas bodyguard, they were not used to such resistance, they turned to go.

"Tell Dorana," shouted Namdarin. "That I am the nemesis of the Zandaar, and I have come for him." Lorik looked back over his shoulder and muttered something about Dorana teaching the insolent a lesson they would not live to remember. To which Namdarin laughed loudly, though he was not as confident as he hoped the laugh sounded. Herding his friends back into the house Namdarin said,

"I think we most certainly have attracted Dorana's attention. Now he must kill me, or his bodyguards will never believe in his power again." Once they were all safely inside they started to make plans for the night, which was rapidly falling.

CHAPTER SIX

Lorik and his four accomplices almost ran to the newly built temple of Zandaar, they scrambled through the door as if the demon was chasing them.

"Master. Master." Shouted Lorik running into the small study were Dorana habitually stayed. As Lorik stumbled into the room, Dorana said,

"Be careful, you fool. What are you running for?" Lorik stood just inside the door way with his four friends waiting outside, he looked down into the cold blue eyes of the old man who was Dorana. Dorana was sitting calmly in the high backed wing chair by the fire, only his face was visible the rest of his body being completely shrouded in the black garb of the Zandaar priest, the sharp contrast between the black of his robes and his pasty white and wrinkled face, made him look more dead than alive. The only colour about the man was the cold blue chips that were his eyes and the bright golden buckles of his shoes. Lorik took two long slow breaths before speaking.

"The strangers are not all they first seemed master."

"Don't talk in riddles, idiot, tell me now."

"The youngest is Morgan, the woman looks like Jayanne, who was chased away for killing the chief elders son, and the other is a stranger who says that he has come to kill you, he says he is the nemesis of Zandaar."

"How ridiculous. They must be made into a final example for everyone, tonight when they sleep I will kill them all. Now leave me, I must prepare myself." Lorik almost ran from the room, so pleased not to have invoked Doranas anger for his failure to return with either the strangers or the silver, he did not realise that Dorana never really expected him to succeed. Dorana climbed slowly to his feet and went into the body of his temple to stand before the altar, he stared up into the centre of the symbol of Zandaar, the five yellow lightening bolts and the five red flames began slowly to revolve against the electric blue background. Dorana sank to his knees and concentrated hard on the symbol, he pushed the rotation faster and faster, until it appeared to be a colourless blur, from the centre expanded a small disc , that grew until it filled the spinning symbol, in the disc he could see a room with four occupants, two women, one old and wearing drab clothes, one young wearing furs and holding an axe, two men both with swords, the four were talking about something that was very important to them. Dorana could not hear the words he could only see the picture, concentrating on both keeping the window open and reading the lips of the people in it was such hard work that Dorana started to sweat, his breathing became coarse and ragged, "This is a task for two at least." he whispered. Almost as soon as he had the picture steadied and focused sharp enough to see the lips of the people clearly the older of the two men jumped to his feet and shouted something that Dorana did not see, the others froze, saying nothing. The man swept the room with his eyes, he was searching for something, on the second time around, he found it. The man looked straight into Dorana's eyes, cold blue ice met cold blue ice, then the heat of rage and hate poured through Namdarin's gaze, the red anger was so strong that Dorana was distracted and lost the delicate balance of his visionary window, it slammed shut with an almost audible crash, the spiralling symbol spun first one way then the other in complete confusion, a surge of fear filled Dorana as he collapsed to the floor, drained by the effort he had just expended to see his foes. Laying still for a few minutes while his breathing and heart slowed down enough for him to attempt to arise he thought about the power he had seen, a hate so strong and an anger so intense that it had actually attained a colour all of its own, a red so hot that a forge could never match it, a red so bright that it made the noonday sun seem dim. He knew then that he was about to face the most difficult task of his life, this man was not going to lay down and die like the others had ,this one would fight. Dorana hoped that his training and experience would be sufficient to defeat the strange power of this man, who he now saw, could be the nemesis of Zandaar. Dorana struggled to his feet and staggered into his study taking his book of the teachings of Zandaar he read the three chapters that he needed to concentrate his resolve and strengthen his mind, eating some almost dried plums to give his body the energy it would need.

Having seen off Dorana's bodyguard Morgan and Namdarin went back into the house and settled down to discuss tactics for the up coming battle.

"I think that you have definitely attracted Dorana's attention." Said Morgan.

"Yes" replied Namdarin, "just as I intended, now he will have to attack us. If his bodyguard are made of the bravest of his supporters he will have to do it himself."

"How will we defend our selves, you must have some sort of plan."

"Not really. I will be the one to go to sleep, the rest of you must stand guard, and stay awake. If any of us sleep we will be attacked, I would rather it were me, because I have come up against their illusions before."

"How did you defeat them last time?" asked Betty.

"More by blind luck than anything, though I did have the illusion beaten before the monk producing it died. Before I go into this battle I have some very specific instructions that must be followed. Do you all understand?"

A chorus of nods.

"Right, here goes. After we have eaten I will go to sleep, Jayanne you will watch over me, and Morgan you will saddle the horses for all of us to leave in hurry, do not forget to fasten the biggest of our wild pigs to Arndrol."

"Why would we leave?" asked Morgan, looking very confused.

"If I lose the first round and Dorana kills me, it is vital that we all leave at the greatest possible speed, you will have to strap my body across Arndrols back, then you ride. Ride hard and fast up into the forest, find a quiet spot and drop my body and the pig. Do not bury me or the pig. Then ride on up to the pass. When the sun comes up release Arndrol, I should return to the pass by noon, if I don't then ride away and forget your home, make yourselves a new one elsewhere."

"You talk like a mad man." said Morgan. "How can you come back from the dead?"

"I do not know how it is done, only that I have died twice and returned. Once a man plunged a sword through my heart, and once the priests of Zandaar burned me with their black fire. On both occasions I returned to life, but all around me the flesh of living and dead animals had been destroyed. A friend thought it might be something to do with an oath I swore on a altar dedicated to the old gods. If you stay near me your bodies may be consumed and I could not bear to loose any more friends, so please follow these instructions very carefully."

"Very well," said Betty, "we will do exactly as you say. I have heard many old tales of these gods and they certainly seemed to be very powerful for many years. If you swore an oath to them they may choose to help you, and their help can take the strangest forms. It is said that they taught the birds to fly and the fish to swim."

"This is lunacy." Said Morgan.

"My son." Said the old woman with a firm commanding tone, "You will do as your friend says, not because he saved your life, but because I say he is right. Do I make myself perfectly clear?"

"Yes mother, I am sorry that I doubted you Namdarin."

"You have good reason to doubt, or I also doubt. I begin to hate the oath I swore in grief and anguish, I hate the power it has over me." Namdarin stopped talking all of a sudden and jumped to his feet, he looked all around the room.

"What is wrong?" asked Jayanne.

"Someone is watching us. I can feel it, I think it is Dorana." Turning slowly around he scanned the room again, this time more slowly. He stopped when he saw what appeared to be two blue eyes, no face, just eyes, staring at him from the middle on a wall. Two pairs of eyes locked onto each other, Namdarin knew that this must be Dorana, he felt the hate rushing into his brain, he felt the hot red fire of anger swell in his chest, holding on to the hate and anger with his mind he hurled it at the eyes. The blue eyes on the wall blinked and disappeared.

Namdarin slumped into his chair, the emotion drained.

"I saw eyes in the wall." said Morgan, his voice quivering.

"So did I." Said Betty, "This Dorana has strange power at his command. You must rest now Namdarin or he will certainly beat you later." Betty went into the kitchen to see to the meal while the others sat in absolute silence, Morgan was very frightened by the disembodied eyes of Dorana, Jayanne was worried about Namdarin's fate in the fight with Dorana, Namdarin was merely exhausted. Betty returned from the kitchen saying, "Dinner will be ready in a few minutes, while we are waiting, Morgan." the young man looked up from his boots, "Go and saddle the horses, and load them for travelling, we may not be coming back. Jayanne, you go upstairs to the front balcony and keep a watch on the street. Namdarin we must talk." Morgan and Jayanne showed no signs of moving to follow Betty's orders, so she said, in a forceful tone "In private." The two young people glanced at each other, but said nothing and departed with speed.

"Now that we are alone, tell me of the oath that drives you." Namdarin spoke at some length of the exact circumstances of his oath and of the bones that are all about him when he awakes. When he had finished Betty thought for a while before saying anything, and finally she nodded as if having made a decision.

"I believe everything that you have said, I think that the old gods are keeping you alive so that you can kill all the Zandaars, but probably not entirely for your purposes. According to the legends they were never terribly forthcoming with their favours, they tended to grant peoples wishes only when the causes were their own. You must find the help of a magician to discover the exact nature of the oath."

"I was going to see Granger before I was distracted to come here."

"I have heard of him, he is said to be very powerful, I believe that is where Morgan was going for help with Dorana. When the situation here is sorted out you must go and see him, do not be distracted elsewhere."

"I will do that, if I survive." He looked ruefully at the floor.

"Confidence is everything, young man." She said. "You must convince first your self, then Dorana that you have nothing to be afraid of, then you cannot lose."

"But there is much to be afraid of."

"This is your fight, if you lose, we will merely run away."

"Then we shall see how well I can fight my fears." He looked up into her wrinkled face and saw the intense life in her eyes, they were soft and brown but fiercely alive.

"That is better. Now let's eat." She rose from her chair and stalked into her kitchen shouting of the others to come to eat. After an enormous meal of pork and vegetables they relaxed near the fire in the living room. Morgan passed round a large brown stone jug of a fiery liquid that at first brought tears to the eyes then a lovely warm feeling to the belly.

"Better not drink too much of this if we are going to stay awake all night." he said.

"I don't think this will take all night." said Namdarin. "Dorana will want this over as soon as possible." He took a long drink from the jug then gave it back to Morgan, who corked it and put it under his chair out of the way.

"Namdarin," said Betty, "You lay down on this couch and try and go to sleep. We will watch over you have no fear." Once he was comfortable on the long couch she covered him with a blanket and turned to Jayanne.

"You can tell us about everything that has happened to you since you left us, especially about that beautiful white bearskin. I presume it is a bearskin."

To the soft and gentle sound of Jayanne telling the others of her past few weeks Namdarin gradually drifted off to sleep.

The swirling black cloud of sleep engulfed Namdarins brain, the electrifying blues and greens soon gave way to a chaotic scene, a jumble of images from his past flashed through his consciousness, his father, a pet dog, a sunny day, a thunder storm, a spiralling morass of history, that finally spun down into a vortex of falling, the endless helpless drop went on for what seemed like hours, until he fell through a blue sky onto green grass. The grass was a deep green, of the sort normally reserved for the leaves of trees, the sky appeared to have a texture not unlike blue silk blowing in the wind, a wind that could not be felt. As Namdarin walked across the grass he felt a little disturbed by the fact that there was light all around him and no apparent source, he could see a few yards in every direction but at the limit of visibility things were blurred, almost unformed. "This a strange place to be, but if this is a dream then it could be anything, I wonder how one goes about finding a priest by the name of Dorana, who may or may not be hiding in this dream?" he asked himself in a very small voice.

"You need look no further." said a deep rough voice behind him. Namdarin spun round to see a man in black robes in the act of stepping out from behind a large group of rocks that had not been there when Namdarin had walked past the spot where they now had appeared.

"You are Dorana?" he asked.

"Who else could you be expecting? You are possibly awaiting some assistance from elsewhere?" Asked the figure whose eyes glowed a bright and sharp blue from deep within his cowl.

"I will need no help to defeat you." Said Namdarin with false confidence, he did not know how to proceed, what does one do in a dream.

"I do not have your bravado," said Dorana, "I have brought a little helper with me, come closer and see." Dorana held out his cupped hands towards Namdarin, who was pulled forwards towards the man in black. In Doranas hand he saw a small white nearly round object, at first it made no sense at all then a tiny crack appeared in its surface and Namdarin then realised it was an egg. Slowly the crack widened and stretched, until the crack was the size of a mans head, the egg had swollen until it was the size of a man. From the crack something flickered, a quick flash and then it was gone, again it flickered, this time Namdarin was able to resolve the image it was a forked tongue, a snakes forked tongue. Knowing the nature of the little helper Namdarin stepped backwards away from the egg, as a head pushed it way through the opening, a large head covered in diamond shapes of blue and red and yellow. He had seen this snake before, in the monastery, then it had been an illusion, now it was part of a dream, where illusion is real. While he backed away from the snake, it climbed sinuously from its egg, until it was fifty feet long and its body was as thick as mans. He turned and ran from the snake, across the green grass, under the blue silken sky he ran in fear.

"If only I had my bow." he thought, trying to run faster because the slithering of scales against the grass was getting louder, a quick glance over his shoulder revealed much, the snake was close, but no closer than it had been, and Dorana was standing still behind it, he was moving at the same speed as both Namdarin and the snake but he was not running. Dorana was floating along a whole foot above the grass. "If only I had my bow." Thought Namdarin again, and there it was just ahead, resting on the grass as if it had always been there, alongside the huge bone bow was a quiver of long arrows, without slowing his headlong flight Namdarin stooped and snatched up the bow and quiver, then continued to run. Holding quiver and bow in the same hand he took an arrow and set it to the string. Rallying his courage he stopped, turned pulled the bow to the limit, and released. The bow kicked hard against his left thumb, the string twanged and the arrow screamed, it jumped the short distance separating it from its target in the blink of an eye, a green streak in Namdarins vision, that went right into the snakes head, above and between the eyes. The snake faltered in its sinuous slide, it shuddered, and began to writhe in pain. It coiled itself into knots and died.

Namdarin knew that the snake was dead because it stopped moving then dissolved slowly into the grass. Namdarin stared at it in disbelief for a few moments then nocked another arrow and let it fly at Dorana, mid-flight the arrow changed into a bolt of light, a gold and green spiral that plunged towards Doranas chest. The Zandaar simple waved his hand and a bolt of black fire leapt out and engulfed Namdarins light bolt. Namdarin was shaken by this turn of events and he felt the icy hand of fear on his heart, as Dorana waved again and this time the black fire of Zandaar came at Namdarins head, fear overcame Namdarin completely and he froze like a statue, the fire struck and spread over his whole body, entwining him in pain, he remembered the agony of fire and by remembering died.

In Betty's house the people sitting around the fire talking about Jayannes fight with a white bear, saw Namdarin twitching in his sleep, then he screamed and breathed no more. The three sat in shocked silence for almost a minute, they had not really expected Namdarin to lose the battle with Dorana.

"Right," said Betty finally, "he's dead, let's move. You two carry him into the stable as he said. We leave when you have done that." Morgan and Jayanne carried Namdarins body between them, Jayannes tears fell gently onto Namdarins upturned face, she was very sad to see him dead, killed by a dream, and she did not believe as he did that he would return. She knew that she would miss him tremendously. She hoped beyond hope that his story of resurrection was true. When they got into the stable they had to lift Namdarin up unto Arndrols back, the problem of the horses size was compounded by the fact that Arndrol was very confused by his friends total lack of movement, the horse kept moving around to sniff at Namdarin. After four attempts to put Namdarin across his saddle Morgan said, "Help me get Namdarin on my shoulder then you can hold the horses head."

This was of course much easier said than done, even with Jayannes help Namdarins body was a limp dead weight that seemed to deliberately make things difficult, eventually Morgan dropped the body into the saddle and tied his wrists and ankles together under the horses girth. Untying the other horses in readiness for their departure Morgan said. "I wonder what is keeping mother?" Jayanne made no answer as she was too wrapped up in her own world of grief. After a period of time that to Morgan felt like hours, but was in fact only minutes, Betty appeared from inside the house, "Everything is secured, here is all the silver that is left, you look after it, Morgan." she said tossing a small box to her son. She walked over to the main stable door and set the locking mechanism, "Once we shut this door it will lock itself, then if we do come back we will have to smash our way in. If there was one thing other than mining that your father was good at it was designing impregnable houses. The fires and candles are out, the shutters and doors are locked, now let us leave." To Morgans intense gaze his mother seemed to tremble slightly, as afraid.

"How can you be so calm leaving your home for so many years, knowing you will not be coming back." he said with a shaky voice.

"Who says I am calm, and who says I wont be back."

"What do you mean?"

"I am not calm, I am angry beyond measure. If Namdarin does not return to rid us of Dorana then I will do it myself. Who would question an old and frail woman hobbling into the temple to pay homage to that bastard Dorana. I will totter up to him on my shaky old legs then carve his heart out and show it to him before he dies." There was no mistaking the surety of her resolve.

"But his friends will kill you."

"I care not." He saw the determination in her gaze and knew not to question her further. She slowly mounted the horse that was to be hers.

"Jayanne." said Betty in a loud voice, waiting for the younger woman to look up and acknowledge her, "Be ready with your axe there may be some who don't want us to get away."

"Then they will die." Was all the answer that Jayanne had.

The three of them left the house that had been home to two for a long time, without so much as one backward glance, their attention was entirely encompassed by their surroundings and the fact that there may be some resistance to their somewhat precipitous departure. As it happened they saw nobody until they reached the gate, there the gate keepers saw the axe swinging slowly in Jayannes hand and decided that being alive was better than following instructions, the newly restored gate pole was opened as soon as they were near it. A single glance from Jayanne had the gate keepers running for the safety of their little hut beside the road. Once they were clear of the village without incident they headed for the woods as Namdarin had told them. The biggest of the moons gave them more than enough light to see by, deep into the woods they went, their passage was noted only by the night hunters, a fox and a few owls watched them as their funeral procession passed. Betty was leading them as she appeared to know where she was going, the other two were deep in their own thoughts. Long before midnight they arrived in a small clearing high on the slopes of one of the highest of the mountains around the valley.

"This is a place that will serve Namdarins purposes more than adequately," then to Morgan specifically, "Your father and I used to meet here, even though my parents disapproved of him." Morgan nodded and cut the ropes binding Namdarins limbs, then he unfastened the ropes holding the pig onto Arndrols rump. Namdarin and the pig dropped to the ground together, both dead.

"Now up to the pass." said Betty. They set of up the trail that Betty knew lead directly to the pass. Both Morgan and Jayanne kept looking back to the dreadful sight of Namdarin lying beside a pig. As soon as they could no longer see the clearing Betty kicked her horse into a trot, this pace was maintained until they reached the summit of the pass. Here Betty called a halt and told Morgan to light a fire so that they could stay warm during what remained of the night.

When they tried to settle down near the fire Arndrol became very skittish, he was having problems understanding why Namdarin had been left behind, he refused to stand still and kept trying to go back to Namdarin, until Jayanne took his reins in hand and held him close to the fire, in the flickering light the grey appeared almost a ghost, sometimes clear and solid sometimes not. Jayanne stroked Arndrols nose and caressed his neck to try and calm him. The three people sat close to the fire, which though it roared high and hot could not warm the ice from their hearts. Around them stood seven horses, nervous horses naturally afraid of the fire, but still comforted by the presence of people. Not one word was spoken for the rest of the night, they sat silent awaiting the first light of a new day and the hope that it could bring.

As the pre-dawn lightening of the sky in the east caused the birds to start practising their songs for the day Betty said to Jayanne, "Release Arndrol. Let him go and find Namdarin if he lives, and hope that he does." Jayanne stood up and tied the big greys reins to the saddle horn saying. "Go and find Namdarin."

Arndrol remain exactly where he was, he had been held there all night and did not see why he should move now. "Go and find Namdarin." Said Jayanne again, this time slapping the horse firmly on the rump and stirring him into action.

Arndrol tossed his head, snorted and set off down the path by which they had all come to the pass. After Arndrol had gone Betty went to one of the pack horses and started to make breakfast for every body, it was to be bacon and oat cakes, a typical travelling breakfast for people of the mining village. The horses could easily find their own forage as the snow on the pass was not too deep to hinder them in any real way. Morgan disappeared for a while to bring some more wood from the fringe of the forest that ended just below the summit of the pass where they had lit their fire. The depressed atmosphere continued even through a very tasty breakfast, none of the people about the fire seem interested in talking, they held their silence in their own thoughts. Thoughts of a friend they hoped to see again, of the actions they would take if he did not return, and in the case of Jayanne, what the hell was she going to do with her life now? When she met Namdarin her only thoughts were of surviving the winter, then she had his cause to fight for, now if he is gone then should she carry it on? Or should she stay here and fight for her village, not that it had ever really fought for her. If he did not return she would go back into the village and help Betty to kill Dorana, then if they survived she could visit her mother for a while and put off any major decisions until then. She thought of her friends, there where only three or four depending on Namdarins revival.

Morgan was most definitely a good friend, he sat across the fire from Jayanne munching slowly on one of his mothers tasty oat cakes that had be dipped in the bacon fat in the frying pan, his young face was distorted by a deep frown, his brown eyes fixed on the flames, his brain stuck on the worry of his mother, his father was already dead so nothing could be done for him but she needed protection which was now Morgans duty, her fight is his. Jayanne saw his slight nod, then he rose, went to his horse, took his whetstone from the saddlebag, returned to the fire and started to sharpen his sword with slow and deliberate strokes of the stone, the edge soon began to glitter and gleam in the red fire light, almost to the hue of fresh blood. Betty was also a friend to Jayanne, if only because she had saved her sons life, she was an old woman but she had a raging fire in her heart, she would kill or die, a friend with little hope of survival. Her third friend was not of flesh and blood, it was her wonderful axe, stolen for her by Namdarin, it had never let her down, it struck where she wanted exactly when she needed it to. It never seemed to need sharpening as Morgan was still doing, its curved beauty flashed in the fire light, looking into the flat of the blade she saw her own green eyes staring back at her, the axe as usual showed no sign of age or wear, it still looked newly forged. The fourth friend was of course Namdarin, who may return at some time today, how her heart leaps at the thought of him coming galloping up the slope on that beautiful grey horse.

The sun came up over the mountains and lit up the pass with the red light reflected from the snowy caps, the birds in the trees below them started to sing in earnest, glad for the coming of a new day and that the search for ripe pine cones and acorns and nuts of all varieties could begin again, for the ones that were staying needed stockpiles hidden away and the ones that were leaving need fat for the long journeys they had before them. The three around the fire knew that without Namdarins return their journeys were likely to be very short.

"Jayanne." said Betty, "What is Namdarin like when he meets the Zandaars that he hates so much?"

Jayanne thought about this for a moment then told them about the monastery, how Namdarin had destroyed its inhabitants, and how he had tortured the monk to gain information.

"So he can be very cruel if he wants to." Was all that Betty had to say for the moment. They remained by the fire watching the sun lit patch of the mountainside gradually extend towards them, the red tinge of the newly risen sun was long gone, and so was half of the morning when the sun finally reached them, even so it gave very little warmth. Suddenly Morgan looked round.

"Did I hear thunder?" he asked, listening very carefully.

"I didn't." said Jayanne. Then there was a distant rumble that they all heard.

"I hope we don't get caught in a storm up here." Said Jayanne looking around for storm clouds and finding none. The rumble sounded again, closer this time, and longer as well, in fact it only faded and didn't go away completely. When the sound grew louder again it ceased to be a rumble and became a rhythmic pounding, Jayanne jumped to her feet and stared intently at the forest, hoping and dreading simultaneously. A flash of grey, then a huge horse came into view, galloping up the slope like the wind, carrying a man, the horses mane was streaming in the rushing air of its passage, its somewhat stubby tail trying to look grand flying flat in the wind behind. The horses chest was flecked with the white foam of a hard ride. The man on its back was Namdarin, a joyous grin on his mouth and a wicked gleam in his eyes, pounding towards the fire they came with no apparent intention of stopping, Arndrols hooves throwing up great clods of earth and snow until he was almost on top of the fire, then Namdarin hauled in the reins and Arndrol slid to a halt on stiff legs, then reared over his friends heads and waved his forelegs in salute. Namdarin slid from the saddle before Arndrol had all four feet on the ground again, he rushed up to his friends and tried valiantly to embrace them all at once. He silenced their babble of questions with one of his own, "I can smell bacon, is there any left? I'm starving." Betty tossed the frying pan back on the fire and said, "Men. All they ever think about is their stomachs." When she turned back to Namdarin she saw Jayanne hugging and kissing him, "or almost all." she continued with a far away look, of distant memory. Namdarin felt the passion of Jayannes embrace, and was amazed by the strength in her arms, when she kissed him her mouth was open and her tongue flickered on his lips and then she stepped away with a little smile. The passion in Namdarin's groin caused him to blush a bright red colour at which Jayanne turned away with such a flick of the head that her long red hair cascaded about Namdarins face. Total confusion swamped Namdarin's brain, this sudden passion from Jayanne was so unexpected that he stood like a stone statue unmoving for a minute until Betty said "Your breakfast will be ready in a few minutes, I want to know something, what is it like to be dead?" The question shocked Namdarin from his reverie.

"I am sorry to say this," was his reply, "but you really don't want to know."

"Yes I do." she said almost vehemently.

"You will find out only too soon, and who can say that what I have experienced is the real death." Betty did not like this answer at all but made no further comment. While Namdarin was eating a hearty breakfast of bacon and oatcakes, they talked about the rest of the day and what was to be done with it.

"Well," said Namdarin, "you three have had no sleep, so if you camp here for the rest of the morning, then we can all go back to see Dorana this afternoon."

"And what will you be doing whilst we are asleep?" asked Morgan suspiciously.

"I think I should go into the village and raise a little hell."

"How?"

"I walk in through the gate and the ones that know I am dead will be very afraid, and I have some important news for Dorana."

"What is this news?"

"I know that it is fear alone that can kill a person in his dream, fear is the weapon he used on me, and now I am going to use it on him while he is awake."

"That sounds like a reasonable plan." said Morgan nodding his head slowly, "Though it would be better to have somebody to watch your back."

"I think I can manage quite nicely on my own, just for a change." So it was eventually agreed that Namdarin was to go into the village alone, and come back for the others early in the afternoon. He trotted away from the camp on the big grey horse, with his bow strung and his sword loosened in its scabbard. By the time he reached the gate it was mid-morning, all the miners should be down in their tunnels hard at work, so the number of people actually moving about the village should be quite low. Still the gate was manned. Edran was one of this mornings gate keepers, the approach of a rider brought both keepers out from their small hut, they stood firm in the middle of the gate. Edran was almost sure that he recognised the horse, but he knew that it could not be that one. As the horse got nearer Edran recognised the long bow, but he could not see the man's face as his hood was pulled well forward, and he was looking down at the ground.

The slowly walking horse came to within a few feet of the gate, Edran getting more and more nervous with each of its steps, until it was almost touching the gate and then the man looked straight into Edrans eyes. Edrans face turn pale as ash, his mouth dropped open and his breathing ground to a shaky halt.

"We meet again, Edran." Said Namdarin in a voice of such low pitch that it seemed, to Edran at least, to come directly from hell. The second gate keeper realised who this man must be and fainted dead away, the thud of his body hitting the floor triggered Edran into action, he took control of his lungs and filled them completely with air, Namdarin knew that he was going to shout or scream or otherwise attract un-necessary attention.

"Be silent." he said in his best graveyard tone. A strangled gurgle issued from Edrans throat as he too fainted. A small chuckle came to Namdarin as he looked down on the two sleeping guards, "Fear even works on some that are not asleep." He said quietly, cutting the rope that tied the gate shut and letting Arndrol push it open, as usual Arndrol was very careful not to step on the sleeping forms or at least not to step too hard on them. Walking the horse through the quiet almost empty village Namdarin made the decision not to find Dorana immediately but first to look around and see what was to be seen. He noticed a building with a high chimney that was emitting black smoke, "That might be a foundry or a smithy, I think I will look there first." When he went around the building he found that there where four entrances, a large door on the front, another with a rutted roadway that came from the mine at the back, and two small side doors. Dismounting at one of the side doors he told Arndrol to wait and went inside as quietly as he could. There were several people inside but none of them noticed Namdarin's black garbed figure moving slowly about. Two men were unloading a low wheeled truck that had obviously come in through the back door, they were taking large and apparently heavy boulders to a big metal pot, the twin of which was resting on a bed of hot coals underneath an enormous cowling that led the oily black smoke up the chimney. Namdarin could hear the steady roar of air being blown upward through the coals, a flow so steady that it had to be a mechanical air pump .The temperature was so high in this area that Namdarin was beginning to get very sweaty, he could feel it trickling slowly down his sides and his back. Beyond the forge Namdarin could see the place where the molten silver was poured into the moulds, a few of the cast pieces were lying around on the benches against the opposite wall, as close as Namdarin could tell they were flames and lightening bolts as he had seen in the Zandaars monastery.

"Probably something to help them concentrate their power." He whispered making his way back to the door by which he had come in. He knew that he had to stop this foundry from operating, but how was the question. The logical choice was the air pump. On the other hand if he killed Dorana then perhaps the villagers would prevent the Zandaars from getting any more of the silver. By now it was almost an hour before noon, time to find Dorana and frighten him, Namdarin walked alongside his horse to the temple, where he knew that Dorana would be, putting an arrow to the string of his bow he went straight to the front door and walked in, ahead of him was the altar, it was large and well decorated, covered with white silk and silver ornaments, ornaments in the shape of flames and lightening bolts. To the left of the altar was another door, as Namdarin walked towards it a black robed figure came through the door and walked to the altar, the figure didn't appear to notice Namdarin's presence at all. The figure stood for a moment before the altar then knelt on the floor, in the attitude of prayer. Namdarin moved until he was directly behind the priest who he thought to be Dorana. Taking very careful aim he pulled his bow string right up to his lips, kissed it then shouted "Dorana!" The man in black jumped to his feet and spun around to look into Namdarin's eyes, Namdarin let fly and the arrow whistled through the air, an inch to the left of the priest's head and buried itself in the wall behind the altar, before the priest could move another arrow flew into the wall an inch from the other side of his head. Dorana glanced over each shoulder at the arrows and saw that either of them could have taken his life if the bowman had so intended.

"Who are you?" asked Dorana. Namdarin threw back his hood

before answering.

"You were told who I am only yesterday." Dorana stared intently at the man's face until suddenly the light of recognition sparked in his eyes, rapidly followed by a whitening of the face.

"You are dead. We fought and you lost. Your body was observed slung on the back of your horse. You are dead." His voice was weak and shaky, as he leant against the altar, without which he would have fallen to the ground.

"And you are beginning to repeat yourself." Said Namdarin with a cruel smile.

"You are dead, I killed you."

"For some that condition is not always permanent."

"You are dead, I watched you burn."

"You are wrong, it is you who is dead, you just forgot to lie down."

"How can this be?"

"I have taken it upon myself to destroy all Zandaars. You will not be the first, nor do I think you will be the last. I care not where we meet next, your dream or mine, the outcome is certain, you lose." The effect of the shocks that Namdarin had caused were beginning to wear off, and Dorana was gathering his wits together, this was obvious from his face, the colour was returning and his eyes finally glanced away from Namdarin's face. Namdarin reached out with his right hand as if grasping for something, Doranas hands flew to his throat in fear that Namdarin was going to strangle him, even though he was still fifty feet away. Namdarin reached out with his mind, and called to his arrows, wished for his arrows, begged for his arrows. Both of the arrows, though buried four or five inches into the wall, slowly slid out into free air and drifted gently across the room until they snuggled into Namdarin's hand like lost kittens. Dorana fell to his knees in front of his altar grabbing a silver lightening bolt as he dropped, lunging forward he flung the glittering ornament at Namdarin, once it had left the monks hand it emitted sparks in showers, like a firework. Doranas aim was off, the lightening struck a few feet short and to the left of its intended target, exploding on contact just like the bolt it was masquerading as.

Namdarin looked at the remains of the stricken chair, a few blackened sticks of wood, smoking on the floor, then he looked at Dorana grovelling on the floor in front of the altar and said, "The next time we meet you will die. Forever." Then he turned and left.

Running from the temple he vaulted onto Arndrol's back and galloped out of the village. The gate was closed again and the guards stayed safe in their little hut as the big grey jumped over the gate without so much as breaking his long and flowing stride. Cowering in the hut Edran listened to the awful sound of Namdarin's maniacal laughter fading as he moved away, the frightened man decided to leave the village immediately, by the other road, but not until he could no longer hear the pounding beat of Arndrol's hooves.

While Namdarin was riding up to the pass to where his friends were sleeping Dorana struggled to his feet, frightened to his very core. Standing before his altar he knew that he needed help to face the demon that had just run from his temple, the calling of such assistance would be strenuous. He went into his study to rest and eat, reading his book all the while, looking for some reference to a being that when killed in a dream later comes back to life. He found no information to help him and finally tried to contact the abbot of the monastery that had assigned him to this village, as it had been for some days he could not reach through the intervening space to the abbot, all that he could find was an empty blackness. The darkness puzzled him. Thinking slowly through his problem he felt almost as if the abbot were dead. The only way to test this theory was to contact someone he knew to be dead. Reaching far back into his past he thought of a monk he had trained with when very young, a man that he had tried to nurse to health after he had caught a terrible fever in one of the swamps of the far south, a man that he had nursed until he died. Picturing the face of his friend Dorana reached out with the arms of his mind, straining hard to find the long lost friend, Dorana's body was pouring sweat into his black robe with the effort of the summoning, but all he could find was the soft velvety blackness. Both his friend and the abbot were dead of this there could be no doubt. The demon must have come through the valley of his monastery and killed the abbot on his way here. Perhaps he wants the silver for himself, no he has said that he is the nemesis of Zandaar, he wants to kill us all. Why destroy a whole monastery, all the monks there must be dead or one of them would have contacted Dorana to inform him of a change of abbot, then come to an isolated village to kill one priest? It didn't make any sense. Surely the monastery must have given him some information about much more important targets than this one here. Unless the demon has no real plan and has been brought here by his companions, now that is possible, then they are his weak spot. Dorana strengthened his resolve and reached out for Betty, the old woman must be sleeping as she was awake all last night, concentrating on her wrinkled face and her hard blue eyes he felt around the area and found her dreaming of her husband, a moments preparation then he plunged into her dream only to have it shatter about him. Returning to his own body in front of his altar he was now certain that Namdarin was a demon because he seemed to know in advance exactly what Dorana was going to do next. Dorana went back into his study to rest and recuperate before the fight that was to come.

Namdarin galloped hard up to the pass and his friends camp, he was afraid that Dorana might try to harm them while they slept. The rumble of Arndrols hooves had Jayanne on her feet with her axe ready before she was really awake. Morgan woke before the big grey had slid to a halt. Namdarin jumped to the ground and went quickly into the tent and shook Betty until she opened her eyes. She looked into Namdarin's blue eyes and her own filled up with tears,

"I was dreaming of Rolarn, we were in a meadow and we were young again. Why did you wake me?"

"I am truly sorry. But until I have killed Dorana dreaming could be fatal."

"Was he surprised to see you?" asked Morgan.

"He wasn't the only one who was, almost everybody I met knew that I was dead. Someone had been spreading the news during the night. Edran the gatekeeper nearly wet his pants when he recognised me. I also found out why they want the silver, it is a weapon. Dorana threw a small piece of your silver in the shape of a lightening bolt at me and while it was flying through the air it changed into a real lightening bolt, I am lucky that his aim was upset, it burned a chair to a crisp in an instant."

"So what do we do now?" asked Betty.

"I am afraid that you must stay awake until I have met with Dorana again."

"Well we have had about four hours sleep, that will just have to be enough." said Betty in a very unhappy tone. Then she went on, "It's all well and good for you youngsters, but I need my beauty sleep." and she smiled, all three laughed at her small joke and the way she was fiddling with her grey hair as if trying to force it into some form of tidiness in front of a mirror. Namdarin stared intently at the old woman and thought that while there was such humour in the face of adversity there was hope, these people would not surrender they would fight to the end.

CHAPTER SEVEN

It was decided that if the final show down with Dorana was to take place on that night they may as well return to their home, more accurately Betty's home. They broke camp and went back down to the village, when they came to the gate they found that it was unmanned.

"I wonder where they have gone?" asked Betty.

"I think something frightened them away." said Namdarin with a smile, to which the others laughed softly while Namdarin opened the gate and waved them in. On arriving at the house Jayanne asked. "How do we get in?"

"When I said that the doors and windows were all securely barred," said Betty, "I was speaking for eavesdroppers, there is a way to open the rear gate, my husband was very good with locks and other mechanisms, one simply opens a concealed hatch on the wall and turns a handle inside and the door unlocks itself, but first we must be sure that no one is watching." The three of them clustered around Betty to obscure her actions from any prying eyes, they saw nobody watching but could not be totally sure. Returning to the place where he had so recently been beaten by Dorana caused Namdarin to shiver. Morgan saw this sudden tremble and asked, "Did somebody walk on your grave?"

"Somehow," answered Namdarin slowly, "I fear that will never be true."

Morgan could find nothing to say to comfort his friend so he went to help the women open all the shutters, and some of the windows, to bring some light into a gloomy house. Namdarin started the fire in the living room and sat down in one of the large comfortable chairs in front of it, the roaring flames did little to warm him. He took the book of Zandaar from inside his jacket and flicking through the pages tried desperately to make some sense of it, the neatly copied text still remained complete gibberish, long study of any one page brought no patterns to mind to help in the deciphering. The letters of the writing were utterly unlike any of the scripts he had ever seen. Morgan came back into the room and saw Namdarin staring at the book, "What is that?" he asked. Namdarin snapped the book shut the tossed it into Morgans hands saying

"It is the teachings of Zandaar. I think all the priests have one." Morgan opened the book and glanced at a page or two before saying, "Can you read this?"

"No. It means absolutely nothing to me." said Namdarin shaking his head.

"But," he went on, "it is definitely central to the beliefs of the Zandaar. It is part of their power and understanding it is going to be very important, I am hoping that Granger can help me to learn its secrets."

"If you beat Dorana, no, when you beat Dorana you could always stay here." Morgan's offer was very serious, a man like Namdarin would very quickly be voted chief elder, and thereby the village would be secure from the Zandaar.

"Thank you." said Namdarin, "But my war against Zandaar must continue until I have killed them or been killed, those are the only two possible endings to this." A deeply sad look came over Namdarins face as he returned to his worries, the sounds from the kitchen indicated that Betty and Jayanne were cooking and chattering about nothing and everything, recipes and weather, men and their many failings. The atmosphere was very nearly that of an ordinary family, but a depressing background was always hanging just out of sight, the moment the talk stopped the darkness became more obvious, then the chattering would start again if only to drive away the feeling of hopelessness. In this manner the day passed slowly for all the inhabitants of Betty's house, Morgan spent most of his time with horses, grooming and feeding and grooming again, until Arndrol became upset by all the attention and pinned Morgan to the side of the stall with a shoulder squeezing the young man until breathing was almost impossible.

"Let me go you stupid animal, and then I will leave you alone." he said but the horse leaned harder against him. Struggling for breath Morgan said, "I'm sorry I called you stupid." To this comment Arndrol tossed his head and snorted loudly, then stepped away from the wall releasing Morgan, who slapped the big horse on the rump affectionately and departed, leaving the horses to their own devices. The stable quickly settled down to the quiet sounds of horses relaxing and mice scuttling about in the hay. Inside the house proper the tension was rising as night time approached, the time of the battle would soon be at hand, Namdarin was as ready as he could be.

Dorana was standing in front of his altar again, watching the light in the western window slowly fading as the sun went down below the mountains, the red light pouring through the windows made the temple look like a dim and dangerous place, a quiet cave full of dark shadows and darker thoughts. In an effort to improve his morale Dorana lit all the candles on the altar and along the white painted wooden walls. The flickering illumination did little to help his mood, he knew that he was to face a foe that had the power to beat him, if the foe could hold on to his sanity, madness was to be the weapon that Dorana was going to use against Namdarin. Dorana was fighting for his life, with no possibility of help from any quarter. Filling the small golden brazier in the middle of the altar with aromatic wood chips and some oil he set it alight, a puff of white smoke rose quickly to the ceiling as the wood caught fire, the red tongues of flame consuming the wood and liberating a rich and powerful odour. Once the fire had settled to a steady low flame Dorana took from inside his robes a handful of leaves, long pointed leaves from rare plant, rare in these mountain parts at least. Placing a slotted lid on the brazier Dorana inhaled the heady smoke of the slowly burning leaves, the smoke coming from the brazier started to swirl and spin about the man in black, soon he was completely engulfed in a spiralling grey cloud. Using the distorting effects of the smoke Dorana moved his mind into the Betty's house, to find that Namdarin had just finished a large meal and was resting in front of the fire. Namdarin was not actually asleep but he was daydreaming, his concentration on reality was so loose that Dorana wreathed him in the smoke and spirited his mind away, and threw it into a nightmare of Doranas creation.

Namdarin was quietly relaxing in a chair in front of a roaring fire thinking of nothing very much, only the wonderful feeling of a full stomach, not really wishing to worry about Dorana, his consciousness was drifting randomly from one thought on to the next totally unconnected thought, until he was suddenly ensnared in a roiling black cloud. Feeling the initial rush of fear Namdarin knew that this was some new attack by Dorana, controlling the fear he allowed the energy of it to rise and rise, but never out of control. Using the energy of fear he pushed hard against the cloud, trying to disperse it, to find Dorana who was obviously hiding somewhere near. The cloud refused to be moved, it clung to Namdarin in stubborn spirals, abruptly gravity vanished and Namdarin was weightless. Weightlessness was something that he had only ever experienced when falling, so his mind automatically assumed that this was happening, fear surged utterly uncontrollable. Fear of falling is an unusual feeling, in that the fall itself is not the cause of the fear, it is the worry about the landing that is the root of the fear. Under Doranas clever manipulation

Namdarin felt that he was falling backwards, no matter how he twisted and turned he fell backwards, and so his fear, his greatest fear was at his back. Dorana snatched at this terror and amplified it. Pictures of spikes and jagged rocks flashed through Namdarins distressed mind. Glimpses of blood splattered floors and smashed quivering flesh pushed the terror he felt higher. When the fear had reached high enough Dorana gave it a little twist, the terror of the fall onto his back switched instantly into the fear of being hunted, and chased. The thing of fear was still behind him but now he was running from it, in order for Namdarin to run from something it was necessary for Dorana to give him somewhere to run. Namdarin was running on a flat grey featureless plain under a flat grey featureless sky, being chased by some horror that he had not as yet seen. The last thing that Dorana wanted was for Namdarin to die, he wanted Namdarin to loose his sanity because death had been tried and failed, Dorana was trying to drive his mind into a corner and then force it to retreat inside itself, this is the only way to deliberately cause insanity, to this end the nature of the pursuing horror was essential.

Though Namdarin was wary of snakes and spiders and rats, none of these actually terrified him, slime and muck he found unpleasant but not inherently frightening so Dorana was forced to invent something that was a conglomeration of some of these things. Namdarin was running hard pushing his legs as hard as he could the monster that was chasing him was only yards behind, a glance over his shoulder revealed the nature of the threat, a hideous beast with eight long furry legs, a huge bulbous body, a long snake like neck, and a head that was Namdarin's, not the face he saw in the mirror but the face his mind saw when he thought of himself, this was his very identity that was chasing him, warped and twisted by Doranas influence but himself all the same. The mouth of the beast opened to show long white fangs that dripped thick red smoking blood splashing on to the grey ground. Namdarin stumbled at the sight and the beast gained a yard before he recovered his feet and ran harder than ever. Namdarin tried to concentrate on his legs to keep them running as fast as he could and to drive the thoughts of the beast away, but the rustling of its legs and the hissing of it breath seemed to keep getting louder. He realised that this nightmare was being dictated by Dorana and that it was time to fight back, but how?

"I will start with something small." He muttered in between ragged breaths. Thinking hard of the horizon ahead, looking at an imaginary line where the sky joined the land he thought, "In a moment I will see a green line appear on the horizon, it will be long green grass growing tall and straight." Then he counted down slowly from ten knowing that when the count reached zero the line of green would appear. Zero, and there it was a faint green line a long way off but getting nearer by the moment, the lush green grass rushed towards him until it was passing under his pounding feet. "Next a break in these clouds." he thought clearing his mind of the greenness of the grass and filling it with the blueness of the sky just over the horizon, the same steady count to zero, and a blue line appeared. Rapidly the sky filled with a clear blue colour, like a hot sunny summers day, looking down Namdarin saw his shadow upon the grass and felt the sun warming the back of his neck. Namdarin's next problem was to change the scene in such a way that it would work more for him than for Dorana. Keeping the grass below his feet and the blue sky above his head, required very little thought, but what to do next? "A small wood." He muttered. "Like the ones near my home." Remembering clearly the shape of one of the copses near his house was very simple. The same concentration and the same steady count down and over the horizon appeared the wood and along with it a gentle rising of the ground this made the running harder but also brought the horizon nearer, things could begin to happen much quicker now. The control of this nightmare was almost all Namdarins now. "Around the wood and up the hill on the summit will be the standing stone were I made my oath." He said it and it was. Pushing hard up the hill with the beast following, but not gaining, the sound of its running like dry sticks shaken in a sack. "From the stones I will be able to see my house at the bottom of the hill." Namdarin said in a loud and clear voice, the rhythm of his words governed by the thumping of his feet on the grass. Cresting the hill in between the standing stones he looked down onto the high white walls of his home. As the picture had been in his mind the drawbridge was down and the gates open. Now he had a real idea of how he was going to defeat the beast, running down the hill towards the drawbridge and the gate he thought of the courtyard inside, the cobbles and the large flagstone he fixed in his mind along with to door to the tower, the one in the far corner of the yard, it would be open. The heavy wooden planks of the drawbridge boomed under his feet, under the arch and into the yard he ran, his footsteps echoing about the empty court. Behind the open door would be the spiralling stairway that lead upwards into the tower and it was. The beast was closing slightly but the turning of the stair kept it just far enough away. At the top of the stair would be a door, a door to the armoury. When the door came into sight Namdarin had his hand set to wrench the handle around and fling the door open, as the latch cleared his shoulder hit the hard wooden door and bounced it open, the door recoiled from the wall and was almost shut behind Namdarin as the beast reached it. Dodging between the racks of weapons Namdarin went to the far wall where his fathers broadsword was hanging in its scabbard. Taking the silver wire bound grip of the long sword in both sweaty hands he pulled it from the wall and turned in a single fluid motion, swinging the sword in a long arc that intercepted the neck of the beast and chopped its head clean off, black sticky ichor poured from the stump, spraying like an awful fountain , its legs quivered as if undecided about which way they should be going and it sagged slowly to the ground. Namdarin held the sword high over his head and brought it down with all his strength into the middle of the disgusting body cutting it into two portions, green slime gushed over the floor making the floor too slippery to walk on with any surety so Namdarin left the armoury dragging the sword with him its hard steel point cutting a groove in the stones and clattering down the stairs behind the tired and gasping man. Half way down the stairway he paused to think, "Dorana must be behind all this and so I must believe that he is now standing in the courtyard waiting to meet me." Holding tightly onto this belief he continued down into the yard and sure enough standing in the middle looking for an exit was a tall old man in black. Namdarins blue eyes swept around the courtyard and everywhere they passed details that were missing from the scene appeared, small clumps of grass grew between the flags, the stones of the walls sprang into sharp relief and the trapdoor to the cellar appeared in the corner right where it belonged. Dorana turned towards the gateway where at a glance from Namdarin the portcullis dropped with a resounding and final clang.

"How does it feel to be trapped in someone else's dream?" asked Namdarin with a cruel smile.

"I can walk away from this any time I wish." Dorana replied, "For instance there is a door in that wall behind you." But Namdarin did not need to look, he knew that his visualisation of his own home could not be altered by a stranger, this image needed no concentration at all to be stable beyond the reach of even Doranas mind. Doranas only hope of escape was to destroy the mind that sustained the image. With a swirl of long black sleeves Dorana produced an egg from inside his robe, an egg like one that Namdarin had seen before, the egg cracked and Namdarin made no move, the snake emerged from the widening opening and Namdarin remained exactly where he was. The huge snake uncurled from the egg to its full length of over fifty feet, pushing the first third of its body up into the air and bending into the s-shaped curve of an impending strike. Namdarin stood calmly with the point of the long sword resting on the stones between his feet and both hands on the pommel, he looked up into the unblinking eyes of the serpent and he waited. The muscles in the snakes body tensed, standing out like steel hawsers, the long tongue flickered and the head moved away a fraction, Namdarin likened this movement to the backward twitch of a crossbow bolt just before the mechanism releases the string, he knew that the strike was on its way, he also knew that once the snake had its mouth open to strike it could no longer see him. The snakes wide mouth flew open, to show off its impressive collection of teeth, and plunged down as if to swallow the man whole, but he had already moved, not away from the snake but towards it, he stepped in underneath the line of the strike and swung the huge broadsword in a long glittering arc, an arc that crossed the path of the snakes head severing it neatly from the body. Both head and body fell to the stones without so much as a twitch, just a brief instant of pumping blood that quickly faded away like a snowball dropped into a smiths forge.

"That makes three times I have killed that snake," Namdarin giggled, "and each time it gets easier." Standing calmly resting the point of the sword on the ground again he stared coldly into Doranas intense blue eyes and saw for an instant fear. "What will you try next, Dorana?" The old priest tried the thing that had beaten Namdarin last time, he threw a bolt of black fire, a long stinking black streak across the space separating the two, it flew leaving an oily black smoke in the air and it flew at Namdarins head. Namdarin ducked a little and the black bolt hit the cross of the sword where it caught and settled in an attempt to melt the sword.

"This sword was forged in the stars, it carries the heat of the gods, your feeble fire will not harm it." Namdarin said as the blackness lost its energy and slid down the blade to leave a small black stain on the stones. Dorana gathered another bolt of liquid blackness and projected it at the sword, then another and another each attempt depleting Dorana's energy. The black fire merely coalesced on the blade and settled slowly to the ground like thick cold tar, until the blade was completely covered in the thick black mess when Namdarin picked up the sword and with a rapid flick of the wrist flung the viscous muck back at Dorana, setting fire to his robe around its hem. Dorana looked down at the blazing garment for a few seconds and then it simple ceased to exist, not bothering to remove it he had just sent it into oblivion. Dorana held his hands high in the air as if pleading with the gods on high, for many moments it appeared to Namdarin that no aid would come until the ground beneath his feet began to pitch and roll like a ship on a stormy sea. Holding onto his fathers sword as if it were an anchor he fixed his feet to the ground and gradually took control of his twisting dream, slowly pushing the distortion away until it was only a distance blurring of the walls of the courtyard.

The desperation in Doranas eyes was obvious, he was looking about like a caged animal, searching for an escape he felt that he was going to loose this battle, and that meant death. He walked slowly to a wall, his brow furrowed with the effort of thought and his body tense with expectation, nearing the wall a dark patch slowly faded into view, Dorana saw a faint hope of escape into the black cave that he had created in the wall. He was only seconds away from escape when the wall slammed back into place with a loud crash. Namdarin laughed, "This is my house as it was before your kind burned it, this one you cannot destroy. You are now on my home territory, you have no hope of winning, you have come here only to die."

"Why do you hate me so much?" asked Dorana, his devious mind not giving up while there was still life.

"I think that I may be able to show you. Watch the door in the bottom of the tower, from it will walk a procession of people." Namdarin summoned up images of all the people that he could remember from his home, a sequence of servants and soldiers, of farmers and their wives, of friends and relations, they all trouped slowly into the courtyard. "These were the people of my household." They stood behind Namdarin in a disorganised group. Then a woman and a boy walked from the tower and stood to his left and right.

"She was my wife, he was my son." He looked at his loved ones and tears came to his eyes, pouring down his face in rivers. "All these were killed when your brethren burned this house with black fire, and you ask why I hate." Namdarin looked into the eyes of his wife and put his arm around the shoulder of his son. Unable to restrain himself any longer Namdarin released the hate and the anger from within, a roaring red tide filled his brain, a red flame of power blossomed in his mind, he raised the long sword and pointed it at Dorana, a howling red light reached out from the sword to engulf Dorana. Dorana struck back with bolt after bolt of black fire but the inexorable advance of the redness would not be halted. Dorana was encased in a raging red fire, in an instant his whole body burst into flames and was consumed by fire of anger and hatred. Dorana died in pain. Namdarin turned to the image of his wife and kissed her then bent down and kissed his son, "The lure of this dream is almost irresistible." he said, his voice catching in his throat, and then the dream collapsed about him, a deep blackness with an almost solid texture overcame him.

Namdarin opened his eyes but the darkness did not abate, he tried to move but could not, panic began to set it. Inhaling slowly he stopped the advance of fear and spoke softly to himself, "Is this some other manifestation of Dorana's power, or is it something more normal." Testing first his right arm he felt a soft but heavy weight attached to the wrist, the left was the same, his ankles had a similar restraint attached, he felt a cloth pressing against his face, and thought, "I have been tied up, and blindfolded. By who and Why?" Then he heard a soft and beautiful voice very close by, "Namdarin are you awake?"

"Yes, I believe so. Though I don't seem to be able to move."

"Are you sure that you are awake and in full control?"

"I am awake and what little movement I can generate is controlled by me." He answered gently before continuing, "I do not like being tied up like this and I could quite easily loose control if this condition does not disappear." A rising note of anger was creeping into his voice. The tension on his left arm eased a little and suddenly a bright light streamed into his eyes blinding him. Namdarin blinked hard several times before vision returned. Looking about he saw that Morgan was holding his left wrist in both hands and pinning it to the floor, Jayanne was similarly attached to his right wrist, Betty was sitting on his legs just below the knee, none seemed much inclined to release him. The room was a wreck, broken furniture was scattered everywhere, it looked like a battlefield. Namdarin judged by the actions of his friends and the destruction all around that he must have been the cause of it all.

"What happened to me?" he asked.

"You turned into a wild thing, attacking everyone and everything." Said Jayanne with a deeply concerned look.

"I am very sorry." he said, "I hope that I didn't hurt anyone. I did beat Dorana, I think he is dead." Morgan thought for a moment then released Namdarin's arm, the two women then did likewise.

"I think we ought to go and find out if he really is dead." Said Morgan.

"We can clean up this mess later." said Betty, going into the kitchen to make sure that nothing in there could set itself on fire. When she returned Morgan had his sword in his hand Jayanne had her axe hanging in its usual place with her bow in her hand, Namdarin was shaking the stiffness of confinement from his limbs his sword was in its scabbard and his bow ready in his hand.

"A fine group of warriors we look." Betty said laughing at the serious faces around her. Once they were outside in the street Namdarin was amazed how quiet it was, they saw no-one about at all.

"Everybody seems to obeying the curfew." said Betty, staring hard at closed curtains in all the windows, all with lights showing from inside. The streets appeared completely empty all the way to the temple, although Namdarin did stop and turn around once when he thought that he heard running feet behind them. The temple came into sight and they saw that there were many lights inside, shining in beautiful patterns through the stained glass of the windows. On the steps in front of the temple was a small group of people, they were armed with swords and long handled axes. Namdarin recognised Lorik as the leader so these must be

Doranas body guard.

"Return to your home." Shouted Lorik, "The curfew is now in force."

"Enforced by whom?" asked Morgan.

"By Doranas word." Answered Lorik as the rest of the bodyguard spread out to give themselves room to fight.

"I do not think that Dorana will be saying much," Shouted Namdarin, "because he is dead."

"No, he is inside and has said that he must not be disturbed, by anyone."

"You have nothing to fear, he cannot possibly be disturbed. You on the other hand can very easily be dead." Namdarins threat was backed by a drawing of swords and Jayannes passing her bow to Betty then hefting her axe with a loving smile.

"Dorana will protect us, you are his enemies and will die."

"Dorana is dead, and once your friends and relatives realise that he can no longer protect you I am sure that they will want a long talk with all of you, a long and painful talk." The brave men of Doranas bodyguard began to look very insecure, looking more at each other than their enemies in front of them, so Namdarin continued, "We wont tell them for a few minutes yet so if you start running now you might just stay alive a little longer." At this Lorik sensed that he was losing control and he shouted, "He is lying, Dorana cannot be dead we have guarded him well since I last saw him. They are trying to frighten us away so that they can get in and kill Dorana."

"Namdarin," Said Jayanne, "This worm is beginning to irritate me, I think it is time he died." She strolled forwards and stood directly in front of Lorik, the head bodyguard was a little confused by the fact that neither Morgan nor Namdarin made any attempt to protect the woman, but still she was only a weak woman, she was tall but only a woman, he looked up into her eyes and smiled his confidence was blatant.

"This is your last chance worm," she said quietly, the axe swinging gently in her hand, "run or die, your choice." Lorik laughed, Namdarin moved to the right and Morgan to the left, they made no actual attacking motions but were standing ready should the rest of the bodyguard decide to join in. Betty had an arrow set to the string of Jayannes bow and she was ready to fire. Jayanne was standing out of reach of Loriks sword, but as his sword was longer than her axe she would have to move inside his range before she could strike him. She grasped the haft in both hands and slowly raised the axe clear over her head, all the while Lorik grinned, with a half step forwards she heaved the axe downwards straight at the grinning head, Lorik moved, in a flash of steel his sword was above his head to parry the feeble blow of a mere woman. Namdarin understood his confidence, with that sort of speed he must be a formidable swordsman. The sword and the axe met in a shower of sparks, the steel of Lorik's sword howled as it shattered into a thousand pieces, the axe did not falter it drove downwards into Lorik's head, through flesh and skull in went without slowing, through ribcage and spine, and finally his pelvis. The passage of the axe was hidden from the others by the sparks that were the remains of Lorik's sword. The sparks scattered to the ground all about, and then Lorik fell into two discrete heaps, each heap topped by a half smile. With the axe head swinging slowly between her knees Jayanne said, "Fool." then looked up at the other members of the bodyguard, they threw down their weapons and ran for their lives. She spat on the remains of Lorik, and stepped back to avoid the slowly spreading pool of blood.

"Let's go inside and see what has happened to Dorana." Said Namdarin sheathing his sword and walking slowly up the steps to the door. He flung the door wide open and looked down the length of the temple, he saw a small column of smoke rising from the altar and what looked like a pile of rags in front of it. He walked along the centre aisle, his boot heels thudding on the polished wooden planks of the floor, up the three steps to the platform and the altar, he turned over the pile of rags and inside it was Dorana, his blue eyes still open staring their cold malice out on the world even in death.

"Well that's the end of him." Said Namdarin, "What now?"

"This village needs putting back in order," said Betty, "I think we should have a town meeting."

"That's a good idea," said Jayanne, "When?"

"Right now," answered the old woman, "Morgan go and ring that bell until I tell you to stop." Her son ran off through a door and in moments the bell started to ring loud and fast, almost like a fire alarm. Betty stood in front of the altar astride Doranas body, Namdarin and Jayanne sat on the altar one to each side of Betty and together they waited for the villagers to arrive. After three or four minutes a timid face peered around the door.

"Come in," shouted Betty, "come in and sit down. There is much to do and little time to do it." She shouted this greeting several times before a steady stream of people made it unnecessary. The temple was very nearly full by the time that the people stopped arriving. Betty went in to the bell tower and told Morgan to stop ringing, then returned to her place in front of the muttering crowd.

"Dorana is dead." She shouted, her words fell into a sudden silence.

"Namdarin here," She waved her arm in his general direction, "killed him in a dream, by the same method that he killed all those who spoke against him. All his ridiculous laws, curfew and trading bans and whatever else, are rescinded. Anyway his brave enforcers have all run away. Now the very least that must be decided here tonight is a new chief elder, I think that Kironand was killed by Lorik and buried quietly somewhere nearby. Do I hear and proposers?" After a moments silence an unidentified voice spoke from the crowd.

"The man who killed Dorana should be the one." The crowd mumbled in agreement. Namdarin jumped down off the altar and said, "When everything here is sorted out I will leave because there are more of these Zandaars for me to kill." He emphasised the statement by kicking Doranas body down the steps.

"Namdarin rejects the nomination." said Betty, "Any others?" A different voice shouted, "Betty should be chief."

"That is a silly idea." she answered, "If you pick me you will be faced with the same decision in a year or so when I die, I am sorry but I cannot accept."

"Let it be Morgan." Came a shout, which was followed by a loud cheer.

"I accept the proposition, depending on a vote of course." he said.

"All those in favour of Morgan being elected as Chief elder raise their right hands now." Shouted Betty over the hubbub. A forest of arms appeared above the heads of the crowd.

"Carried unanimously. Now that decision has been made I think that the rest can be left up to the family heads and the new chief. So if everybody else can leave and go home then the real business can be sorted out, of course any major decisions will be put before a full town meeting tomorrow evening." At this point the family heads rose almost as a man and ushered their respective families out of the temple, in only three minutes a town meeting was reduced to a much more manageable size as there were only forty or so families in the village.

Discussions went on long into the night, for there was much to be done. Many of the people wanted the temple burned down because it stood for Doranas power, but they were out voted by the ones who said it would be useful if only as a place to hold town meetings, previously they didn't have a building big enough. Pardons were issued for the surviving members of Dorana's bodyguard, depending very much on good behaviour, but they would be allowed back. This brought up the subject of banished people being present in the village.

"I presume," said Morgan, "that you are referring to Jayanne. When she was sent away from here last time she was unarmed and alone, now she is neither. The last person who attempted to stop her doing something she wanted to do was Lorik, you passed him on your way in here tonight. If any you want her to leave you are more than welcome to ask her, but she may not take it too well."

The old man in question looked for a moment into Jayanne's calm green eyes then thought the better of his rash words and said so at length. The next topic of discussion was the redistribution of the silver collected by Dorana. The final decision on this matter was a complex mixture of giving some back to the families that claimed it was stolen from them and the chief keeping a fair sized fund to help families that will suffer difficulties as the winter deepens. By the time all this had been arranged it was very nearly dawn, the family heads were told to inform the respective families of all the decisions made and to meet again at sundown to sort out any further problems. Once these had left Betty invited Namdarin and Jayanne to sleep at her house, Namdarin accepted without a moments thought but Jayanne said that she ought to go and see her parents, after all she had been here two days and not said a word to them. As the four of them were leaving the temple three young men came in, they said that they had been sent to remove Dorana's body, before it starts to stink.

Namdarin smiled and told them to put out the candles on their way out .At the bottom of the steps outside all that remained of Lorik was a dark stain on the hard ground, the three had obviously been busy here as well.

It was after midday before Namdarin, Morgan and Jayanne met again, the first good nights sleep they had had for three days left them feeling really alive, full of energy and ready for anything, or very nearly. They met in Betty's house.

"How did your parents take your return, Jayanne?" asked Namdarin.

"They seemed pleased that I was still alive, but not too happy to have me around. I think my presence made them uncomfortable, after all they did reject me in front of the whole village. I don't hold it against them but they just cannot forget it." she said with a deep sigh, she knew that she would be unable to stay here for much longer without conflict breaking out between her and her parents.

"How do you feel about being made chief?" Namdarin asked looking closely at Morgan.

"I'm not sure, it sort of dropped on me suddenly. I think mother engineered it deliberately, I am most certainly the youngest chief elder ever. I have no idea at all how I am going to cope with the responsibility of running this village and looking after everybody in it. It is very frightening."

"I am sure that your mother knew what she was doing, and that she will be able to help you for many years to come." said Namdarin who had run a small community of his own.

"Yes I know but what am I going to do?" asked Morgan looking very puzzled.

"Basically," said Namdarin, "you do as little as you can. The fewer things you interfere with the fewer mistakes you can make. The idea is that you leave people to get on with their lives and they won't bother you with petty troubles, this way you only get real problems to deal with. These are the most difficult to resolve but by far the most rewarding."

"Saying it is easier than doing it."

"That will always be true, my friend. All I can say is good luck, you'll need it."

"Namdarin," said Morgan, "I know that you will have to leave soon but I would like you to stay a little while at least until things are more settled."

"Morgan, my friend, you have nothing to fear. Your mother will be of great help to you, so you have no need of my advice."

"I don't think it is advice that I will need, I think it is your sword."

"The whole village elected you as leader, you will lead them well because you care so much, and a good leader will always find the backing he needs amongst his own people, to use an outsider like me to enforce your rule would be a very serious mistake. This is an enormous challenge for you but you must take it by the horns and shake it until it surrenders."

"How can I thank you for all the help you have given me and my people?"

"That's very easy, just make sure that the Zandaars don't get any more of your silver, in their hands it becomes a most formidable weapon. I know that you can't stop them getting some, but if you don't sell large quantities directly to them they won't be able to mass it too quickly."

"You have my word on that, we will not sell to Zandaars even in tiny grains."

"Good enough for me. I think that tomorrow I will go and look for Granger, I seem to have been after him for a long time and getting no nearer." Jayanne who had been listening carefully to their conversation interrupted.

"I will go with you." Namdarin stared into her green eyes for a minute that felt like an hour, his heart was racing and his breath shortened by the prospect of travelling with her again. "Don't you want to stay with your people, I am sure that Morgan could arrange it."

"They are not the people I used to know, Dorana has taken away all the strong ones, all those that resisted him are dead. The ones that are left are frightened to even look at me."

"They all saw what you did to Lorik, of course they are frightened, but that should pass in time."

"No, I will travel with you for a while, if you will have me."

"Of course, I am very glad that you have decided to come with me. I could not stay because I have a job to complete, but leaving you behind would have been almost impossible." He reached out with both hands and took her small hands in his large ones, he pulled her slowly towards him until they where almost touching then he leaned forward and kissed her slowly. Their lips met and a fire awoke in them both, the kiss stretched on into eternity, their breathing getting ragged and hoarse until a delicate cough from Morgan reminded them of his presence, they broke apart blushing bright pink, and stuttering in complete confusion. The pair of them looked for all the world like guilty teenagers caught in their first kiss by a watchful parent, they refused to meet anyone's eyes, not each others or Morgan's. Morgan watched them struggling with their feelings for a moment then burst into an enormous laugh that ran on and on, until he could hardly breathe at all, once the fit had subsided he said,

"You two will get along just fine, together you could conquer the world."

Jayanne was very confused by her reaction to Namdarin's kiss, she was sure that she hated all men because of her flawed marriage, but this one made her feel very strange inside, a sort of warm and yet urgent need filled her when they kissed. She had been sure that she never wanted a man to touch her again but this one was different. Namdarin's confusion was just as bad, he was fighting the Zandaars because they killed his wife and child it was love for them and hate for the Zandaar that drove him on, so how could he feel any love for another woman? There was no doubt in his mind that he did feel something very strong when he looked at Jayanne, his heart beat faster and his breathing became disturbed, his body behaved like a lovesick child. He had no place in his future for love, only hate could sustain him in the fight to come, of this he was sure, these feelings would have to be suppressed. He turned and left the house quickly.

Jayanne was very upset by his sudden departure, she looked at Morgan who had a very surprised expression. "What is wrong with him?" she asked. Morgan shook his head and finally said, "I don't know, he's running away from his feelings. Maybe you frighten him, you certainly appear to frighten all the other men around here."

"But not you?" The question was entirely in the tone.

"Sometimes you frighten me, you can be so savage."

"My savagery is nothing compared to his hatred, you didn't see him torture the monk in the monastery."

"You are both intense people, you feel things very strongly and react in an extreme manner to everything. Possibly he is frightened of hurting you." She took his words entirely the wrong way and hefted her axe,

"He would have a fight on his hands then."

Morgan smiled and said, "Not physically, I can foresee nothing that would make Namdarin attack you. But, if you become emotionally involved and then he gets killed, as he is expecting, you will be hurt again."

"He worries too much." She snorted before leaving to seek her own council.

The afternoon passed swiftly for everyone, Namdarin and Jayanne were walking around the village him thinking grim thoughts and her greeting people she knew, they managed to avoid each other until it was time for the meeting in the temple or the new town hall. They arrived separately at the town hall, a few minutes apart but still much earlier than was necessary, they walked in to find Morgan talking to the family heads, primarily to ensure that the meeting would bring no surprises. Namdarin came in first and stood near Morgan , listening to the way he handled the people around him, Morgan seemed to be dealing quite easily with the family heads, he talked calmly and reasonably to all, smoothing over what difficulties he could, and ignoring the petty family arguments. When Jayanne came in she stood beside Namdarin for a minute or two, he was faintly disturbed by her presence, he smelt the wet fur of her white cape, he heard the soft rustling of her boots and she shifted her weight, he felt her green eyes staring at him, but he didn't look at her. She reached out with one hand and took hold of his, saying softly, "We must talk." He looked into the green eyes and followed as she towed him towards Dorana's study.

Once they were inside the study with the door firmly shut she spoke, slowly and clearly,

"I know that you have some feeling for me," he drew in a breath as if to say something, "no, don't interrupt, let me finish. I know that you excite me in ways that I have never before experienced. This may or may not be love." She sighed. "This could easily complicate our relationship, you still love your wife, and I still hate men in general. We must not let these feelings destroy our friendship. I think that we should leave here tomorrow, together and continue your fight together, until we both understand how we really feel and can come to some sensible agreement. What do you say?"

"When we kiss I feel like a young boy again, it feels very good. I cannot envisage a life without you, this is how I test for love. If by imagining the sudden absence of someone life has no meaning then the feeling must be love. I have tested the way I feel about you and I have no doubt that I love you, though it feels wrong, I should love my wife though she is gone and my life continues. I hoped that you would come with me when I leave here, because I could not face being alone again, and I hoped that you would stay because of the danger into which we both will travel. You say that you will come with me and my heart is filled with joy, I agree we leave tomorrow and go to find Granger."

She smiled and nodded then stepped towards him and tilted her face upwards to be kissed, their lips met and the rush of their passion was a roaring fire that consumed them, the rest of the world was shut away from them for the duration of the kiss, it was only a minute but seemed like hours, they went no further than a single kiss. When the kiss was finished they went into the body of the town hall to find the meeting in progress and going nicely, so they kept on walking hand in hand out into the street and back to Betty's house.

CHAPTER EIGHT

The following morning both Namdarin and Jayanne got up before the sun and set about the preparations for their departure, before the others were up for breakfast the packing had been done and the horses loaded, Jayanne had decided that they would need at least one pack horse so she picked the biggest and healthiest leaving all the others that they had brought for Morgan and Betty. After a quiet breakfast, no one really felt like talking, Namdarin and Jayanne dressed in their travelling clothes and went into the stables. Goodbyes took a long time but eventually they rode out of the big double door and up the street to the gate which had still not been repaired, and none showed any willingness to repair it. As they crossed the broken gate Namdarin looked back to see Morgan standing in the main street waving, both Jayanne and Namdarin raised an arm in salute of the friend they were leaving behind, Morgan's task would be safer than theirs but just as difficult. Namdarin kicked Arndrol into a trot and towing a heavily laden pack horse the two of them went up the trail to the pass, the weather did not look too threatening, but the strong wind meant that things could change very quickly. They didn't talk much going up the trail to the pass, they were thinking about the place they had just left, Namdarin of the friend he had left behind and Jayanne of her family, they were almost to the summit of the pass before Namdarin finally spoke,

"Did you say goodbye to your family?" Jayanne looked serious before replying,

"Yes. The only night I stayed with them the goodbyes were said then."

"Were they unhappy to see you?"

"I think they were unhappy that I was still alive. They blamed me for all the problems that they had been having since I left."

"Will they be able to last out the winter?"

"I don't really care, but I am sure that Morgan will look after them."

"When you went to see Granger, which way did you go?"

"You remember the gully where we met Blackbeard and his men?"

"Of course."

"Well before we get to it we turn south along the top of the escarpment, which will bring us to an easier way down onto the plain near the ford, then we can cross the river and turn north up into the mountains again, hopefully without meeting Blackbeard or his friends."

"That sound sensible enough to me, how long will it take to find Granger?"

"On horseback, three days maybe four." Namdarin nodded and said no more, returning to his thoughts. He thought of the help that he was going to ask Granger for, what form it could possibly take was a complete mystery. So far in his meeting with Zandaar priests he had prevailed when surprise was on his side and when the conflict was one to one, but when more than one of the priests faced him he lost, if only temporarily. Dorana had beaten him on the first meeting but not the second, Namdarin was learning at every contact with the priests, perhaps Granger could teach him without there being any risk to Namdarin or Jayanne, and risks to Jayanne were becoming of major importance to Namdarin.

By the middle of the afternoon they had reached the top of the gully and turned south, the strong cold wind had not abated at all, though it had brought no really bad weather, just the occasional heavy shower of rain that passed in minutes, leaving them a little chilled but not really cold. They made camp for the night beside a small lake near the edge of the escarpment, Namdarin left the task of lookout to Arndrol, who did a quite good job, he only woke them once, when an inquisitive fox got too close for his comfort.

Namdarin woke in the morning very early, before the sun was up, in the cold of the pre-dawn light, he studied the sleeping face of the woman nestling in his arms, she was snoring softly, her clear pale skin excited him, and the warmth of her body resting against his made it clear that he was not going back to sleep now. He closed his eyes and daydreamed about her, he saw her coming out of a lake where she had been bathing, her long red hair was plastered to her head in long curving waves, it disappeared behind her white shoulders, the muscles of the upper arms rippled as she pushed the hair back from her face, her green eyes flashed in the sunlight. As she walked towards him she flicked the water from her arms with a graceful swish that caused her small breasts with their prominent pink nipples to bounce gently, he watched them jiggle as with each stride she came further from the water, her flat belly was slowly revealed with its clearly defined musculature then the bright red bush of her pubic mound and her strong thighs, the light sparkled on the drops of water falling between those long legs. She walked towards him with her arms outstretched, a vision of glorious beauty, an invitation that could not be refused.

Jayanne turned over in her sleep and caught Namdarin with the sharp point of her hard elbow just beneath the rib cage, this shattered his dream into a million little pieces and left him gasping for air. His discomfort woke Jayanne from her quiet dream of nothing in particular to find him struggling for breathe, she pushed him roughly onto his back and rapidly examined him for any injury, finding nothing obvious she stared into his eyes and noticed that he was trying to smile, she frowned in confusion. Namdarin finally managed half a lung full of air and Stammered, "You hit me in your sleep."

"I am sorry." she said, the concern was plain on her face.

"I am sure that I deserved it." Said Namdarin his lungs starting to work in a more relaxed fashion, "It is time we were moving anyway." He continued.

Together they broke camp in a matter of four minutes, the practise they had on the way to the village made them an excellent team. They had breakfast on horseback, biscuits, cold meat and water from the lake, simple but filling fare.

They made good time as they travelled towards the river, less than an hour from breaking camp they were looking down from the high banks into the river, it was about half a mile wide here with high banks both sides and a wide bar of gravel reaching across, making an excellent ford. Upstream of the ford the river was so wide that it appeared to be stationary and not flowing at all, but when it reached the gravel bar it rushed over the rocks making a soft but constant hissing sound. The horses found an easy way down to the water and walked carefully across, the gravel did not give very good footing, the stones were quite large and prone to suddenly turn over under the weight of a horse and rider, the water was only a few inches deep on average but it did have the occasional deep hole. By the time they climbed up the opposite bank both the people were wet to the knees and the horses were beginning to show signs of being very cold. Once on the grassy plain they picked the pace up to a slow gallop to help the horses warm up, well two horses were galloping but Arndrol was going scarcely faster than a trot. When the horses had been thoroughly warmed up they walked them for a while, then started to alternate between trotting and walking, this would give them a good speed without straining the horses, and leaving them plenty of energy for a gallop if needed. It was during one of these slow walks that Jayanne asked a question,

"This morning you said that you deserved to be hit by me. What did you mean?"

"I was having a very improper dream which you interrupted at just the right moment." he answered slowly.

"What do you mean by improper?" Namdarins answer was even slower this time.

"Well, I would rather not answer that, you might be offended."

"I really want to know." She was adamant and kept on asking for a few minutes until Namdarin finally had to give in. He went to great pains to point out that this was only a dream over which he had absolutely no control, he made this very clear before going into the details of the dream. He told of his vision of her coming out of the lake, he left out none of the details and none of his feelings about her beauty. When he had finished he looked at her to find her green eyes boring into his, he looked away quickly and his cheeks flushed pink. She thought for a while about what he had said, she found it vaguely exciting that he was dreaming about her but also was slightly disconcerted about the nature of the dream. She reversed the roles, she closed her eyes and thought of him walking slowly out of a lake naked and dripping, she saw his broad shoulders with their clearly defined muscles, his wide chest with its sparse mat of black curly hair, a band of which reached down across his flat belly to a thick bush about his manhood. His penis hung small and soft with a droplet of water glistening on its tip, not the hard symbol of male dominance she knew, this was gentle and calming.

These thoughts and the slow backwards and forwards rocking motion of the saddle beneath her brought a deep warm feeling, a slow excitement that she had not felt before, concentrating on the rapidly intensifying heat in her belly she was astounded by the speed with which this feeling took over her body and made her tremble as if in fear. With a sudden shudder it was over leaving a slow quieting of the heart and the breathing, and a warm feeling of dampness between her legs. "This feels good." she thought to herself, "How can something this good be improper?" She wondered about the way these feelings were associated to men and women, her knowledge of this sort of relationship was very sure, first the man would get drunk or excited about nothing, then he would beat her and strip her clothes from her, then he would throw her to the ground and drop his trousers to release his hard and throbbing manhood, then he would get down on top of her and force it inside her, thrusting harder and harder until with a grunt he withdrew leaving a milky stickiness and pain, he would stagger to his feet and call her all kinds of revolting names and beat her some more. How could women enjoy this enough to actually seek out the man of their choice and capture him deliberately? Jayanne considered this question for a while before deciding that men must not be all the same in this aspect of their behaviour, some must actually bring pleasure to their wives, the only pleasure her ex-husband had ever given her was the day he gurgled as he struggled for breath and spat hot red blood all over her as she twisted her knife in his guts and screamed at him to die. This brought a blazing fire to her blood and made her feel strong, stronger than him for the first time in her life, this was the first time that she had taken control of her own life, she now realised that she could have just left him and gone away, but then he may have done the same to some other woman and that could not be allowed. Namdarin would not have behaved in this way, he is a kind and gentle man, true he has cruel part to his nature, but he has undertaken a quest that will probably end his life and all for revenge against the people who killed his wife and son. A man who cares so much for his family could not possibly harm them, so perhaps he did not hurt his wife even when he made her pregnant. This thought went completely against everything she had experienced of men, her only experience being her husband.

Namdarin was almost sure that she had fallen asleep, her eyes had been closed for a long time and her breathing was slow and steady, but the horses had rested enough and it was time to pick up the pace again, so he said loudly, "Jayanne, its time to go quicker again." She opened her eyes and looked at him for what seemed to be a long time and said, "Right let's go," with a quick heel to the ribs her horse almost jumped forward into a quick trot, leaving Namdarin behind for a few moments before Arndrol gathered himself and caught up with a surge of power that surprised Namdarin enough to make him grip extra tightly with his knees. Jayanne continued to talk, "A dream cannot be improper it merely is, a persons actions or words can be improper but thoughts kept private cannot."

"You have no objections to me dreaming of you in a lustful way as I have described?" he asked, a little surprised by her statement.

"How can I object to a dream? What good would it do? A dream cannot be controlled, I can't control my own dreams how can I expect to control yours?"

"But I can control my dreams, I fought against Dorana in my dream and won because my control was better than his."

"That is different, that was a dream of combat in which you had a definite opponent, in an ordinary dream you would be fighting against yourself, a battle you could not hope to win. If lust is part of you, you will not be able to suppress it. Reality is entirely different."

"Things that happen in dreams occasionally do happen in reality."

"Very occasionally." she said quietly looking away and switching her concentration to the task of riding, she wondered for a while about the nature of dreams, could they be alternative realities, or mere fantasies, or even the raving of a temporarily deranged mind. These thoughts are unimportant, the most pressing priority is to find Granger, urging her horse into a gallop she left Namdarin to follow.

Namdarin looked at Jayanne ahead of him, her round backside bouncing in the saddle of her horse, he was amazed how quickly his thoughts turned to sex when the immediate threat of battle was removed, if his relationship with her was to go any further he would have to be very careful, she was right about reality being different. The reality in question was that if he pushed her too hard she would kill him in a moment, this was a serious challenge, one that he could not walk away from, he would have to try, but there was no hurry.

Arndrol did not like to follow any horse so he accelerated until he was alongside Jayanne's horse and then slowed down to match speed. Namdarin looked across at Jayanne, her red hair flying in the wind , a joyful grin on her red lips, the pleasure of riding fast was plain to see in her eyes, even the horses seemed to be enjoying a change of pace. Namdarin felt Arndrol's huge ribcage start to flex to its limits and he knew what was going to happen next, the horse was building up for a surge, Namdarin leant forward in the saddle, gave rein and said softly into the horses right ear, "Go on, run my friend." He felt the horses rump drop as it tensed for the kick and then it let go, a single kick of the rippling hindquarters and the man and horse were ahead of Jayanne, a second kick and they were starting to get going, Arndrol's big hooves cutting great clods of earth and grass and throwing them high in the air, a third and a fourth big kick and the surge was gone only a steady acceleration was left, in only ten strides Arndrol was at full speed, he was flying over the grassy plain. The cold air was making Namdarin's eyes stream with tears, but the horse kept on running, this was what he was bred for, to run hard for a short distance, because of his size he was strong and fast over a sprint, but his endurance at high speed was lacking. After only two minutes running flat out Namdarin looked over his shoulder and saw that Jayanne had given up the chase, her small horse and the pack horse had no chance at all of catching the big grey. Namdarin did not like the idea of Jayanne being out of sight and she was getting awfully close to the horizon already, he pulled hard on the reins and turned the big horse around and galloped back towards Jayanne, she too had been upset by the fact that he was running off without her, seeing him turn back caused a sigh of relief and a smile.

Arndrol pranced alongside Jayannes horse, he was sweating profusely and breathing very hard, blowing long plumes of steam from his flared nostrils.

"He is just a big show off." Said Namdarin patting the horse on the neck in an effort to calm him down. "He has been penned up too much recently, he likes to run and run, these slow horses get on his nerves." He continued with a huge grin.

"He is not the only show off around here." Said Jayanne, "You enjoyed that run as much as he did."

"Very true, the wind rushing in your face feels really good. The pounding of a strong horse gets the blood moving in your veins." He said whilst wiping the tears from his face with the sleeve of his coat.

"I think now might be a good time to stop for a rest," said Jayanne, "the horses will certainly be glad to rest for a while, those last few miles at a gallop has really put a strain on them, even that big grey monster of yours."

Arndrol tossed his head and snorted loudly, then jumped forwards again to show that he was not tired, Namdarin pulled the reins and stopped him going any further. Jayanne laughed, "I am sure that horse understands every word I say."

"Of course he does." Said Namdarin as Arndrol flung his head up and down as if nodding. They dismounted and allowed the horses to roam free grazing as they would in the certain knowledge that Arndrol would bring them all back when they were called, Namdarin and Jayanne ate from their packs and sat in the tall grass staring up at the sky, it was blue with a few clouds rushing across, the cold wind was racing over the plain, blowing the grass in waves not unlike the sea, the grass was beginning to turn brown as the cold of the middle of winter approached.

"How much further to the mountains?" Asked Namdarin.

"We will start to climb steeply sometime tomorrow, if the weather holds."

"Are we far enough away from the Black Crow?"

"Yes, I should think so, we are about fifteen miles away, so we shouldn't meet any of Blackbeards friends."

"The horizon looks like it is ten miles away, they could see us from quite close to the inn."

"The grass is deceptive, the horizon is only five miles away, and for them to see us they would have to be at the top of one of these gentle rises and looking our way as we crested the rise that we are on, this is very unlikely."

"Unless they are keeping a deliberate watch for travellers."

"Why should they do that?"

"Because they are bandits." His tone of voice became that of an impatient adult explaining something to a slow child for the thousandth time. Jayanne's eyes narrowed as she stared at him, her face flushed red with a surge of anger.

"I am not completely stupid." She said in a cold and ferocious voice. Namdarin realised that he had upset her with a simple phrase said wrongly, he apologised profusely and often, but it was nearly an hour before she would talk to him properly. It was the middle of the afternoon and they were still pounding across the grassy plain before she finally gave him the bright and sunny smile that meant he had been forgiven for his error, Namdarin filed the incident away in his memory to remind him never to be patronising again, it was just not worth the trouble it caused, and he didn't want any bad feeling between the two of them. They made rapid progress across the plain and into the slowly rising foothills of the mountains, before the sun had gone down they decided to camp for the night in a small clump of trees. The trees had long since lost all their leaves, deposited on the ground to give a rich deep covering that was warm and comfortable to sleep on. After a wonderful red sunset and a hearty meal they were sitting near the roaring fire when Arndrol stamped his feet and shook his head.

"What is wrong, Arndrol?" asked Namdarin, the only reply was another stamp though the horse did seem to be looking at something out in the darkness.

"Hello the camp, may I approach." Shouted a voice from amongst the trees.

Namdarin rolled to his right and snatched his bow, nocking an arrow as he came to his feet, Jayanne got up slowly and held her axe in both hands.

"Who are you?" asked Namdarin.

"I am called Poredal, I am alone and friendly."

"What are you doing in this wilderness?"

"I am a travelling minstrel and I am, well, travelling."

"Approach slowly." Out of the darkness came a tall thin man in a red coat and red pants and red boots and perched upon his head was a red felt hat with a long red feather, he was leading a horse that was very nearly red. Slung on the man's back was a five stringed instrument not unlike a guitar. He seemed to carry no weapons other than heavy handled short bladed knife at his belt. Once he and his horse were inside the circle of the firelight he tied the horse to a tree, before saying to Namdarin, "Your cautiousness is perfectly understandable, there are bandits about in these parts. May I ask who you are?"

"I am Namdarin and this is Jayanne, we are also travelling."

"Shall we sit down?" Asked Poredal, sinking slowly to the ground beside the fire, "I am going south and east, looking for news to tell and songs to steal."

Both Namdarin and Jayanne were completely disarmed by the minstrels relaxed and confident manner, Poredal started to chatter about nothing and anything, he didn't seem to stop for breath, he just talked incessantly. He talked about the weather, he talked about the roads, he talked about people he had met recently, he talked. Namdarin became more and more relaxed by the constant drone of the mans soft and silky voice, he was almost asleep when the minstrel took his instrument from his back and started to play and sing. He played soft ballads and sang in a crystal clear delicate tone perfectly in tune with the guitar. After singing five or six songs he stood up and started to dance along to the music, he jigged around the fire, round and round he went, one moment he was in front of Namdarin the next he was behind him. Poredal danced in the red firelight and threw his long feathered hat to the ground, and he danced behind Namdarin, and then behind Jayanne, who was staring intently into the flames, concentrating hard on the music. In one of the natural pauses of the song Poredal yanked his knife from its sheath, turned it and rapped Jayanne firmly on the back of the head, she collapsed in an unconscious heap beside the fire. Namdarin rolled to his feet attempting to draw his sword on the way up, he was almost upright when he felt a blinding pain in his right leg, he looked down and saw an arrow which had gone right through the meat of his thigh, Poredal kicked him hard in the chest and rolled him on to his face then hamstrung him with a swift slice of the knife.

Namdarin was helpless on the ground, screaming in agony, watching the blood pumping out of the wound at the back of his right knee, he reached down with one hand and placed it on the pressure point at the top of his right thigh pushing hard stopped the blood flow, but any relaxation caused it to start again. Men came running into the fire light from the surrounding trees, amongst them a huge man with a thick black beard, this one looked closely at Namdarin and said,

"You and her killed many of my friends, it looks like you will die, and she will beg to die before we have finished." Blackbeard kicked him in the ribs, which dislodged his hand from his groin and another squirt of red pumped towards the fire. More men were coming forwards and they brought horses,

"Mount up.", shouted Blackbeard, "we should be back in camp before morning. Bring her and leave him to die." The men mounted their hoses and Jayannes limp form was thrown over the rump of a pack animal, and as suddenly as they had arrived they left, Namdarin knew that he would die soon, he hoped that he would be reborn so that he could go after this band of criminals, though there was no obvious supply of living or dead flesh to help with the regeneration, this worried him. Over the thunder of departing hooves he heard some raised voices, shouting and complaining voices that seemed to be having some trouble with what sounded like an angry horse .After a few screams the voices gave up and left. Namdarin hoped that Arndrol was still free and alive, he said a small prayer and whistled, it was not the usual clear shrill tone that brought Arndrol running but it still worked none the less. Within moments he heard the returning hooves of his friend, the crackling of the wood on the fire made the big horse jittery but he still came right up to Namdarin and nuzzled his face.

"Oh. My friend, how it hurts. Go and find me another horse quickly." Arndrol remained standing and flicked an ear, he blew hot breath into Namdarins face.

"Now is not the time to be stubborn. Go." The grey turned and went in to the darkness of the trees, Namdarin said another prayer, then thought that he was becoming far to religious. He pulled a knife from his belt with his left hand and cut free the belt, still using only his left hand, his right being occupied keeping the blood in his leg, he tied the belt around his right thigh just above the wound. Tying knots with one hand is very difficult but when your life depends on it you can achieve miracles. Even when tied the belt was still too slack to stop the blood flow, so Namdarin pushed the knife handle under the belt and twisted the belt up into a bigger knot, thereby making it tight enough then he wriggled the handle under the belt to stop it slipping. Gently he removed his right hand from the pressure point and was surprised to see that no new blood came from the wound. He began to wonder where his horse had got to, it was certainly taking him a long time to find the pack horse that had got lost when Blackbeards gang had stormed into the camp, he hoped that the bandits had not captured the pack horse and taken it away, listening very carefully he heard the sound of returning hooves. Arndrol came into the light of the fire leading the pack horse by its reins.

"Well done, give me those reins." said Namdarin in a shaky voice, loss of blood was beginning to make him a little weak, but he knew that he could not give up, he had to stay awake and get off after Blackbeard as soon as possible. Taking the reins in his left hand he pulled the horses head towards him and took a knife from the remains of his belt.

"Arndrol," he said, "go for a long walk and don't come back until I whistle."

The horse shook its long mane but left the fireside slowly and disappeared into the gloom of the trees. Namdarin pulled the reins tight together under the horses chin and twisted them as hard as he could, so that the only way that the horse could relieve the pressure was to fall over, and this it did, though it did fall half across Namdarins useless legs, causing a huge wave of pain that almost rendered Namdarin unconscious. Once the pain had subsided a little and thought became a realistic possibility again, Namdarin turned his mind to the old gods, the ones that he believed to be the guardians of his oath, they had healed him three times now, though this time he did not want to wait until he was dead, he wanted to be healed now then he could chase Blackbeard.

"Old gods," he said, "you have helped me three times in the past, help me now in my hour of need. I cannot wait to die for you to heal me, so please do it now. I offer the life of this horse though it has served me well in life let it serve me better in death. I give you its blood and its breath, its heart and its spirit, its strength and its power, give me what I need." So saying he sliced the horses neck, the horse twitched and struggled but Namdarin hung on, it kicked its legs but Namdarin hung on, its warm red blood pumped from the wound in its throat, pouring all over Namdarin as he lay helpless pinned beneath it. He felt the warmth of the red tide and tasted the hot coppery tang of blood in his mouth. Gradually the horse got weaker and weaker as its life blood poured all over the ground, Namdarin waited for the gods to intervene but nothing happened.

For what seemed like an eternity nothing out of the ordinary occurred, the horse lying on top of him began to cool and a whirling blackness engulfed the man.

Jayanne regained consciousness to find herself hanging over the back of a horse looking down at the dark ground going past at quite a speed, she tried to struggle off the horse but was tightly bound hand and foot, the horses movement was making it difficult for her to breathe, the back of the saddle was digging into her ribs. A gruff voice said "Sit still and you wont get hurt." So she decided to bide her time and wait for a better opportunity to escape. The ride appeared to go on for ever, the pain in her ribs was getting worse with each stride the horse took. She was almost happy to see them arrive in a camp, the camp site was a sprawling affair in a clearing in a wooded valley, a small river ran down the middle of the clearing providing water for both people and horses.

The man on the horse with Jayanne got off and went to talk to somebody that Jayanne could not see, not even his boots. The man came back and undid the ropes fastening Jayanne to the horse, she fell to the ground in a heap, the lack of circulation to her arms and legs meant that she could not stand up at all, a roaring wave of pins and needles coursed through her body, she was picked up by two of the men and carried to a place near the fire, this short journey gave her an opportunity to look about the site, she saw no women, no buildings, only tents.

This was a temporary raiding camp, it could be moved in a matter of hours.

"I hope Namdarin comes soon." she thought , she was certain that he would come to rescue her from this predicament. They arrived near the big central fire, that seemed to be used by everybody in the camp, Blackbeard spoke to her," You have killed many of my men and now you must be taught a lesson."

"There is nothing you can teach me."

"We will teach you pain and death."

"I know pain very well, and death rides this way for you to learn."

"You will know pain that you cannot imagine. You mustn't joke about death or he will come for you and you will beg him to take you."

"I don't joke about death. His horse was not amongst the ones that rode into this camp tonight, so he must be riding it and he will be following you, to kill you and all your men."

"You are talking about your companion, he is dead my lovely, his legs were cut off and he died." Blackbeard smiled expecting this statement to crush her resistance.

"He has died before, but he always returns, he will come here and kill you all, if you are lucky. If you are unlucky he will release me and then I can kill some of you very slowly, he is much too quick about these things." While they were talking some of the men were driving four stakes into the ground close to the fire, Jayanne wondered about their purpose but knew it was not going to be to her liking. Blackbeard noticed where she was looking.

"You will be tied to those stakes and you will amuse the men as you have no doubt noticed they have no women here." He laughed loudly as the two men holding her up dragged her over to the stakes, where her clothing was cut from her and she was tied spread-eagled naked on the ground, a set of dice were produced from a pocket and a game ensued over the honour of going first. The ropes that tied her to stakes were far too strong for her to break but by a steady application of pressure she made one of the stakes move a little. Relax then pull, relax then pull , the stake was getting looser in its hole, but long before it had any chance to come free a winner was decided. The winning man was a small and evil smelling individual, though to Jayanne all these men smelled bad.

"So you have been chosen by chance to die first." She said in a calm and clear voice that shocked the man. He lowered his trousers and revealed a huge throbbing erection that twitched with a life of its own. He knelt down between her spread thighs and pushed his penis inside her, quite roughly, then he began slowly thrusting in and out. Through all this Jayanne kept her eyes firmly closed and made no sound or other acknowledgement of the man's presence. Soon he climaxed and was gone, to be replaced by another man from the head of the queue that had formed, Jayanne opened her eyes just once to memorise his face, then she said ,"I know your face and I will kill you." He looked down into her eyes and saw none of the fear he expected, only hatred was there glaring back up at him and then it was gone as the lids slowly closed on the green eyes. For her this was easier than her marriage had been because there was no violence only violation. The line of men waiting soon diminished to nothing and the last man threw a blanket over her, they didn't want her to die of the cold before they had all had their pleasure with her. She lay there unable to move and prayed for Namdarin to come, she looked up into the slowly lightening sky and knew that the sun would be up before long. "Today is the day that he will come." She whispered to herself, a man beside the fire looked at her but said nothing, he was thinking of his wife and children back at the main camp, he was wishing to be there instead of here. He had nothing to do with the rape, he was only part of Blackbeards gang of outlaws because he could not get any land to farm for himself. He slowly got to his feet and looking all around her walked over to Jayanne and gave her some meat to eat, and some wine to drink, "I will have no part in making war on women." he said quietly.

"If you wish to leave do so now, you may not get another chance, when Namdarin comes he will come with death in his eyes, and he will not know which have been good to me and which have not."

"You keep a false hope, he is dead."

"Did anyone capture or kill his horse?" she asked.

"Three tried to catch that beautiful grey, but it nearly killed them so they gave up."

"If Namdarins horse is alive he will be riding here right now."

"I think I feel a sudden need for the comfort of my wife's arms." He stood and walked over to the picket lines where the horses were kept mounted one and left at a slow walk so as not to attract so much attention.

Jayanne dozed for a while and the next thing she saw was the sun shining down on her face as the blanket was ripped from her, a tall but fat man was standing between her ankles he pulled down his pants to expose another rampant penis, she had lost count of the number that she had seen recently, the fat man fumbled himself inside her, the weight of his fat and sweaty body made it almost impossible for her to breathe, she had to time her breathing to his thrusts, each time he thrust the breath was pushed out of her lungs. The fat man was almost done when there was a commotion amongst the trees surrounding the clearing and a man staggered into sight, he was carrying another man who appeared to be dead.

CHAPTER NINE

Namdarin awoke to find himself covered in the bones of a horse, his brain was confused by this for a while then his memories came rushing back in a tangled jumble that took some short time to sort out. The fire was still burning strongly and the woods about were still very dark, so only a little time had past, he breathed a huge sigh of relief, then whistled for Arndrol. He heard an answering scream from the horse and then the pounding of hooves, Namdarin got to his feet, took the remains of his belt from around his now healed right leg, he retied the belt so the knot where he had to cut it was at the back, this made things a little awkward because the place where his scabbard should hang on his left hip was now occupied by his belt buckle. He had these things sorted out before Arndrol came into the view, the horse trotted towards him slowly and nuzzled his face, the horse seemed happy to see him. Namdarin searched around the campsite quickly, picking up the items that he would need, his bow, her bow, both quivers full of arrows, his sword and her axe. When he finally climbed up onto Arndrols back he looked like and army all on his own festooned all about with weaponry. Though it was still dark he had no problem following the trail left by Blackbeards men, it was five yards wide and littered with all sorts of garbage, from discarded wine jugs to horse droppings, "A blind man could follow this bunch of idiots." Kicking the horse into a gallop he followed the trail, he could tell by the spacing of the hoof prints that they were going much slower than he was. "If they were to arrive at their camp before sunrise, and are going much slower than me I should catch up with them before they get there." he said with a wicked smile on his lips.

    The trail remained easy to follow until it crossed a short boggy area and went onto a large platform of stone, this appeared to Namdarin to be many square miles of unbroken rock. The horses he was following left no visible tracks on the hard surface, he had lost the trail. He could not track them over rock at night he would have to wait for the sun to come up, from the look of the sky in the east this would be an hour or so yet. He got off the horse and sat on the ground were the gang had left the bog and gone onto the rocky pavement. The gradually increasing light of the rising sun gave him a better view of the rocky surface, he could now see small patches of the mud scattered on the rocks going in a clearly defined direction. He followed the patches of mud, which became wider separated very quickly until he could see no more of them, the mud must be shaken off the horses hooves very quickly on the hard surface, but he had a rough direction in which to go so he went that way all the time praying that they band of outlaws did not change their course. It was full daylight when he crossed the edge of the rocky area into a grassy valley, he could see no evidence of the gang having passed this way, a moments desperation struck him.

    He decided to follow the edge of the rocky area first on way then the other until he found the tracks, this was going to take some time, time that he was not sure was available, judging by the size of the tracks they had left before the rocky area he set off at a trot, hoping that he would not miss any tracks. After only a few moments he realised that he had not marked the place where he had started ,with no starting place he could search the same piece over and over again. He stopped the horse and dismounted, taking the axe he made two deep cuts in the grass, to form an x.

He should be able to see this even when riding past quickly, remounting he looked down at the mark and shook his head, it was just not noticeable enough. Cutting a long twig from a tree he tied a small piece of his shirt to it and stuck it into the ground in the centre on the x.

"That I will see at a gallop." he said, and set off again, after five minutes travelling in one direction he marked the end of his run with another stick and galloped back to the first one, he stopped by this and pulled it from the ground and continued on much slower so as not to miss the tracks. Five minutes after picking up the first flag he planted it again and set off at a gallop to the second flag. This meant that he was covering the same section of ground over and over again, but this was better than choosing the wrong way first and riding half a day before turning back to try again, as it was he had found the track in less than a hour. Dropping his flag he proceeded with new hope after the gang of bandits. Their tracks seemed to be leading up the valley toward a large wood that completely filled the valley floor, he entered the wood slowly and carefully, knowing that there would be guards about, long before he saw any guards he smelled the wood fuelled fire in the middle of their clearing. He dismounted and approached the smell cautiously on foot, ahead of him he could see that the trees thinned out and stopped, and then he saw a man riding towards him, the man did not see Namdarin as he crouched down in the sparse undergrowth, he rode past slowly as if trying not to be noticed by anyone. Less than a minute after he had past him Namdarin heard the snort of Arndrol, the man on the horse had obviously stumbled upon the big grey, Namdarin was going back into the wood to stop the man from reporting back to his friends when he heard a single set of hooves going away from the camp at high speed, he found Arndrol undisturbed eating the spare grass under the trees.

"That must have been somebody leaving." he said quietly. He went back to the edge of the trees to spy on the camp, peering through the undergrowth beneath a tall oak tree he was looking down into the camp, he saw the tents arranged in a rough circle about a large fire, off to one side was a picket line with horses tied to it, about thirty horses, all unsaddled with only halters on their heads holding them in place. Beside the fire was a blanket that appeared to be staked to the ground at each corner, while he watched a man came from one of the tents and went over to the blanket, he flung the blanket aside to reveal a red headed woman tied to the stakes, Namdarin knew that this was Jayanne, the man dropped his trousers and got down on top of the woman , Namdarin watched the man's white buttocks heaving up and down, he felt the bile rising in his throat, he felt the anger come in a great rush, he moved from the tree. From the corner of his eye he saw something move he turned towards it and saw a man coming towards him, he must have been on sentry duty watching the perimeter of the camp he was not close enough to be sure that Namdarin was a stranger so Namdarin shot him with an arrow. The man saw the bow being pulled and screamed, the scream was cut short by the arrow, but the noise had attracted another of the sentries from nearby, Namdarin reached out and pulled the arrow back to his hand and ran into the woods so as not to be seen by the sentry who was coming towards the scream.

Namdarin watched the second sentry pick up the body of the first and carry him down into the camp, Namdarin moved around inside the trees to where the second sentry must have been keeping watch and crept to the edge of the trees to see what was happening in the camp.

The man wobbled slowly down the hill towards the fire and deposited his load as gently as he could near the fire, Blackbeard came out of a tent and walked slowly over.

"What happened?" asked Blackbeard.

"I heard him scream," said the sentry, "then I saw him fall, in his chest was an arrow with green and yellow feathers. When I got to him he was dead and the arrow was gone."

"How can an arrow just disappear?"

"I don't know, but I swear there was an arrow in his chest when he fell. You can see the hole it made." At this point Jayanne laughed aloud.

"What do you know of this, woman?" demanded Blackbeard, prodding her in the ribs with the toe of his boot.

"It means that my friend is out there in those trees, he has come to kill you all."

"The man is dead, it must be somebody else, who is it woman?" This time he put the sole of his right boot on her right breast and pressed down hard and twisted the delicate flesh from side to side until she screamed.

"He is death," she sobbed, "He comes for you. For the rest of today he will pick you off one by one with his bow, and tonight he will send the nightmares against you and tomorrow he will ride in and kill whoever is left alive."

"Nobody could hit us from those trees without being seen."

"Tell your best bowman to put an arrow in the trees if he can."

Blackbeard waved at one of the men standing nearby ,the man ran to a tent and came out carrying a bow, he stood near the fire and shot an arrow towards the trees that the dead sentry had been guarding. The arrow landed fifty feet short of the first tree.

"Pathetic." Laughed Jayanne. The bowman tried again, this time giving the arrow a much higher trajectory, it fell only about twenty feet short. The bowman shook his head in disgust and tried again. Namdarin watched the bowman and wondered what was going on. The man appeared to be shooting at the trees, then the thought struck him this was a challenge. As the third attempt flew through the air and got tangled in the branches of the very oak tree were Namdarin had been hiding earlier, Namdarin got to his feet nocked an arrow, pulled the bow until his arm was almost screaming in pain, aimed a foot over the bowman's head and fired.

The bowman watched his third arrow fly slowly up in a long arc and come down in the branches of a tree, he turned and smiled at Blackbeard, "I hit it," he said "but I don't think it's dead." Blackbeard nodded, then heard a strange hissing noise, a green and gold streak came from the trees to his right and struck the bowman in the chest, the man fell to the ground with the arrow sticking up out of the middle of his chest. The feathers of the arrow twitched to the bowman's slowing heart beat, all the people around gasped and were silent. The arrow started to twitch again as if the bowman were coming back to life and then it slid slowly from the man's ribcage, it struggled a little when it caught between two ribs, but it soon came free and sailed slowly into the trees.

"He will never run out of arrows," said Jayanne who was as shocked as the rest by the arrows sudden departure, "his bow has certain magic properties, it is very powerful, has an extremely long range, and its arrows always return." Blackbeard turned towards her and looked stunned into her laughing eyes, his jaw hanging open in shock.

"You four go and get him." He said indicating four of his men, the four in question drew their swords and ran towards the trees screaming, two of them fell with arrows in them before they had gone twenty strides, the other two dropped to the ground before the arrows could get them. Blackbeard watched his brave men come crawling back to the fire on their bellies in the mud. He looked at the dirty faces and said, "Take two others and go the long way round, through the trees, bows don't work to well when trees get in the way." The two shame faced men selected two others and went into the trees on the other side of the clearing.

Blackbeard looked down at Jayanne whose green eyes flashed with mirth, "I could kill you now before he could stop me." He drew his sword to emphasise the fact.

There was a blur and an arrow buried itself in the turf between his feet, then drifted away like a huge dandelion seed blowing on the wind.

"He is saving you for last," said Jayanne, "he has something special in mind for you." Blackbeard said nothing, the men all stood around waiting, the tension in the air kept on rising, a few small fights broke out, but these where quickly suppressed by a single word from the black bearded leader. After a hour of waiting two men came out of the trees near the spot where Namdarin had been shooting from, they walked slowly into the camp, their heads hanging.

"He shot the other two," said one of them, "we never saw him, we heard his horse once, but we never saw him. He must be the devil himself."

"No," said Jayanne, "I have told you, he is death."

"The witch could be right."

"Once it goes dark," said Blackbeard, "he wont be able to see enough to shoot any body, we go in, in force, and find the bastard. I will hang him by his ankles and set fire to his head." The men all around the leader cringed in fear, they had never seen him this angry before, or perhaps he was just covering up his fear, so a few of the most frightened dared to think.

"Get what sleep you can," shouted Blackbeard, "its going to be a busy night."

He retired to his tent.

Having killed two of the men sent into the woods to capture him Namdarin returned to his station by the big oak tree, this was the highest section of the forest rim, which meant that his arrows had their maximum range from here. Inside the camp he saw that the men were not straying too far from the centre, they were keeping an alert watch on the entire perimeter, there was no way that

Namdarin could sneak into the camp without being seen, so he decided to wait where he was and see if he could pick off a few careless ones. One such happened early in the afternoon, a large man came out of a tent and walked towards Namdarin, when he was about fifty feet away from the camp he turned round and dropped his trousers, this was the latrine that the men used, Namdarin looked down at the huge white rippling flesh of those buttocks and recognised them, he had seen that backside this morning, it had been pumping away on Jayanne at the time.

"Oh." whispered Namdarin taking up his bow, "What poetic justice." He pulled and took careful aim, this was a tricky shot to attempt even at close range, he let out the long slow breath that calmed his heart and steadied his hand, then released. The arrow sailed through the air humming like an angry bee, it travelled under the fat man's buttocks, pierced his scrotum and cut his penis off cleanly at the root. The fat man gasped, reached down and picked up the damaged part and tried to stagger into the camp, his pants tangled in his legs, he didn't get very far at all, with the amputated item in one hand and the other hand covering up the bleeding hole, before he bled to death. Jayanne lifted her head when she heard the arrow in the air and she saw it strike, her body shock with paroxysms of mirth, she laughed until she cried, Namdarin heard her cackling laughter from his concealment in the trees. When she had control of herself again she shouted as loud as she could, "A good shot my lord, a very good shot."

Blackbeard stormed over to where she was staked out and another arrow hit the ground very near him, being careful to make no seriously threatening move he spoke to her in a very husky voice filled with emotion, "What manner of demon is this lord of yours?"

"He is death." was the stock reply.

"Why does he attack us?"

"You attacked him first, once in the gully and for the second time at our camp. As you did not learn to leave us alone after the first disastrous meeting then you must be too stupid to live."

"How can we avoid this conflict?"

"Twice now you have tried to kill us, if what you say is true you have succeeded at least once, you cannot avoid it, all you can do is die."

"No. As soon as it is dark we will get him, and then I will have to think up something really special for you."

"Then I have absolutely nothing to fear." Her answer came with a smile.

He turned to the men who were staring in fear at the body of their fat friend and said, "You men get some sleep!"

Namdarin watched as the men dispersed into the tents, except of course, the guards, they moved about the camp in short runs, which ended in quick dives into the grass, they were making themselves as small a targets as they could. Namdarin thought about all the men down in their tents who would soon be sleeping, if only he had the power of Dorana to enter their dreams, the process of invading dreams must be relatively simple because Dorana was able to do it all alone, with no apparent aid from complex magic, could it be that it was merely a question of belief? Did knowing that a thing could be done qualify as enough belief? Namdarin was sitting with his back to the old oak tree, safe from the view of the guards around the camp, he relaxed slowly and concentrated on the typical dreams of men, dreams of rampant women, dreams of successful combat, and dreams of wonderful wealth. With an almost imperceptible slowness a dream began to form in his minds eye, it seemed to centre on a woman with improbably large breasts, Namdarin tried to latch onto this dream but in doing so he appeared to chase it away, it vanished like the dream that it was.

"If that was one of their dreams I was seeing, then I will not have to chase it so hard next time." He said, Arndrol who was standing behind the tree snuffled in the grass. Namdarin relaxed himself again and tried to conjure up exactly the same sequence of feeling that brought the first dream, he had no success until he tried to think of another dream, afterwards he would realise that dreams are over in moments to attempt to return to the same dream was foolish. The second dream that he encountered started with the sound of swords clashing, feigning no real interest he drifted gently towards the sounds, the scene that he found was two men fighting over a barrel full of jewels, there were diamond and emeralds and sapphires as big as goose eggs. Which of the two combatants was the dreamer and which the dream? One of them was crystal sharp in all his features, the other had only a sharp sword and a sharp face, all other aspects of his person were indistinct and blurry. Namdarin thought as quietly as possible ,"How do I influence this? What I need to happen is for the dreamer to loose the fight. If the dream man had two swords and knew how to use them he should win." Looking hard at the dream man Namdarin could see his right hand very clearly, so he looked at the blurred left hand and thought of it as hard and strong as his own, the hand slowly changed until it matched the picture that Namdarin wanted for it. It looked clear and purposeful, in the hand that was now more his than the dreamers, he pictured a sword, a long and shiny sword with broad blade and a sparklingly sharp edge. The dreamer suddenly stepped away from the dream man, who now was wielding two swords, one of them like a master, the dreamer tried to disengage but the dream man kept following him, the dreamer did not dare to turn his back to the dream man, he knew that the two swords would chop him to ribbons. The dreamer fought on with more and more desperation, he made wild slashes, and savage lunges, none of which found any target but air. The fight went more and more the dream man's way, he was becoming clear his blurrs were fading into sharp outlines, the colours of his clothes became well defined, the hiss of his harsh breathing whispered in the ears of the dreamer. Namdarin understood that the dreamer must believe totally in his dream for it to kill him, so he tried to make the dream completely real, the grass crunched underfoot just like untouched grass does, it even smelled like freshly trodden grass. Once the scene was truly set to be as real as possible Namdarin made the dream man strike with a swirling blade he disarmed the dreamer, whose sword flew many yards through the air, paused then plunged the blade into the dreamers chest, there was a shock and then darkness. Namdarin opened his eyes and looked down on the campsite, nothing had changed none of the guards had moved, but possibly one of the sleeping men would not wake up. Namdarin wondered about the ease with which he had invaded the mans dream and killed him, "Could it be that by surviving two of Doranas attempts my mind has been opened to this sort of activity?" he asked of no one in particular. He stopped thinking about this and relaxed, closing his eyes he reached out for another dream, the next one came in flash, it needed no chasing and no subtlety at all, but then it was not a very subtle dream. The dreamer was in the process of raping a beautiful woman, she was struggling but her wriggling only made his enjoyment more intense, Namdarin was so shocked when he recognised the face of the woman that he almost fell out of the dream, she was Jayanne. Namdarin moved very close to the pair and the dream Jayanne saw him and her green eyes pleaded for help, he stared into those green pools for a moment then he twisted her face into the form of a giant serpent, its head was black and gold and three feet across. The dreamer reared away from the serpent and screamed , the serpents head struck, and the darkness fell again.

Namdarin opened his eyes, and heard a distant screaming, a man came rushing from his tent , he seemed very frightened about something, he walked slowly over to Jayanne and stopped a few feet out of reach, Namdarin picked up the bow. The man said something to Jayanne, she laughed and he ran back to his tent. Namdarin settled down again, "I went too quickly that time and didn't give him time to believe in the snake, I must remember not to rush things. I wonder what he said to Jayanne? It certainly seemed to amuse her." Namdarin relaxed again and reached out for another dream, he was really looking for Blackbeard, but he didn't find him this time, he found another man in a very strange dream which was a confused jumble of places and people, the colours were distorted and only the dreamer himself appeared to remain constant. Namdarin could make no sense of this at all and couldn't find a way to turn it against the dreamer so he just set fire to it all , he enclosed the dreamer in a gradually shrinking circle of fire. The dreamer ran from the flames , and ran from the flames until there was nowhere for him to run to, the flames caught him and he burned with a horrid scream.

Namdarin opened his eyes and heard no scream, there was no rushing around in the camp so another of Blackbeards bandits was dead. The next dream that Namdarin caught was very surprising, the dreamer was female, she was a very plain female with straggly red hair, he knew that she was Jayanne. She seemed to be waiting anxiously for something, he decided that rather than invade the privacy of her mind he would depart this dream without effecting it at all, he opened his eyes and was still by his oak tree looking down on the camp, the sun was beginning to descend towards the mountains so he decided to try for one more dream, he relaxed and reached for the dream of Blackbeard, he pictured the face of Blackbeard, he filled his mind with those dark eyes and that thick black beard that frames that wide face. This time he found the dream he was after. Blackbeard was riding his horse across a wide plain, his men were behind him, they were some way off, Namdarin took a very direct course of action in this dream, he thought of himself as a tall thin man dressed in a long black cape who will appear in front of Blackbeards galloping horse just about now.

Blackbeard was galloping across the plain, he was chasing something that he knew was valuable, he was not sure what it was exactly but it was worth the chase, suddenly there appeared in front of him a tall thin figure wearing a long black hooded robe.

"Who are you to delay my chase?" He demanded reining the horse to a sliding halt.

The man in black threw back his hood to reveal the face of one of Blakcbeards own men.

"What are you doing in that ridiculous religious robe?" asked Blackbeard.

"I am dead, Namdarin has killed me." Said the figure ,then his face slowly faded into the form of another of Blackbeards men, "and he has killed me too." the figure continued.

"Who are you?" asked Blackbeard, the sweat was beginning to show on his face.

"I am death," said the figure the face fading again into a naked skull.

"What do you want with me?" asked Blackbeard not really wanting to know.

"What does death ever want with men," the skull changed into a reflection of Blackbeards own face, "I come for you." Blackbeard screamed. Namdarin opened his eyes again and looked down on the camp to see Blackbeard come staggering out of his tent and go rushing over to Jayanne, they spoke for a while then Blackbeard went to the fire and added many logs and hunched over the roaring flames as if he was cold.

After the death of the fat man the camp settled down into a watchful and tense alertness that Jayanne found most entertaining, it amused her enormously to watch the men moving around looking over their shoulders and scanning the trees all the time for incoming arrows. Her situation had not changed since she had been brought into the camp, she had not been released from the ropes even for a trip to the latrine, consequently she was beginning to smell quite awful, she found this very unpleasant but it did have the advantage of discouraging any of the men from further sexual advances, though she was beginning to itch terribly and she was very hungry. The afternoon passed slowly with very little action, except for an occasion when a man came running out of his tent, he looked at her and walked over to her, he stopped a few feet away.

"You are a snake goddess aren't you?" He asked, still shaking from his dream.

"That may be true." she answered with a huge smile.

"You tried to eat me." he said.

"If I had really tried that you would be dead." She laughed long and loud, until the man ran back to his tent. Jayanne tried to wriggle some circulation into her cramped arms and legs, she had some success but not much, the feeling returned to her fingers and toes, but the pain of their awakening was hard to bear. Once the pain had subsided to a dull throbbing she tried to get some sleep. She dozed and drifted in and out of consciousness all afternoon, it was very nearly sundown when Blackbeard woke with a shout and came out of his tent and walked over to talk to her.

"I have just met your friend death in a dream." He said, his voice quaking.

"You are lucky to be alive. You are not the only one though, at least one of those ruffians of yours also met him and he accused me of being a snake goddess." Her tone was calm and confident.

"He told me that two others were dead."

"Have you checked them to see if it is true?" she asked, a cruel smile twisted her face.

"No. I know now that it must be. He is certainly a demon of the very worst kind, I have no idea how we will kill him, but we must try."

"You cannot kill death, you could try running away as soon as it goes dark. If you leave me behind unharmed he may not follow you." she suggested knowing that if they released her she would follow and kill them.

"That would be the end of my life, for me to run from a single man, one that all have seen bleed like a real man, even though he be a devil. If I run then the men that follow me now will loose confidence in me and I will soon cease to be the leader. That I cannot countenance."

"If you go into those trees in the darkness your men will die, he will probably let you live until tomorrow. The dark is his natural element, you would not try to out swim a fish or out fly a bird or out run a horse, in the darkness he moves like a ghost, you will not see him but he will walk amongst you."

"I have no option I must try."

"When you go into those trees tonight he will kill some more of you, he has already killed one third of your band. Tomorrow he will ride into this camp and kill the rest. Look up at the sun, watch the sunset behind the mountains, you see the last sunset of your life. Run and you may see another."

Blackbeard stood and walked over to the fire, he threw on it many big logs, he watched the flames eat into the wood and felt the heat on his skin but his heart was still heavy and cold with fear, he hunched down beside the roaring fire and stared into the flames hoping for inspiration. Staring into the flames he heard a distant almost musical ringing sound, like an extended ringing of a small bell, not the strike and fade away of a normal bell but a long slow ring followed by a quick fade. Blackbeard stood up and looked around for the source of this strange sound, he looked up towards the oak tree, underneath the wide spread limbs of the old tree he saw a man sitting on the ground with his sword braced delicately across his knees, he was passing a whet stone down one side then the other, this was the ringing in Blackbeards ears. Behind the man was a big grey horse it was standing still and watching the man. The man under the tree was finally satisfied with the edge of his newly honed sword so he got to his feet and wave the sword in the air, the last rays of the sun flashing red and orange off the shinning edges, the man walked into the trees and the horse followed him. Blackbeard now knew where Namdarin was and once the light had faded enough he sent his men out to each side of the oak tree hoping to catch Namdarin between them.

Namdarin walked into the trees with the horse behind him, "Blackbeard now knows where I am," he thought ,"I think it is time to move. He will attack this area as soon as he can so I must get round to the other side of the clearing before he and his men start moving." Once he was out of sight of the men in the clearing he vaulted onto the horses back and galloped off away from the camp he had to get far enough away so the horse would not be heard as they came around to the other side. As the light faded Namdarin had to slow down or risk being thrown from the horse by a low branch or a sudden pothole, to Namdarin his progress seemed woefully slow. He reached the edge of the trees long after full darkness had descended on the clearing, he could see the fire still burning, but nothing around it was visible, his plan was to sneak into the camp and kill as many of the guards as he could without being seen, and then possible release the horses or if he could get close enough Jayanne. Leaving Arndrol by a tree with precise instructions about noise Namdarin crouched low and moved slowly down the hill towards the fire. The line of the bandits horses stood between him and the fire and he knew that they would be guarded so he headed for one end of the line moving as slowly and carefully as he could, which was carefully indeed. He made almost no noise at all as he approached the first guard , the man had a quite pronounced cough, Namdarin held the cure in his hand, eight inches of shining steel, "Damn." thought Namdarin as he plunged the knife into the soil. "I hope that blade didn't flash any light towards the guards." It hadn't, there was no reaction from the guards. Namdarin dropped down onto his belly as he crawled through the wet grass , he was listening very intently to the sound of the soft breeze blowing in the trees, the rustling of the few remain leaves covered the small noises he made. Namdarin crawled behind the guard who seemed more interested in watching the horizon than the ground nearer to him, he glanced around occasionally but the sweep of his eyes was so fast that he could not have seen anything that was stationary and nothing moving smaller than a man. Namdarin was moving very slowly and was smaller that a mouse at the time he came directly behind the guard, Namdrain reached up and grabbed the man with his left hand by the face, covering his mouth and nose, the guard fell over backwards and Namdarin plunged his knife into the belly, then turned the blade upwards, puncturing stomach then diaphragm then lungs then heart, the only noise that the guard made to attract any one attention was a single small liquid gurgle, this sound was completely drowned by the nearby stream. Namdarin guessed that there would be another guard at the other end of the line of horses so he crawled that way. The horses were only a little disturbed by his passing and they didn't make enough noise to attract any one, Namdarin arrived at the end of the line and crawled around for a while but found no guard, he was eventually forced into the conclusion that there had only been one guard on the horses. Creeping through the trampled grass near the camp was more difficult than the longer grass, concealment in this shorter grass would be almost impossible, so Namdarin opted for the other sort of concealment, he hid himself from view by being someone who belonged in the camp, he hoped that he was almost the same size as the guard he had already cured of his cough. He stood up in plain view of any who may be watching and he walked around the fire, keeping as much of his face concealed as possible, Jayanne was too near to the fire for him to attempt a rescue while any of the guards were still alive, so he went into a tent, luckily it was empty, he decided to commit some minor acts of vandalism, he slashed the bedding and emptied a water jug all over it. He left the first tent and went on to the next he did the same in that one and then went on, until all the tents had been visited, the only ones he left undamaged were the ones with the bodies of the men who had died in their sleep. No one would use their bedding for fear of catching what ever had killed them. He left the tents knowing that any of the men out in the woods hunting him would return to a very uncomfortable night.

Walking slowly away from the tents he headed to the horses,

his plan was to release them and so keep the bandits from running away. As he came to the line of horses he heard some heavy footsteps behind him, he rested his hand as casually as he could on the knife in his belt and kept his back to the approaching man.

"You really shouldn't leave your post you know." said a deep and resonant voice. Namdarins reply was a grunt and a nod, the man was still too far away.

"If Blackbeard catches you wandering around he will hang you up by your thumbs for a week." The voice continued getting nearer all the time. Again Namdarin nodded and grunted. The man was beginning to get suspicious.

"Are you alright? Friend, you sound sick." A large hand grabbed Namdarins right shoulder and spun him around. As he turned Namdarin pulled his knife and plunged it into the man's belly. Unfortunately the man was wearing a wide belt with and enormous metal buckle the point of Namdarins knife caught in this buckle and the only damage it did to the man was to knock all the air out of him. The man stepped backwards from the blow and let out an immense groan, which was heard by the other guards around the fire, they jumped to their feet and started running towards the tussling pair, Namdarin was trying to get in another cut with the knife but the man was hanging on to his knife arm. Namdarin shook him off with a swift kick to the groin, then he dropped the knife and drew his sword, in the remaining instant before the guards arrived he whistled for Arndrol. The guards arrived in a fast running bunch, their swords were drawn but they were in each others way. Namdarin jumped to his left and the man at the end of the approaching group ran straight onto his sword, with a quick twist and flick of the wrist Namdarin had his sword freed from the man's ribs and was ready for the next onslaught. The four remaining men stared to circle around Namdarin, who tried to keep moving so that his back was clear but he failed.

First one then another of the men became brave enough to slash warily at Namdarin, who parried each stroke in time to parry the next he could find no real openings into which to press an attack. Namdarins posture became more and more defensive as the circle around him tightened, Namdarin was getting dizzy with the constant turning when he heard the thunder that he was awaiting, Arndrol came in amongst the men, he knocked one down and kicked out at another who blundered into Namdarins sword and died. As Arndrol came to a halt beside him Namdarin grabbed the prominent saddle horn and swung himself up onto the horse, who spun around in a most alarming fashion for any man standing too near. This spin was a standard tactic for remounting in battle, the man swings up and the horse spins lashing out with feet and head, this creates a small clear space which the horse then uses to escape, hopefully. The moment that Namdarin was firmly in the saddle he snatched the axe from it place hanging on the horn and began slashing about himself. One of the men tried to grab the reins near the bit, but he got too close and lost two fingers to Arndrol's huge yellow teeth.

The noise in the camp brought Blackbeards men running from the woods, there would be too many for Namdarin to take in the dark so he guided Arndrol across the stream with a single bound and away from most of the bandits, he did manage to run down two more of them before he got to the trees, when he reached the cover of the trees, he dismounted, took the bow from the saddle and put the axe back, slapped Arndrol on the rump and climbed a high tree.

From his vantage point in the tree he heard a lot of running and shouting as the bandits tried to catch the horse, Namdarin knew they had little if no chance of actually trapping the horse in the dense woodland. Finally he heard a shout from deep amongst the trees, "Damn it. The bastards not even on the horse, he must be hiding some where, find him." A deathly silence descended on the wood, all of Blackbeards men were trying to be as quiet as they could hoping to catch Namdarin making some noise. Slowly Namdarin went down the tree until he was lying along the lowest and biggest branch, he was eight feet from the leaf littered floor, he slowed his breathing down until he began to hear the sounds of people moving about, well he assumed they were people because the noise they had been making previously must have driven all the animals away. After a few minutes patient waiting he heard delicate footsteps crackling through the dead leaves towards the tree he was hiding in. When the person passed under the branch Namdarin reached down and cut his throat with another knife, he felt the hot blood spray over his hand and wrist and presumable up his sleeve, he dropped to the ground and wiped the sticky mess from his hand and the knife handle before running softly to another tree and climbing again. The thud of the falling body and the sound of Namdarin running soon brought somebody to investigate, the man arrived carrying a flaming torch, he held the torch high over his head, Namdarin let him get very close to the body under the tree before putting an arrow into his head. The branches of the tree restricted the power of the shot and almost caused Namdarin to fall, he was still scrabbling for his balance when another of the bandits arrived. When the man picked up the torch and stamped on the dried leaves that had started to burn, Namdarin saw that it was Blackbeard. From his current position hanging upside down from a branch there was little that Namdarin could do other than remain a still as possible and hope that no one noticed him. Blackbeard raised the torch high and waved it from side to side and shouted.

"Every body out of the trees, return to camp immediately, we will get the bastard later." Then Blackbeard ran from the wood and kept on shouting the same message over and over until all his men had left the forest. Namdarin crept to the verge of the undergrowth to try and find out what was happening. He could see a group of men with torches about fifty feet from the trees, they seemed to be discussing some plan or other. Suddenly the men started to move, they scattered to the left and right of his position, running towards the trees they flung their torches high over the trees. The plan was now obvious, they intended to burn him out. Namdarin ran away from the edge of the trees, deeper into the wood, he whistled for Arndrol, he didn't want the horse to die in the fire. Moving through a forest at night is not easy, but running and whistling made it almost impossible, finally Arndrol found him and together they tried to out run the fire. Blackbeards plan was fortuitously assisted by the wind that was blowing the fire away from the clearing and towards Namdarin. High in the upper branches the fire was out running the horse, the occasional burning twig and branch would fall set fire to the ones lower down, Namdarin angled the horse so that they were still running mainly down wind but moving slowly towards the stream, the heavy ground hugging black smoke was making them both choke. Crashing down a high bank they splashed into the shallow water of the stream, the horse stumbled on the slippery rocks of the stream bed, almost dropping Namdarin into the icy cold water, once they had crossed the stream Namdarin slowed the pace down, the stream would act as a barrier to the fire, or so he hoped.

Blackbeard watched the fire start, he thought for a little while that it wasn't going to catch but eventually it started to spread , all the little puddles of flames joined together to make a good sized fire. He listened to Namdarins whistling, which was slowly getting further away until it suddenly stopped, he could not be sure that Namdarin had been caught by the flames but he could at least hope. Calling his men together he went down into the camp to find out just how much damage Namdarin had done. Glancing into the wrecked tents and staring at the dead near the horses, he was astounded that one man could make so much harm in so short a time. He posted guards all around the camp, with threats of awful punishment to those he caught asleep. The men were very tired most of them had had no real sleep for two days, Blackbeard knew that their alertness would be very low no matter what sort of threats he made. Blackbeard planned to search the ashes in the morning hoping to find at least three sets of bones. He went to sit beside the fire, he was cold and hungry and tired, he wanted to sleep but did not dare, if Namdarin had not been killed by the fire he might get into his dreams again, this thought gave him just enough fear to keep him awake.

"He isn't dead." said Jayanne startling the black bearded man.

"How do you know?" he snapped.

"His horse runs faster than the wind, I have seen it."

"No horse can run fast in a forest at night."

"That one can, it may not be as manoeuvrable as a small horse but it only has to run around the big trees, the little ones it runs straight through. In the morning he will return and kill all of you that are left."

"Woman your constant babbling is making me very angry."

"What do I care for your anger?"

He jumped to his feet and flung away the blanket that had been covering her, he looked down onto her naked body which was now stained by the mud and excrement that she had been lying in since the night before. She saw the hatred in his eyes and thought that she was about to be raped again, she closed her eyes because she didn't want to see this happen to her again. He watched her slowly close her eyes then pulled back his right leg and kicked her hard in the crotch. A white bolt of pain filled her brain, for a few seconds she knew nothing but screaming agony, she gasped sucking in cold air trying to cool the raging fire of pain in her groin.

"See," he said, cruelly, "That hurts you just as much as it would me. Perhaps you will learn when to keep your mouth shut." He stamped away leaving her writhing in pain. When the pain had subsided a little, she forced herself to relax, breathing in a slow controlled rhythm she forced her brain to ignore the steady throbbing of her delicate genitals, she felt a slow dripping of blood that made her think that the kick had cut her quite badly. Trying desperately to think of anything other than the pain she shifted her thoughts to the ropes holding her to the stakes. When she pulled on the rope holding her right hand she felt a little give in it that had not been there the last time she had tried. Perhaps the sudden jerk caused by that kick had loosened the stake a bit, she thought. She began a slow series of tension and relaxation to the suspect stake hoping that the varying movement would slacken it more. She was very tired and weakened by lack of food but she kept on working at the rope until it eventually gave way, the whole stake came out of the ground. She reached across her body and untied the left hand , then untied the right hand from its rope. She put the stake back in the ground and held the ropes in her hands to rest for a while to recover what little strength she had. She did not realise just how tired she was, within moments of shutting her eyes she was asleep.

Namdarin made his way through the trees until he was once more looking down into the camp. There was no activity that he could discern, the guards that he could see near the fire seemed to be awake and perpetually scanning the tree line, a few of the tents had piles of what must be shredded bedding outside them. He decided that the best time to attack would be just as the light is coming up, before the sun comes up. Resting on the verge of the trees he catnapped, always keeping one eye open, his body was resting but his mind was not. The time passed very slowly for Namdarin waiting for the light under the trees, the men in the camp only numbered twenty two, they would be as tired as he was, they would be as hungry as he was, and they would be as frightened as he was. He waited and waited, the wind made the trees rattle, it was getting stronger and changing direction, the good weather that they had been having for the last few days was about to change, this late in the year the only possible change was to snow. Namdarin prayed that it would not come before the dawn, his arrows could go astray in a blizzard. When the clouds in the sky started to show the first signs of lightening he got to his feet and stretched the cricks out of his back and arms, he turned to see Arndrol looking at him, the horse seemed to know that battle was about to be joined, he was stepping from one foot to another the way he usually did when he was excited. Namdarin removed the horses reins, and his halter and stowed them in a small pouch behind the saddle. Now the horse knew that it was not going to be any practice this was for real. Without the bridle and bit nobody but Namdarin could ever control this horse. Arndrol started to snuffle and snort , Namdarin was forced to cuff him on the head and tell him to be quiet, he jumped into the saddle, set the sword to one side and the axe to the other, taking the bow in his left hand and setting the quiver where he could reach it easily he was ready. With the light slowly rising he walked the horse slowly around the clearing until the wind was at his back, it was cold and strong with a definite tang of rain. His slow movements were ignored by the sleepy guards, they were nodding or fast asleep all around the camp. Turning towards the camp he started shooting arrows into the guards, he knew this was going to attract everyone's attention but he had to kill some of them before he got in amongst them. Four arrows hit four of the men, two in the head who were not even aware that they had died, one in the throat, who tried to shout a warning before he drowned in his own blood and failed, and one in the chest he made some noise before he died, now the camp started to come alive. Spurring the big grey on he galloped into the camp, one of Blackbeards men ran in front of the horse and tried to grab the reins, he was astounded to find that there were no reins to grab and died under Arndrol's hooves with the surprised expression still on his face. Namdarin went around the circle of tents chopping at guy ropes as he went the confusion that this caused for the people still inside the tents was all to Namdarins advantage. He went towards the fire in the centre of the circle and cut down two more men that were trying to run away, he was shocked to see Jayanne sitting up trying to unfasten the ropes at her ankles, he galloped past her and dropped the axe well with in her reach. With two fast strokes of the superbly sharp axe she was free, she staggered to her feet , her legs were very weak because of the length of time she had been motionless, Blackbeard had finally escaped the wreckage of his tent.

"Will one of you idiots shoot that man!" he shouted, but none of the bandits had a bow to hand, two men where trying to get back into their tents when Namdarins sword took them in the back.

Jayanne had convinced her legs that they ought to be working by now and she moved to attack a group of four men who thought they would be safe in such numbers, Namdarin watched with one eye while riding down some of the guards from the other side of the camp, Jayanne stalked towards the group swinging the axe in long lazy circles first forehand then backhand then the same left handed, she stamped her bare feet in the cold mud to bring the circulation back to her legs, pain she was not interested in feeling only causing pain interested her now. The four spread out in a line with drawn swords, Jayanne stopped just out of reach of the raised swords and she waited. She knew what she was waiting for and she knew it would come soon, these brave men would decide to attack her all at once, and to be sure that their timing was exactly right they would look at each other for a signal to start, she looked into their eyes and they looked into hers, until they all looked at the man standing in the middle of the line, she took a half step forwards and swung the axe in a low sweep that took both legs out from under the leader of this small group, the axe flashed red for an instant then shiny steel, she turned with the follow through and took the next man in the belly, the sound of steel grating on his spine was clearly audible over the mumbling of the first man who had now landed on the ground. The third man swung a savage blow at her head which was blocked by the wide blade of the axe, the resulting shower of sparks hid her next swing, a short backhand stroke that hit the ma's sword arm and left the greater part of it in the mud. Then she spun round to see the frightened face of the other man, he didn't move at all until the up swinging axe hit him in the groin, it smashed through his pelvis and his abdomen and finally it lodged in his ribs. Jayanne was amazed by the noise that the axe started to make, it was stuck firmly in the man's ribcage, there was no blood coming from the wound and the axe appeared to by making small slurping noises as if it was drinking the blood that should be pumping from the gaping hole in his body. She wrenched the axe clear and turned to look at her vanquished foes. Two were dead but two still had a few minutes to live. The one with stumps for legs was one of the ones that had raped her so she hit him on the head with the flat of the axe and took a knife from his belt, she cut away his trousers and chopped off his manhood, this gory trophy she placed in his hand where he could find it if he regained consciousness. From the man with the missing sword arm she collected another similar trophy before she went in search of more prey. The next man she met was a good swordsman but his sword was not good enough to take a slashing blow from the axe, she cut through his leather armour and caved in his chest, again the axe stuck and slurped the blood from the wound, Jayanne felt a strange surge of energy as the axe fed, it seemed to be taking energy from the dying man and passing it on to her. She pulled the axe free and waved a cheery hand to Namdarin who was sitting astride Arndrol who was stamping on a lump in a tent until it stopped moving. She reached down into the hole in the chest of the man at her feet and smeared his blood all over her body, until her hair and body were the same colour, blood red. Her white smile and her green eyes were the only none red parts of her body, there was one small patch on her back that she could not reach but she decided not to worry about that, feeling almost dressed again she moved on with a bounce in her stride and a savage song on her lips. The song sounded like a rowing song, it had a steady beat that she used to time the swing of the axe, she strode about the camp looking for all the world like a she devil, chanting her song and dealing death to all that stood before her, whenever she came upon one of the men who had raped her she cut off his penis and left it either in his hand or his mouth, she smiled if they were still alive when she performed her simple surgery, she like to feel them squirm under the edge of her knife. Being a dead rapist did not save them from her mutilation.

While Jayanne was collecting Namdarin was equally busy, he was storming around the camp, chopping heads from necks and riding down the ones running away , this was a battle on a small scale, so it was over very quickly. Soon there was only one bandit left, a huge bear of a man with a thick black beard.

"You can have him," shouted the red faced she devil, "I think I have killed all the rapists."

"There are a few over there you haven't finished with yet." Answered Namdarin waving a hand to indicate the guards he had shot on his way into camp.

"Who are you two?" demanded Blackbeard, "You fight like devils." Namdarin dismounted and strode confidently towards the last of the bandits.

"I am Namdarin and she is Jayanne, I have no idea what else she has told you."

"She said you are death."

"She may be right, I appeared as death in somebody's dreams recently, I believe the dream was yours."

"She said that you had died and then returned."

"She told no lies there."

"How can I fight a man who cannot die?" asked Blackbeard passing his sword from one hand to the other nervously.

"Oh I can die, it just tends not to be permanent." He thought that Blackbeard was making far too much of his fear. And then the ex-bandit leader lunged, moving surprisingly quickly for such a large man he hoped to catch Namdarin unawares.

Namdarin merely fell back and took his stance a stride further away.

"I had thought that we were talking not fighting, you obviously wish to do both at once." He said engaging in a series of flashing attacks to all parts of Blackbeards body. The speed of Namdarins wrist was far too much for Blackbeard, his sword could not keep up with the weaving point of Namdarins wicked blade, when Namdarin disengaged and stepped back Blackbeard was panting as if he had run a mile and his sword arm had two cuts that bled a little but the worst of his wounds was to his right thigh, this one was pumping a small river of blood that ran down the knee and into the tall black boot.

"You may be very strong but your reactions are a little slow." Mocked Namdarin. Purple rage filled Blackbeards face and he charged at his tormentor with his head down and his arms spread wide, Namdarin stood his ground and waited until Blackbeard was almost on him then he plunged the point of his sword into Blackbeards massive shoulder between the collarbone and the shoulder blade, the big mans own momentum drove him onto the blade, the point ripped through a lung, a beating heart, a churning stomach and a kidney before it came out of his lower back, only when the shoulder hit the hilt did Blackbeard realise that he was dead. Blackbeard slumped face down on the ground at Namdarins feet, his legs twitching and blood bubbling merrily from the hole in his shoulder.

"Well I think that is the end of your activities." Said Namdarin to the dying bandit. Then he looked around to see what Jayanne was doing, she had finished her dismembering of the dead and dying and was walking slowly towards him. He was very glad to see her alive but a little unsure of how she would accept the time he took to rescue her. She looked a fright covered in blood that was now drying to an almost black colour, the axe dangling from her right hand and a dripping knife in her left. She walked calmly up to him and dropped the knife on the ground, she flung her arms around his neck and whispered into his ear,

"I knew you would come for me." Then the sobs started to shake her whole body, Namdarin held onto her and rocked her from side to side, saying all the silly things that are used to calm crying children. Arndrol may have been hit by a pang of jealousy because he came over and rested his nose on Namdarin's other shoulder, the tableau held for many minutes until Arndrol broke away and snorted loudly and stamped his feet. Namdarin scanned the edge of the trees and saw what had attracted the horses attention, five horsemen were coming into the clearing, they weren't coming quickly but they came with a purposeful stride and five abreast at a steady walk.

CHAPTER TEN

The five men jumped their horses over the stream and the noise of their landing attracted Jayannes attention. They had spread out into a line and came towards the pair at a steady walk, Jayanne's axe was dangling at the end of its wrist thong until she flicked her wrist and the haft jumped up into the palm of her right hand, the slap of wood on skin made Namdarin start from his reverie as Jayanne moved away from him to give herself some space in which to swing. The five slowed their horses to a very slow walk and then stopped only feet away, Jayanne glanced at Namdarin confused by his lack of response to this new threat. One of the men looked down at Jayanne with large blue eyes and smiled a knowing smile that generally melted the hearts of all the ladies, Jayanne felt a momentary weakening of her intention to kill him, then she shook her head and reminded herself of the last few days.

"My." He said in a smooth and soft voice, "I'll wager that you are a real beauty if you ever have a bath." He moved his weight forwards in the saddle so as to dismount.

"Be careful Mander," Namdarin said, "if you touch her she will probably kill you. She has no love for men." Mander settled back into his saddle.

"My lord Namdarin can you not protect me from this savage woman?"

"You can protect yourself by telling us what to are doing in the camp of these bandits."

"Namdarin my friend," Jangor responded, "we have come on a commission from a local baron, we have come to bring a gift to the baron."

"What gift?" demanded Namdarin, his hand on the hilt of his sword.

"The baron offered us a thousand silver pieces for the head of Blackbeard." He laughed, "It appears that the man in question has no more need for it, you and your lady friend are quite welcome to share in the reward." Namdarin smiled and nodded.

"How kind of you to offer us a share when we have done all the work."

"I think that is a very kind offer don't you?" said Jangor looking at his fellows, who grinned.

"Well," said Namdarin with his fists planted firmly on his hips. "You can at least help with the tidying up. Come on let's see what we can salvage from their belongings." The men dismounted and began to search the bodies of the dead, they were more that a little disturbed by the mutilation of some of the corpses.

"Who butchered these men?" asked Jangor.

"She did." said Namdarin waving an arm in the direction of Jayanne, who still had not moved. "They raped her and she didn't like that." Jayanne was watching the five new arrivals very intently, she was unsure of their intentions, she especially did not trust the one called Mander.

"Namdarin," she said , "Who are these people?"

"They are friends I met on the road soon after I started my quest."

"Can they be trusted?"

"Yes, they are honourable men, they are ex soldiers and now mercenaries. Did you kill that minstrel Poredal?"

"No I didn't see him." She replied thoughtfully, "I didn't see him here at all, not even once."

"Damn. He must have gone somewhere else, we owe him for the nasty trick he played on us." By now all the dead had been moved down wind and piled up in a heap, Jangor and his friends returned to the fire where Jayanne and Namdarin were talking.

"Madam?" asked Jangor almost diffidently, "May I borrow your axe to remove the head from this corpse?"

"No you may not." She snapped. Her tone caused Jangor's eyebrows to rise, she seemed to very attached to the axe, she looked away from his slightly shocked face, and brought the axe down in a smooth one handed stroke right onto the nape of Blackbeard's neck. The axe made a solid thunk as the head rolled slowly away from the body, she pulled the axe from the turf and left behind a three inch deep scar in the grass.

"You are stronger than you look." Jangor nodding appreciatively.

"The axe is sharper than you can imagine." She replied, "It is mine now and no one else may use it." Her stubborn stare was almost a direct challenge to Jangor a challenge that said "I dare you to try and take it away from me."

"Jayanne," said Namdarin, "I have told you that these are

friends, now please be less aggressive. I have no wish to see your or their blood spilt." She glanced at Namdarin with cold green eyes, and nodded.

"If Namdarin says that you are friends then your are friends, I should not be so un-trusting but I have had a bad time with men recently." She said to Jangor, who chose to look on this as an apology, it was obviously as near as he was going to get to one anyway.

"Why don't you go and get cleaned up?" asked Namdarin, "And we will see if we can find you some suitable clothes to wear." She turned and walked to the stream the blood had now dried hard and black and itchy. It took her quite a while to scrape off all the hardened gore, when she can from the cold stream he skin was almost blue and she was shivering very hard. She walked into Namdarin's arms and he wrapped her white bearskin around her.

"Blackbeard had decided to keep this for himself."

"I am glad it is still here." she said rubbing herself all over with the soft white fur.

"We have found some clothes for you to choose from, they are over there by the fire." He took her by the hand and led her towards the fire, where the others were sitting. Mander looked up and said, "I was right you are beautiful." His huge smile made her nervous but she responded with a quick grin. While she picked through the pile of clothing the men talked about the things they had been doing since they last met.

The mercenaries had gone south down the red river then east picking up the occasional job, escorting caravans, guarding rich men when they were travelling, guarding gold shipments and important peoples wives, but where ever they were and what ever they were doing the Zandaar priests always seem to find them and cause trouble for them. They were chased from job to job across the countryside, the priests never laid any specific charges, but always the mercenaries lost their current employment. Their last job before their current one had been guarding a lords horses, the herd was several hundred strong. The lords prize mare was in foal and died giving birth to a stillborn foal. A local Zandaar started ranting about witchcraft and curses, and pointed to the only strangers around. Jangor and his fellows left the area without being paid and at a gallop, stakes had been set up and bonfires laid.

"That is not my idea of a good barbecue." Said Jangor with a huge grin. "So we left in a great hurry. We went north for ten days until we came to a great manor house three days south of here, the lord of this manor said that he was having a little difficulty with a group of bandits led by a large black bearded man, he offered us a thousand silver pieces for the beard so long as the head was still attached, you have saved us a great deal of trouble. Why were you after them?"

"They attacked us probably with the intention of separating us from our wealth and when we beat off their first attempt they came after us again, the second time they captured Jayanne and tried to kill me. I was forced to go and rescue her. You arrived just too late to help."

"Have you solved your little problem yet?" asked Jangor, uncertain as to how much Jayanne knew.

"I still haven't found Granger, though I now know where he lives, I have killed a few Zandaars and learned to use some of their tricks against them, I am certain that the old gods are protecting me, and most probably using me for their own purpose. I know where to go to cut off the Zandaars head, but other than that I am no nearer a solution."

"Which way will you be going when you leave here?"

"I think we will go with you at least until we find the lord who hired you, Blackbeard has been a problem around here too long for him to suddenly act to remove him, I think that the lord's intention was to remove you, my friends. According to the people that live hereabouts Blackbeards gang have been robbing travellers for years."

"That is true, at least five years." said Jayanne. Jangor frowned, it seemed to him that his reward was going to be difficult to collect.

"He is not going to want to pay us is he?" asked Stergin.

"No I don't think he is, but I feel that we should be firm in our dealings with him and insist that he keeps his word." Said Jangor taking his dagger from his belt and polishing it on his thigh. Mander laughed, and Kern grinned saying,

"I looks like things are back to normal again."

"Jayanne," asked Jangor, "where did you meet Namdarin."

"I was having a little problem with the previous owner of this hide and Namdarin helped him to see things my way." Her green eyes sparkled with the enormity of the understatement.

"The owner in question," said Namdarin, "did not like being woken from his hibernation by a woman armed only with a knife, he thought that she should have waited until he was dead before trying to take his fur." Namdarin completely failed to keep his face straight and fell about laughing.

"You can't mean that the bear was still wearing his skin and she tried to kill it with a knife." Said Jangor, to which the only reply from the two gigglers where rapid nods and more laughter. Jangor shook his head saying, "You two are utterly insane."

"Oh, but what a sight it was," said Namdarin, "I first saw her standing with her back to a rock wall fending off this huge bear with only a small knife, she looked very impressive."

"I am sure she did." Said Mander with a look of admiration. Jayanne was warm and dry by now so she got dressed in a motley assortment of mismatched clothes taken from the tents of the bandits. The six men watched her getting dressed, their eyes intent and their thoughts lewd. When she was dressed she went to the pile of weapons that the mercenaries had stripped from the dead and selected a broad belt and four good knives to hang from it, then she went back to the pile of clothing and searched for a soft leather belt or possible some trousers. None of the belts she found were soft enough for her liking so she cut a good pair of trousers into pieces. The five mercenaries looked on in confusion, but Namdarin knew what she was doing. In a matter of a few minutes she had cut the strap to the right length and formed the pocket to her satisfaction, she walked over to the stream bed and selected a few small round stones, after a few practise swings she hurled the stones and blinding speed into the stream, striking splinters from the rocks she was using as targets. When she was sure of the aim and power of her new sling she wrapped it around her head and tied the long unruly red hair back with it, then filled a pocket with more of the stones that she had been using.

"When do we start moving?" She asked walking back to the group of men sitting around the fire, "Or are you going to sit around like oldsters for ever?"

"As soon as we have loaded our newly acquired horses with our recently obtained trade goods we can leave." Said Jangor. It took them quite a time to saddle and load all the bandits horses, most of the morning was gone before they were ready to leave.

"Well Namdarin," said Jangor, "I think we ought to stay together for a while, because every time we meet I end up with an excess of horses and some quantity of metal to trade."

"We end up with extra horses and metal." Answered Namdarin with emphasis on the first word.

"Of course I meant we. We have so much here that we may be able to buy some of that iridescent silver that the Zandaars prize so much."

"They will be willing to pay even more for it now," Namdarin spoke softly, "we have cut off their main supply. But no matter how much they offer I will not sell them any."

"Why not?" asked Stergin.

"Because they make awful weapons out of that silver, they make lightning bolts and flames that can be held in the hand and thrown at their enemies. The silver lightning bolts change into real lightning bolts when thrown, this I have seen, and I presume the flames work the same way."

"Kern," Shouted Jangor, "Take the point as usual, the rest of us will follow."

"Which way?" asked the quiet scout.

"South to the manor." Kern wheeled his horse about and trotted out of the clearing heading towards the sun, the rest mounted and with the bandits horses all tied together they set off after Kern. Kern quickly found a track heading through the forest in the direction they wanted to go, it was a well used path, quite broad, wide enough for two horses to walk side by side, and very level, as if it had been in use for many years. All through the morning the wind had been getting stronger and stronger, now it was shaking the trees, and making some of them lose branches, one enormous branch fell alongside the line of empty horses and caused them to panic, they all tried to run in different directions and ended up tangled in the trees. Before they had the horses freed from the trees the sun had been covered by huge black clouds, and a light snow had started to fall, not much of the snow made it down through the trees, but they knew that once they left the protection of the trees it was going to hinder their movements. When evening came they had reached the edge of the forest, but decided to camp under the last of the trees rather than go on any further through the snow , which was a foot deep beyond the trees. They set up their tents in a small clearing, once the fire was lit water was no problem, simple throwing snow into a bucket near the fire provided enough for all the people and the horses. Four tents were erected around the central fire, and after a meal they all went to bed. Despite hopeful glances from Mander, Jayanne went into a tent with Namdarin who was more than glad of the company, but had nothing on his mind but sleep, it had been three days since either of them had slept properly. They wriggled into their bed rolls and went to sleep so fast that neither of them remembered anything of the night . The next thing that they knew it was morning and Jangor was shouting as was his wont, "Out of your pits you lazy blackguards. The sun is up and you are not. Move it, move it ,move it. " Moans and grumbles came from the other tents, Stergin was complaining about Kerns snoring keeping him awake all night and Mander was moaning that Andel was nowhere near as warm as a woman to cuddle up to. Namdarin and Jayanne listened to the early morning routine that their friends always seem to go through , there was a lot of noise but nobody took any of it seriously. When Namdarin and Jayanne left their tent Stergin and Andel were already making breakfast, and Kern and Mander were stripping down tents, Jangor was checking over the riding horses hooves. Namdarin dismantled and packed away their tent while Jayanne went to help with the breakfast.

"Namdarin," called Jangor, "You will have to check your own horse I am afraid, he just wont let me near him."

"He is always like that, I be there in a minute." He finished fastening the tent to a pack horse and went over to where Jangor was standing beside Arndrol. Namdarin bent down beside the horses shoulder and tapped him gently on the leg, Arndrol lifted the leg up and presented the hoof for inspection. In only a minute Namdarin had checked all four hooves and found no problems.

"What could be easier than that?" he asked Jangor.

"The brute kept trying to stamp on my feet." Answered the soldier. The pair laughed together as they went to fire to have their breakfast.

Once they left the forest they discovered that an extra six inches of snow had fallen in the night, the horses were now tramping through a foot and a half of cold snow, luckily the wind had dropped and the people were considerably warmer than they had expected to be.

"At least there is one good thing about this weather," said Jangor, to no one in particular, "Blackbeard's head wont start to smell before we get to the lords mansion house." The morning passed very quickly with constant changes of pace, they would trot for a while then walk, they could not afford to push the horses too hard in the cold weather, if a horse got sweaty in this weather and then it got cold it would almost certainly catch a chill, and that would make it completely useless. Arndrol seemed to like the snow, he kept kicking huge clods of it at the other riders.

"Namdarin, can you not control that big stupid horse?" said Andel after a particularly large lump of snow fell down the back of his neck, "The damn thing is almost keeping me awake." The others laughed because they knew that he was lying, it took more than a little bit of snow to keep him awake.

"I have seen you sleep standing up in a blizzard," Said Mander, "so stop moaning."

"I remember that blizzard," said Andel, "I was standing in that blizzard because you had sneaked off into the scullery with one of the serving girls, perhaps I should tell one of your wives about that."

"The girl was ill and needed some care and attention."

"And I am sure she got it, and so did you."

Mander kicked his horse and moved out of earshot.

"How many wives does he have?" asked Jayanne.

"I think its four." Said Jangor.

"How does he manage that?"

"He moves around a lot, since we started travelling he has probably picked another one or two, but we don't bother counting, neither does he."

"How can he love all these women?" she asked.

"One at a time obviously."

"What will happen when one finds out about the others?"

"He will die." Laughed Jangor, "But he will die happy, and so will most of his wives."

"It is a very strange life that you lead."

"I cannot argue with that." The two of them lapsed into silence, each being content with their own thoughts at this point.

The rest of the day past without incident and they set up camp beside a frozen stream for the night as travelling in the dark of night could be very dangerous in these wintry conditions. Namdarin and Jayanne had some time for conversation before sleep over came them, they talked together in a small tent illuminated by a single candle.

"How can one man keep so many wives happy?" she asked.

"Some women are easily pleased by a man who is only present some of the time, it means they can still have the title of married women and lead a life of their own choosing, Mander probably picks his wives careful from those who feel that being married to any one man is too restricting."

"So when ever Mander decides to arrive upon the scene, his wife has to suspend her choice of life until he goes away again?"

"Possibly, or perhaps if it is inconvenient for her to do that at the time she just sends him away, quoting undeniable infidelity, that way she can be married and have absolutely no ties. I would think that the first time a woman sends him away is the last time she sees him."

"That is a very strange way to live."

"Not really, Mander has the advantage of never being truly lonely, but never being truly tied into a marriage. The woman in question has the advantage of being married if suits her, and divorced as soon as she feels like it. You must remember the awful pressure that is applied to unmarried women. They must settle down and choose one man, most likely a man from their own village, none of whom they find satisfactory, a quick marriage to a man like Mander removes all this pressure, they can then wait until a man that they like appears in the area. Mander has the advantage of almost always having a roof over his head and a warm woman to make the nights pass pleasurably."

"How do you mean pleasurably?"

"You have been married you must remember the pleasure of the matrimonial bed."

"No. I remember only pain."

His look of complete amazement shook her, she looked into his eyes and saw pity so intense that she had to look away as her face reddened with her ignorance. It took Namdarin some minutes to recover from the shock and realise that she had been so badly treated in her innocence, by the monster that her parents had chosen. Unbidden to his mind came the memory of his wedding night, the shy retreat to the nuptial bed chamber of the newly married couple, the quiet cheer and toasting of the guests they left behind in the main hall of the house. His mind brought him vivid pictures of the almost ceremonial disrobing, he seemed to be forever waiting for her to catch up, she had so many more clothes than he did the, long white dress and what seemed like a hundred petticoats underneath. He was down to his under garments in a matter of a few seconds and then he stood to watch the gradual revelation of the body of his bride, the excitement brought an intense swelling to his manhood and a shortness to his breathing, a tension that could not be denied, an urge older than life itself. Jayanne had been denied this all her life, she saw the distracted look in Namdarins face and the tiny smile induced by the memories. He remembered the force of the feelings that coursed in his veins as she removed the final veil and he removed his breeches. They stood together in their nakedness, they stared at each others bodies, he saw the boyish hardness of the muscles of her abdomen and the beginnings of the womanly roundness of her hips, he looked at the soft delicate pubic mound, with its dusting of soft golden hair, he saw the upturned hardness of her young breasts, the nipples standing firmly to attention under his intense gaze. Althone blushed red when she saw the eagerness of his passion causing his penis to twitch, his young body had almost no hair only a soft down on his chest and a small tuft about his loins , the constant pulse of his manhood as it jumped to the rapid pounding of his heart held her eyes, the fascination was almost unbreakable. He stepped towards her and they kissed, the temperature around them seemed to rise with their twinned passions. They spent the night in glorious exploration and discovery.

Tears came to Namdarin's eyes as he thought thus of his wife, Jayanne saw the water running down his face and held him in a tight and comforting embrace, his arms enfolded her in a warm embrace, he wanted more than comfort and she felt his need but could not respond to it, she released him and tried to push him away for a moment he did not feel the rejection, then with a deep and meaningful sign he relented and turned away from her, the tears came in floods. She thought of the pain that had been evident on his face and the causes for it. She did not understand in any way what had brought on his sudden melancholy. She was more used to him being a strong and stable figure in the turmoil about them, to see him break down and cry shook her confidence, but it also enhanced his humanity, he now showed himself to be a man like any other with fears and pains, with a past that could still reach into the present and effect him terribly. She put her arm around his shoulder and pressed herself against his quivering back, she held him so until the shaking subsided and he fell asleep.

"In some ways you are like a small boy that occasionally needs a shoulder to cry on." She whispered, he made no response. She soon fell into a deep sleep and deeper dreams, she dreamt of being rescued from a wicked fate by a tall man with a kind face sitting on a tall grey horse. The dream ended in a slow ride on the grey horse as together the set off into a new life.

The next morning came with a raw wind and blowing snow that cut under the flaps of the tents and made them all very uncomfortable, it was hard for any of them to leave the warmth of their beds, Namdarin and Jayanne held each other tightly without speaking until final a shout came from Jangor, "If we stay here we will waste a whole day, so everybody out." Dressing quickly whilst still in their beds they finally made it out of the tents and into the raging blizzard.

"We cannot make the horses stay here in the open." Said Kern. "They will freeze to death if they don't start moving soon." He went around the horses shaking the snow from their blankets and checking their legs for any signs of lameness.

Today Arndrol decided to co-operate with the gentle scout and allowed his legs and hooves to be examined, the knowing touch of the big man calmed the horse and made the job of packing and loading very much easier. The small party mounted and set off at a slow walk towards the manor house that belonged to Melandius, the man who offered a thousand pieces of silver for Blackbeards head.

After a morning trudging slowly through a raging blizzard they stumbled almost blindly into a large group of evergreen conifers, once inside the outer layer of trees the wind lessened and the snow disappeared completely, the temperature began to rise and a quietness descended like thick tar over the group, the horses stumbled as if asleep on their feet, the people on their back's began to nod as if they had not slept in days.

"I am falling asleep." Mumbled Kern, his normal alertness eroded away to nothing. Jangor stirred suddenly at this as if noticing for the first time that he was in danger of falling off his horse. He shook his head hard from side to side, trying desperately to shake off the lassitude that was gradually overcoming him. He took in a deep breath and shouted,

"Wake up everyone, something is trying to put us to sleep." He reached over and cuffed Andel on the back, then reached to the other side and struck Mander none too gently. Mander slid from his saddle and landed on the hard ground with a solid thump, and a snore. Namdarin saw a few moss covered skeletons half buried in the ground, it appeared to him that both animals and people just lay down and went to sleep until they died. His slowing brain came to the conclusion that something nearby was killing any living thing that came too close, having arrived at this momentous insight he decided, "Who cares."

As his head fell forwards against his chest he rallied for a moment, slowly he pulled a knife from his belt and very deliberately cut his left forearm, a short and shallow cut that bled freely and hurt intensely, the white light of pain exploded in his brain and he was suddenly very much awake. With the rush of sensation came an impression of a sinking feeling that emanated from the only tree that was not a conifer, the immense weeping willow looked like it was crying as its branches shuddered in a non-existent breeze, it moaned like a sobbing child, Namdarin's eyes started to close. Another slash with the knife, and he woke again, he reached over to Jayanne who was rocking in her saddle and slapped her hard across the face, she muttered but came no nearer to her senses, he struck her again and again, until her face reddened by the stinging of his bare hand she opened her eyes and slapped him back, his head jarred to the right by her strong right arm, he shook it and said, "Pain can keep us awake, but that willow must be destroyed now, or we will all die." Jayanne's horse fell asleep on its feet and collapsed slowly to the ground she rolled free before it hit taking her axe from the saddle horn, she staggered to her feet and Namdarin fell from his saddle and joined her as they walked together towards the tree, they kept on slapping each other until they were underneath the writhing branches, Jayannes face was red and sore, Namdarin was bleeding from nose and mouth, Jayanne seemed to have difficulty hitting his cheek, but the pain that they shared was enough to keep them awake. Once they were inside the circle of waving branches the influence of the tree was such that a mere slap on the face could not keep them awake, Namdarin began to use his knife again first on his forearm then on Jayannes left thigh. The five strides to the trunk of the tree left them each with five new cuts, the pain brought a sudden brightness to the mind that vanished like a stone down a deep dark well. Jayanne braced her legs and swung the axe high away from the tree, and at the instant that Namdarin's knife bit into her leg again she struck, a blinding light of rage and pain filled her brain as the axe swung down to its collision with the tree, it bit deep through the bark and into the white wood underneath, the tree shook as if in a gale, the end of the branches lashed about them like a hundred whips, the small cuts that they caused only strengthened the pair as Jayanne wrenched the axe clear and struck again, this was no stroke intended to cut a tree down she was striking for its heart. The whistling of the axe was completely drowned by the noise of the branches rattling like dry twigs. The blade struck in the same place as the first stroke, through the white wood and deep into the heartwood of the trunk it cut, the blade almost disappeared inside the tree, a strong smell of rich green sap came from the gash, and a sharp smelling sticky goo oozed out. The ground beneath their feet bucked and trembled like a ship in a storm, they could see the shallow roots of the tree curling up in a effort to reach them. Jayanne felt a rush of energy that was coming from the axe, holding the haft in one hand she reached to Namdarin with the other, as their hands touched a sparkle of electricity jumped between them, the somnolent effect of the tree disappeared in the instant that they touched, holding hands firmly they rode out the storm as the tree slowly died, its struggles getting weaker and weaker until it merely twitched, when Jayanne could no longer feel the energy flow from the axe she released Namdarin's hand and pulled the axe from the tree. Arm in arm they staggered out from underneath the slowly swaying branches and collapsed in an exhausted heap only a few feet from the trees reach. Jayanne recovered first, she wrapped a scarf around the leg to stem the bleeding and went to find out how the others had fared, she found the mercenaries and all the horses fast asleep on the ground where they had fallen. Standing as still as she could she watched each in turn, their chests were all rising and falling with their breathing so she no longer feared that any were dead. She walked over to Jangor, and gently prodded him in the ribs, he moaned a little but did not awaken, she kicked him and he grunted, so she kicked him harder, he rolled away from her foot and staggered to his feet, he swayed and rocked like a drunkard.

"What's going on?" He asked, his speech slurred nearly beyond recognition.

"Namdarin and I need help now, the others are only asleep so don't worry about them, we need bandages quickly before we bleed to death." Her calm clear voice and the slowly spreading red stain on her leg eventually reached into his befuddled brain, he shook his head savagely from side to side in an effort to clear the residue of the tree's influence. Once his eyes had cleared of their confusion and he had gone to one of the snoring horses, she returned to Namdarin's prostrate form and attempted to stop the blood running down his arm. She clamped her hands hard around the muscles of his upper arm and the flow of blood to the arm stopped so the bleeding stopped, but if she released the arm it would start again, so she waited until Jangor arrived to help. When the old mercenary had shaken off the lethargy caused by the tree he moved very quickly indeed, in only moments he came to her side and was cleaning the wounds on Namdarin's arm and binding them tightly with a broad clean bandage from one of the horses packs, he kept glancing from the wounds to the bloody blade of the knife that was lying on the ground where Namdarin had dropped it.

"Did he cut himself?" he asked sounding more than a little confused.

"Yes, and me as well."

"Why?"

"It was the only way to stay awake. The pain cancelled out the trees effects, it just didn't work for very long, that is why there are so many cuts."

"I see." He nodded. "That is the best I can do, you release his arm and lets see if it still bleeds." She let go of his arm and watched for a minute but the bandages showed no signs of any major bleeding.

"You are next." said Jangor removing the scarf from around her leg, the scarf looked like it had been washed in a red stream, it dripped bright red droplets everywhere. He made her sit down and showed her where the pressure point was in her groin that would stop the bleeding, she leant on this point with both hands while Jangor cut away the leg of her trousers.

"Ye gods." he exclaimed, looking an six parallel gaping wounds the red flesh pulsing in time to her restricted heartbeat. He shook his head saying, "I am going to need help with this, can you hold on for a minute while I rouse the others." She nodded. He jumped to his feet and ran over to his sleeping friends. He slapped Kern hard about the face, until he saw the eyes open, "Get your sewing gear and hurry." He let go of the front of Kern's jacket and Kern fell to the ground only to roll to his feet and wobble over to the pack horses, next Jangor went Mander and Stergin and Andel, each received the same rough treatment that brought them to their senses in the shortest possible time. Andel was given the task of fire making and food preparation, Stergin was sent to find some liquor or some other pain relieving substance, and Mander went with Jangor to prepare Jayanne for the ordeal that was about to begin. Andel had a small fire blazing when Kern brought his needles to be cleansed in the red fire, once they were red hot he plunged them into cold water and they sizzled merrily, the thread he was going to use was a fine spun cotton which he put into pot of water that was placed over the fire to boil. When he went to where Jayanne was lying on the ground Stergin had already poured half a flask of Wandras down her throat and she was quite drunk, Stergin passed her a rolled up glove saying, "Bite on this it will help." He placed it between her teeth and held her head firmly. Mander held her leg above the cuts and pressed on the pressure point at the same time, Jangor held her knee so that she could not move. Kern calmly examined the cuts and decided to start with the one highest up her thigh, he was glad that all the cuts were straight and clean, though fairly deep in places. He started the gory task of sewing her leg together, the pain of the needle going in and out of the flesh was nothing compared to the pain caused by the cotton rubbing through the trembling edges of the openings, long before he had finished the first and longest of the cuts she passed into total unconsciousness. Half an hour later when Kern was just starting the last of the gashes Namdarin woke up. He staggered to his feet and said, "What is happening?"

"We are patching up the mess you made of your friend, I hope I never get to be that good a friend of yours." Said Stergin without looking up from the peaceful face that he held on his lap.

"I had no idea I cut her that deeply," Namdarin replied, his voice shaking with emotion, "I was not even sure that I could stay awake."

"You certainly ensured that she did, she even made sure that you were alright before looking to her own wounds."

"Is she going to be able to walk?" Asked Namdarin's small voice.

"She should have no problems," said Kern, "she will be scarred and will have to rest here for a few days, but she will be able to do everything that she used to, in a while." Namdarin sat down nursing his own injuries and feeling very ashamed that he had hurt her so, he hoped that she would be able to forgive him, he knew that her understanding was all important to him now. When Kern had finished stitching up the last of the cuts he examined them all closely,

"I think that should be enough, Mander release that artery and lets see if we have any leaks." With a swift muttered prayer Mander let go of her leg, together they watched the pink colour slowly replace the drained pallor of her skin, one of the cuts wept a little blood but that soon stopped on its own. Kern reached down and put his hand inside her boot, "Her foot is warming up nicely, she will be fine." He turned towards Namdarin ,"You are next." Jangor removed the bandage that he had put on Namdarins arm to let Kern have a good look.

"Those are not so deep but they will heal quicker if they are stitched."

Namdarin nodded he knew that he could not afford to be disabled for a long period, though he did not see that the wounds were bad enough to warrant sewing, "Could it be that Kern is using it as an excuse to inflict pain by way of payment for the damage he did to Jayanne," thought Namdarin while staring into the steady eyes of the taciturn scout. "No, such was an unworthy thought. If a man like Kern wanted to hurt him for Jayannes injuries he would have struck him or refused to help him. Kern saw the necessity of Namdarins actions even if he did not like the results." Namdarin sat as still as he could with Mander and Jangor holding his arm while Kern went back to his work.

"Thank you." Said Namdarin when the needlework was done, "You are a most surprising and useful person to have as a friend." The sweat of the pain was pouring down Namdarins face, he turned to Jayanne who was still sleeping on the ground her head still in Stergins lap, she was twitching and fidgeting almost as if looking for something.

"If she moves too much she will break whose stitches and I will have to start all over again." Said Kern.

"I know what she wants." said Namdarin walking over to the tree where she had dropped her axe, he stooped deeply under the branches, still not trusting them even though they had been quiescent for well over an hour, lifting the axe by its leather wrist thong he took it to her and placed the haft against the palm of her right hand, the fingers clenched hard about the wood until the knuckles whitened and then they relaxed, her breathing slowed and she rested much more peacefully.

"They have become almost as one." Said Namdarin. Camp was set up around the sleeping woman, the horses seemed to wake up as soon as they were touched, Arndrol came crashing to his feet the very instant Namdarin laid his hand on the long grey neck, the horse jumped around as if looking for foes, seeing none he seemed confused then he stood stock still with only the muscles of one shoulder twitching with agitation and he looked about to see they other mounts still sleeping where they had fallen. Arndrol turned his big brown eyes on to Namdarin and then lowered his head almost to the ground, looking up into the man's calm blue eyes like a chastened puppy.

"Its all right, my friend." Namdarin said calmly. "It's not your fault, you had no defence against the tree." This did not satisfy the horse, he did not like being considered the same as all the other horses. His head still hung down as if he had disgraced himself.

"Even some of the people fell asleep, so there is nothing to be ashamed of, now cheer up and stop being so silly." said Namdarin slapping the horse on the neck and pulling his ears. It may have been merely the tone of his voice or the smile on his face but the horse was cheered by his friends words, and stood in a more normal posture, not quite with his usual proud curve to the neck but certainly less depressed.

"I hope that Jayanne is going to be as easy to mollify." said

Jangor.

"That is a hope beyond hope I think." Answered Namdarin. The camp had only two difficulties, the first was putting up a tent around Jayanne without waking her, the second was the fact that the nearest water was about half an hours ride away. The first was overcome with teamwork, the second was deemed to be just one of those things that had to be lived with, Jayanne could not be moved today so water would have to be brought to the camp. Andel was given all the canteens and sent to get it.

"If you feel the slightest bit drowsy turn round and come straight back, there could be more of these dreadful trees." Warned Jangor as he left.

"How will he tell?" Asked Mander, "He is always drowsy."

In the depth of the trees darkness came early and it almost beat Andel into the camp, his horse walked into camp loaded down with the water he had brought, Andel himself seemed asleep in the saddle, his head forwards and his chin jogging gently against his chest with every step the horse took. Mander intercepted the horse and pulled the reins from Andels limp hands, then he tried to push his friend from the saddle, Andel suddenly looked up and shouted, "Ha. Fooled you. You thought I was asleep. Not this time my friend, not this time."

"I knew that you had not been caught by a tree because the horse was still awake." Said Mander trying to recover some face .Andel just giggled and set about cooking a meal for them all. By the time they had eaten the forest was completely dark, the deep blackness that only trees seem to accomplish.

"I don't think we need to worry about guards for tonight," said Jangor, "this wood must be well known as a place to stay away from." The men all nodded and went to their respective tents, except Namdarin, he sat by the fire for a while longer, his thoughts turned to the tree. What had it been doing here? Perhaps some one had set it here to guard something. What if somebody else knew what it had been guarding? They could be waiting outside its influence for it to die. If this was true then they, whoever they were, would be coming here very soon.

Namdarin decided that somebody ought to stand watch, but he could not justify waking up everybody else on such a feeble string of what if's. He must stand guard himself, all night if necessary, the pain from his arm would restrict his sleeping anyway so he would not be loosing much. He went to the tent that he and Jayanne usually shared, opening the flap he held his breath and listened, her breathing was slow and steady, he could imagine a beautiful smile on her lips as she slept like an innocent child. Sitting down in the mouth of the tent he faced towards the fire, it gave him no real warmth from this distance but it gave enough light to show most of the area nearby, though the trees did restrict the horizon very quickly, his only blind spot was directly behind him, the sound of the wind in the trees would cover the noise of anybody approaching that way, but there was no way that Namdarin could cover all the forest on his own so a small blackspot would have to be acceptable.

CHAPTER ELEVEN

Namdarin was sitting in the dark mouth of his tent looking across the slowly sinking fire, the sound of the wind in the tree tops was whispering indecipherable words in his ears, he was thinking about his friends sleeping in their respective tents. He let his mind start its casual drifting, he was intent on finding their dreams, he considered this invasion of their privacy a necessity if he was going to improve his skills, Jayanne was nearest to him the dark relaxation of her slumbering mind was like a quiet cave into which one could retreat to hide from the world, leaving this he went to look for the others. Mander was dreaming of a woman who had no face, Kern was hiding in the trees hunting for some undefined game, Andel was drifting aimlessly through a green woodland, Stergin was watching the birds flying free in the sky, Jangor was trapped in a dark dungeon, he was fastened to a rack the pain in his arms and back was howling in his head, he was waiting for the tormentor to come and turn the handle one more time, Namdarin decided that intervention was needed, reaching carefully into the dream he released the ratchet that held the cogs of the rack, Jangor felt the sudden reduction of the tension and said a quick thank you to the gods, he recovered his sword from under the rack and plunged it into the surprised tormentor, who was an enormous man with a hard and savage face. Namdarin walked away from this dream knowing that Jangor could deal with all the problems that would come up. Namdarin was almost surprised by the ease with which he had penetrated his friends sleeping minds, he wondered if it was possible to reach a waking mind, slowly he expanded the range of his search pushing outwards and feeling for any intelligent contact at all. He felt the touch of something large and slow, it felt like an amorphous mass but it did contain small centres of brightness. One of the centres recognised him as he passed, the brightness approached and spoke to him in a series of complex gestures and strange sounds, suddenly in dawned upon him that this was a herd of horses, the part that recognised him was Arndrol, he had not realised that horses lived in such intimate contact with each other all the time, they seemed, on this plane at least, to be parts of a much larger whole, the centres that Namdarin observed around him exactly matched the number of horses in their camp but further off, though still within reach of the herd were other spots of brightness, these must the horses belonging to other people, they were within the reach of Arndrols mind but well out of Namdarins sight, Namdarin rushed back into himself totally amazed by what he had learned about the herd nature of horses, he thought about cattle and flocks of birds and wondered if they had the same sort of contact with each other. This contact between separate groups of horses could be of use if only some method of communication could be found. Putting this idea to one side he relaxed his mind and reached out again, hoping to find a mind further away that he could feel. Beyond the horses and deep into the trees he detected a swirling blackness, that might be a mind, it was far too active to be invaded, he could barely keep up with the switches and changes of direction, it appeared to jump from one thought to another in an instant, though all the thoughts were of a uniform darkness, this mind felt like an awful sewer, full of the sludge and slime of existence. Namdarin felt the necrotic nastiness rubbing off onto himself, he felt depressed and distracted, he broke the tentative contact that had existed between himself and the stranger. He could not come to a decision about the stranger, was he human or not? Namdarin could not be at all sure. Getting quietly to his feet he went to the horses and removed his bow and quiver, moving slowly he returned to the darkness of the tent. Sitting cross legged in the tent , with the bow across his knees, an arrow set to the string, he felt a little better, or at least a little better prepared. Clearing his mind he reached out for the swirling darkness of the stranger, instantly he felt the vertigo of the turning and shifting morass of the strangers thoughts, he was closer than before and getting nearer all the time. Wrenching his mind away he heard the horses shifting and stamping as if in fear of some approaching danger, scanning the trees Namdarin searched for any sign or glimpse of the stranger, the flickering light from the sinking fire made all the shadows unsteady, he kept jumping from one twitching shadow to another, until he saw a region of darkness that moved smoothly and with purpose, it moved towards the camp. Namdarin could make out no real details about the shape, it was man sized and moved like a man, its outline was distorted by a long dark cloak that reached down to the ground, its footsteps seemed unsteady and uncertain, almost jerky. The shape exuded a feeling of intense fear, it was terrified of the place it had put itself in but something was driving it on. For many minutes the shape flitted in and out of the trees around the fire, it was trying to make sure that everyone in the camp was asleep. Finally it made its move towards the fire, Namdarin let it get far enough away from the trees so that it could not dive into cover and then he stood up, aimed and pulled the bow shouting, "Do not move whoever you are."

For an instant the shape froze like a stone statue then it collapsed into a black heap on the ground and remained there muttering softly. Jangor and Stergin were the first to get clear of their tents they came out at the run with swords ready for battle. Seeing Namdarins arrow pointing at the black hump on the ground they approached it carefully, Jangor flicked back the man's hood with the point of his sword, and Stergin placed cold steel against the wrinkled neck underneath.

"Stand up very slowly." said Jangor, his voice cold, his arms and legs were starting to tremble with the cold , he had not bothered to dress and his underclothes were no where near warm enough for the cold of the night in the middle of this harsh winter. The man tottered to his feet, his back was hunched and his face a prune of enormous age.

"I mean you no harm." The crackly voice struggled out over the noise of the fire.

"What do you want creeping into a camp after dark? That is a particularly dangerous activity." Asked Jangor in a more gentle tone.

"I felt the tree die and wanted to find out how it happened."

"Who are you?" asked Namdarin.

"My name is Crandir, I am a woodcutter who lived many miles away from here but I heard a tale of great riches hidden in this forest, I did not have the courage to come and investigate myself but my sons did, all three of them came here and did not return. Finally I had to come to find out what had happened to them. As I walked into the forest I felt a strange force that was trying to put me to sleep. I moved away from the effect and waited outside its influence, hoping that it would go away. After a few months waiting some Zandaars arrived and asked me what I was doing they said that the influence I had felt was a tree set to guard a treasure that was theirs. Over the last thirty years of my waiting they have appeared four or five times a year to check on the tree. They never actually go near it they send in a sensitive like me then he returns to tell them that the tree is still alive. When you killed it I felt its effect disappear and came as fast as I could to find out what happened to my family."

"They fell asleep and died , their bones lie in the moss you see all around here." said Namdarin, "What did the Zandaars say the tree was guarding?"

"They did not say exactly, it is a great treasure that is theirs alone, no other man can touch it so they say."

"Well if they want it so much I will not let them have it."

By the time that Crandir has finished telling his story the sun is almost beginning to rise, the mercenaries get up and start to make their breakfast, Crandir is invited to join them, Jangor decides that they can take a few days to find the treasure while they are waiting for Jayannes leg to heal. Namdarin goes into Jayannes tent and finds her sleeping peacefully with the axe still held firmly in her right hand, he nudges her gently until she wakes up. She yawns and stretches somewhat gingerly.

"How are you feeling?" he asks softly.

"My leg is sore but not as painful as I expected, I feel weak and tired, but other than that I feel fine." She smiles at him and her green eyes flash in the early morning light streaming through the tent flap.

"I am sorry that I cut you so deeply." he says his head hanging, unable to look into her eyes, he is frightened of the rejection he may find there.

"Some times a little pain is essential to stay alive, in fact I could almost say that pain is an affirmation of life in itself. Without pain there can be no life. You did exactly what needed to be done, most men would not have been strong enough to do such a thing, you acted with the best intentions and achieved what was needed." He looks up into her green eyes and is dismayed by the intensity of her trust .He scrambled from the tent with tears in his eyes and called for Kern to inspect her injuries, the quiet scout goes into the tent and unfastens the bandages, he lets out and involuntary shout of amazement that brings the rest of them to the tent at a run. Only Kern and Jangor can fit into the tent with Jayanne the rest have their heads clustered in the opening. A clamour of voices all asking the same question but with different words "What is wrong?"

"There is nothing wrong, except that these wounds look to be at least four days old, even though we all know that they were only stitched up last evening. Namdarin let me see your arm." Namdarin pushes his arm into the tent and allows Kern to cut away the bandages. The removal of the bandages reveals bright red cuts with high ridges and leaking a thin watery blood from the ends, Namdarin swallows hard at the sight of his own damaged flesh.

"That is how they should look after only a nights healing, Jayannes leg looks four days better." They all compared the wounds, Jayannes were pink not red, they had only slight ridges and no leakage at all, the edges were tightly sealed, and they showed absolutely no signs of infection.

"Those stitches have to come out now." Said Kern, "or they may never come out at all if she continues to heal at this rate." He took a small knife from his pocket and gave it to Jangor, "Burn this clean." Jangor returned in only a few minutes with a knife that was so hot that it still steamed even though it had been quenched in icy cold water. Kern took the knife and inspected it carefully, it showed no signs of contamination or dullness.

"Cutting the stitch will cause almost no pain at all," he said holding his voice as calm as he could, "but the pulling of the stitch will cause some pain though this should subside very quickly." She nodded and began to breath long slow relaxing breaths, Jangor took her left ankle in both hands and pressed it hard into the ground. Kern slid the point of the knife under the first stitch, and paused to allow Jayanne to prepare herself, she felt the warmth of the knife against her leg and then he pulled it through the knot and her whole thigh twitched. A small gasp escaped her lips but she made no other noise. Kern carefully inspected the two ends of the stitch, he chose the roughest of the two to pull so that the smoothest would pass through her skin. He bent forward and kissed her soft white thigh, taking the end of the cotton in his teeth, this was the only way he could be sure to hold it tight enough and pull it out all in one go, to take two attempts would only cause her more pain. Suddenly he pulled his whole body away and the stitch came out, Jayanne let out a short squeal of pain. The place where the stitch had been only showed two small spots of blood. The process was slow and painful for Jayanne, though it also caused to pain for Namdarin, mainly the pain of jealousy. He was jealous that Kern was getting so close to a woman that he wanted for himself. All the time that Kern worked on her leg she kept a tight grip on the haft of her axe, it seemed to comfort her. As Kern progressed further and further up her thigh Namdarin found it harder and harder to watch, eventually he left the tent and went to sit by the fire.

As he stared disconsolately into the red flames he could not help thinking that something was missing, after a few minutes he suddenly realised what it was. Crandir had disappeared. Namdarin jumped to his feet and rapidly scanned the trees, he found nothing. After a few moments thought he went to look amongst the remains of the willow tree, as he approached he was astounded by the changes that had come over the tree, it now looked as if it had been killed years ago, the ground beneath it was littered with broken twigs and branches, the leaves had completely disappeared, patches of white heartwood were showing on the trunk where the bark had fallen off. Looking beyond the scabby trunk he saw the old man's black cloak and realised that he looked very much like a Zandaar, he seemed to be digging beside the tree. Drawing his sword he put the point to the hunch in the old man's back.

"What are you doing?" he asked through tightly clenched teeth.

"I am searching for the remains of my sons." was the tremulous answer.

"I am no fool," said Namdarin harshly, "your sons could not possible have made it this close to the tree without falling asleep, what do you seek ,Zandaar?"

"If you don't know then I wont tell you."

"You will tell me , or you will die and I will have to find out for myself."

Crandir turned slowly towards Namdarin and stared into the younger man's eyes, while they stared at each other Namdarin saw the old man's eyes fade from a watery blue to a deep black, they seemed to spin and turn, Namdarin felt a sharp tug of vertigo and snatched his eyes away, the old man had been trying to hypnotise him.

"If you try that again I will cut your head off." Namdarin prodding him in ribs with his sword. Taking a knife from his belt Namdarin cut the bindings of the man's cloak, inside he found a book fastened into a harness, the book was the teachings of Zandaar, Namdarin recognised the markings on the cover even though he could read them.

"I already have quite a collection of these." He said with a snort. Prodding Crandir with the sword he guided the old man's wobbly footsteps back to the fire, once Crandir was sitting by the fire Namdarin asked Stergin how the removal of Jayannes stitches was coming.

"Its all finished now, Kern is just renewing the bandages. What is going on with the old man?"

"He is a Zandaar, he was digging by the tree, I am going to find out why."

"Is he willing to tell?"

"No, I don't think so."

"Oh," said Stergin with a disgusted look, "I can't bear to watch that again, I am going for a walk."

"What do you mean?" asked a nervous Crandir.

"Oh ,the things he does when people will not talk to him are awful. I once saw him cut out a man's guts fry them in front of him and feed them back to him before he died, it was horrible. The worst thing is if he gives you to his lady friend, I saw the results of some of her butchery only a few days ago, she beat some robbers in single combat then cut off their genitals and choked them by pushing their own penises down their throats. She is really cruel. I am going before things get messy around here." Turning his back to Crandir he walked towards Namdarin and winked hugely then walked away stopping to have a word with Jangor. Jangors face went pale and he came over saying, "Can't you take him away from the camp first, it took days to get rid of the stink last time."

"If I take him away from the fire he might catch his death of cold."

Jangor just snorted. Mander came over and asked "What is happening?"

"Namdarin is going to interrogate the old man." Mander looked from one to the other in shock, his face turned pale, he started to gasp, "Oh, No." then he ran off into the trees and they heard the sound of him vomiting.

"Has he got a weak stomach?" asked Crandir.

"No." answered Jangor, "judging by the throw I would say it was fairly strong, it just gets a little queasy when Namdarin indulges his talent for torture."

The horror was plain for all to see on the old priests face, he was trembling with imagined pain already.

"All right." he said with the sweat pouring down his florid face, "I will tell you what you want to know." He looked into the icy stares all around him, swallowed nervously, cleared his throat noisily and started to speak.

"The treasure that is said to be hidden beneath the tree is mainly a weapon that only a god may hold, along with this are said to be other more mundane treasures, gold, gems and other such valuables. I have been instructed to recover the weapon and take it to our chief in Zandaarkoon. You may have all the rest but the weapon I must take to the chiefs."

"You offer us a deal that you have no power to enforce." sneered Nadmarin.

"If you kill me the priests of Zandaar will hunt you down where ever you may go, you cannot hide from us."

"I don't see what difference one more dead priest will make," said Namdarin, "my tally is over fifty now."

"How can you have killed so many of us and not be know to me?" asked a stunned Crandir.

"I don't leave any survivors behind and I don't give the ones I kill any time to contact their friends."

"I have already reported the death of the tree, an honour guard will be on its way here to escort the weapon to Zandaarkoon, there will be many good warriors in that guard."

"I have nothing to fear from them, I have beaten your priests in mortal and magical combat, I will wait here for them and kIll them all." Crandir was shaken by the vehemence of Namdarin's rising voice and he began to cower away from the angry man. He appeared to shrink in every bodies eyes until he became as a small black smudge beside the fire. Jangor watched amazed as Namdarin jumped to his feet and stormed around the fire vilifying the Zandaars in gradually rising tone. Crandir had been unmoving and unspeaking for almost five minutes then Namdarin's ire suddenly ground to a halt. Namdarin stood stock still as if listening for something, the others around the fire held their breaths in expectation. Namdarin kicked the old man hard in the ribs, Crandir rolled onto his back and stared calmly up into Namdarin's irate eyes, Crandir was smiling.

"You have made a serious mistake." he said, "Now we all know who you are and who your friends are. The honour guard is riding hard to catch you here, and they are coming ready for battle. Our soldiers are coming from all around, you cannot possible escape the net that is closing as we speak. You will all die at the hands of nightmares. I will not allow you to kill me." Crandirs calmness lent credence to his words.

"How can you stop me?" asked Namdarin with his hand on the hilt of his sword.

"That is quite simple." the old priests tired eyes locked onto the younger man's sharp blue ones, "I die." Crandir's eyes rolled backwards to reveal yellowed whites and his chest collapsed as it released its last breath. Namdarin's eyes widened in shock, the old man had chosen to die and done it. Then a howling black wave descended on his brain, a blackness deeper than night and darker than the spaces between the stars filled his mind. Namdarin struggled and searched around in the blackness for some light that could show him a way to escape the darkness that Crandir had inflicted as his last act.

Jayanne limped from her tent in time to see Crandir die and Namdarin fall, her natural inquisitiveness had been aroused by the raised voices. Namdarin's friends rushed to his aid as he fell to the ground, his eyes were open but obviously saw nothing , his breathe came in short shallow gasps that seemed completely inadequate to support life. As Jayanne struggled around the camp fire to where all the commotion was occurring Jangor slapped Namdarin's face but his eyes did not even blink, Kern squeezed his injured arm but got no reaction at all. As Jayanne passed the body of Crandir she was almost sure that she saw him breath out of the corner of her eye.

"He seems to be alive but his mind is elsewhere." Said Andel.

Deep inside his own mind Namdarin was still looking for some illumination, and then he found it, far away he saw a tunnel of golden light, it was getting closer with every instant that seemed to pass. The closer the light came the faster it approached, Namdarins need for the light appeared to be pulling it towards him, or maybe him towards it. Accelerating rapidly towards the immense golden void that was the tunnel, his path was suddenly blocked by a huge head, a male and bearded head, Namdarin's progress towards the light stopped in an instant.

"You must not pass here." said the huge and sepulchral voice of the disembodied head.

"Who are you to deny my right of passage into the light." asked Namdarin, he was amazed how thin and empty his voice sounded.

"I am Xeron, one of the ones you call the old gods, the priest Crandir seems to have bypassed your oath to me with his own sacrifice. The path before you is the path of the dead, this is where they begin their journey into the next plane. If you truly wish to go that way I cannot stop you, but you must understand that there can be no return, if you go into the light you will forget your previous life and your oath, if you choose to return to your world you can fulfil your oath and perhaps even find some happiness. The choice must be yours and freely made."

"I wish to return to my own world and the friends I have left there."

"Then you must go into the darkness, deep in the dark is the yellow light of your sun and there it shines on your world, it is far away but in this form you can travel very quickly." A hand appeared and pointed the way. Namdarin turned away from the tunnel of light and set off in the direction that the hand had indicated. In a moment he met Crandir, whose face was split by a huge smile.

"I had hoped to meet you here." said Crandir reaching out and grasping Namdarin's wrist with such speed that Namdarin could not react.

"Now we travel into the light together." Said Crandir.

"No." Said Nadmarin. "I will go back to my world, I still have much to do." He struggled hard and tried desperately to pull away from Crandir as the pair of them started to drift towards the tunnel of light.

"I am afraid that the imperative of a soul to pass on exceeds your choice," said Crandir, "we shall pass on together." The inexorable acceleration toward the light continued.

Jayanne looked down at Namdarins dying body and knew that he was failing because of something that Crandir had done. Checking the old mans chest very carefully she saw it flutter as if his heart was still beating under those ribs.

"What ever it is you have done to him it must be stopped." she muttered and to the surprise of her friends she lifted the axe high over her head and caved in the old priests chest with a single blow, blood splashed from the wound, some fell sizzling into the fire, filling the air with a rich coppery taste. Crandir gurgled and died finally.

Namdarin was fighting like a madman in Crandirs grasp, he desperately wanted to return and finish his task, suddenly and enormous gash appeared in Crandirs chest, he howled in agony and their progress towards the light halted.

"No, No." Shouted Crandir in horror as they started to move away from the light, Namdarin had thought that his earlier travelling towards the tunnel had been fast, but the speed they were making now was truly amazing. The medium through which they were moving was as thin as air but pressure of their passage was like a hurricane pushing against them, the medium began to scream as they rushed through it at an ever increasing velocity. Crandir was struggling and screaming to escape the force that was pulling them towards what Nadmarin now saw to be a small yellow light, they entered it at blinding speed and fell into a blue green sky. As they neared the white snow topped trees Crandir became so transparent, as if his substance was being eaten away, that Namdarins wrist passed straight through his clenched fist. Namdarins essence flashed back into his own body and he took his first breath for what seemed to be hours. Namdarin shook his head to remove the remaining disorientation and looked up into Jayannes concerned green eyes. Her hand was resting on the haft of the axe that was still buried in the chest of the dead monk.

"Now I have another piece of useful information." Namdarin said, as he wobbled slowly to his feet.

"What is that?" asked Jayanne.

"The god that I swore my oath to is called Xeron. Crandir just took me into the place where the dead go and Xeron told me to come back here. From what he said the oath prevents me from going there and returns me to life. Crandir found a way to get around the oath but it cost him his life, he had to die and take my soul with him into the light."

"If what he said about the soldiers is true then we must leave here immediately" , said Jangor.

"No." said Namdarin "I want that weapon, we probably have a day or maybe two, before they get here, if they were any closer they would not need to station a watcher."

"That is logical, but we can't always rely on these religious people to be totally logical." Said Stergin.

"Well I think we can risk half a day to search for those riches that Crandir spoke of." Said Namdarin.

"Right," said Jangor his decision made, "but let's make this as quick as possible. You three," he indicated Mander ,Andel and Stergin, "break camp, we will ride at midday. Jayanne you rest, we may have to ride fast this afternoon." With the instructions given Jangor went to the pack horses and removed two spades, "We have some digging to do." he said tossing one of the spades to Kern, and walking towards the willow. Namdarin went with them though he was too injured to do any real digging he would at least have some feel for any magical traps that they may find. Beside the tattered trunk of the willow they found the small hole that Crandir had dug with his bare hands.

"Let's assume that he knew where to dig shall we." Said Jangor to Kern, "you can go first." Kern shrugged resignedly and attacked the mossy ground with gusto, under the moss was a layer of soft black earth that was rich in all forms of creeping and crawling life.

"It looks like the sleep spell only worked on mammals and such," said Namdarin, "the population of insects seems to be better than normal."

"I hate creepy things." Kern said, with a meaningful shudder.

Six inches into the earth Kerns spade hit a rock with a mighty clang. Working quickly Kern cleared the stone with ease, it was four feet square and seemed to have the remains of an iron ring in its top surface, the iron was reduced to a red stain in the grey rock.

"Dig this side clear and then we will have to lift it." Said Jangor pointing to the side nearest the ring. Kern looked at him for a moment then said, "Is all this digging making you sweat?"

"I'll dig it clear then." Said Jangor using his spade for the first time, as anything other than a prop to lean against. He chopped the soil away in huge lumps, Namdarin knelt by the rock inspecting it closely, he was looking for engravings, the stone had been buried so long that he could not be sure if the roughness of the surface was eroded chisel marks or just the natural finish of the stone. As Jangor dug down the side of the slab it rapidly became obvious that they would not be able to lift it, it was seven inches thick and must weigh half a ton.

"This is going to take all of us to lift." Said Jangor, "That is of course if we can get hold of it. It is sitting on top of another block and there is no gap to get even a finger in."

"If we drive a wedge into the crack," said Namdarin, "and then use a long branch as a lever we should be able to get a rope around it, then a horse could pull it over for us."

"Good idea. Kern you find the tree splitting wedges, I'll find us a lever, and I presume the horse in mind is a big ,ugly ,grey one." said Jangor smiling at Namdarin.

"Of course," laughed Namdarin, "he has done this sort of thing before." While the others went to get the things they needed Namdarin knelt by the slab, he cleared his mind of the clutter of thoughts and reached out to the stone trying to feel it in his mind, it remained as dead and empty as any stone anywhere. Kern came back first with the wedges and an iron headed hammer, he tapped the wedges into the crack, one at each edge. Jangor came back with a seven foot long pine branch, he propped it against the willow trunk and checked the placement of the wedges , nodding to Kern in agreement he turned to Namdarin.

"Have you checked it for magic?"

Namdarin shrugged his shoulders and said, "As far as I can tell it feels as if it has no magic at all, but I could be wrong."

"Right. Kern drive those wedges in and let's see how high it lifts." Starting slowly Kern hit each of the wedges in turn and gradually they slid under the slab until they had produced a four inch wide gap. Jangor pushed the pole into the gap ,it was tight but it did go in. Namdarin whistled for Arndrol, the horse came at a trot and stood by patiently. Namdarin uncoiled a rope from the saddle and said, "If we push the rope under the edge with the lever and then when you lift the slab clear of the wedges I will be able to pass the rope around the corners and tie it across the slab, then we can leave the hard bit to Arndrol."

Jangor nodded and allowed Namdarin to position the rope and the lever, once they were all satisfied with the placement of the lever Jangor pushed a short fat log under it to act as a fulcrum. Jangor and Kern got hold of the raised end of the pole and pulled it down , they pulled so hard that their feet were almost leaving the ground. With a slight creaking the slab started to rise, as soon as the space was large enough Namdarin wriggled the rope around the corners and shouted "Let it down." When Jangor and Kern released the pole the slab crashed down with an awful thump, which dislodged one of the wedges, the wedge fell down inside the hole, it made a loud clatter.

"At least it didn't splash down there." said Kern.

"It sounded like it landed on stone." agreed Jangor, as they let Namdarin secure the rope to the horse, they sat beside the tree while the big horse attempted to lift the slab. After three tries the horse looked back at the rock and snorted, shook his mane and flicked his ears, Namdarin could see that he was getting a little irritated by that rock, to Namdarins soft encouraging words Arndrol walked forwards again, he leant on the rope until it sang in the gentle breeze, his powerful hindquarters hunched and trembled, bunched and rippled, and then he kicked, his wide rear hooves cut deeply into the soft turf, his fore hooves rose into the air as he pushed with all his prodigious strength until, the edge of the slab started to rise, Arndrol knew that he had moved it and was not going to let it fall back , maintaining the force the slab continued to rise, slowly at first but with ever increasing speed until it reached the apex of its curve and crashed to the ground with a resounding thump, to the joyous applause of the whole camp, every one had come to watch the competition between the big horse and the bigger rock. Even Arndrol joined in the celebrations, he pawed the air and screamed his loudest challenge to the whole world. Stergin came over with a burning log from the fire to use as a torch, they all looked down the square hole, it revealed a short shaft about twelve feet deep with small steps cut into the side, Jangor climbed down and Stergin dropped the torch to him, he caught it deftly in his left hand while his right sat on the hilt of his sword.

"There is a tunnel here that goes straight under the tree." said Jangor as he waved to Namdarin to come down. When Namdarin had reached the stone floor of the tunnel Jangor pushed the torch through a fine net of tree roots, they blazed nicely and opened up in moments to reveal another net three feet further on, the roots seemed to be growing down through the cracks in the slabs that formed the roof of the tunnel. The walls of the tunnel were dry and so was the floor, Jangor thought this a little strange, if roots can get in so can water. Casting about with the torch he found a small gap at the bottom of one wall, there was a patch of damp sand in front of it.

"Who ever built this place even installed drains." He said as he set light to another invasion of roots.

"The air is surprisingly good down here." said Namdarin.

"Maybe the builder also put in ventilation."

"No." answered Namdarin, "the flame goes straight up, and only the smoke near the roof goes back towards the entrance."

"How far does it go?" came a shout from above ground.

"Not far." Shouted Jangor, hopefully. He burned another group of roots and saw a wide space beyond. If was a room about fifteen feet on a side, they came into it through a door in the middle of one wall. The room was amazingly clear of roots, in one corner was a pile of sacks, well what used to be sacks, the gold coins had spilled out onto the floor as the sacks had rotted away, tatters of cloth and leather were still visible but they did nothing to restrain the glittering of the gold in the flickery light of the torch.

"There is gold down here." shouted Jangor as he stirred the coins with one hand, he picked one up and bit it, it was soft and shiny, pure yellow gold of that there was no doubt in his mind. Against the wall facing the door was a table or possibly an altar, and on this there was a long wooden box. Unlike the sacks the box showed no signs of age, it was made of an unusual black wood with a smooth almost oily finish not unlike burnished steel. The yellow flames of the torch showed the remains of an iron catch on the front of the box, amongst the red rust below the catch where particles of gold, the catch had obviously been guilded, though the catch had rotted to almost nothing the box was as hale and strong as the day it was crafted. Namdarin ran his hands along the smooth black wood, he felt a tingle and a thrill of electricity, the oily texture was so smooth as to be almost frictionless. Namdarin grasped the ends of the box with his out stretched hands, it was six feet long and a foot wide, the corners were still sharp and dug painfully into the bones of his hands as he tried to lift the lid. The muscles of his shoulders bulged as he increased the force against the stubborn lid , with a creak and a groan the lid rose slowly, pivoting about concealed hinges the front edge came upwards. The blackness of the wood was continued inside with a lining of shiny black cloth, nestling in a groove in the lining was a broadsword. The uncertain light of the torch revealed a sword five feet in length, the blade appeared to be a vague colour but it was definitely not rusty, the grip was long enough for two very large hands and bound in black wires, the cross piece was wide and thick and polished to a mirror like finish, the pommel was a single multifaceted stone the size of a fist, it was black like jet or polished coal. Namdarin snapped the lid down and turned to Jangor, whose mouth was hanging open, "I will take this."

"It is very pretty, but does not look terribly practical." said Jangor, ever the military mind. Jangor put the torch in a holder on the wall above the altar and went down the tunnel into the light, he looked up into five anxious faces.

"How long before noon?" he asked.

"An hour or two," answered Stergin, "Why?"

"There is more gold down here than our horses can carry, so get some bags for it, but remember we may be going into battle soon, so the horses must be able to run, and run fast."

"If we are going to be carrying gold we can lose some of this steel, can't we?" said Kern.

"Of course, but no overloading!" Jangor emphasised the last word. Andel, Stergin and Mander began unloading the steel that they were to leave behind and collected some bags to put the gold in. It did not take them long before they were rushing back to the hole with empty bags over their arms, Kern was already down in the tunnel waiting for them and Jangor had just come to the opening with two heavy sacks that were intact. Kern took the sacks one at a time and tossed them up into the waiting arms of his friends, once Jangor and Kern had gone into the tunnel to collect some more gold Namdarin came staggering in view carrying the box, tucking it tightly under his good right arm he struggled up the steps at the end of the tunnel, he refused all the offers of assistance with the heavy box. When he was out of the hole he moved a little away from it and put the box down, he opened it again. The steady sunlight showed the blade to be four feet long and nearly triangular in shape, it was six inches across at the hilt and tapered down to a half inch point, the body of the blade was a strange blue colour, that faded to yellow at the edges, the yellow was ripply and appeared to show the blows of the makers hammer. The black gem in the pommel glittered like midnight in the weak winter sun filtering down through the trees.

"That is indeed a weapon for a god." said Jayanne looking over his shoulder, "It looks heavy."

"It certainly is that, I don't know if I should touch it, but I am sure that Zandaar mustn't get it."

"I agree," she nodded, "Crandir was far too anxious about it." Namdarin closed the black box and tied it with a rope then fastened it to Arndrols saddle. In half an hour Jangor and the others had five large bags of gold distributed amongst the pack horses, the camp was cleared, the fire out, and everybody mounted.

"Which way should we go?" asked Jangor.

"Somebody still owes us some silver for Blakcbeard's head." said Mander,

"I never thought I would say this," chuckled Jangor, "but do we really care about a few pieces of silver."

"Its not the silver it the principle." Said Mander.

"Since when did you have any principles?" Sneered Andel.

"I have more principles than you, you lazy lout."

"And they are all more flexible than mine."

"Enough ." Shouted Jangor. "You two begin to wear on my old nerves. Mander is right however, there is a principle involved, the baron sent us hoping that Blackbeard would kill us. We owe him the opportunity to complete the job himself or to hand over the reward he promised."

"I also wish to see this baron and his house," said Namdarin, "I believe that we will find someone there who played a particularly nasty trick on Jayanne and I, he is a minstrel that goes by the name of Poredal, he wears entirely red clothes and rides a red horse."

"There was a red horse in the stables." Said Mander.

"What, or who, where you doing in the stables?" Andel asked.

"She was the cooks daughter, I think." answered Mander with a distant smile.

"No more morals than a tom cat."

"Will you two never stop squabbling?" asked Jangor. The two in question looked at each other and shook their heads.

"That is settled then, we go and collect our rewards from baron Melandius." He continued. They pulled out of the camp in the usual formation with Kern scouting ahead. It was just after midday when they left the protection of the trees, the view that met them was a crystalline expanse of pure white.

"We can't hide our tracks in this." Said Kern.

"So we make the best speed we can." Said Jangor, kicking his horse into a fast trot. Arndrol decided that this must be a race and paced alongside Jangors horse for a few minutes then began to lengthen his stride, reaching out with each forefoot the grey began to pull away from Jangor, but didn't actually break into a canter, "Namdarin." shouted Jangor, "That pace may be fast enough for a monster like that but these more realistic sized horses need to go a little slower, if you don't mind?"

"My mind isn't the problem," said Namdarin, "it is his that is the problem." He slapped the horse on its neck and said, "Slow down, stupid." With a loud snort of derision Arndrol shortened his stride until even the loaded pack horses could keep up. Andel was the last man in the line and when he looked over his shoulder he saw the tracks that they were making in the virgin snow, the scars in the pristine surface would be visible for many miles. Heading south almost directly into the sun their forward vision was seriously restricted by the glare flashing from white fields of snow. Arndrol enjoyed trotting through the deep snow, he loved to throw great clods of it every where.

After an hours travelling at a constant trot Jangor suddenly called a halt. As all the riders hauled their mounts to a standstill, Jangor signalled to Kern and indicated the eastern horizon. "I thought I saw a flash over there." he said. Kern scanned the horizon and saw nothing, he shook his head saying "I see nothing, but all this glare could hide an army."

"Let me try." said Namdarin.

"What do you mean?" asked Jangor.

"I have an affinity with horses, I may be able to feel their mounts."

"What can we loose?"

"Right." said Namdarin, "Everybody quieten down the horses make them stand very still and quiet." Once they were all settled he unfocussed his eyes and cleared his mind, reaching out as he had the night before he felt around for the herd consciousness of the horses. He found the close brightness of their own mounts very easily then he searched for the next nearest concentration of horses, sure enough there was a strand of the collective mind that reached away to the east, Namdarin followed the strand until he came to a group of eight bright centres of awareness, their colours seemed somewhat wan and watery, Namdarin assumed that they were very tired. They were heading northwards, for the forest. Carefully Namdarin followed the herds mind back to the west and into his own. Opening his eyes and taking a deep breath, that his body seemed to need almost desperately, he said "There are eight horses over there, they are going to the forest we have just left, they are going fast and are very tired."

"They will probably see our trail within the hour." said Kern.

"They will then be two hours behind us, and their horses will need rest, if we carry on at our current pace they will not catch up today and only catch us tomorrow if they can ride through the night. Let's ride on and hope for a change of weather or terrain that will help us." Said Jangor.

"They may find our tracks ," Said Namdarin, "but they will still have to go into the forest to check that vault. That will put them a further two hours behind, unless they want to split their already small force."

"Let's keep moving then." said Jangor laying his heels into his horses flanks, knowing that the others would follow him.

CHAPTER TWELVE

An hour later they were trotting through a narrow valley, all their gear jingling and jangling like a peel of bells, when Kern saw a trail ahead, it was the track of a lone horseman who had moved from the bottom of the valley up the left hand side, he had gone high up into the rocks above them, and judging by the way the horses hooves had slipped in the snow he had been pushing very hard.

"He is hiding up in those rocks." said Kern as the others all came to a halt behind him.

"Who ever he is, he heard us coming and got frightened." Said Jayanne.

Namdarin unslung his bow, strung it, and set a long arrow to the string, he muttered to Arndrol, telling the horse to stand still. His sharp eyes caught a movement in the rocks, with a fast smooth action he pulled, aimed and released. His arrow sailed upwards, humming its song of death, but the target had already moved on.

"Namdarin." Said Jangor, "You really can't go killing everyone we meet, it is a most unfriendly attitude. We should talk to them first and then kill them, if it is absolutely necessary."

"It does become habit forming." Said Namdarin by way of an apology, and he called his arrow back, he enjoyed the look of disbelief on his friends faces as the arrow drifted gently into his hand, Jayanne laughed and said, "You are just showing off." Somebody else had been watching the arrow as it went passed his hiding place, he was so busy following its sedate flight that he stood up to get a better view. Jayanne saw his head appear above a rock, in a blurred instant of motion she snatched her sling from her head, a stone from her pocket, and spun the leather strap once, up to release speed and the stone flew in a long curve that intercepted the mop of brown curly hair with an audible thud, followed by a second quieter one.

"Now who's showing off?" asked Namdarin looking into Jayannes smiling eyes.

Jangor gestured to Stergin and Andel and the two jumped from their horses and ran up the rocky slope to the place where the man had been hiding. They returned with a young man almost dangling between them, his feet were dragging two ruts in the snow. Andel rubbed snow into his face and woke him up.

"Who are you and why are you spying on us?" asked Jangor.

"I am called Crathen by my people."

"And what of your purpose?"

"I was merely trying to avoid being robbed."

"So you think us robbers do you?" Jangors voice was harsh and cruel.

"What other band would be abroad in this weather?"

"You for one."

"I am a band, a band of robbers." said Crathen laughing, "Do you fear me so much?" he shook his arms free and thrust out his chest like a strutting cockerel.

"We tremble in our boots at the mention of your name."

"Well I am no robber or bandit but I do seek a certain bandit, he is a large man with a blackbeard, have you seen him?"

"Oh yes, we have seen him. He is in fact part of our group." Crathens face froze for an instant and his hand flew to his sword hilt, Stergin's hand was far quicker and the sword was not drawn, the younger man's wrist was held in a vice like grip. Jangor continued, "Part of him is part of our group." Mander pulled Blackbeards head from its covering and dangled it by the hair so the young man could see. Crathens mouth fell open, then snapped shut and fell open again.

"He looks like a fish." said Mander.

"He wriggles like one." said Andel.

"I presume that a certain Baron Melandius offered you some silver for this small piece of a large bandit." said Jangor. Crathen nodded, still staring into Blackbeards dead eyes.

"How much?"

"A hundred pieces." Stuttered Crathen.

"A whole hundred." Said Jangor, "He offered us ten times as much and expected never to see us again, he was laughing at you."

"Then I must kill him, I bid you good day." Jangor shook his head and the young hothead could not get his arm free of Stergin's grasp.

"If you rush off now you will die before you even see him. So why not calm down and come along with us, we will get our thousand and your hundred and then you can kill him." Crathen ceased his struggling and thought for a moment.

"Fine." he decided finally, "I will come with you. You might need an extra sword." Stergin released his arm and laughed aloud, the others smiled but Crathen completely failed to see anything funny.

"Are you all laughing at me?"

"You are a very young man," said Jangor, "you are mistaken if you think you are a match or any of us. Namdarin's bow almost caught you, Jayanne subdued you with a single stone, and you haven't seen the way we fight with swords."

The young man was obviously upset by the way Jangor dismissed his skill, his only skill.

"We may be riding into danger," continued Jangor, "we might have to fight against the priests of Zandaar before we get to the house of Melandius, you will get the opportunity to display your courage then. Do you still wish to ride with us?"

"Of course, I am not afraid of a few old men in black."

"Be afraid." said Namdarin, "Be very afraid and you may stay alive." Crathens only answer to the dire warning was a serious frown.

"See Namdarin," Said Jangor, "simply by asking a few polite questions we have gained another sword and more importantly a living arm to wield it." Turning to Crathen ,"Go and fetch your horse then we can leave." Crathen scrambled up the tricky slope and returned in moments with a large brown mare in tow.

"Mount up." shouted Jangor in his best military tone, "We must keep moving or the Zandaars will catch us standing around and chattering."

They resumed their journey towards the house of Melandius, Crathen took the time to introduce himself to each in turn and to tell them something of his life story. They found that he was the fifth son of a small landowner, not that his father was small but that the amount of land he owned could not be shared amongst five sons and each part remain viable, so Crathen left to make his living away from farming. He had been fairly successful so far, his young face was always a favourite of the ladies, most wanted to mother him or take him as a lover, the first case being profitable and the second both profitable and dangerous. His skill with a sword was better than most, so he said, to a derisory noise from Stergin. His time in any one of the houses that had employed him was usually short, his contracts were generally terminated by a jealous daughter or suspicious husband. Gradually the whole group began to warm to the young man, his soft charm entranced them all, even the suspicious Jayanne. Her attentiveness and her flashing eyes soon had Crathen hopelessly ensnared, Namdarin grew rapidly more distant from the chattering pair, he felt the jealous tide building inside him.

Jangor turned his thoughts to the invasion of Melandius's house, the more he thought the more he became convinced that they would not be able to get through the heavy wooden gates, as soon as they were recognised the gates would close and open only when a ambush was waiting them inside. He discussed his feelings with Kern at great length and together they decided that a frontal assault was out of the question, some subterfuge was needed but exactly what they had no idea. It was clear that they not only had to get inside but they had to take a hostage to ensure their own safety, it would have to be a high ranking hostage, Melandius was the most obvious choice. When they rested as the sun went down in a narrow snow choked valley Jangor mentioned the problem to the others and asked for suggestions.

"The small gate to the stables might be a way to get in." Said Mander.

"You always know the sneaky ways in and out don't you?" Said Andel, scathingly.

"And you always find them useful." The two stared at each

other but said nothing more.

"What sort of gate is that?" Jangor asked.

"It is wide enough for a horse and tall enough for a mounted man, it is not as well guarded as the main gate, and has a small gap at the top where the door does not fit properly, a thin person may be able to wriggle through."

"What about the approach?"

"I don't know, the corner towers may watch that wall but if they do they can't watch it all at once."

"So. If we sneak into the stable in the middle of the night could we get to Melandius without being seen?"

"If the timing is right almost certainly." said Crathen.

"How do you mean?"

"Well. The guard change shifts at the third hour after midnight but their last patrol should be finished by an hour before that. If we go in when the last patrol is over that will give us an hour to creep into Melandius's chambers."

"How long should it take to get from the stable to Melandius with out making too much noise?"

"Normally only a minute or two, but in the dark, without lights or noise, we could need half an hour."

"Are Melandius's rooms guarded?"

"Yes, but if we get there just after the change over, then we will have a whole hour before the lost guard will be noticed by a patrol."

"That may give us enough time to complete our business and depart."

"They may want to chase us and get back their leader or the silver that they don't agree is ours." Said Kern.

"If they send a party after us, it will only confuse our trail and the Zandaars, who have potentially far bigger numbers, may just loose us."

"If we ride the best part of the night," said Kern, "we should get there long before sun down and be able to check for observers on the back gate."

"Well then, let's keep moving shall we?" said Jangor, and they all followed him into the deepening gloom, the night looked as if it would be clear, it was already very cold, and the stars could be clearly seen, even though the sky was not fully dark. The snow scattered by the horses hooves became sparkles of light in the air, the moon rose above the eastern hills, huge and yellow but it soon returned to its more usual silvery shade, the snow picked up the moonlight in deep relief and showed sharp shadows and bright snow fields, the cold became so intense that the riders faces started to ache and then went completely numb. The muzzles of the horses became festooned with icicles and the peoples faces white with frost. Long before the moon reached it highest point in the sky Jangor had decided that they could not continue in these conditions, "We need some shelter and a fire." he shouted through the pain in his cheeks, his lips were cracked and bleeding. Kern grunted and waved towards a thick stand of trees half a mile away turning the horses they walked slowly up the slope into the trees, the cold had driven all thoughts of caution from their brains, they stumbled in amongst the tall evergreens with none of their usual watchfulness, but on this occasion it was not needed. Once they were well inside the trees Mander and Andel dug a deep pit in the snow, they dug until they had reached good, if frozen, ground.

Together all the travellers helped to build an enormous fire, they gathered fallen branches from all around and stood about the fire bathing in its rich red glow. As the heat reached into their outer layers they finally began to talk and think, Jangor became nervous of the fire, he wondered if they had built it far enough inside the barrier of trees so that none of its light could escape. He knew that once the sun came up the column of smoke would be visible for many miles as would any light that escaped during the darkness.

"I have never known it so cold." Said Mander.

"I have only felt this cold once before." said Jayanne, "That was about five years ago, it only lasted for two nights and then the temperature rose until it was merely freezing."

"Two nights of this will kill us all." said Jangor.

"Tomorrow night we will be inside Melandius house, it will be warmer inside those thick walls." said Andel.

"I was planning to leave the horses and at least two people outside."

"Well you won't get any volunteers for that."

"I wouldn't expect any in this weather, we'll just have to hide quietly in the stables. The only visitors at night are going to be illicit lovers and they should be easily subdued and not missed by anyone."

"A couple of the under grooms sleep in the stalls." said Mander.

"Did you have to bribe them to go away then?" asked Andel acidly.

"No. But a token or two will keep them quiet."

"Or a tap on the head." said Kern.

"A gentle tap I hope." said Crathen, not liking the blood thirsty tone that was creeping into the conversation. A large patch of snow had melted and sizzled into the fire, leaving enough rapidly drying soil for them to all sit down on, though there was still not enough space to set up the tents. Kern suddenly thought of the injuries of his friends, "Jayanne let me look at your leg." Jayanne immediately walked over to Kern and dropped her trousers, much to Crathen's amazement, his jaw fell open like its strings had been cut and his eyes bulged at the sight of Jayannes' creamy white thighs. Andel nudged Crathen in the ribs with an elbow saying, "You look like a fish again." The young man's teeth clacked together and his face turned a bright red. Kern pronounced her fully healed, and called Namdarin over. Namdarins arm was another matter entirely, it was no longer bleeding and showed no signs of any infection but it was still a long way from healed.

"Another three or four days for these stitches." said Kern re-wrapping the arm. Jayanne smiled at Namdarin and said, "You worried too much about my leg, it is your arm that you should think about now, you might not be able to shoot too many of your arrows before it gives way."

"I will rest it, but please don't nag." She took pity on his long face and put her arm around his shoulders and hugged him, she kissed him gently on the cheek and he held her tightly for a moment or two. His passion began to rise and his pulse to race, he let her go before things could get out of control, he wanted her now more desperately than ever before. Crathen saw the feeling that passed unspoken between the two and his face fell, he wanted her himself but knew now that her feelings were for Namdarin alone. Crathen turned his back on the fire and looked outward through a circle of horses legs, they had all gathered as close to the warmth of the fire as they could, the view was very restricted but it did make him think of the horses, they had had nothing to drink all day, eating snow is no good for them so they don't do it, he took a large pot from one of the pack horses and filled it with snow, setting it by the fire to melt he went to collect some more, soon the pot was full of warm water which he gave to the horses. They clustered about the pot and gulped the water down as fast as they could, between them the horses drank five such pots full of water. Taking a hint from the younger man's thoughts for the horses Mander and Andel made some soup for the humans to drink, the hot lumpy liquid soon warmed their inside to match their rapidly roasting outsides.

"We may as well get some sleep if we can." said Jangor. Kern helped Crathen to wrap the horses in their blankets before they all retired to the respective bundles of blankets and furs, Namdarin and Jayanne shared her bearskin and were quite warm cuddled against each other, the rest did not feel so friendly towards each other and so remained as small separated cloth wrapped lumps about the roaring fire. The warmth of the fire soon sent them all to sleep, even the horses heads nodded as they fell into their own semi-alert sleep state.

In the pre-dawn light, Kern was the first to awaken, he sat up with a start, and scanned the trees rapidly looking for the disturbance that had woken him.

The only unusual thing that he could see was a white grouse that was pecking in the soil that had been cleared of snow by their fire. Kern reached out and threw another log on the remains of the fire, the grouse caught his sudden movement and took to the air with a clatter of its short wings, they showed a few brown feathers that had not yet been replaced by the wintry white, before the bird was over the trees the others were all awake.

"We really must remember to post guards when we are resting." Said Jangor, shaking his head, "Someone may catch up with us when we are asleep."

"Asleep or awake, it makes no difference for some people." said Mander looking pointedly at Andel.

"I am surprised to see you wake up alone, did you not manage to find a warm bed for the night?" Here the usual argument ground to a halt, their hearts were not in it, the cold had sapped their strength.

It was a weary bunch of people that mounted on their tired horses and left the small oasis of warmth, they all looked back with longing glances at the sinking fire, pushing the horses up to a slow trot soon warmed them up, though they were beginning to show signs of weight loss, the food of the last few days had been of a very poor standard, nothing at all like the horses were used to.

The sun rose over the snow capped mountain peaks, and travelled slowly up into a clear and crystalline blue sky, there was not a single breath of wind for which they were grateful, even so the mere fact of passing through the cold air caused ice to form on their faces and about the horses muzzles, any exposed skin rapidly lost all feeling, the cold was seeping into their bones and freezing their brains, thoughts fluttered slowly though their heads like lost bats blinded by the hard light of the cold sun. Jangor began to worry about the Zandaars that they knew were pursuing them, looking over their mounts he could see quite plainly that a long run was just not in them any more, he dropped back down the line of riders and paced along beside Namdarin.

"Can you feel how close the Zandaars are?" he asked quietly, so none of the others could hear.

"I can't even feel my own backside." Was the sullen reply.

"Try." The desolation in Jangors voice stirred Namdarin, he looked into Jangors worried eyes and nodded. Slowly he emptied his mind of the clutter of distracting thoughts, he closed his eyes and felt for the horses. He found them, as usual the brightest were the nearest, though they had dimmed considerably since the day before, their bright colours of yellow and white and gold were now much softer, yellows and oranges fading to reds, and one that was such a cold green that Namdarin knew it had to be sick, beyond their own small herd they could reach no other, it seemed that the cold had isolated them from the bigger herd.

Giving up the search for the mounts of their followers Namdarin focused in on the green aura of the sick horse, he could not make out exactly what was wrong with it but it was obvious that the horse could not last much longer in the cold. Namdarin returned to himself and opened his eyes.

"I could not reach any horses other than ours, but it could be that the cold affects the herding instincts. Our horses are taking this cold very hard, one in particular is sick, that one there." He pointed to one of the pack horses.

"Kern." shouted Jangor, "check that horse, Namdarin says it is ill." Their whole column stopped while Kern examined the horse in question.

"It will go lame within the next day, it is very cold and tired, it needs a warm stable and some good food."

"We cannot afford to go any slower. It must keep up or die." Crathen was shocked by Jangors harsh judgement, he felt a deep pity for the poor horse, but knew that Jangor was right. Kern quickly looked over the other horses and said,

"The others are better but weakening fast, they all need rest."

"If our horses are struggling with this cold, those Zandaars horses will be almost dead. If we go slower how long will they last?" asked Jangor.

"They might make it through another night, but we will be betting our lives on it."

"Perhaps the weather will break before then." said Jangor scanning the horizon but finding no clouds that would indicate such a change. Continuing at a walk the party hoped and prayed for a break in the weather, if the horses died underneath them, they would not survive for long on foot. Before the sun had reached its height they heard a sound like a soft wind moaning in the trees, but they saw no trees and felt no wind. Arndrols ears started to flick from side to side, he was listening for something, one of the pack horses suddenly skittered to one side.

"Beware." shouted Kern, "something is disturbing the horses." Frightened eyes scanned the horizon as the sound came again, nearer and louder this time. It was followed by a series of sharp yaps.

"Wolves." shouted Kern, "Make a circle, we cannot hope to out run them." They fought the frightened horses into a rough circle, surrounding the pack horses so they would not break away and be eaten by the wolves, the mercenaries drew their swords and sat on the nervous mounts waiting to see the wolves that they knew were hunting them. Jayanne had her sling ready, Namdarin tied his reins to the saddle horn then let them drop, he did not want to spare the time to remove them entirely, Crathen had his bow strung and ready before Namdarin. The three armed with the long range weapons moved around the circle to the eastern side where the noise was coming from. Over the crest of a hill came a rushing white tide, difficult to see against the white glare of the snow, it quickly resolved into a group of about twenty white wolves, huge they were, four feet high at the shoulder, black tips to their ears, black flecked tails streaming out behind them, huge yellow eyes and long lolling red tongues, they poured down the hill like a river, a river of running death. Namdarin's bow sang first, sending a humming messenger of death, then Jayannes sling started to turn, its stones whizzing through the air to strike at heads and mouths and legs, Crathen was the last to stir from the shock of those awesome hunters, his bow buzzed a much lower tone than Namdarins, but the lesser powered bow had the same effect at the rapidly shortening range. Four times Namdarins bow jumped and four corpses rolled in the snow, four times Jayannes sling spun and four more hungry mouths died in the cold, three times Crathen fired and two wolves fell, this was the first time that Crathen's life had depended on his accuracy, the third arrow injured a wolf, but it was by no means out of the battle. The fallen wolves did slow down those following but only for a moment each time, Namdarin was forced to drop his bow and draw his sword. Arndrol felt the bow fall against the saddle horn and knew that he could now move, with the squeeze of Namdarins knees the big grey plunged towards the charging pack, he was screaming and kicking and biting, the strongest hatred of his breed was for the stealers of foals, he gave vent to this hatred in the only way he knew, he killed. The pack was split by the sudden counter attack and swirled around the circle of horses in opposite directions. Jayanne followed one half and Crathen the other, Namdarin was left stranded by the passing of the tide, suspended by his own indecision, Arndrol quivering with the excitement beneath him, he failed to decide, Jayanne he knew could defend herself, Crathen he was unsure about, Jayanne he didn't want to loose, and Crathen he didn't really care about. The need for a decision was removed by events, firstly Stergin separated from the circle and went to aid Crathen chasing the wolves clockwise, and secondly a white shape carrying one of Crathens arrows leaped from the snow towards Namdarin, the man slashed at its head with his sword, the jaws snapped shut and broke the blade, driving a piece deep into the wolves brain, this left Namdarin unarmed but the wolf fell in an unsightly heap to the snow. Turning his horse about he saw that Jayanne was being pressed very hard by the snapping wolves all around her, it looked as if her horse would fall at any moment. He thought of the broadsword in the box behind him and twisted in his saddle, he attack the ropes with a knife and when the ropes had fallen away he prized open the box and flung the knife away. His hand leapt to the sword hilt, without thought and the sword hilt leapt into his hand with out moving, he felt a thrill at the contact, a rush of energy that sent him into battle to free Jayanne, the long sword cut blue arcs in the air, at left blue after images in everybody's eyes, where a blue stroke intercepted a white body it killed, the merest scratch was instant death, and every death pumped energy into Namdarin's arm, his savage approach divided the group attacking Jayanne and her axe was then able to take a serious toll upon them, caught between the green eyed woman and the blue eyed man, between the silver axe and the blue sword the pack died. Crathen and Stergin made quick work of their smaller group of wolves, but before they could go to Jayanne and Namdarins aid the battle was finished. The pack horses in their tight little circle were stamping in fear at the smell of blood all around them, Kern took their reins and guided them away from the scene. Jayanne turned to Namdarin, she saw then a fierce light in his eyes, the lust for battle was plainly written on his face.

"How good is that new sword?" she asked.

"It seems to have a similar effect to your axe, every wolf I killed gave me some of its energy, and any injury appeared to kill almost instantly, I am going to have to be very careful not to scratch any of my friends with it."

"It looks heavy?"

"Not really, I didn't even notice the weight." At this point Jangor arrived, he picked his way through the scattered corpses with great care, his horse was nervous enough without actually stepping on one.

"Are you hurt?" he asked staring at the two. Namdarin looked at Jayanne and noticed for the first time that both she and her horse where splattered with blood. She looked at him and saw a similar picture, together they laughed loudly.

"I will take that as a no, shall I?" Their smiling faces told Jangor everything he needed to know. He left them to their mirth and went to check on Crathen and Stergin, he found them both in a similarly jubilant mood, though they had each suffered a minor injury or two. Crathen had a small slash in his left thigh and Stergin had a piece of his right boot missing.

"Those hounds were hungry." said Stergin looking down at is damaged boot, "they took a few small bites from my horse." Jangor examined the horses wounds.

"You will have to swap horses, this one will need a little rest."

"I'll have one of the pack horses, their loads are lighter than me." He set off to where Kern was looking after the horses.

"That cut doesn't look too bad, a bandage should suffice." Jangors comment made Crathen look down at his hurt leg and nod.

"I'll be fine," he said, "I have never seen wolves like that before."

"I have heard of them," said Jangor, "but never this far down the mountains, they are said to stay up in the permanently frozen parts, I wonder what brought them all this way down. Perhaps it was the cold." Namdarin returned the sword to its box, and refastened the lid, he called his arrows back from their targets and replaced them in their quiver.

"I think that all the excitement is over for now, so let's get moving." Said Jangor in a voice loud enough to be heard by all. Moving at a quick walk they left the scene of their latest victory, looking back the wolves blended into the snow beautifully, except for the splashes of red that where spreading slowly from their wounds. During the walk Namdarin attacked his scabbard with a knife, he opened up the seam all the way down one side and widened the mouth, moving the metal retainers inside the scabbard and resewing them was difficult on a horse, but possible and before the sun was half way down he had a scabbard that would take his blue bladed broadsword. Taking the box from behind him he put it across his knees, it was beautifully made and a fitting home for such a sword. Should he really put the sword in a drab, badly stitched, leather scabbard? It would be much easier to draw in a hurry, the box was difficult to open and had to be tied to the saddle. Anyone who saw that black hilt with it shining gem would know that it was valuable, but then the box alone was worth a lot. Jayanne came alongside him while he was thinking about the sword, she saw his puzzled face, "What is wrong?" She asked.

"I don't know whether I should wear the sword on my hip, where a sword belongs, or leave it in its box, where it looks more at home."

"My axe only feels at home when it is hanging from by wrist, so that is where I generally keep it." She lifted her right hand, which held the axe, and placed the flat of the blade gently against Arndrols flank, just where a patch of wolves blood was marring his grey coat. When she took the axe away the stain was completely gone.

"Its thirst does have a use." she said, "If you put that sword in a scabbard on your left hip, you will get your legs tangled in it when dismounting, and it will probably drag its point on the ground when you walk." He looked at the open end of the scabbard and thought of the eight or nine inches of blade that would show through. He nodded, "It will have to stay in the box then." he sounded a little disappointed.

"If you fix the scabbard diagonally across your back it shouldn't get in the way at all, though it may be a touch more difficult to draw in a hurry." He thought about this for a while, then decided that she was right, with some more work he soon had the scabbard along a wide belt that draped across his right shoulder. The hilt of the sword sat six inches above the shoulder and could be drawn with reasonable speed providing that he remembered where it was. All the time that he was working on the scabbard Jayanne was walking alongside, she was thinking more of his safety than anything else, but before long her thoughts turned inwards to consider her feelings for this man. She thought about life without him and found only an empty void, she was completely unable to visualise a life for her in which he had no place. "Is this love?" she thought, "If he is so important to me it must be, from what I have been told of love." She was of course confused only by the spiritual nature of love not the physical acts, of them she was certain she wanted no more. She was sure that she could devote her life to supporting Namdarin in his cause, but she was equally sure that there could be no actual love between them, there was absolutely no possible cause for her to submit to that ever again. Her memory of the time with her husband came back to haunt her again, her more recent time in Blackbeards camp improved her feelings in no way at all, she remembered his return from the tavern on the night of their marriage, her mother had warned her that there may be some pain and a little blood the first time that they where together in the matrimonial bed. She had heard of the pain of the first penetration from other sources as well, but this did not prepare her for the actuality of marriage to the man they had chosen. She had left the marriage feast quite early, the wine and food had made her very tired, she had expected him to follow soon, she knew nothing of the harsh looks he ignored whilst drinking with his male friends, she had almost fallen asleep waiting for him to come to her, she heard the door slam open then close with equal ferocity, the crash of the wooden door meeting its frame woke her from the gently doze that had overcome her. She smiled softly to herself and listened to the sound of his footsteps getting closer. Slowly he came up the stairs, the beat of his feet on the stairs was uneven and unsure, she assumed he was as nervous about this night as she was, but she had no idea just how wrong she was. He had listened to everything his father had told him, he had kept his ear to the wall in the night and imagined the games of his parents to be real. His father had told him only the night before to make sure that the wench knows who is in charge of life for them both, he flung the door of the bedroom open, so hard that it crashed against the wall, she was surprised by the look of hate in his eyes, she had expected love and understanding but got none. He pulled the covers from the bed to reveal her naked form, he stared for a moment at the luscious young body reclining before him then he removed his shirt and the belt that held up his trousers, the belt was draped over his shoulder before the rest of his clothes were dropped on the floor in an untidy heap.

"Tidy this room up." he demanded pointing to the pile of discarded clothes on the floor. Confusion and rebellion fought in her mind for an instant, rebellion won.

"It is your mess, you move it." was her reply, the defiance surprised him, he had assumed that her naked posture showed complete obedience, he was determined that no woman was going to get the better of him, he had been told that once you let a woman take control you would be forever under instruction, they could find a man things that must be done immediately that he had never even dreamed of, and all these tasks would fall to him.

"Do as you are told, woman." He shouted, already on the verge of loss of control. She pulled the bed covers back over her nakedness and turned on her side as if going to sleep, though her mind was in turmoil. This total disregard for his orders was more than he could stand, he heaved the covers into the corner of the room and grabbed her wrist twisting it savagely up her back, he forced her face downwards upon the bed, and he beat her with the belt. He had hoped that she would not be like his mother, he had hoped that she would be as obedient as his mother was when the belt was so obviously ready for use, Jayanne had never seen a belt used as a means of punishment, but now she felt its painful results. This was not the intensity of pain for which she was prepared, blinding flash of the belts strike almost took away her senses in their entirety. He watched the welts rise on her round buttocks, and across her white thighs, he was astounded that she did not surrender immediately after the first impact, she made no sound at all, the only noise in the room was his laboured breaths, the swish of the belt and the crack of leather on skin. The sight of her trembling and quivering buttocks with their criss-cross red stripes made him very excited, his manhood rose and pulsed, it twitched and trembled with every fall of the belt, finally he could stand the tension no more, moving over her body he pushed his knee down between hers forcing her legs apart. Keeping the pressure on her arm he spread her legs further and knelt down between them, using his knees he forced her thighs to part until he could clearly see the soft red pubic hair that covered the mound of her sex. The sight drove him almost insane with passion, he lifted her up by the hips until she was able to support the lower part of her body on her knees, pushing her face down into the bed with one hand he reached between her buttocks and cupped the bulge of her vulva in his other hand, it was warm and wet with blood from her bleeding backside, roughly he spread the thick lips and plunged two fingers inside, he felt the muscles of her back writhe as she tried to move away from the invading digits. The soft warmth enfolding his fingers was very interesting, he moved them back and forwards, in and out, experimenting and enjoying her suffering, this was control and power that could not be beaten, he felt strong and invincible. The aching of his manhood finally made itself felt and he removed his fingers and thrust his penis into her. He failed to notice the momentary resistance deep inside her, nor the blood of her virginity when he withdrew spent after only five rapid thrusts, he stared down at his rapidly shrinking cock, it was pink with mixed blood and semen, her body was shaking with silent sobbing, and he realised that in all this she had made no sound, not a single noise had escaped her lips, only the occasional gasp of pain, for some reason this seemed to take away his pleasure. Taking her by a leg he threw her onto her back and grabbed her right breast, he pulled and twisted it savagely, but she remained silent in her torment, her tear streaked face and her wriggling body drove him on, only when he looked into her eyes did he stop, he was expecting to see defeat and surrender, but her hard emerald eyes only projected hate. Her body was his, for the moment, but her mind would be always free, and it would beat him. In an instant he felt fear, then the usual response took over, anger roared through his brain, he called her whore and witch, he cursed womankind back to the beginning of time. He told her that if she told anyone of what had happened he would say that she refused him and that she was no virgin, this gave him the right to punish her. She was his forever and she would learn to love him, or die. This was the threat that sealed his fate, she planned from that instant to kill him. He tied her to the bed and left her until the morning when he returned and released her with a huge smile, he enjoyed seeing her struggling to be free.

Just before the sun reached the white mountain tops Jangor called a halt saying, "Melandius house is just over the next rise, we will rest in those trees until it is time to sneak in." Once they where shielded from view by the thick trunks of the trees, they built a fire and had a good hot meal, the horses were watered and left to find what forage they could. The wind moved round to the south and began to strengthen a little, it held a delicate aroma of warmth, the prospect of the cold breaking cheered up the entire party, even the horses.

Namdarin completed his new scabbard after the meal and tried it out, he found that drawing the sword was quite easy, but the presence of the hilt above his right shoulder did make his bow more difficult to remove from its new place across the left shoulder, finally he decide to fashion a holder for the bow and the quiver that could be attached to his saddle so that the horse could carry all this inconvenient hardware, but that would have to wait a while yet. Stergin challenged him to a little fencing practice. The physical activity soon warmed them both up to the point that they had to remove their heavy outer clothing.

"Don't you two tire yourselves too much, we may have to fight later." Said Jangor.

"Namdarin has to get used to his new sword, and I am beginning to feel a little rusty." said Stergin as they drew again and laid about each other with a will. Namdarin found that drawing his sword from over the shoulder was slightly slower than Stergins more practised cross body draw, but it did give the advantage of the sword coming downwards from the draw in a fairly efficient attacking slash that had the swords whole weight behind it. Properly timed this slash could coincide with the wrist of the opponent at the moment he sets it for battle. After practising this technique for a while they found that a quick man like Stergin could lunge forward underneath Namdarins sword and run Namdarin through the chest, but Namdarins sword would be falling straight onto his back and would probably cut him clean in two. Most people are too wary of death to try such a risky tactic.

After midnight the wind had picked up from the south to such an extent that it was noticeably warmer, the snow on the branches of the trees was beginning to melt, icicles were starting to fall, and it was time for them to leave, Jangor made certain that every one checked his gear to eliminate all unnecessary noise, they didn't want to advertise their approach any more than they could avoid. The nearly silent trek from the small wood that had been their hiding place for the last few hours was slow and careful. Over the top of the rise ahead of them they saw the silhouette of the corner towers against the stars. The half full moon stayed behind the clouds that were coming in on the warm southerly wind. Moving down the slope they crossed the open ground in front of the high stone walls, expecting to hear an alarm at any instant. They saw no lights in the towers and heard no noise from the house, the total darkness of the place was eerie, it looked for all the world as if everyone inside was already dead. They had a little difficulty finding the door in the darkness that puddled about the foot of the high walls, they were looking for a dark opening in a black wall, Stergin found it eventually by running his hand along the wall, it was exactly as Crathen had described.

CHAPTER THIRTEEN

The party stood looking at the high wooden door for a moment or two before they saw the gap over the top, it was about seven inches wide.

"I'll go." said Crathen, starting to remove some of his heavy clothes.

"No." said Jangor, in a harsh whisper, "Jayanne you are the thinnest, you go."

"But I know the locks." said Crathen. Jangor just stared at him, waiting for him to understand. When Jayanne had taken off her bearskin and left her axe hanging from the saddle horn she was ready, moving her horse into the doorway she climbed onto the saddle and peered through the opening.

"You don't trust me." accused Crathen.

"Correct," said Jangor. "You are unproven, you have a pleasant face and beautiful words, but we cannot afford to trust you blindly." Crathen sighed and nodded, he saw the undeniable logic of Jangor's words, though he was still hurt by the lack of trust.

"It seems clear." Whispered Jayanne.

"Go then." said Jangor. Taking a knife from her belt and placing it carefully between her teeth she started to wriggle through the gap. The door rattled like the boom of a battle drum, as far as her waiting companions were concerned, but to the rest of the world it would not have woken a sleepy mouse. The difficult moment came when she squeezed her hips through, her still weak and painful left thigh dragged across the top edge of the door, biting hard on the blade of the knife she made only the slightest of grunts. Once she was through the gap she climbed down the twin wooden bars that held the gate closed, these heavy oaken beams had to be lifted and stacked quietly to one side before the three iron bolts could be drawn and the gate opened. Luckily the gate was used regularly so the bolts were well oiled and almost noiseless. As soon as the gate was open Jayanne rushed to her horse and recovered her axe. Kern and Stergin dismounted and went inside to search the stable yard. They returned in a minute to say that it was all clear. The rest of the party climbed down from their horses and walked them very slowly inside, the alarming clatter of hooves on the cobbled floor of the yard seemed very loud to them. Kern lifted the latch on the stable door and he and Mander crept inside, the ones left waiting outside heard a muffled shout and a solid thud and then Mander poked his head around the door waved them in. The taking of the stables made absolutely no noise and attracted no attention from the patrolling guards. Two stable boys were tapped smartly on the head and trussed up like chickens for roasting.

"Crathen." Jangor said, "You will now have the chance to prove yourself. You are the only one who knows this place properly, you must guide us, If you lead us wrong you will be in the front of the fighting."

"Your lack of trust hurts me," answered the young man, "but I will guide you as best I can. We must start in soon."

"Mander, Andel. You two stay here, look after the horses and make sure that outer door stays unlocked." said Jangor. "Right lead on." Crathen led them across the stable yard to small door that opened onto a stair way. Up the narrow twisting stair they went, Crathen, then Jangor, Kern, Jayanne, Namdarin and finally Stergin. The stairway was lit by small candles scattered along its length in a completely random manner. The soft creaking of the old wooden steps kept their nerves on edge.

"These are the servants quarters", whispered Crathen, "there should be no one about at this hour." At the top of the stair they entered a narrow corridor, Jangor had no idea which way they were going the turns of the stairs had totally confused his sense of direction, they were entirely dependant on Crathen's knowledge of the place.

The corridor was lit by candle at each end, this meant that if someone was standing between you and the candle you were in complete darkness. They passed along the corridor with their left hands on the left shoulder of the person in front, even so Kern's wide shoulders still kept rubbing against the walls and occasionally the doors of the servants rooms. The end of the corridor opened onto another stairway this one went up as well as down. Jangor tapped Crathen and pointed upwards with a serious frown.

"The roof." whispered Crathen to the unasked question. "We go down." He led them down the winding stair, this one was better lit than the other, but it creaked and groaned just as much. As they went down the temperature went up, almost as if they were walking down into the fires of hell. They passed several empty corridors without incident, they saw no signs of anyone about at all. Crathen suddenly stopped in the entrance to one of the long corridors, Jangor peered over his shoulder and saw a candle bobbing along in the darkness, it was going away from them but both he and Crathen held their breathes until the glimmer had disappeared into a room.

"The next corridor leads to the kitchen," muttered Crathen, "there is always some activity there. We must pass it and go down into the cellars, be very careful here." They all heard him, hands strayed to hilts and heads turned one way and another. Stergin tapped Namdarin on the shoulder and whispered a short message, Namdarin nudged Jayanne and so the message passed to the front. Jangor told Crathen that there were footsteps coming down the stair behind them.

"Lets move." whispered the nervous young man. He practically scampered down the stairs, the others following at a more restrained pace. Passed the well lit entrance to the kitchens and down into the cold dark of the cellar. Once they were around the turn of the stair Crathen felt about on the wall for the candles that he knew should be there, finding them he lit one, the tiny pool of light showed them all to be safely in the cellar, it revealed cobweb strewn barrels, presumably of wine or beer. A thick layer of dust covered everything inside their small puddle of illumination.

"We should be safe here for a while, no body ever comes down here."

"What is this place?" asked Kern.

"It is an old wine cellar, its not used any more because it gets too cold in winter and too warm in summer, deeper cellars were dug at the other end of the kitchens. The only ones who come here now are children trying to frighten themselves." Closer examination of the dust showed the numerous disturbances of small rodent footprints, a quiet scampering of claws on the cold stone flags of the floor told them that the rats in question were still watching. Following Crathen's single candle they travelled slowly along the length of the dark and musty cellar, at the far end a wooden door barred their way, it was locked by years of neglect. Kerns heavy shoulder was needed to open it, the creak of the rusted hinges was alarming in its loudness, the open door revealed a stairway leading up into the house, it was narrower than all the others and turned in a tighter circle.

"This is supposed to be a secret escape route." whispered Crathen, "I wasn't sure that it came all the way down into the cellar, I found the upper end but never bothered to find the bottom. This will save us some time, and get us around some of the guards." After they had gone three turns up the steep stair the dust on the floor suddenly disappeared.

"Somebody uses this stair regularly." muttered Kern.

"It is said, in whispers of course, that Melandius uses it to visit the servants quarters in the middle of the night. He goes to the room of one of his wife's hand maidens, though she is no maiden."

"How likely is it that he is there now?" asked Jangor.

"It is not very likely, but if he is we are just unlucky and will have to wait for him to return."

"How does he get past his own guards without them knowing?"

"Where do you think the whispers came from?" Jangor nodded and let the matter drop. They passed two more doors and stopped in front of the third, Crathen motioned them to silence and turned the handle of the door very carefully. It opened without a sound, it had been in constant use. A small crack was all that Crathen needed to see the guards standing outside Melandius's rooms. He closed the door and turned to the group, "The guards are there and seem to be very alert. Now we must wait for them to change over, it should not be more than half an hour now."

"Will the guards check this stair?" asked Jangor.

"I don't think so."

"Who else has rooms in this area?" asked Namdarin.

"I am not sure." Namdarin settled down on the stair while Crathen opened the door again and listened to the guards, they were chattering about nothing in particular, just passing the time. Namdarin decided to pass the time more productively. He cleared his mind and went in search of dreamers. With a sudden rush a multitude of scrambled dreams tried to impinge upon his mind, he pushed them away and tried to focus onto one, it was very difficult to concentrate on one dream when so many were almost clamouring for attention. He rejected one dream after another until he finally managed to enter the one he wanted, it was the best possible dream for any musician, the dreamer was looking down onto a sea of upraised adoring faces, each face shone with an internal light of pleasure, intense ecstasy of the songs of the singer in front of them. Namdarin was standing behind the singer and looking over his shoulder, he swept the crowd with a stare that put out all the lights, the singer became desperate, his singing more frantic, his fingers tangled on the strings of his instrument, his voice choked in a throat full of ashes, in front of his eyes the crowd became an angry howling monster, that was hungry for his blood. The singer backed away from the edge of the stage and blundered into the heavy bars of the cage, glancing sideways he saw the cage extended up to the edge of the stage. The monster opened its huge mouth that completely filled the open end of the cage, a foetid stink of rancid offal, and disgusting swamps engulfed the singer, the red maw advanced, a thick and slimy red tongue flicked itself about his knees and started to pull him towards the green and yellow flat topped teeth. The musician fell and lost his guitar and any control that he had over the monster, the mouth closed with a black finality that could not be denied. The dream was ended and Namdarin opened his eyes, Jayanne saw his smile and asked, "What have you done?"

"I may have killed the minstrel." She smiled and nodded, hoping in one moment that this was both true and false. She hoped that he was dead and yet she wished to kill him herself. Crathens look of total incomprehension was understandable, he did not know anything of the methods of the Zandaars or that Namdarin had now taken them for his own, "How can you have killed him?" he asked.

"I turned his dream against him and it swallowed him whole."

"And this will kill a person?"

"If the person truly believes that the dream has killed him, he will die."

"This is wicked sorcery."

"This is necessary to our survival, that's not quite true, Poredal's death is an act of vengeance. He killed me so I killed him, he used deceit and a knife, I used magic and a nightmare. There is little difference in our actions. This is more easy for you to understand because you have not experienced the dream war as I have."

"Can you find out if Melandius is sleeping?" asked the young man.

"I don't think so," answered Namdarin, "I only latched onto the minstrels dream because he was dreaming of singing, Melandius could be dreaming of anything."

"Even singing?"

"That is a possibility." Namdarin nodded but showed no real concern for Melandius, even though his death would seriously effect their plans.

"I can hear the guards coming up the main stairs." whispered Crathen, putting his finger to his lips to indicate silence. The company held their breathes while the guards changed places.

The quiet words of the guards were audible but indecipherable. Two pairs of heavy footsteps faded away down the central stairway.

"Any plans?" asked Crathen.

"We must entice at least one of them into this stairway." said Jangor, "Kern you be a rat and make one follow you down, and we will drop something heavy on him from above, Namdarin probably." Most of the group retreated up the spiral until they were out of sight of the door, Kern stayed by the door and waited until Jangor indicated that every thing was ready. Kern squeaked like a rat and scratched softly at the door. His imitation was so good that Jayanne was looking about nervously, thinking that there was a real rat some where near. Namdarin stood on the stair just out of view of the door and drew his blue broadsword, when he saw Kern move away from the door he eased himself forwards and waited. The light from the corridor spilled into the dark stairway and a guard shuffled in muttering about horrible rodents and winter, he followed the noise of the imitation rat down the stair, as he passed through Namdarins sight Namdarin swung the sword down, he was holding it by the end of the blade, the heavy black jewel of the pommel caught the guard just behind the ear, he groaned and fell down the stair with a loud clatter until Kern caught him and stifled his twitching body with a solid hug. The second guard had heard him fall and called softly, getting no reply he came to investigate and a second time the blue sword fell and another guard collapsed on the stair. Namdarin jumped down after him and caught him before he landed on top of Kern. Kern carried one body while Namdarin and Stergin shared the other. Crathen scampered down the hall way and having checked that the main stair was clear waved them towards Melandius's rooms.

The barons rooms were opulent to say the least, there were silks and tapestries hanging every where, almost no wall could be seen in between the bright colours, here and there a dim painting of a dark face peered down on them, most probably the ancestors of the current baron. The only things that looked out of place were the two sleeping guards dripping their thick blood from scalp wounds into the deep pile of the patterned carpet. Jayanne cut down some curtain cord and trussed them up like joints for roasting, a gag was stuffed into each mouth to ensure their silence.

"Very pretty." Whispered Stergin, fingering a particularly lively green silk, which had a picture of trees drawn on it in dark blue ink. This was the barons private receiving room, where he would meet guests to discuss things not for the ears of the people. The bright illumination came from two large oil lamps suspended from chains attached to the ceiling, the glass globes of these lamps were completely clean, there was no evidence of soot on them at all.

"Either they have just been cleaned in the last half an hour, or they burn an oil that makes no smoke." Mused Jangor, he had never seen a completely smokeless lamp oil before but doubted that the lamps had been cleaned in the middle of the night. Near the mechanism that lowered the lamps for fuelling and cleaning he found a bottle of a clear slippery liquid, which had almost no smell, he stuffed it under his belt for investigation at a latter date. Crathen opened the only door other than the one they had come in by, and crept slowly into the dim room it revealed. In the middle of the floor was an enormous bed, fully seven feet on a side, curled into a small ball in the middle of the immense expanse of red satin covers was a middle aged man, he looked weak and defenceless. The large fireplace cast a flickery jumping red light about the room, which revealed even more portraits, some so darkened with age and smoke that they seemed almost blank, others bright and new. The newest of the paintings appeared to be not relatives of the baron but were of people cavorting in all sorts of sexual poses some involving animals and demons.

"Quite a collection he has here." Stergin said, taking a serious liking to one of the picture of three women who seemed to be raping a man.

"Give me our little present." said Jangor, and Stergin removed to bag from his belt and handed it over .Kern and Namdarin grabbed Melandius by the arms and rolled him onto his back, Jangor clamped a heavy hand over his mouth and dangled Blackbeards head in front of his eyes. The baron struggled for a moment, then he recognised the face in front of him. His eyes went wide and flicked from side to side, looking for a way to escape.

"Remember us." Said Jangor. "We have now delivered that item you asked for and you now owe us a thousand silver pieces and this young man a hundred. Do you wish to pay up?" The baron nodded his head as far as he could considering its restraints.

"If you make a noise we will kill you." said Jangor, the baron shook his head emphatically.

"Where do you keep the money?" asked Jangor, in a forced whisper, removing the hand that was covering Melandius's mouth.

"In a strong box in the next room." Jangor moved away from the bed so that Kern and Namdarin could lever the captured baron upright, his arms were twisted savagely up behind his back and fastened there in one of Kern's large fists.

Melandius was walked into the next room his toes barely touching the floor, most of his weight being supported by Kerns strong right arm. The smaller room that they all entered now was even more plushly furnished than the anteroom. This was where Melandius kept his favourite treasures. Against one wall stood and enormous iron bound chest, it was big enough to be a coffin for a man as big as Kern.

"Open it." commanded Jangor.

"The key is on a chain around my neck." whispered Melandius. Jangor pushed his hand inside the barons night shirt and found a thick silver chain on which there was indeed a key, with a snap of the wrist the chain broke and cut into Melandius's neck at the same time. Jangor bent down in front of the chest and put the key into the lock.

"Wait." said Namdarin as loud as he dared. "What about a booby trap? He gave in too easily." Jangor looked up into Melandius's eyes and saw the fear there.

"You open it." He said, Kern threw Melandius to the ground in front of the chest, Jangor put his knife against the barons kidneys and watched very carefully while the old man opened the lock, the key was turned twice the wrong way, then once the right way and twice the wrong way again.

"What would have happened if I had just unlocked it?" asked Jangor.

"The chest would have thrown two hundred poison tipped darts around the room, I would have been just as dead as you, had I not taken the antidote with my supper as usual."

"I would have killed you just the same." said Jangor.

"The poison is so fast that you would not even have noticed the fact that you had died."

"Then you were in no danger, why did you open it."

"It has been so long since the mechanism has been checked that I did not want to risk a miss-fire, the poison may have lost its effectiveness, so might the antidote, these are too many chances to take all at once. If I see another day you can be assured that it will be checked more regularly."

"That is of little comfort now. You have no real need to fear for your life. Once you have paid us for the head, that is a thousand silver pieces for us and a hundred for Crathen we will leave, you will be bound and gagged but that is all. If how ever you decide to send men after us we will of course be forced to come back and deal with you on a more permanent basis. Do you understand?"

The baron nodded and pulled two sacks from the chest, "The big one should be a thousand and the small one a hundred." He handed them to Jangor.

"How very tidy." said Jangor, "Now take us to your minstrels room, Namdarin has a debt to pay to that wicked songster." A deep frown crossed Melandius brow but he continued to lead them, out through the anteroom, where he stared for a moment into the eyes of his captured guards, they knew that they would be punished if they were allowed to live. Down the corridor towards the stair by which they had come up to this level, the baron stopped in front of the door that was exactly opposite the door to the stairway.

"This is the one." he said. Namdarin stepped forwards, placed one hand on the door and closed his eyes, a look of total concentration flooded his face, after an instant he stepped back and nodded to Jangor, "It seems safe." Jangor tried the door handle and found it locked, Kerns heavy shoulder soon removed to latch from the door frame, they all walked into the dark room, Kern lit a candle and Melandius gasped at the scene that was revealed in the small pool of light. Lying on the bed with his hands outstretched and hooked into claws, his eyes wide open in fear, and his mouth open in the shape of a scream that was never heard was Poredal, the ex-minstrel.

"It looks like he died of fright." Stammered Melandius.

"Yes." said Namdarin, "The only thing wrong is that he didn't know why. I wish I could have told him, but then he is dead and that is good enough for me."

"How did you kill him? His door was locked and I know he has the only key, it is there on that table."

"I sent one of his own nightmares to kill him." Answered Namdarin in such a calm and clear voice that Melandius could not help but believe him.

"If you or your men follow us then you will die in fear like this." Said Jangor pointing to the cold form on the bed.

"If I never see you people again it will be three days too early." Answered the shaky baron. Jangor escorted him back to his room and tied him up next to his guards, when he was sure of the ropes and knots he said, "Your next patrol will find you in a while, but we will be gone. Remember what we said about pursuing us, it would be fatal." He left the door closed on his way to his friends who were waiting on the stair. The way back to the stable was uneventful, they followed the same path but met absolutely no one. Once mounted they left at a gallop and looking back saw no lights or alarms of any sort. When they had cleared the rise and were out of sight of the house Jangor waved them down to a quick trot. He rode alongside Namdarin and they discussed the way forward.

"I refuse to be distracted any more I am going to look for Granger." Said Namdarin firmly.

"I agree, we will come along with you, if you don't mind that is?"

"Of course. I expected you to have something better in mind than a trip into the mountains to hunt for an old mystic."

"Every time we meet I make a profit, generally with a little risk, but that is business."

"I don't foresee you making any profit from Granger."

"No, but we have attracted a lot of attention recently, it might be a good idea to disappear for a while, a lonely trip up a mountain will do as nicely as anything else."

"Right, then it is settled, we go on together. I think we should ride through as much of this night as we can and rest in the morning." Jangor agreed with a simple nod and silence descended like a thick woollen blanket. The crunch of the horses hooves in the thawing snow and the rush of their breathing was the only sound. The biggest of the three moons came out from behind the rapidly thinning clouds, it seemed inordinately large as it was only a few degrees above the horizon, while Namdarin stared at its glowing white half circle, a small black spot raced across its face, this was the smallest and fastest of the moons, it was rarely seen because it was so small, the occasional glimpse as it came over the horizon at sunrise or set was all that most people ever saw of it, to see it cross the biggest moon was said to be either a good omen or a bad one depending on which part of the world you happened to be in. Namdarin paid little attention to the fortune that it would bring and only marvelled at his fortune in seeing such a rare event. Before the sun came up the wind shifted around to a more southerly direction and picked up to a stiff breeze, a breeze that carried even more promise of rising temperatures, Jangor knew that when the sun came up the temperature change would be quite dramatic and all the snow they had been walking through for the past few days would vanish into the ground, taking their tracks with it, Jangor breathed a huge sigh of relief at the thought of the difficulties their unwanted followers were about to encounter.

They were travelling eastwards into the mountains as the sun appeared above the snow clad caps of the high peaks, they felt its warmth on their faces and rejoiced at a temporary respite from the cold, they knew it was only to be short lived because they were going up to where it never actually got warm, high above the tree line was where Granger lived, Namdarin thought about this for the first time, if there is constant snow there can be no trees, if there are no trees what does Granger use for fuel to keep him warm? This question kept buzzing around in his head, it perpetually wanted an answer, but no logic of Namdarins could come up with one.

"Jayanne," he asked, "How does Granger keep warm up here where there are no trees for fuel?"

"I have no idea," she said after a moments thought, "but when I met him I was beginning to get cold enough to hunt a bear, and he was wearing only a light shirt and pants."

"How old was he?"

"He looked both old and young, his face was lined with age but he moved like a man of your age, he looked intense and relaxed at the same time. It is very strange, even though it was only a few weeks ago when we met I have difficulty picturing his face." She shook her head and said nothing more. Namdarin continued to puzzle on the old man's preference for living in the perpetual ice of the mountains, he finally came to a tentative conclusion that it was the seclusion and freedom from interruptions that must be his overriding reason.

The day started to warm up once the sun was well clear of the mountains, Jangor asked Jayanne for directions to Granger's lair, they turned a little north and started to climb up through the gentle foothills, the high peaks were soon lost in a rolling landscape of white snow and brown bracken interspersed with the occasional group of trees, some stripped by the winter and others still carrying their evergreen leaves. Stergin kept a close watch on their back trail, he saw no signs of pursuit at all. Just before noon they set up camp in a small depression in a hillside, a bank of thick gorse bushes protected the little dell from the warm south wind, they shovelled the snow out of the dell and piled it around the edges to give extra protection from the wind and to help hide their tents from the view of anyone coming up the valley. They had a quick meal of cold meat and biscuits and curled up in their respective tents. Namdarin and Jayanne shared their tent as usual, as he rolled himself up in the huge white bearskin and put his arm protectively about Jayannes' shoulders, she wriggled her body tightly against his, this brought a warm feeling to the pit of his stomach, it was really good to have someone to look after in this way, it at least partially filled the hole left in his life by the death of his family. As soon as he thought this he drove the thought away with a ferocious shake of his head, nothing could possibly replace his family, his wife and his son were the whole reason for this quest. "Vengeance must come first, then I can think about starting again." he whispered, his agitation was somehow sensed by Jayanne even though she was fast asleep, she wriggled against him and pulled his arm tighter about her breast. The hardening flesh of her warm nipple pressed against the pulse on the inside of his wrist, a rush of hot animal lust coursed through his body driving logical thought away, his confused brain started plotting and planning a seduction that would have this wonderful woman begging for his attentions, the transition from waking to dreaming caught him completely by surprise. The dreams continued the thoughts of his waking mind, lust and sex consumed his brain in a spinning tide of pink and red flesh, a hard pink nipple and a tightly curled red bush of hair, a damp warmth enfolding his manhood, his breathing raced and his pulse pounded, faster and faster, until at the moment of release he came to startled consciousness, and rolled away from Jayannes' naked body and spent himself in the bearskin far enough away so that she should never know. Calming himself down as quickly as he could, taking long slow breaths, he hoped that she would not wake up, when she started to move he held his breath until his lungs started to burn, she turned towards him and put her right arm across his chest, he felt her right breast resting against his arm and her hand brush slowly across the course black hairs on his chest, her gentle fingernails tracked around his hardening nipple and then down his trembling torso, her fingertips trailed across the depression of his navel and came to rest just inside the thick bush about his manhood , which was once more firmly excited. "What is she dreaming about?" He thought and decided to try and discover exactly what was going on inside her brain. He struggled for many minutes to achieve the detached clarity of thought necessary for dream invasion. The mere presence of her hand, resting on his lower belly, though now utterly unmoving, made concentration very difficult, the slow rise and fall of his chest caused the hand to slide first down then up, though the movements were impossibly small they were incredibly exciting. Berating himself soundlessly for his lack of control, he thought of the cold ice of the night before, and the crystal clarity of the indigo sky above, the calming twinkling of the stars slowly pushed all thought of the body from his mind and he reached as gently as he could into the mind of the sleeping woman, to whom he was very close both physically and emotionally, the flickering thought of physical proximity almost shattered his concentration, but he held on and pushed gradually into the rich red warmth of her dream. The dream was soft and pink, it was blurred and slightly confusing for a while until he centred himself on Jayanne, she was holding in her arms a small baby who was no more than a few days old, standing a little away from the pair was a dark figure of a man he carried a long bow and a huge sword. Namdarin saw the man was himself, Jayanne had the baby to her breast it was sucking hard on her nipple, she was stroking its head with her right hand. Namdarin had never before seen Jayanne in this maternal light, she seemed to be truly content, a small smile played on her lips as she looked down into the puckered face of the child which was valiantly attempting to get the whole of her breast into its mouth at once, Namdarin felt a slight surge of jealousy towards the dream child as he noticed the swollen size of her milk filled breasts, they were bigger than her current ones and lined with delicate blue veins just beneath the surface, the nipple not in use oozed a slow drip of sympathetic milk. Namdarin wanted to reach forward and take that vacant nipple for his own, but felt guilty about stealing food from a baby and so resisted the impulse. Jayanne looked up at the Namdarin figure and he solidified with startling rapidity, the sword and bow disappeared and the heavy clothing with them, naked he walked towards her and took both the woman and the child in his strong arms, an embrace filled with such love and tenderness that Namdarin felt almost as he had when a little boy peaking through a knot hole in a wall to watch the ladies getting ready for a bath. Briefly he considered staying and watching how the dream developed, but with a shake of his head he turned away before he could take the first step towards reality a large bearded face appeared before him.

"Xeron." he whispered.

"That is correct." came the impossibly deep response.

"Why are you in Jayannes dream?"

"I am not, I am in yours."

"Why mine?"

"There is something you should know."

"What?" Namdarin was amazed by the curt attitude he was taking towards a figure he knew to be a god.

"This woman is sometimes a seer."

"This dream is a picture of the future?"

"One of the many possible futures."

"How do we reach such a conclusion?"

"Who is to say if that is the conclusion, it may be just another step along the way."

"Then how do I follow the path towards this way?"

"That is much more difficult to define, are you sure that you wish to go that way? Having another family will open you to the same sort of danger as you are now in. If they are harmed you will follow the road of death and destruction again."

"I want my family back, this cannot be so I will start again if I survive."

"The woman is a true seer, if this dream is a sight then it will come to pass, if it is only a dream then it might come to pass, if it is a nightmare in the making then it shouldn't come to pass."

"How will I be able to tell the difference?"

"If she remembers the dream when she wakes up it is most likely a true vision."

"How does my quest progress?"

"It goes much as to plan, you have so far met all the necessary challenges."

"What should I do next?"

"That would require a direct answer, and to give the answer would be interference, so I cannot tell you."

"So you can give no direct advice and no actual help. You are not of much use to me, are you?"

"Given the right conditions you will not die, your oath binds us both."

Namdarin saw that the conversation was going nowhere so he said, "Be gone."

Xeron went.

Namdarin opened his eyes and looked into the sleeping face, framed in unruly red hair. Gently he shook her and whispered her name, "Jayanne." Her startlingly green eyes flew open and she reached for the axe that was at her side.

"Relax." he said ,"there is no panic."

"Why did you wake me? I was having a lovely dream."

"What were you dreaming of?" The intensity of the question shocked her for a moment. Her face reddened as she remembered some of the details of the dream.

"Never mind." he said, knowing that her embarrassment could only be made worse by further questions. "Go back to sleep, I am sorry for waking you." She stared at him for an instant and then settled down with her head on his chest and her arm across his body. Namdarin resigned himself to the function of pillow. He held her tight and stroked her hair until he fell into a dream all of his own. His dream was sharp and clear, it was a picture of himself as a boy, he was in his fathers library, through the open windows streamed golden sunlight and the laughter of playing children, his friends were outside having fun and he was stuck inside. He didn't want to learn to read, he saw no need for it, most of his friends showed no intention of learning to read and write so why should he. His father explained at great length that men who wish to rule a house or even a small farm should be able to read then they can deal with other reading people at a distance, much more profit can be made in this way, he may have to learn to read and write and speak in different languages in the future and to learn someone else's language one must first understand ones own. The sulky child would much rather learn in the cold dark days of winter not when the sun was warm. No arguments were going to get him out of the library so he had to give in and learn of letters and words and the sounds they make. The smell of books and dust always brought back memories of these days, once the child's interest in words had been fired it refused to go out, he learned fast and forgot little, this knowledge was to stand him in good stead in later life. He woke with a start. It had been some time since he had smelled the dusty aroma of a library but now it seemed to be hanging thick in the air, he moved his foot to bring back the feeling that had disappeared while he had been sleeping, he softly kicked a large heavy lump with the movement. It was the huge book of Zandaar from the monastery. With a gasp things suddenly fell into place, he must learn to read the book of Zandaar, the dream was probably sent by Xeron, not direct information, just a prod in the right direction. Who could teach him though? Granger was the only answer that held any hope, certainly no priest of Zandaar was going to help him, so Granger it must be. Closing his eyes again he drifted into a deep and now dreamless sleep.

 Namdarin awoke to the sound of a soft snore, Jayanne was still sleeping even though the daylight was streaming through the gap in the tent flap. He studied her innocent face in the weak light reflected from the floor of the tent. Her pale skin showed no signs of tanning despite its constant exposure to the elements, her hair was as tangled and twisted as normal, her narrow upturned nose gave her an almost child like look. Listening carefully he heard no sound from the rest of the camp, except for the occasional shuffle of a bored horse. Pushing aside thoughts of Jayannes body next to his, he cleared his mind of as much of its normal clutter as he could and tried to search the surrounding area, horses he found but only their own, he felt the thoughts of a small hunter as it scampered through the deep snow, it was intent of supper and spared no time for the invisible watcher. Reaching up into the mountain pass before them Namdarin encountered no presence that he could interpret only a vague feeling of unease, he could find no focus or centre for it but there was something that felt wrong. Returning his senses to his body he found that it had suffered none of the usual shortage of air that normally accompanied his jaunts, he was still just as calm and relaxed as he had been before he left.

"I must try and do this next time." He whispered, "What ever it was that I did right." He was still frightened that when he left his body unattended it could die, or be killed. "I must remember to set some one as body guard." He chuckled quietly at the unintended pun. These thoughts sent a chill racing through his body, he pulled Jayanne closer in an attempt to drive away the cold that was not physical. His fidgeting woke her partially, she turned tighter in towards him and slide her leg over his, the feel of her soft thigh sliding over his and her knee dropping into the space between his legs brought and intense excitement and an instant erection. He could feel her stiff pubic hair pressing against his thigh. "Gods I must have this woman." he thought. "I must not frighten her." With his free left hand, the right one being trapped under her body, he lifted her chin and kissed her softly on the lips, her mouth was closed and warm, she drew the deep breath that indicated she was about to wake up, she moved towards him pressing her lips against his, her leg slid up his until her thigh was pressing against his manhood and her pubic mound against his hip. Her eyes opened slowly and the soft light illuminated the deep green pools, she looked into his blue eyes and realised that this was no dream, in an instant her whole body became as tight as a pulled bowstring, this was the moment that Namdarin was waiting for.

"Shhh," He whispered, "I will not hurt you, and I will never rape you, that will be your choice not mine, though it will be very hard for me or any man to resist you." He leant towards her and kissed her again before turning away and pulling her arm around his chest, he relaxed as much as he could and pretended to be asleep. He could feel the tension in the muscles of her arm, her confusion appeared to come and go in spasms, eventually the periods of tension became shorter and more spaced out, until he was able to believe that she was sleeping. His belief was completely mistaken, the turmoil in her mind gradually subsided as she began to believe what he had said. Never before had she experienced a man with such control of his sexual urges, when she awoke to feel his hardened manhood pressed against her leg she was sure that he was going to rape her, and yet he had merely kissed her and turned away. His need was perfectly obvious even though he was pretending to be asleep, she could feel the muscles in his back contracting and relaxing aimlessly, a certain sign that he was not asleep. Her fingertips resting gently against the course hairs on his chest revealed to her his pounding heart, the twitch of his buttock against her leg jumping to the pulse in his erect maleness. The feeling of safety that grew in her belly made her feel warm, his words had calmed her moment of terror, she began to wonder how far his resolve would reach. Looking back over the sexual experiences of her life all she found was male need and her pain, none other than Namdarin had ever put her feelings before their needs. The warmth in her belly seemed to concentrate itself into a hard centre of unnameable need, that settled into the seat of her womanliness and gave her a damp and uncomfortable feeling between her thighs, this reminded her of a sensation she remembered from a recent horse ride whilst thinking of Namdarin. Her thoughts turned to the pleasing dream that she had been rudely awoken from. She remembered the soft, warm pink lighting, the wriggling infant in her arms, sucking strongly at her breast, the hard muscles of a man's arm around her shoulders, this was Namdarin and his child, it was her child as well. If this dream were to be true, sometime in the future, and it carried all the usual signs, it was clear and sharply focused, it had no confusion about it at all, it was slow and steady, it just had to be one of the dreams that become reality given enough time. Her age in the dream did not feel much more than her age now, so it cannot be long to wait. But for her to have Namdarin's baby in her arms she must have sex with him, she had vowed never to allow another man to tie her down and rape her, yet Namdarin had left the choice up to her, she did not understand how she could have his baby if he did not have sex with her, he said that he would not hurt her, but she could not submit to that degrading process again, and never by her choice. The confusion raged in her brain for a long time until she was forced to the conclusion that she was missing some important information, she could not understand how the survival of the human race depended on so many women surrendering to the ropes and the whips just so they can have babies, some of which are bound to be male who will do exactly the same things to other women, this did not make any sense at all. She wished intently for another woman to talk these problems over with, but she was surrounded by rapists. She thought of the animals she had seen mating, the horses and the cattle, always the males with their enormous weapons extended chase the females until they surrender and stand still, to be mounted, she would never stand still, while she was able, she would fight. She desperately needed someone to share her difficulties with, Namdarin had said that he would never rape her, could he be trusted? He was after all only a man. She had to sort her feelings out or she would probably go insane, she would have to talk to Namdarin.

"No time like right now." She thought and shook Namdarin gently saying "Wake up. I have to talk to you." He had only been dozing so he woke very quickly.

"What is wrong?" he asked.

"Why do women want babies?" The bluntness of the question stunned him for a moment or two, he had trouble assembling an answer in his shocked brain.

"I am no woman, as you may have noticed, so I cannot really answer that, I will try, babies are a joy to their parents, but also a serious trial, they are the future for the human race or the family or the man and woman involved. Some view child bearing as the final declaration of love between a man and a woman."

"This is not how I see it. How can rape and pain be associated with love?"

"You have had entirely the wrong experience of love, it is something soft and gentle between two people who share a feeling for each other. What you have seen is not an act of love nor really an act of sex, it is more about the domination of one person by another, that is power not love."

"So you say that this act of love is without pain."

"For some women it is a little painful the first time, and there are some who actually enjoy pain, but to inflict pain on an unwilling partner is a criminal act in my view."

"How ever you see it, it still involves putting that large piece of a man into a small hole, that hurts." He smiled indulgently then prayed that the light was such that she did not see it.

"Did you mother not tell you of these things?"

"I asked her a few times, but she changed the subject, she seemed to be embarrassed."

"That place on a women is very flexible, don't forget that when a woman gives birth the baby comes down the same passage, and it is far bigger than any man."

Jayanne gasped she had never thought of this before.

"A newborn baby is bigger than a bulls thing." she whispered hoarsely.

"But a baby is nowhere near as long."

"What a horrible thought."

"No. It is completely natural, these are the wonders that the female body can perform, it produces live and kicking babies, females generally have much better stamina than males, they have a higher tolerance for pain, they survive harsh conditions far better, and the human race needs them all, if almost all the men were to suddenly drop dead the race would survive and be back up to strength in only a few years, if the women die the race dies with them."

"This still does not explain why a woman would want sex for anything other than having babies."

"Sex gives the most wondrous pleasures, to both men and women."

"It does?"

"Oh, yes. The pleasure cannot be described, it is like a joyful rush of the brain and a glad seizure of the body."

"I don't believe you."

"I understand, it is entirely unbelievable, only experience reveals its truth."

Namdarin said nothing and Jayanne was deep in thought, how could she believe him? He told her things that she had no knowledge of, no background for, and only a few hints that they might be facts. Could she bear not knowing for sure? No, she could not.

"I want to learn this pleasure, but I am frightened." She said.

"I would like to teach you if you will let me."

"You must."

"Very well, but remember this, I will not hurt you and if you say stop I will stop immediately." He pulled his right arm from underneath her and propped himself up on it, "Close your eyes and try to relax." he said, her eyes closed but her body remained tight, "I am going to touch you with my left hand only, there is nothing to be afraid of." He brushed a few of her hairs away from her face then placed the warm palm against her cheek, after a few gentle strokes across the quivering flesh of her face he moved the hand down her neck to the shoulder, here he reached around to the nape and tried to massage away the tension that was holding her head still, first one side then the other, until the muscles of her shoulders began to relax.

"Is that good?" he asked, getting a small nod as the only reply. Her breathing was slow and even, almost to the verge of sleep when he stopped rubbing her neck and moved his attentions to the hollow at the front of her long neck, with the lightest of touches he traced his fingertips around the her throat and down the breast bone, slowly and softly down in between the twin mounds of her breasts.

Pausing for a moment he rested the palm of his hand over her heart, the thump from beneath the ribs was slow and strong, not in the least excited. Sliding the hand under her right breast he slowly cupped as much of it as he could, which was by no means all of it, her breath caught in her throat as he captured the nipple between finger and thumb and rolled it softly from side to side, he watched the other nipple respond in a similar manner to the one he was holding, its soft pink bud gradually hardened and lengthened until the urge to take it in his mouth and suck it firmly was almost to much to bare. Switching from one to the other the whole of each breast seemed to harden under his knowing touch.

"Does that feel good?" he asked.

"It feels strange and exciting." Leaving the breasts to their own devices his hot sweaty hand slid down over her trembling belly, which jumped away from his touch occasionally, his fingers found the depression of her navel and explored it thoroughly, she wriggled and giggled at the sensation of another's fingers. He heard her laughter as small bells in the air, a joy to hear and a pleasure to ring. Sliding his hand slowly over the hard muscles of her lower abdomen his fingertips encountered the coarse and curly red pubic hair of her glorious triangle. Her breath was rasping in her throat, her body remembered the pain of a man's touch, but her mind was caught between two choices, there was no pain here and pleasure had been promised. As if he had read the indecision in her mind, or the responses of her body he asked, "Stop or carry on?" Her mind was made up and fear was to be banished, "Carry on." His fingers gently twisted the red hairs in to tiny spirals and tugged them into spiky towers.

"You will have to open your legs just a little." His excitement was almost at the same feverish pitch as hers, his aching penis was causing him some serious distraction, he knew he had to ignore its demands and concentrate hard on hers. He felt her knees lift one after the other and separate by about five inches, with now exaggerated slowness he moved his hand until it cupped the entire mound of her sex, her breath stopped and her legs snapped shut, trapping his hand in their soft fleshy folds.

"Stop or carry on?" the whispered question came again. No verbal answer was forthcoming but he felt a forced relaxation of the muscles and a slow separation of her legs, taking this to be a carry on instruction he increased the pressure until he could feel the hot dampness against his palm, then he began to rock his hand backwards and forwards, not moving across the surface just shifting the pressure. The presence of his hand reminded her of the way a saddle moves when the horse is walking slowly, the constantly changing pressure caused the soft innards of her sex to rub very gently against themselves, the sensations this produced were indescribable, Namdarin saw the flush of pink in her shoulders and across her breasts, he felt the lips of her sex swell with the rush of blood, he knew that the time was near. With great care he slowly spread the index and third finger of his left hand, opening her throbbing centre to the cold air of the tent, he felt a slow trickle of her lubricating fluids as the crack opened and a small tremor of her belly as she lifted her hips to push against the intruding fingers, he slid his middle finger into the opening until he could feel the swollen nub of her clitoris, five quick strokes against its sensitive surface and her body clenched in a spasm of pleasure, her hips lifted clear of the furs under her, her thighs clamped shut imprisoning his hand again, he felt a warm rush of fluid pour out of her like the gush of a hot geyser, her breath was held in her lungs and then released in a long low moan, the sight and sound of her pleasure was too much for him and his throbbing penis spat its sticky cargo over her thighs. The slow descent from the heights of passion seemed to take forever, no words were spoken until the their panting had ceased and their hearts were beating at a more manageable pace, together they lay still and rested, unmoving, her arms spread wide and his hand still trapped between her legs.

"Was that a pleasure beyond description?" he asked, he voice husky with emotion. Her answer was many moments coming.

"It was indeed something I had never experienced before, it was like a soundless buzzing that fills the brain, a painless agony that swamps all feeling, a raging fire that burns within."

"But is it good?"

"I do not feel that it is good or evil, it just is."

"It is not something that you fear then?"

"Rape is all I fear." He slowly pulled his hand from its warm nest and taking her right hand he placed it on his shrunken manhood saying, "That is not something to for you to fear from me," he chuckled, "in the days of my youth the mere presence of a ladies hand would have brought that particular monster back to life in an instant, now I am old and slow."

"How can it be that you are so spent?" she asked holding him gently in her warm hand, the sticky residue of passion on her fingers.

"There is more pleasure in giving than taking." He held his left hand to his face and smelt her fragrance on it then taste the salt tang of her juices, with a huge sigh he said, "We must get some rest, tomorrow we ride into the mountains to find Granger and make him help us." He turned away from her and they settled down to sleep through the rest of the afternoon and the coming night, the morning after would bring a new challenge.

Printed in Great Britain
by Amazon